I0762774

PRAISE FOR

THE DIAMONDS SERIES

Rebel Heiress

"*Rebel Heiress* is a page-turning delight of a historical romance, elegantly undergirded with themes of individuality, diversity, and the power of following one's star. I loved it from the first line and couldn't put it down until the last."

—**MIMI MATTHEWS**, *USA Today* bestselling author of *The Siren of Sussex*

"Simply brilliant. Howard returns with a clever, banter-filled, meticulously researched tale so swoon-worthy readers will be left utterly starry-eyed."

—**ANGELA MONTOYA**, award-winning author of *Carnival Fantástico*

"Smart, romantic, and utterly inspiring, with a plucky, progressive heroine you'll cheer for. Another triumph from Amalie Howard!"

—**ALEXANDRA VASTI**, *USA Today* bestselling author of *Ladies in Hating*

Lady Knight

"The chemistry practically crackles between the clever, indomitable Zia and the wickedly charming Rafi. A wildly exciting page-turner!"

—**LIANA DE LA ROSA**, *USA Today* bestselling author of *Ana María and the Fox*

"A ridiculously romantic, womanist, hilarious, and hugely entertaining romance that had me smiling and swooning from start to finish."

—**ELIZABETH EVERETT**, *USA Today* bestselling author of the Damsels of Discovery series

"Amalie Howard's delightful *Lady Knight* is a winning combination of romance, good causes, and great friendship."

—**Erica Ridley**, *New York Times* bestselling author of the Wild Wynchesters series

Queen Bee

"A refreshingly updated historical that has quickly become one of my favorites!"

—**Jennifer L. Armentrout**, #1 *New York Times* bestselling author of *From Blood and Ash*

"Immersive and inclusive. Amalie Howard brings a new twist to Regency romance in this intriguing story about deceit, bitterness, vengeance . . . and finding true love."

—**Brigid Kemmerer**, *New York Times* bestselling author of *Defy the Night*

"Amalie Howard brings a much-needed breath of fresh air to Regency romance in this buzzy revenge romp rich with feisty characters and unexpected friendship."

—**Stacey Lee**, *New York Times* bestselling author of Reese's Book Club Pick *The Downstairs Girl*

"Funny, smart, and enchanting. Thoughtfully handled moments of grief and friendship and a swoon-worthy romance make this novel difficult to put down."

—**Krystal Marquis**, *New York Times* bestselling author of *The Davenports*

"A divine dip into Regency waters! *Queen Bee* takes flight."

—**Jodi Picoult**, #1 *New York Times* bestselling author of *Wish You Were Here*

REBEL HEIRESS

Rebel Heiress

AMALIE HOWARD

JOY REVOLUTION

Joy Revolution
An imprint of Random House Children's Books
A division of Penguin Random House LLC
1745 Broadway, New York, NY 10019
penguinrandomhouse.com
getunderlined.com

Editor: Bria Ragin
Cover Designer: Michelle Cunningham
Interior Designer: Michelle Canoni
Production Editor: Jamie Johnson
Managing Editor: Tamar Schwartz
Production Manager: Tracy Heydweiller

Library of Congress Cataloging-in-Publication Data
Names: Howard, Amalie author
Title: Rebel heiress / Amalie Howard.
Description: New York, NY : Joy Revolution, 2026. |
Audience: Ages 12 and up | Summary: "A young heiress must disguise herself to attend a prestigious, all-male university, where she unexpectedly falls for her handsome tutor"— Provided by publisher.
Identifiers: LCCN 2025026372 (print) | LCCN 2025026373 (ebook) |
ISBN 979-8-217-02416-2 (hardcover) | ISBN 979-8-217-02417-9 (ebook)
Subjects: CYAC: Romance stories | Disguise—Fiction | Heiresses—Fiction | Universities and colleges—Fiction | Great Britain—History—Regency, 1811–1820—Fiction | LCGFT: Romance fiction | Historical fiction | Novels
Classification: LCC PZ7.H83233 Re 2026 (print) | LCC PZ7.H83233 (ebook)

The text of this book is set in 11-point Sabon MT Pro.
Interior art used under license from Adobe Stock.

Manufactured in the United States of America
1st Printing

The authorized representative in the EU for product safety and compliance is Penguin Random House Ireland, Morrison Chambers, 32 Nassau Street, Dublin D02 YH68, Ireland, https://eu-contact.penguin.ie.

FOR ANY DIAMOND WHO NEEDS TO HEAR THIS:

No one else can shine like you, so shine proudly.
The world needs your light!

Dramatis Personae

LADY ROSALIN CHEN / ROZ

A Seasoned Debutante, Scholar-in-Disguise, and Amateur Astronomer

MR. TARIK ST. CLAIR

Master's Degree Student, Tutor, and Second Wrangler at Trinity College, Cambridge University

LORD BLAKE CASTLETON

Lady Rosalin's Best Mate, Shameless Gossip, and Unapologetic Rake

LORD ANSEL CHEN

Dearest Cousin and Unfortunate Doppelgänger

VISCOUNT WILLIAM HUMBOLT

A Newly Minted Gent and Fellow Student at Trinity College

MR. HAROLD JENNINGS

A Second-Year American Student at Trinity College

MR. KLAUS AND MR. KRISTOF BLENDEL

Third-Year Roguish Norwegian Twins and Students at Trinity College

SIR JAMES LOWRY

Master's Degree Student and Third Wrangler at Trinity College

Marquess and Marchioness of Ridley (Keston and Ela)

Lady Rosalin's London Set and High Society Friends

Viscount and Viscountess Hollis (Rafi and Zia)

Lady Rosalin's London Set and High Society Friends

Duke and Duchess of Delmont

Parents of Lady Rosalin and Lord Bowen,
and Uncle and Aunt to Lord Ansel

Lord Bowen Chen

Rosalin's Baby Brother and the Duke of Delmont's Heir

Anna

An Exceptional Lady's Maid

Henry

A Loyal Groom and Coachman

Miss Caroline Herschel

A Legendary Astronomer Nicknamed the "Hunter of Comets"

Mr. George Peacock

Tarik's Mentor and Fellow at Trinity College

Dr. Christopher Wordsworth

Master of Trinity College

Mr. John Pond

Astronomer Royal

PART I

I was therefore entered at Oxford
and have been properly idle ever since.

—Jane Austen, *Sense and Sensibility*

CHAPTER ONE

We are to admit no more causes of natural things than such as are both true and sufficient to explain their appearances.

—Isaac Newton

London, 1820

When my cousin asked me to dance, I let out the smallest of sighs. I brushed the satin and tulle skirts of my new gown and reached for the cool, practiced poise of Lady Rosalin Chen that had become second nature by now. I was certain the request was made under duress from his mother, my aunt, again. Not that I minded—Ansel was a safer partner than anyone else.

Glumly, I followed him to the middle of the ballroom floor.

Truth be told, I was getting rather sick of this game I'd been playing for so many years—acting like a besotted gentleman-obsessed fool, while chasing any serious and usually ill-matched suitors off in secret, with everyone else none the wiser. Not even my best friends knew of my scheme. All the *ton* saw was poor Lady Rosalin . . . the eternal bridesmaid and never the actual bride.

Little did everyone know that I *chose* to be unwed. Because, honestly, who wanted to be married off to a troglodyte of a peer who thought the Earth was flat or an abacus was a type of fungus?

Not me.

This season, subdued because of King George III's death, did not have the same vibrancy and color of previous years. For obvious reasons, since the entire country was in mourning following the passing of its monarch. Months had passed, and while some events had started to resume, there was a lingering cloud of somberness over the *ton*.

My father, the Duke of Delmont, had to be here for Parliament, and while there had been some deliberation between my parents about remaining in West Suffolk out of respect for the former king, in the end my woefully unwed *status* had forced their hand. So, here we were. Back in Mayfair. With new wardrobes and a slew of freshly renewed hopes—at least on their parts.

Though this year was different. My normally too-busy father had suddenly taken notice of my impending spinsterhood, and *that* was immensely dreadful. What the duke wanted, the duke got, and if that meant a husband for me, my efforts to stave off marriage didn't stand much of a chance. I shivered. This was it—this was the year that I might be wedded to an absolute dunce for the sake of precious aristocratic bloodlines, if I couldn't secure an acceptable match on my own.

The mere thought of it made me wither inside.

Technically, this would be my fourth season in the *ton*. Unheard of, really. I'd had my first at sixteen, and now at nineteen, I was firmly on the shelf. I fought back a grimace of dread, keeping my face neutral and pleasantly placid. By all accounts, I couldn't even be called a spinster . . . I was practically a fossil. An old-maid fossil—passed over, discarded, and deemed utterly undesirable. I squashed down the pervasive trepidation creeping through my veins.

It wasn't that I *didn't* want to marry. I did . . . eventually. But I'd always hoped for a love match. A true connection with a person—intellectual, emotional, and physical. That magical space where that special someone understood, appreciated, and celebrated all your complexities. Like binary stars, existing in each other's orbit.

Silly, I knew.

Because the truth was that falling in love simply wasn't as easy as all the poets made it out to be. I could simper and swoon with the best ladies of London high society, but when it came to stifling my intelligence, together with my tendency to fixate intently on an interesting subject, I could come across as off-putting. No gentleman wanted to be humiliated by a woman who understood the world better than he did. I'd even gone so far as to simplify my opinions, to distill them down to barely any hint of provocation.

I was smart. Prodigy-level smart, especially when it came to numbers. I was able to calculate sums in my head without resorting to parchment or an abacus. I'd inherited the skill from my father, who was a genius with figures. Our estate ledgers were unfailingly correct, and from the time I'd been a small girl, he'd allowed me to sit on his knee in his study and check his work for fun. Papa would test me, too, hiding incorrect numbers in the columns, beaming with pride when I pinpointed the errors.

My proficiency for numbers had been a delightful novelty as a child . . . not so much as an adult woman whose only goal was to ensnare a titled husband. I'd taught myself to be coy and play the ingenue, but something in my expression would invariably display some veiled contempt that a puffed-up gentleman could sense. They wanted to be fawned over and coddled. Finding a diamond suited to me, even one in the rough, had been next to impossible.

And I did not want an arranged marriage.

Oh, I supposed an arranged match had turned out fine for my parents. They got along well, even if they weren't the most passionate of people. My father traveled far too much, and my mother was quite busy with family obligations and her numerous charities. However, they'd conceived me, and then my little brother over a decade later, so some measure of intimacy had to have happened at least twice.

The thought of my straitlaced parents engaged in any romance was laughable.

Though I'd been an only child for the first fourteen years of my life, until Bowen was born, my cousin Ansel lived with us. After a tragic carriage accident that claimed my uncle's life when Ansel was young, he and my aunt had moved in. It'd been nice during my childhood years, though the competition between us was brutal at times, especially in the schoolroom. I wasn't officially allowed to attend Ansel's lessons, though that didn't stop me. I copied whatever I could find and memorized his schoolwork.

My cousin would show me the problems, and we'd race to complete them. I held my own, especially in mathematics and physics. I *relished* beating him at sums, and later on, more complex equations and problems. When he went off to Cambridge University three years ago, I'd been left behind, forced to supplement my education with books from my parents' extensive library and stealing Ansel's rather sparse notes when I could. I was livid that girls were denied any right to enroll—the injustices to my own sex a bitter pill to swallow.

But swallow it I had, just like every other woman born in England before me. I loved Ansel dearly, but I also deeply resented him. I begrudged his autonomy because he was male, which granted him the freedom to travel and be who he wanted, the ease to flirt and converse with whomever he desired, the ability to go to *Cambridge* and study whatever he wished.

Gracious, I'd sell my soul to go to university even for a day . . . a measly *hour.*

I loved reading about intrepid women who defied convention—where there was a man theorizing about some academic subject, there was usually a woman in the background going toe-to-toe with him. No one ever heard about *them,* of course. Émilie du Châtelet, a woman I greatly admired, was a capable mathematician in her own right, though most only knew her as the French philosopher Voltaire's mistress. If she'd been born a man, her writings and works would have been revered. I once read that she had commissioned men's clothes to enter a meeting place that welcomed only male scientists!

How wickedly audacious!

Émilie believed that women had just as much value as men and that true social exchange would only be a benefit to expand knowledge. But history had always been biased against women, especially intelligent, opinionated ones who did not fit the mold of what dutiful, quiet, demure ladies should be.

Just like me.

Émilie wasn't the only one who defied convention. I've had a sneaking suspicion for years that our family physician—Dr. James Barker—was born a woman. I'd learned that he had received a degree in medicine at twenty-two from a medical school in Edinburgh and was exceptionally competent. He was small in stature, had enviably smooth skin, looked young and boyish, and had a high-pitched voice. Given his skill, however, his personal history was no one's business.

Swallowing my scowl at the unjustness of it all, I gritted my teeth as my cousin finished the last turn of our requisite dance, nearly tripping over my own feet in my burst of irritation. Ansel deposited me back to my usual alcove and was on to his next dancing partner quicker than I could blink. Well, at least Mama would be happy that I'd danced.

With a sniff, I smoothed my glossy blue-black hair over my ear, though not a strand was out of place, and pasted on my best, most demure smile. I waved to Zia, my bosom friend Ela's new sister-in-law, as she danced past. Zia had made her own match last season to arguably the biggest rake of the *ton,* Mr. Rafi Nasser.

Hearts had cracked galore when he'd been taken off the marriage mart. While Mr. Nasser was indeed handsome and clever and had progressive views of women, I didn't want a rake, not even a reformed one. I wanted a gentleman scholar who wouldn't be put off by a partner who was his intellectual equal. Surely, that wasn't too much to ask for?

Sadly, in the aristocracy, most scholars were snubbed. Even the boys enrolled in university weren't interested in finishing their study. Becoming a man was about social connections, not scholarship. It was infuriating that they had such opportunity at their fingertips and threw it away for trivial, frivolous diversions. In fact, all any eligible gentleman seemed to care about these days was going on their grand tour.

Case in point—my dear cousin Ansel, unbeknownst to his parents, was about to embark on a five-country revel, celebrating his journey to becoming a man. *While a lady's journey covers the hearth, home, and needlepoint,* I thought sourly.

Notwithstanding that Ansel was in his third year of Cambridge and leaving the Easter term unfinished, everything seemed to be on a strange, mournful hiatus this year with the death of the king. All the social events thus far had been rather restrained out of respect to the crown. No wonder my cousin and most of his set wanted to escape to Europe. The air of decadence in Italy or Greece would hardly be diminished by the death of a ruling British monarch.

"Roz, you haven't moved an inch from where I left you."

As if my dour thoughts had summoned him, Ansel reappeared like the devil himself, flushed and tousled from a rousing quadrille, spectacles askew on his nose. Other than the glasses, which everyone knew were an affectation to make him appear more erudite, we could be siblings. Our fathers had been identical twins, with mine being older by nearly an hour.

Considering we were born barely a month apart, even our parents hadn't been able to tell us apart as babies. As children, we'd switch places to play pranks on new servants, or even tutors, with me attending maths lessons while Ansel ran off with his friends.

I'd *loved* that!

As we got older, people often mistook us for brother and sister, instead of the first cousins we were. We had the same sleek black hair with its striking midnight-blue sheen that was parted in the middle—though his was a good twenty inches shorter than mine—oval faces with light brown complexions, round cheekbones, plump lips, and expressive dark-brown eyes. We also had a similar rectangular build, whereupon my waist had to be severely cinched to be visible, and to compound things, we were of a similar height—five feet and ten inches—which I knew irritated my cousin terribly.

I sucked in a shallow breath. "I'm biding my time," I said with a toss of my chin.

"You won't find a husband standing here."

I glowered and rolled my eyes before I remembered that someone was always watching with the intent of spreading gossip, and that was the last thing I needed. "Go away, Ansel."

"Would you like to dance again?" he asked, and I narrowed my gaze at him in suspicion.

"Why are you being so nice?"

He shrugged. "Perhaps because I will be gone for several months, and you will be alone without me all season long. Though it might not seem like it, I will miss you, Roz. I want you to make a match and be happy."

"Don't pretend like you actually care," I told him sullenly. "And I've decided that the perfect gentleman is a mythical creature, as illusory as a unicorn."

Ansel pouted and peered at me with a puppy-dog expression. "Come now. You're my favorite girl cousin. Don't give me the cut direct in front of everyone."

"I'm your only girl cousin," I replied grumpily, and then relented. Who *would* take pity on me and ask me to dance when Ansel left? My waltzing options were dire . . . unless Ela and Zia forced Lord Ridley or Mr. Nasser to take pity on me. Pity dances were the worst. At least Ansel appeared to come on his own instead of being coerced. I might as well enjoy his company while I could.

"Fine, but don't step on my toes," I groused.

"I make no promises." Ansel grinned, and once more, I envied the reason he was so joyful. Who wouldn't want to go to France, Italy, Greece, Belgium, and Austria looking at art and architecture, and learning about history and culture? I would do anything to escape the parochial fate I'd been born into. Offer up an organ . . . sell my soul.

In reality, I wasn't *that* rebellious. I knew my place, so I could only hope to compromise.

Exhaling a breath, I concentrated on the three-beat count of the music and not flubbing the steps. This waltz had only just begun and already felt interminable. All I wanted to do was sulk in a quiet corner.

I'd researched every single eligible gentleman on the marriage mart with meticulous detail—preparation was the key to success—I knew the state of their finances, their family histories, their interests, their vices, their strengths, and their weaknesses. I was very well aware that my extensive *groundwork* was a touch extreme, but I knew what I wanted.

And marriage in the *ton* was for forever.

Until death, as they said.

I sighed. My carefully thought-out plan—a series of five tests that each marital prospect needed to pass—had thus far been a dismal failure. It wasn't even that difficult.

- *Scholarly aptitude and ability to engage in intellectual discourse—multiple questions in mathematics, physics, and philosophy*
- *Progressive stance on women's status and rights in the aristocracy*
- *Emotional breadth and depth—must be compassionate and kind*
- *Political views in favor of changing antiquated laws*
- *Physical compatibility*

Honestly, on the last test, were butterflies too much to hope for?

Every gentleman I'd met faced the same inquisition. If they failed, which many did, I quickly moved on. If they passed, other subsequent stages would weed out any prospects who might allow me only a modicum of educational and personal liberty. But season after season, not a single gentleman had ever met my full expectations.

It was entirely disheartening.

In fact, the only person who had come close to my impossible dream had been my best friend, Lord Blake Castleton . . . a flirt through and through, with an incisive brain he preferred not to use. He'd nailed my academic questions without blinking, and I'd been buoyed by his views on women—that they shouldn't be pigeonholed into archaic roles. He was compassionate *and* stood for change. My hopes had exploded, and the next step had been to see if we had physical compatibility.

Alas, there was none. Not a butterfly in sight.

Honestly, if falling in love was to be determined by kisses, I was positively doomed. My overly methodical brain had dissected our experimental kiss until it had become a clinical study—of touch, texture, and taste—observations that led to the conclusion that it was nothing to swoon about. That said, I'd been willing to accept Blake, even with the mediocre kisses, until I realized to my dismay that he was emphatically not inclined or ready to settle down with anyone.

Thereafter, I was forced to face the facts that I might be too picky, and my standards were unreachable. Was something wrong with me? Was my desire to find my perfect person so impossibly daunting? Certainly, I'd deterred the fortune hunters and the suitors who didn't seem to have any interest in me as a person. But surely there was someone I might have some common ground with on a cerebral level or even some infinitesimal semblance of a spark?

With the way things were looking, it seemed being unapologetically myself meant being alone. A fact that was fine by me, but not with my parents. Or the *ton*, for that matter.

Finally, the everlasting dance ended. Ansel's gaze narrowed on my flushed face. "You're looking a bit peaked, Roz. Shall we get a drink?"

I nodded. That sounded like a capital idea. Perhaps afterward I could slip away unnoticed. As he escorted me toward the refreshments room, I peered at him, a wave of envy washing through me. "Are you excited for your trip?"

"Beyond," he replied. "It will be magnificent, and I shall return a sophisticated, mature, and cultivated man."

"So you say," I muttered. "I envy you, you know."

"Why?"

My brows drew down. "What do you mean why? In what world do you see me getting to do something like that?"

"Well, it's not safe, is it?" he said matter-of-factly as he handed me a glass of water. "You're a girl. You could not travel on your own. Who would look out for you?"

"Women are just as capable as men," I replied, and sipped. "I bet Lady Zenobia could hand you your pride with fencing, and some of her friends, like Miss Sorenson, could probably wipe the floor with you, using just her fists."

"But you're not them, Roz," he noted, the light reflecting

off the clear lenses of his spectacles in a way that hid his true thoughts. "Besides, Auntie Susu and Uncle Lan would be lost if something happened to you."

My stomach roiled. "And yet, they're frantically trying to get rid of me and marry me off by the end of the season. An egregious irony, if you ask me. I'd rather take my chances on the Continent. Maybe I could even become a pirate like Anne Bonny or Mary Read. Did you know they both pretended to be men on the high seas?"

"You would make a dreadful pirate. You get seasick, remember?" Ansel pursed his lips, forehead scrunching in thought. "They only want to see you settled. All parents want that for their daughters, especially in the *ton*. You know how this works, Roz." He refilled my glass from a pitcher before handing it back to me. "What's really the matter?"

"It's not fair," I murmured. "You get to go off on your adventures while I'm stuck here. All because I have a bosom."

He snorted. "Not really, if we're being objective."

"Ouch," I said in fake outrage, but it wasn't as though he was wrong about that either. Most of my stays had been tailored with cleverly lined bust enhancers to supplement my distinct lack of curves. I wasn't *flat,* but I certainly wasn't going to win any décolletage contests.

My utter lack of an ample chest, cinched waist, or curvy hips had always been points of insecurity for me, though my self-confidence had blossomed in the past two years with my dear friend Ela at my side. Poppy Landers used to tell me I resembled a tall, shapeless potato and was lucky I had a pretty face.

I was glad she was gone, ousted for trying to ruin Ela's reputation. Twice! Poppy was a terrible person with an ugly heart . . . and she was also the reason I didn't have many friends, outside of Ansel and Blake and, more recently, Ela and Zia. It was hard to trust people when someone had made me feel small for so long. In hindsight, Poppy had done that on purpose—kept me isolated so I would have no one else but her.

Pink blanketed my cousin's cheeks. "I beg your pardon," Ansel said. "Not that you don't have *them,* but that they're not obvious." When my brows jumped even higher, he released an aggravated noise, going even redder with mortification. "It's just, you're hardly buxom, so if you weren't in a gown, we could be twins." His cheeks were practically on fire now. "That came out wrong . . . Oh, sod it. You know how we used to pretend to be each other as children in the schoolroom? You could be me and not a soul would guess."

Regrettably, I understood. "I'm only teasing you, I remember."

But as I sighed, the childhood memory of our underhanded switch also inspired a rather brilliant, albeit completely scandalous, idea. One that made my heart thump with illicit excitement, because I still *could* be him . . . with no one the wiser. If a woman like Émilie du Châtelet could do it, why couldn't I?

Only the real Ansel would know, and he'd be far away on the Continent, having his fun and living his best life. I could be living *my* best life, too.

If I took his place at Cambridge University as Lord Ansel Chen.

Facing him, I smiled with every ounce of charm I possessed. "Cousin. *Cousin.*"

He peered at me, dark eyes going wide, and immediately shook his head. "No. Whatever it is you've concocted in that devious brain of yours, the answer is no. I *know* that look."

"You didn't even hear what I have to say," I protested.

"I don't have to," he said. "You've got mayhem written all over your face."

I arched a brow. "Fine, then. I'll just let it slip to Papa and Mama that their precious nephew is taking a secret trip to the Continent."

"Roz, you wouldn't!" He looked so betrayed that I felt a rush of guilt, which I squashed immediately. He would have no such compunction if our roles were reversed.

I wrapped my arm around his. "Let me be you, Ansel, just for the term while you're gone. You know I'll probably get better marks than you. It's a win-win. No one will worry about your whereabouts or contact the duke about your absence, and I'll get my adventure."

Ansel's brows crashed together. I could see him considering the merits of the idea, but then his face fell. "We might look alike, Roz, but we're not identical. People who are aquainted with me will *know.*"

My mind raced, mulling over potential options. "What if you switched campuses for this term? I know it's quite untoward to move between colleges within a university, but you're almost done anyway. No one would care, especially if the instruction came with Papa's ducal seal. How about . . . Trinity? It's close enough to St. John's. And it's still under the Cambridge University umbrella."

Ansel shook his head, looking reluctantly impressed. "You are diabolical, cousin."

"I prefer quick-witted," I said, hope soaring inside. "So, you're in?"

He didn't answer for a beat, but then he nodded. "Fine, but do *not* get caught, or it will be my hide as well. Roz, I am serious. This could end badly for both of us."

"I won't get caught, I promise. No one will suspect a thing!"

CHAPTER TWO

To explain all nature is too difficult a task for any one man or even for any one age.

—Isaac Newton

Everyone's going to know.

Gritting my teeth, I swallowed past the lump of fear lodged in my throat that was growing larger by the second and shoved my fake spectacles up my nose.

No one's going to know.

I tugged on my too-tight cravat as I strode confidently across the perfectly manicured grounds of Trinity College toward my new lodgings. Well, toward Lord *Ansel's* new temporary residence. He, ergo me, would have a quiet place of his own to study for a few days per week . . . and of course, to keep all my academic contraband away from prying eyes at our London home. I'd have to be careful, but I'd found that with meticulous planning down to the minute and obsessive attention to detail, the most impossible feats could be achieved.

While Cambridge was a good sixty miles from London, it was close to our ducal seat in Newmarket. I could go from the college to London—six hours by carriage—without too much undue notice with a small detour. It was a long ride, but that would give me ample time to study and read through any discussion notes.

Besides, our coachmen were already accustomed to going back and forth from our country seat to London during the season, since my mother had been satisfactorily convinced that I was needed there for important charity work with the local parish—which *was* true for a handful of hours. The rest of the time, however, was free, and as long as I was back in Mayfair by Friday afternoon in time for my weekend social obligations, what Mama didn't know wouldn't hurt her.

Thankfully, with the somber sluggishness of the current season, due to the king's passing, I would not be missed in London during the week, though I had to be diligent with any of my social appearances on the weekends. While my father was mostly oblivious or absent, my mother *would* notice if I didn't show my face at the larger events. Especially since this was my supposed last-ditch chance to find an acceptable husband.

I ignored the guilt that slid through me.

Falsely assuming a peer's identity had to be a crime, even if it was one's own cousin. The newspapers would have a field day. My father would be furious. My mother would have conniptions. Lady Rosalin Chen would be absolutely, unequivocally ruined.

No one will find out, I repeated firmly, rolling my neck.

Fortunately, the housing for my cousin's attendance at Cambridge University was already paid for by my father—the general rule was that if an aristocrat resided at the college for two years, any degree conferred upon him was automatic and he would not have to take the exams that everyone else did. Technically, Ansel had fulfilled that residency requirement, though he had yet to formally withdraw, which worked out perfectly for me. Because while he was off on his secret grand tour, I'd take his place here.

It was up to me to seize the day.

Seize *my* day.

So here I was . . . gripping it in a chokehold, despite fighting to cast up my accounts with each step while the cloth padding in my shoulders shifted precariously beneath my coat. Inhaling deeply, I slowed my gait and tightened my spine. My disguise *would* work. It had to work.

But everything felt dodgy . . . from my stuffed shoulders to the spectacles that refused to stay put on the slope of my nose, and the false facial hair that suddenly felt quite itchy. I pressed a damp finger to each of my carefully applied sideburns. The fake mustache tickled my nose and the too-tight cap that held in my braided, pinned wealth of hair also felt nailed to my skull. Better than the alternative of being too loose, but it still hurt.

You're fine, Roz. Everything's fine. Breathe.

My camouflage was top-notch. I had a scrupulous plan. I was aggressively prepared.

Besides, it wasn't as though anyone would connect Ansel and me, especially at a different college. His preferred fields of study were philosophy and the classics, and my true love was astronomy. The forged ducal paperwork had made the enrollment switch easy. It wasn't common to change colleges within the university, but having a powerful, rich duke for a father tended to make all obstacles disappear. I was also well aware that forging my papa's signature and using his wax seal was also a crime.

I cringed with a sigh.

Add that to my growing list of transgressions . . .

Speaking of the duke, I was also counting on the fact that my father would be much too busy traveling to keep a close eye on the expense ledgers. At the end of the Easter term in June, no one would be the wiser . . . and I would have had a small, unforgettable taste of university life. And by the time Papa's steward reconciled the accounts, the term would be over. Perhaps then, if any concern arose, I could convince him that it was an accounting error. These things happened all the time—and a reminder of the duke's generous donations to the college would soothe all ruffled parties.

In the meantime, I'd have my own unique grand tour.

Confidence bolstered, I fixed my cravat again—how did boys endure these?—and adjusted my billowing dark robes. A quick glance in the windowpane of my hired carriage earlier had confirmed that I looked very much like my cousin and not a girl in disguise. Now it was up to me to carry the performance. I was well-versed in masks, having worn them for years, and this would be like all the others.

A show, nothing more.

Right now, I was Lord Ansel, free and unencumbered by any horrid marital expectations. I snorted softly. I'd have to get used to being addressed as a lord, because I would not be readily answering to my cousin's name. Mimicking his walk, which for all intents and purposes wasn't that different from mine, I strolled forward like I didn't have a care in the world. The most notable differences were in the attitude—a lifted chin, a slight swagger with each step, and the innate confidence of a peer who knew the world was his oyster.

An oyster that would be *mine*. For a couple months, at least.

Spine snapping tight as I passed through the majestic and awe-inspiring Great Gate leading into the expansive Great Court of Trinity College, I let myself take it in. I was finally here. Groups of young men dressed similarly to me crossed my path, and for a moment, I was worried that I'd be called out as a charlatan, but other than a few passing harried glances, no one seemed to notice me.

Good, that was good.

Resisting the urge to make sure my facial hair was in place yet again, I adjusted my eyeglasses and pressed on. A stone fountain sat at the center of bright quadrangles of manicured lawn as I made my way across toward Nevile's Court, near the library, where my rooms were located. Though as I opened the door with my heavy key, it wasn't so much plural as it was a single, tiny space with a bed and a desk.

Shelves lined one whitewashed wall, and a large leaded-glass window the opposite. A table with a washbasin stood to my right, and a small fireplace took up the third wall facing the door, though with the spring upon us, it wouldn't be needed. My school clothes—all conveniently purloined from Ansel's armoire—had been neatly stored in the narrow wardrobe, and all my notebooks and textbooks on celestial mechanics were strewn over my bed.

I grinned to myself, a breathless giggle escaping me that I quickly swallowed before shutting my door, lest I be overheard and exposed for the fraud I was. Removing my outer gown, cap, and gold tassels, I loosened the cravat that had been choking me and unfastened my coat and waistcoat. Even with the extra wadded cloth padding the shoulders, it was a snug fit over my tightly wrapped bosom. I heaved the first full breath I'd had since leaving my house an hour ago.

Thankfully, my personal groom and lady's maid were both sworn to silence and amply compensated with my pin money for their confidence. I smiled fondly. Henry and Anna were in love and planned to marry, thanks to my own intervention a summer ago, which had allowed them to spend more time together while tending to me. As a result, there wasn't anything either of them wouldn't do for me, including keeping my secrets.

Watching them fall in love had made my heart twist with envy. But while I'd been deeply envious of their blossoming affair, it had also given me a last ember of hope that there still might be someone out there for me. My very own perfect person—a gentleman who would appreciate my fastidious mind and quizzical nature, who would meet me at every quarter, challenge me and inspire me, one whom I would adore and be adored by in turn . . .

Then again, chances of that happening while I pretended to be Ansel were slim.

Sighing, I glanced at my timepiece and yelped. I was due to meet my tutor, who supposedly had a room at this location as well. While classes and courses of study weren't formal, Ansel had said that impromptu discussions and debates tended to pop up all over the college. Private study was customary, and my assigned tutor would guide me through any difficult texts or mathematical problems. Ansel hadn't known who would be assigned to me, and I'd only received the name of my tutor after my cousin had left for France.

Tarik St. Clair.

My hands practically vibrated with excitement as I packed my books into my satchel, dressed, and refastened my discarded gown. Then I rushed out into the hallway, only to crash into a large mountain, my bag and books flying across the polished wood floors.

"Oh, goodness, I do beg your pardon!" The words flew out of me, and I cursed under my breath, in belated dismay realizing Ansel would never apologize. Boys didn't care if they crashed into people and caused a rumpus.

"Bloody hell, mate! Are you well?" the mountain said, his voice almost a shriek. A mop of wild blond curls tumbled into his brow, a pair of bright blue eyes assessing me from his considerable height. Gracious, he was huge. At least twice the size of me in width. "You came out of nowhere!"

"No harm done," I said as I gathered the notebook and pencils that had slid out of my bag. I kept my naturally husky voice pitched low, leaning in to the performance of being my cousin. Though I wanted to be myself, too. Ansel was much too smooth and grandiose for my tastes. "I was late and not looking where I was going." I peered at him. "You're not Mr. St. Clair, by chance, are you?"

Blue eyes widened comically. "No. He's a . . . Wrangler. I'm only a second-year."

"Do you happen to know where the discussion rooms near the Great Court are, then?" I asked. "There's a lecture I'm supposed to attend that Mr. St. Clair might be leading."

"As a matter of fact, I do."

I chewed my lip and then internally scolded myself for the habit. Thankfully, the boy was distracted, smoothing his rumpled gown. "What's a Wrangler?" I asked as I followed him down the corridor.

He shot me an odd expression, and I cringed, wondering if I'd already given myself away with my ignorance. But then he just shrugged his big shoulders. "St. Clair is a prodigy—a senior scholar pursuing his Master of Arts degree who ranked so highly in the competitive Mathematical Tripos examination it earned him the title of Second Wrangler. Only one other person scored higher than him." He wore an impressed look, so I nodded, then schooled my face to match his, though I had no idea what the Tripos was. It sounded fancy.

"That's remarkable."

"Most scholars at his level are usually encouraged to become Fellows of the university," the young man continued. "Being a Wrangler is a prestigious position to hold, and one of his primary duties would be to tutor and mentor younger students as part of his contribution to the college. I suppose that's where you come in." He pursed his lips. "Are you planning to take the Mathematical Tripos exam?"

I shook my head. Since this whole scheme was temporary, I had no plans to take *any* examinations, but having a tutor who had breezed through a top-level test was an unexpected benefit. That meant he was *smart*. I couldn't wait to pick his brain, particularly about mathematics and astronomy.

The gent smiled and stuck out his hand. "I'm Will, by the way." He wrinkled his brow as if he'd made a terrible faux pas. "Viscount William Humbolt, if we're being formal, which I hope to God we're not. I've stuck my foot in my mouth terribly these past months. The title is new, passed down through a third cousin to me. I'm still learning the ropes of things." The words tumbled out of him in a stream, and he stopped abruptly, shamefaced. "I'm sorry. I've done it again, haven't I? Open mouth, insert entire leg."

I laughed at his aghast expression. This freshly minted viscount and I were going to be *just* fine. "No, you haven't done anything. I'm new here, too. I'm Lord Ansel Chen, also somewhat unfamiliar with all of this, but you can call me . . ." I trailed off, brain blanking for a moment before inspiration suddenly struck. "Roz."

His blond brows jumped up at the moniker that couldn't be any further from my supposed first or last name. "Roz. Is that a nickname?"

I thought quickly and waved a careless hand. "Middle name's Eros. It stuck."

"Eros," he murmured, eyes brightening. "Greek god of love and passion. I do enjoy reading the classics." His face twisted into a grimace. "Much more than mathematical statistics, though my mother insists that I should have a greater understanding of all the subjects a proper viscount should know."

I didn't have the heart to tell him that most viscounts and peers of my acquaintance were experts only in drinking, gambling, and flirtation, and nary a one of them was interested in the pursuit of higher education, least of all mathematics or the classics. For many aristocrats, university was a formality, with little effort required to be conferred with a degree. A farce, actually. Though one that was benefitting me now, so I couldn't be *too* irritated.

"Will you be in London for the season as well?" I asked, pushing up my descending spectacles with one finger. By God, the frames were annoying.

"That is the hope," Will replied. "The intent last year was to make a few friends or connections, but then the king died and everyone went into mourning. Last term was subdued, though university life did continue. It has been much harder than I thought to be accepted as a peer when I wasn't born one."

Will's every emotion was transparent on his round face—something he would have to conquer if he hoped to survive a very vicious aristocracy. His difficulty did not surprise me. The ranks of the *ton* were very insular. Most peers, like Ansel's set, which included the Marquess of Ridley, who would eventually become the future Duke of Harbridge, knew each other from leading strings.

And sometimes the gentlemen—excluding Lord Ridley, my cousin, and any of their friends—could be haughtier than the ladies, sticking their noses up at those they deemed to be inferior or lacking in some way. Ansel could be high in the instep at times, but he wasn't a supercilious toff who looked down on others below his station.

I studied Will, noticing his cravat was askew and that there was a crusty yellowish stain on it—egg from breakfast if I had to guess. His clothes, though markedly new, were rumpled and untidy. He would hardly pass muster at an Almack's gathering, but in truth, I found him adorably endearing, like a giant baby chick I wanted to take under my protective wing.

"The *ton* is peculiar," I said as I kept pace with him down a nearby staircase. "But it will get easier as you find your footing."

He gave a humorless chuckle. "Of course, the way I keep fumbling my way about, I'd be highly shocked if any invitations arrived at all."

I bumped his arm with mine. "Tell you what? Let's stick together. You help me find my way around here, and I'll help you in London when the time comes. How does that sound?"

Incredulous but hopeful blue eyes peered down at me. "You'd do that? But you just met me. What if . . . people shun you by association? They don't call me Viscount Bumpkin for nothing."

Disgust bled through me. Goodness, the dreadful similarity to the intrigues in a London ballroom was too much. Name-calling was a vicious art, and the wrong associations could ruin a girl's come-out before it even began—everything always hinged upon the *right* connections. To think that young men would behave in such a manner at a prestigious university was a shock to me, but perhaps such social hierarchy existed everywhere.

"You seem like an amiable gentleman," I said with a shrug, determined to shore us both up. "Let's leave the judgments for later, shall we?"

Because the truth was if gentle, trusting Will found out he'd been deceived by a lady dressed as a boy, I had no doubt he might not be so friendly or forgiving. In my current happenstance, beneath my false mustache and padded shoulders, I *was* the absolute wrong social connection. However, I'd take allies wherever I could get them, and I suspected Will might feel the same.

At the end of the staircase, we entered a large room for the lecture, which was taken up by over twenty lads of varying ages wearing the same billowing gowns with various hats and tassels, occupying sofas and chairs of all sizes pulled in a haphazard circle. A frisson of excitement wound up my spine at the hum of voices. Will and I crammed into two spots at the end of a sofa. I pulled out my notebook and pencil as chatter flew around the room, and attempted to follow the chain of conversation. My ears perked up. It ranged from gossip and girls to complex geometry and algebra problems as well as celestial mechanics.

I couldn't help the grin that spread across my face at the latter.

Now *that* was what I was here for.

"Gentlemen, come to order," a deep voice said. I couldn't see over the heads in front of me as I scribbled the date on the first page. Someone blew a loud whistle through his mouth. "Gents, quiet!"

Everyone shushed. A tall head of wavy dark hair was the only thing I could see through the gaps in the bodies in front of me, but I was much too focused on writing the date in my new notebook to get a better glance. I only needed to listen after all, and participate should I feel the need. For now, I wanted to soak it all in. There would be time for contribution later—I didn't want to seem *too* eager.

"Let's resume our discussion on analytical versus geometrical approaches to mathematics, and the path our own Mr. Newton has charted. The challenge was that the former is arguably the path forward, and I agree. Algebra and calculus are by far superior for advancement in mechanics."

I blinked. That was an aggressive viewpoint.

The room quieted to an ominous, abrupt hush, heads swiveling in my direction. Will gasped beside me, and I realized that I'd uttered my private thoughts aloud. My stomach fell. So much for not sounding too eager on the first day. Perhaps I'd be lucky, and the discussion would move on if someone else chimed in. But the silence only grew.

"By all means, sir, in the back row, enlighten us," the disembodied voice said, a hint of annoyance bleeding through.

Mortified, I cleared my throat, keeping my voice deep. In for a penny, in for a pound, then. "Calculus might be more elegant, but a geometrical method could prove to be more rigorous for any kind of mathematical proof. One could debate the merits of either, but both solutions are valid."

"Well said," someone to my right observed, and I smiled gratefully in their direction, then I cursed at myself for smiling at all—boys hardly sought approval.

"Advancement in the knowledge of mathematics and the

understanding of astronomy and mechanics is limited with the Euclidian method," the first voice countered.

"Perhaps," I replied. "But that doesn't negate the value of classical constructions."

"Point taken," the leader said, his voice sounding closer than before, as if people in front of me had cleared a path. "Who are you, sir? Introduce yourself."

Horrified, I shrank into my seat, wishing I'd kept my stupid mouth shut, but then the crowd in front of me shifted as if by magic, and any rational thought deserted me completely as my dismayed stare landed on the most beautiful face I'd ever seen. Goodness, speaking of the classics, this boy could be Adonis in the flesh. And I'd seen plenty of good-looking gentlemen.

My throat dried as my bemused gaze collided with a pair of intense blue eyes the color of lapis lazuli gemstones, surrounded by warm russet-brown skin. I'd never seen eyes that color—like a glassy lake shot through with splashes of sunshine on a summer day. His face was square with a strong chin and a bold nose, offset by full lips that were currently pulled into a grimace as he observed me. A wave of the thick brown hair I'd glimpsed before slid into his brow when that fascinating gaze flashed and darkened . . . with *recognition*.

Oh no.

"Lord Ansel," he drawled, making my heart sink precariously even as a part of me cheered that my disguise was convincing enough. Honestly, what were the chances I'd be tested so sorely on my first day? "What are you doing here? Shouldn't you be at St. John's knee-deep in classical philosophy? If I recall, that was your field of study."

I gulped, feeling my face heat despite my internal dictates for it to remain calm. "Er, I . . . transferred."

Whispers buzzed through the room like a swarm of gnats. "That's uncommon," someone remarked from my left side as one behind me barked, "A spy in our midst," while another muttered, "Deuced nob."

I didn't understand the second comment, though it stank of some hidden rivalry, but the last was correct, and I grabbed on to it like a lifeline. I was an aristocrat—I answered to no one. Channeling every titled male of my acquaintance, I lifted a haughty brow, smirked, and slouched back into the sofa cushions. "What's it to you? I am a peer. My interests have changed, and I can do as I please. Who are *you* to question why I am here?"

A few murmurs rose out of that, naturally from the other nobles in the room and the sycophants who wanted to cozy up to them. There might be an underlying intercollege rivalry, but the aristocracy superseded all. I leaned in *hard* to that innate privilege, despite the self-disgust brewing in my gut. I deplored class distinctions and anyone who thought they were automatically better through a fortunate circumstance of birth.

A mocking smile that did not reach his eyes curled his lip. "We've met, but perhaps you do not remember. It was during a rowing competition on the River Cam some years ago." His expression grew arctic. "You toppled me into the river."

Dismayed, I stared at him, wondering what would have

possessed Ansel to do such a thing but leaving my expression blank. Those nearest us stared in rapt attention. "Did you deserve it?"

"You certainly seemed to think so."

I snorted. "Well, then, perhaps the act was justified. Shall we be gentlemen and let bygones be bygones?" I stood and stuck out a palm, tilting my neck to hold his gaze, considering he was several inches taller than me. "Mr. . . . ?"

"St. Clair," he said, his smile growing teeth as his hand grasped mine hard, nearly causing me to wince as the name fully registered. "Your tutor for this term."

CHAPTER THREE

> To every action there is always opposed an equal reaction: or the mutual actions of two bodies upon each other are always equal, and directed to contrary parts.
>
> —Isaac Newton

The dining hall was crowded, the long tables laden with dishes and almost every chair occupied by students, but thankfully, Will had saved me a seat at one end. As I threaded my way toward him, I scanned the seats for the boy who I was certain hated me with the fire of a thousand suns, but Tarik St. Clair was not in sight. My fluttering pulse calmed a smidge as I sucked a gulp of air into tight lungs.

No matter how many times I told myself, *Think like Ansel*—I could not control the way my very female heart responded to the boy. It'd been a week, and I couldn't stop thinking about him. His intensity and his obvious intelligence combined with his striking looks turned my normally unflappable self to suet pudding. Was this what it was like to fancy someone? To be hit with the swooning stick? All fluttery and weightless and unable to draw a full breath?

I'd played the game for so long in the *ton* of the smitten

girl without understanding what being calf-eyed over someone even meant. Not knowing what it was actually like for Ela with Keston or Zia with Rafi. That hopeful, blissed-out look that young lovers wore when their hearts were upon their sleeves had eluded me.

Until now.

This strange fancy felt like I had been struck in the chest by a runaway carriage.

With those lush lips set in a sharp-edged angular face, he was uncommonly handsome—the resulting mix of European and likely Indian ancestry. My beautiful friend Ela was of Indian descent, and though Tarik's complexion was a shade lighter than hers, they shared the same thick hair, defined brows, and obscenely long eyelashes.

Those mesmerizing lapis lazuli eyes tortured me in a storm of my own imagination, boring into my soul and finding me lacking in every possible way. Until they hadn't . . . until they'd burned with something else other than contempt.

He doesn't like you, silly girl, no matter what your fantasies conjure up. You are Lord Ansel Chen, I reminded myself. *You cannot be pining over your tutor, for heaven's sake! Especially when he thinks you're a terribly spoiled, indolent peer who shoved him into a river.*

As much as I loved my cousin, I begrudged him for being such a colossal cad. It came with the territory—his set were the crème de la crème of high society—and though I couldn't possibly condone or understand what might have possessed him to treat Mr.

St. Clair with such callousness, I wished it had been *anyone* else. On top of our awful start, their previous history would make the next few months even more of a challenge for me.

I wanted to learn. I did not want to be ignored or, worse, opposed at every turn because of some absurd feud that I had no part of.

Though I was grateful Mr. St. Clair seemed to be avoiding me at the moment.

"You almost missed dinner, Roz," Will said, his round face lighting up when I plonked down beside him at the very far end of the table and proceeded to fill my plate with enough twice-boiled potatoes, chunky stew, and crusty bread to feed an army. My stomach growled with approval. I was ravenous!

"Thanks for saving me a seat," I told him before tucking in.

Maintaining a disguise and studying complex subjects while hiding from handsome tutors certainly worked up an appetite—and I wasn't a demure lady now who had to mind her manners. I could be as feral as I wanted, within reason, of course. Manners were still important, obviously, but I didn't have to eat like a bird in public. I wolfed down a few mouthfuls, groaning as the rich stew hit my taste buds. It certainly wasn't our family chef's cooking, but it was exactly what I needed.

"Slow down, or you'll make yourself ill," Will said with a chuckle, though he ate as heartily as me.

"Famished," I said, and wiped my plate with a piece of bread before reaching for a second helping. I'd skipped lunch in favor of finishing my reading, hoping to astound St. Clair if and when we next met, and now I was paying the price. I felt curious eyes flicking to me from around the table, but I was too focused on filling my growly belly to pay them any attention.

Will cleared his throat when I glanced pointedly at him. "Roz, may I present Mr. Harold Jennings, by way of America, and Sir James Lowry of Essex. Harold is a second-year like me, though James already took the Mathematical Tripos. He got Third Wrangler, which is a huge accomplishment, and he's pursuing his master's. And those two next to them are Mr. Klaus and Kristof Blendel from Norway. They're third-years, bound for the clergy."

I recognized the first two from the combination room—Harold was a short, dark-skinned boy with a sparse mustache that looked like it was a spider clinging on for dear life, and the vaguely older James was a stocky, freckle-faced redhead with a shy smile showing charmingly crooked teeth and penetrating green eyes.

The last two were identical twins with corkscrew blond-brown curls in the same hairstyle, who were mirror images of each other. They did *not*, however, embody potential vicars. I had no idea what made me think that, only that the mischievous glint in their light blue eyes reminded me of Blake. It would be impossible to say who was who. Given how much Ansel and I looked alike, so much so that I was pretending to be him, I nearly laughed at the irony of becoming friends with a real-life pair of twins.

After dabbing my mouth with my napkin, I stuck out my palm and shook each of their hands. "Lord Ansel Chen," I replied. "But you can call me Roz." I glanced at the twins. "So, who's Klaus, and who's Kristof? How do people tell you apart?"

The one on my side of the table—*Klaus?*—grinned. "They don't, and we like it that way. Keeps everyone on their toes."

With a smirk, the other twin tapped his chin. "There is one way to tell, but well, you'd have to get to know us better. A *lot* better."

I blinked, the suggestive note in his voice causing me to snort—goodness, they were more like Blake than I thought. I certainly felt for their future parishes—men of the cloth with their charm and looks would be taking many a confession.

"Good to know," I said smiling. "A pleasure to make your acquaintance."

"Where are you from, Roz?" Harold asked as one of the subsizars cleared the used dishes from the table.

As I'd learned from Ansel, subsizars, also known informally as scouts, were less wealthy students who worked to cover their school fees and were assigned as helpers to affluent, upper-class students. I'd read that Isaac Newton had been a subsizar here when he attended the college in the 1660s. I admired men like him, who had worked hard for everything they achieved.

With Ansel's station as a peer, he was assigned a scout, but I'd yet to meet them. While the hierarchy did not sit well with me, it was a reality for those who could not afford the fees, while receiving a coveted education in return. However, despite their reduced circumstances, they deserved to be treated with respect and kindness.

"Not far from here," I replied with a delayed start, recalling who I was supposed to be when everyone stared at me. "My uncle's ancestral seat is in Newmarket. He's the Duke of Delmont. Most of my family is in London currently, though. My mother, brother, aunt, and my cousin . . ." I trailed off with a frown. "Er, Lady Rosalin, who is out for the season."

James sat up, expression suddenly speculative. "I've heard of Delmont. He's rumored to be a force in Parliament and focused on trade laws between Britain and the Far East. He's a powerful man, isn't he?"

"He is," I said, proud of my father and his accomplishments.

"Is your cousin attractive?" Kristof said, eyebrows waggling. At least, he was the one I thought Will called Kristof. "Is she unmarried? Promised to someone? Will she visit? I guarantee we can show her an excellent time."

I laughed. "I'm not sure that I want my sweet, innocent cousin around the likes of you lot."

"Sweet and innocent, even better," he said. "We are very pious, my brother and I."

"I'm sure you are," I said while Harold burst into snickers.

"Do *not,*" he blurted, shaking his head, "bring your cousin around these two, not unless you want her to be corrupted or marched to the altar. The number of broken hearts left in these two libertines' wakes is a travesty."

Klaus threw a hand to his chest. "You wound us, dear Harold."

"We're not *that* bad!" Kristof added.

"No, you're worse," Harold replied with a chortle.

Everyone laughed good-naturedly when Klaus poked him and Harold pretended to shove his friend off his seat in turn.

I loved their easy camaderie. Their friendship would be an

added bonus while I was here. My continued presence depended, however, on whether I could handle a tutor who might be motivated to see me fail. I wrinkled my nose at the thought of him and nearly sneezed when my mustache tickled my nostrils. I was still getting used to the extra facial hair and the constant feeling that there was something untoward on my face.

"Can any of you tell me what to expect from Mr. St. Clair?" I asked in a quiet voice. "He's my tutor this term."

Their expressions ranged from alarm to sympathy to mirth. The twins of course displayed the last. James looked like he swallowed something vile, a sneer curling his mouth. They all exchanged silent looks before Harold ventured to speak first. "He's a hard, exacting taskmaster because he was one of the top-ranking students in the Tripos, so he'll likely expect a lot from you. There will be heavy reading, and you will be tested orally frequently."

The twins snorted in unison and Klaus fanned himself, pretending to swoon. "He can test me that way any time."

Kristof rolled his eyes. "True, he is pleasing to the eye, but only if he stays silent. The smart ones always want to show off the size of their brains. So tedious!"

I nearly snorted again. Goodness, they were cheeky.

"One of my mates had him as a tutor last term," James interjected, helping himself to some blancmange pudding that one of the subsizars had quietly deposited on the table after clearing the rest of the dishes from the previous course. "He decided to leave university with no plans to return. Guess who forced that decision?"

My eyes widened. “St. Clair caused him to leave?”

“That’s the rumor. He’s a varlet, nothing but a scapegrace.”

Something in the hissed insult combined with the derisive curl of his lip made me frown. “You don’t like him, I take it.”

“Not particularly, no.” James scowled, then turned to glare at the others. “And before any of you loudmouthed clods say it’s because he got Second Wrangler years ago, and I’m jealous because I got Third, you’re wrong. He’s arrogant and thinks he’s too good for anyone else even though he doesn’t deserve the position he has. He’s a nobody.”

“Why do you say that?” Harold questioned, clearly surprised by the vitriol.

“I was in the same year as him, remember? He *followed* me here, certainly not on his own coattail, poaching *my* fellowship opportunities,” James ground out. It took a minute for him to collect himself. “Everyone knows he was a subsizar who only got special enrollment because of his uncle.”

“He was accepted here, same as any of us,” Harold said quietly. “Financial limitations shouldn’t matter. Within these walls, we’re equal.”

“We’re not, but what would you know? You Americans don’t understand British hierarchy.”

The conceit in James’s voice rubbed me the wrong way, especially when poor Harold hunched into himself, looking oddly humiliated. There was a social structure here, just as there was in the *ton,* but James didn’t need to be so heavy-handed about it. It wasn’t *Harold’s* fault he was unfamiliar with centuries of English bigotry.

I wasn't exactly sure what James was alluding to about St. Clair, but if I was stuck with a knave for a tutor, then I needed to be prepared. "So why did your friend leave?"

"He couldn't keep up, I suppose," James replied, his gaze meeting mine and seeing my troubled expression. "Don't feel too sorry for him either. My friend is a marquess, and an honorary degree will probably be conferred upon him just for living here. Some highborn toffs don't even have to take the examination. A waste of time and coin, if you ask me. Why even attend university, if you're not interested in doing the actual work?"

"An excellent question," Will said, clearly trying to reduce the tension. "Though I must admit, it's much harder than I expected it would be, so perhaps an easy degree is a blessing in disguise. For aristocrats, anyway."

I nodded, thinking of my cousin. "University is the done thing as part of a gentleman's education, at least if one isn't lucky or wealthy enough to go on a grand tour."

The twins sighed in unison.

"I'd give my left arm and leg to be able to go to Europe for a year or two," Kristof groused. "See the Roman ruins, get my portrait painted in Paris, visit Vienna's Schönbrunn Palace, run with the bulls in Pamplona, participate in an orgiastic Dionysus bacchanal in Athens. Now *that's* an education."

I nearly spluttered at the last, feeling my face flame. They were loose with their words, but I was enjoying every scandalous moment. Girls were never allowed to talk like this. Honestly, what *was* an orgiastic bacchanal? I knew who Dionysus was—the Greek god of wine and ecstasy—so it wasn't hard to deduce.

Was *that* what Ansel was doing? No wonder he was so excited about going!

"Why the clergy?" I asked curiously, considering that neither of the twins seemed too reverent in nature, not that I was judging. Perhaps, despite their brazen natures, they would make excellent clergymen.

"We are neither the heir nor the spare in our family," Klaus replied. "As third and fourth sons, we could have bought a commission in the navy or gotten an education to become a reverend, the most prestigious genteel profession, so we chose the latter." He eyed me. "What about you? What's a duke's nephew interested in studying? Shouldn't you be in line for the dukedom?"

Ansel would be in line for my father's seat after my little brother. "My younger cousin is the heir apparent, so I'm the spare," I said. "But my uncle is healthy, and I hope he lives a very long life. As far as study, I'm interested in astronomy, specifically." I felt my cheeks warm with embarrassment. "I should like to build my own telescope one day."

Admiration bloomed in Klaus's eyes. "Capital!"

I peered at the dour-faced James again. "If you're Third Wrangler, are you a tutor, then, as well?"

James nodded, and for a brief moment, I wondered whether I should switch to him, but the way he had treated Harold stuck like a thorn under my skin. It was a gut feeling, nothing more, but something told me I'd be better off with St. Clair. He might dislike me, but at least he didn't seem unduly spiteful.

When a chair scraped loudly against the stone floor, I glanced over my shoulder, noticing that the crowd in the dining hall had begun to thin. My stare snagged on a lone figure on the other side of the room, poring intently over a book, while picking at the remnants of some cut fruit on a plate. My pulse picked up while my eyes greedily absorbed every detail.

As if he'd felt the weight of my scrutiny, Tarik St. Clair glanced up, that fiery blue gaze colliding with mine. Even with three very long tables between us, it felt like he was an arm's length away, the sheer magnetism of him intense and annoyingly overpowering. I could feel his animosity like a tangible touch.

"He really does not esteem you," Will murmured into my ear, making me jump. "If looks could kill, you would be floating down the River Cam."

I didn't think it was *that* bad. I yanked my gaze away and pretended to be unfazed, even though my heart was galloping like a runaway horse in my chest. It thumped even faster when my voice came out unnaturally loud in the suddenly empty, cavernous room. "I don't care what that pompous jackanapes thinks of me."

James brayed with laughter, eyes lighting with malice, and I swallowed my discomfort.

"I think he heard you," Will said, seeming perturbed, but I focused on the table instead of turning back around. "If you're not careful, he could make your life very difficult."

"He can try," I gloated, standing. "But I can handle whatever he throws at me."

The twins chuckled. "You're plucky, Roz. Come out with us tomorrow tonight, after curfew. We're going to a new gambling den that just opened."

I lifted my brows. "Don't the proctors frown on that? You could be fined or face rustication." I'd overheard Ansel bemoaning fines he'd been forced to pay out of his own pocket many a time for flouting the curfew because of the ever-vigilant proctors who kept track of the students breaking any rules, though he'd never faced suspension. One more privilege of being a peer.

"Not if we don't get caught," Kristof said with a wink.

I had a feeling that carousing with those two would be an experience to remember. Grinning at them, I grabbed my bag. "I would love to. But alas, I've been summoned by my uncle to London. Count me in for next time, though."

My skin felt as though it was on fire as I walked past St. Clair's table, the press of his hostile gaze like blades upon my skin. It was a decidedly strange feeling—one I'd never felt before, and I could not decide whether it thrilled me or warned me off. In truth, there was an unhinged part of me that wanted to provoke him further for no reason at all, as if it *liked* being the insufferable center of his attention. Flustered, I hastened my steps but froze when his throat cleared.

"Lord Ansel," he called out. "A moment, please."

I stopped and forced my stare to meet his, inhaling sharply at his otherworldly beauty. I kept my lips pressed together so no sound would escape them—namely, the feminine sigh that would most certainly give me away as I swooned over his elegant features up close. St. Clair's thick, dark hair was rumpled and fell into his brow as if he'd run his fingers through it too many a time. My own fingers itched stupidly to do the same, and I fisted them closed.

In all my seasons, no boy had ever taken my breath away, not even Blake, but the poets could write sonnets about this boy's jawline, sharp cheekbones, and sculpted lips. The romantics would marvel over the jewel-bright glint of those thick-lashed eyes, where blue was too prosaic a word to describe them, and the warm glow of his russet-brown skin, which would make a person dream of sun-kissed beaches and balmy summers.

When he cleared his throat, I gulped and tore my gaze from the mesmerizing landscape of his face. He pushed a thick book toward me with one finger. "Your required reading for this weekend. I expect a lively discussion first thing on Monday."

Jolted out of my trance, I glanced down—its spine was as wide as my forearm. "This weekend . . . this whole book?" I mumbled dully.

His blue irises lit with no small degree of satisfaction, and I cringed inwardly. That haughty expression could rival any condescending blueblood in the *ton*. "Did I stutter? Didn't you just boast that you could handle anything I threw your way?"

"I . . ." My cheeks flamed as I faltered for words with growing distress at the fact that he *had* overheard me and that my bold boast had earned me a task that would take hours to complete. "I beg your pardon, sir?"

"No apology needed. Simply complete the reading and we won't have any difficulties. Monday, Lord Ansel," he said, his eyes falling back to his own open book in a clear dismissal.

"Roz," I choked out. "Name's Roz."

I don't know why I told him that—maybe it was my small attempt to control this untenable situation.

He didn't answer, though he speared a piece of fruit with a fork and ferried it to his lips. I should have taken the volume and left, but instead, senselessly captivated, I stared at his mouth like a smitten fool while he bit into the triangle of pear. He licked the juice off his lower lip, and my entire chest clenched in visceral response.

What would it be like to feel that mouth pressed to mine? To kiss him? The warmth in my cheeks suddenly spread everywhere, from the tips of my ears to my shoulders and torso. My skin felt like it was cinching tight over my bones.

"Lord Ansel?"

My gaze snapped to his in utter mortification at being caught ogling him like some desperate lecher. Heavens, what was I *doing*? "Yes?" I croaked.

He was frowning. "Is there a problem?"

"No, none." I forced my face to convey nothing but cool hauteur, though my insides were churning with shame. Hastily, I snatched the book and hurried away on unsteady legs before I could be caught doing something infinitely worse.

Like swooning.

CHAPTER FOUR

Oh, Diamond! Diamond! Thou little knowest what mischief thou hast done!

—Isaac Newton

Curse this deuced cravat!

Divesting myself of all my garments, including the blasted garrote of a neckcloth and the troublesome, badly fitting eyeglasses that transformed me into Lord Ansel Chen, I sank into the bathtub in my chambers at Delmont Park with a loud, happy sigh. While I loved being at Trinity College in my tiny room and living the true life of a university student, washing in a basin with cold water was not ideal. And despite having a chamberpot in my quarters, I'd been properly horrified at the idea of relieving myself in the public privies.

That would never happen.

I sighed again as my parched skin soaked up the unscented water like a desiccated sponge. I'd had to forego my usual rose-scented soap, but that was a small sacrifice. Though I washed myself properly every day, nothing could compare to a long, hot soak. I recognized the privilege for what it was, and for once was deeply grateful for my station and the luxuries it afforded me.

Anna massaged her fingers into my scalp as she lathered my long hair with the soap my cousin usually used, which smelled of lemon and bergamot. My waist-length tresses hadn't been properly washed for days, and considering they had been tucked up under a wig and then under a hat, it was a wonder they weren't more of a snarly, smelly mess. The relief of not having the tightness of the wig pressing onto my skull felt glorious.

"How was your first week?" Anna asked quietly, with an eye on the other maids bustling about my chamber. "I still cannot believe no one recognized you or knew you were a lady." Her hushed voice sounded scandalized.

Though she was part of the subterfuge, she hadn't been shy in sharing her worry for me . . . and for what the possibility of discovery could do to my reputation as well as her position in my father's household, should he find out she'd been complicit in my scheme. But he would *not* find out, and even if he did, I would make sure that Anna was free of any blame.

"Neither can I," I replied, and then stared grimly at the heavy book resting on the chair near the armoire. Normally, I would be thrilled at the prospect of official study, but there was no chance of *anyone* getting through that entire tome in three days. St. Clair wanted to humble me; I was sure of it. I exhaled and felt the start of a headache. "I suppose it went as well as could be expected—I have a ridiculous amount of reading to complete before the start of next week. An entire book, in fact."

"Good thing you love reading, my lady."

I grimaced. "This, unfortunately, is more of a punishment. I fear I didn't start off on the right foot with my tutor."

"How so?" she asked.

I sighed. "Apparently, he had an altercation with Ansel in the past, so he already does not esteem me. I fear we are bound to be enemies, which does not bode well for my plans."

"You can charm anyone, my lady. You are Lady Rosalin, not your cousin. Perhaps, remember that when you feel discouraged—this might all be a ruse where you look like him, but you are not him. You're *you*. Smart, brilliant, and capable, but also considerate and kind."

"Thank you, Anna," I said, buoyed by her words and the wise reminder that I *wasn't* Ansel, and though I was walking in his shoes, the choices I made were all mine.

"Speaking of being charming, the duchess sent a messenger yesterday, and she expects you in London by this evening," she said, carefully pouring a pitcher of water over my head to rinse the suds away.

I groaned aloud. After my first week at Cambridge, I'd much rather curl up in my bed and get a head start on my reading than put on a pleasant face to try to catch a husband. The mere thought of it was exhausting. "Perhaps I can say that I'm ill."

"The Duchess of Harbridge's ball is important, and your presence will certainly be missed. Your mother will be very disappointed." Anna wrapped a length of toweling around my wet locks and squeezed gently. "And Her Grace might curtail your visits to Delmont Park, if you go back on your word to be present for the season."

"Very well," I said, knowing my mother was single-minded enough to do just that and thwart all my carefully laid plans. "Instruct the cook to prepare a basket of food for us, and Henry to ready the carriage. I suppose I can read on the way."

Not willing to squander the opportunity in my lap, I would make the best of things. Six hours of being cooped up in a carriage meant a stretch of uninterrupted study time. I'd have to learn to manage my reading load as well as my mother's machinations for the season . . . or this arrangement would fail.

Shortly after I finished my bath and dressed, we were ensconced in the carriage on the way to London. I held the worn volume of *Opticks: or, A Treatise of the Reflections, Refractions, Inflections and Colours of Light* by Sir Isaac Newton in my hand and traced the lettering on the front cover. It was an older edition, but it appeared exceedingly well cared for. There were lightly penciled notes in the margins.

I wondered if they belonged to St. Clair. The lettering was precise and bold, the notes encapsulating different calculations as well as general observations. A strange thrill wound through me at the notion of our ideas and opinions intersecting . . . or better yet, clashing. I blinked and scowled at myself.

This absurd, fabricated rivalry I had with my tutor had to stop.

I thumbed through the pages, stopping at one of my favorite chapters. In all honesty, I'd read the book before, though it was some years ago—my father had a first edition in our library at Delmont Park, and I'd adored reading about Newton's prism and lens experiments, particularly about the refraction of white light into multiple visible colors. Some of the concepts were familiar; others were vague, because I had only paid attention to the sections that had interested me.

Like his telescopes.

Older telescopes used glass lenses, which impacted how colors could be seen, and the resulting images were fuzzy and out-of-focus. In truth, Newton's brilliant design incorporated mirrors instead of glass lenses, which reflected the image back to the eye. It fascinated me that his first instrument, built in 1668, was a mere six inches long . . . almost ten times smaller than those of this century.

"That looks like it would give you a headache," Anna remarked from her side of the coach, making me jump. Her brow wrinkled at some of the diagrams.

I smiled and tapped the top of the leather spine. "It's an interesting book. I forgot how much I enjoyed it. Well, parts of it anyway."

"And you're reading it *again*?" she asked with a horrified expression. "For *fun*?"

"As a refresher," I said, lips twitching at her reaction. "When you see the colors of the rainbow up in the sky after a rainstorm, it's because of Newton's experiments that we know they come from white light or sunlight."

"How did he do them?" she asked, curious.

I warmed to my subject. "Via prisms and refracting a beam of light. In the old days, Aristotle and other philosophers thought that the different colors—red, orange, yellow, green, blue, indigo, and violet—came from both light and darkness, from black and white, or from some effect of the rain on the rays of the sun. This author proved that they were all white light when he refracted them back into another prism and sunlight emerged."

"Fascinating," Anna said. "But all that numerical text and those calculations must be boring. Words are so much better, in my opinion. A sonnet is more relaxing than numbers."

"That's because you have the soul of a poet. Sums are not boring at all. I find them quite fun. I suppose I have the soul of a mathematician."

Her repulsed expression made me giggle. "Honestly, my lady, no wonder no suitors ever meet your expectations if this is the kind of diversion you call *fun*."

"Would you rather I spend these hours perfecting my needlepoint?" I replied, feeling the urge to defend my passion. "Hours upon hours punching holes into fabric, not to mention flesh, in my case. How tiresome! I'd much rather stretch the muscles of my brain and learn something new."

"You could enjoy the colors of the rainbow in your fashion or coiffure. They're pretty to look at, and that's all that matters, at least for a lady of your station. Who needs to know where the colors came from?"

"I do," I replied. "I savor knowing how things work, and besides, many men and women are employed as scientists and engineers based on this man's theories."

Anna sniffed and stared pointedly at my plain navy traveling costume. "Perhaps if you also focused on *wearing* those bright hues, you might have more success with attracting a suitor."

"What's wrong with what I'm wearing? You know I prefer dark colors."

This was a bone of contention between my mother and me. It was currently de rigueur to wear Turkey red and saffron yellow, but I despised loud shades. Though the king's death had been sorrowful, I rather enjoyed the reprieve of wearing somber colors. It'd been a blessing in disguise.

However, a return to the season hadn't stopped my mother from commissioning dozens of gowns in colors that were designed to make me stand out like a peacock on display. Fortunately, I'd been able to sneak orders with Madame Marchand for a few other dresses in some more muted colors. Leave the posturing to actual peacocks . . .

At least this long carriage ride meant I would be free of primping for a few hours before I had to concede to my mother's intrigues. I settled in, kicking off my slippers and then tucking my feet beneath me on the squabs, and concentrated on Newton. Eventually, I was lulled by the rhythm of the wheels, my eyes fluttered shut, and I was dreaming of telescopes and rainbows and obnoxious tutors with eyes so hypnotic, a girl could get lost in them.

"I look like a giant pineapple, Mama," I groused, and stared grumpily at my reflection in the mirror. The hexagon pattern of the yellow fabric itself was a problem, though made even worse by the gold-and-green tufted embroidery. This had to be a joke.

"Pineapples are fashionable," she replied while fastening an emerald necklace to my throat, and I nearly wept in horror at the likeness it made to a pineapple crown. "You know yellow is a highly coveted color this season."

"Isn't it too bright? We're still mourning the king, after all. We should be respectful at least for a few more months."

"Mourning is officially over, by the palace's own announcement," she countered. "And we must set our sights on getting you wed. I am certain that His Majesty, may he rest in peace, would understand the circumstances in which we find ourselves with your future. Desperate times call for desperate measures."

I gritted my teeth. "Honestly, what gentleman wants a gaudy pineapple for a wife?"

"The fruit is a sign of wealth, power, and hospitality. Three things that herald our family, and will hopefully attract someone similar." She puffed my sleeves and studied the plume factory of white feathers currently ensconced upon my crown. I was lucky I could keep my neck straight and head high from the weight of them. Who knew feathers could be so heavy? Well, they *were*—especially when encrusted with gems along the rachis. The multitude of hairpins required to keep them in place only worsened my situation.

"Let's be realistic," I muttered. "They're a sign of imperialism."

The maids surrounding us gasped, but they were used to my unconventional opinions.

"Rosalin!" my mother chastised, though she was smart enough to know I wasn't wrong. It just wasn't something any well-bred young lady should have thoughts on.

"Don't worry, Mama, I promise to keep my irregular views to myself," I said as Anna threaded more gems through my hair, which would not hold a curl no matter how hot the curling tongs were. *Clearly, gems were the replacement for ringlets,* I mused wryly. "Though it's not like the Duchess of Harbridge would not agree."

Ela's mother-in-law, Zia's own mama, the Duchess of Harbridge, whose ball we were attending tonight, was a brilliant, forward-thinking activist who led the charge for human rights in Parliament. Despite not having her own seat, since she was a woman, her very influential husband fully supported her recommendations and proposals. Her voice had power, and she wasn't afraid to use it.

"She is a *duchess* and free to speak her mind, my dear. Perhaps you can aspire to such a position, should you find a duke to marry," my mother said. "Women in our position must always find creative ways to have our opinions taken into account."

I blinked at that, narrowing my gaze at my mother, but her expression was placid. What opinions did she have? She never went against my father . . . or so it seemed. Mama was a private person, but she had never been a wilting wallflower.

"There are hardly any good dukes left," I muttered. "Much less ones with two brain cells to rub together or ones whose brains haven't fully developed yet."

Mama arched a thin, dark brow. "The Duke of Bentley is looking for another wife."

I gasped and nearly gagged at the idea of marrying the man in question. Not only was he older than dirt, but he was also of the mind that women should be seen and not heard. No, thank you. "He practically has one foot, and perhaps even the entire leg, in the grave!"

"What about the Duke of Renton? His mother is desperate to see him wed. She asked me last week if you thought him handsome."

My eyelids fluttered shut in disgust. "Mama, he's sixteen with barely any whiskers on his upper lip."

"Beggars cannot be choosers."

I clenched my jaw, mimicking her terseness. "And yet you expect me to choose between a slovenly old toad and a pubescent boy who is an utter greenhorn. How are either of those acceptable?"

"Then pick someone else," she said. "A marquess, an earl, a viscount. Even landed gentry will do."

My eyes stung. "If it were *that* easy, I would have been betrothed years ago."

"You must marry this season, Rosalin. Your father won't stand for his only daughter not to be wedded after a fourth time on the marriage mart. People are starting to think something is wrong with the Duke of Delmont's offspring, and once that gossip takes root, it will be impossible to counter."

"Nothing is wrong with me. I simply cannot abide a narrow-minded, bigoted old fool or a blushing schoolboy intimidated by his own shadow," I bit out. "Would you be happy to see me wither away in misery?"

"I would be happy to see you settled and safe."

I opened my mouth to argue and snapped it shut. That was the way of our world—girls of my station were traded from one keeper to another. Being married was the pinnacle of our existence and, sadly, was the only opportunity to continue to have a voice. At least for husbands who *allowed* their wives to speak. I swallowed the bitterness on my tongue.

My mother had a capable, clever mind of her own, but she often ceded to my father, claiming that he would do what was best, especially politically. Which was true—he was a brilliant politician, and his political legacy was something to be lauded and admired. But that didn't mean he knew what was best for *me*.

Was it so wrong to wish for a husband who could hold my interest with his mind alone?

Most people in the aristocracy alleged that one could not be both a gentleman *and* a scholar, as if the two were mutually exclusive. An aristocrat's primary goals were tied to his estate and title, and for him, university was primarily about making social connections, learning diplomacy and civility, and gaining sophistication.

Then again, Zia's brother and Ela's husband, the Marquess of Ridley, had been made better for his time at Oxford. His intellect served him well, and not just as the future Duke of Harbridge but also as a respected peer. Mr. Nasser also had an exceptional ability to talk about any culture in the world . . . an aptitude that would have come from having diverse family and an extensively broad education. Even Blake, for all his faults, had been shored up by his time at university. He was sharp, with an extraordinary memory.

I hated hiding who I was, hated pretending that I was not intelligent to make others feel more comfortable. Ansel and his friends didn't know how lucky they had it to be unapologetically who they were. I wanted to be seen. Heard. *Respected*.

And more than anything, I wanted to leave my mark on the world, like Newton, or any of the intrepid female scholars

I idolized, like Émilie du Châtelet, Caroline Herschel, Wang Zhenyi, and Sophie Germain to name a few.

But the more I thought about it, the only reason I was able to pass muster at Cambridge in the first place was because my parents—my *mother*—had always encouraged learning. Was this one of *her* creative ways of subverting the patriarchy? Maintaining a well-stocked library of books with subjects girls weren't usually expected to study? In hindsight, she had never prevented me from reading whatever I loved, so in a roundabout way, I owed her for getting me here, for the foundations I had already . . . for making me who I *was*.

Thus, I forced myself to let go of my frustration and smiled at my mother in the mirror, taking in the similarities of our heart-shaped faces, fine noses, and depthless dark eyes. Her hair—much thicker than my pin-straight inky locks—held luscious curls in her carefully styled coiffure. Her silk gown was also striking, and though the blue-and-cream hand-painted pattern was less obvious than mine, it was no less stunning.

"You're right, Mama. I'll try to work harder to make a suitable match."

Something like regret chased over her features but was quickly gone before she gave voice to it. "You look beautiful, my dear," she said instead, and handed me a pair of pale dyed gloves, which I donned. I stared at myself in the mirror. The whole effect wasn't *bad*. I certainly did not resemble my alter ego, Roz, but the bright color complemented my complexion and made the waterfall of raven-black hair falling over my shoulders seem extra glossy.

"Thank you, Mama."

I still felt like a pretty pineapple, but one of my mother's skills was fashion, and if she deemed the gown a standout, then I would concede. Her sense of style was legendary and admired by every woman in the *ton*. Every time the Duchess of Delmont wore a new piece, some version of it would be copied within weeks. As a result, I had no doubt that my entire set would want to embody pineapples come next month.

I swallowed a resigned chuckle as we descended to the waiting carriage.

It was just us attending the ball, as Papa was traveling once more to the Far East on an urgent diplomatic visit. It was a rare thing to see my father at home, and even those times were in passing. He was a stickler for duty and took his ducal obligations very seriously, which was probably why he was now questioning how his daughter remained an unwed spinster after three seasons. Securing my future was also his responsibility, after all.

The ride to the Duchess of Harbridge's residence was quick, considering we lived only a few streets apart in the very desirable Mayfair district of London. Exhaling, I closed my eyes and settled into my recognizable Lady Rosalin persona—the endearingly sweet, marriage-obsessed, and delightful version of myself everyone in our circles knew.

Being viewed as the girl who desperately wanted a husband had a twofold advantage: one, it made some gentlemen avoid me like the plague—*huzzah!*—and two, no one questioned why I was so picky if I appeared to covet them all.

I reconciled myself to the prospect of joining the latest crop of wallflowers lingering on the periphery and counting the minutes until Mama decided it was time to return home. She would expect me to take a turn about the ballroom and be seen, so I couldn't hide the entire time, but I was quite adept at being invisible when I wanted to be.

Perhaps Blake would be in attendance. He was typically a dependable diversion, though he didn't always show up to these events.

I wished that I'd brought *Opticks,* though the brick of a thing would not fit inside my reticule. Suddenly, a brilliant thought occurred to me: *Might His Grace have a copy in his library?* I knew from Zia that her father was very well read and prided himself on the quality of his collection. I could slip away easily by way of the retiring room. I brightened at that idea, the prospect of the evening suddenly seeming less tedious.

We were announced by the majordomo and greeted by the Duke and Duchess of Harbridge. On the way down the staircase, I could see Ela and Keston dancing a set, and I waved as Mama and I made our way through the crowd. Dutifully, I nodded, smiled, and curtseyed when other introductions were made, attempting to be at my most charming so my mother would not find fault and keep an even closer eye on me.

Half the battle was appearing as though I were thrilled to be here—a willing tribute up for offer on the marriage mart with a dowry that made most gentlemen salivate. Though as I caught sight of the infantile Duke of Renton sticking his entire index finger up his nose and then studying the contents therein with great fascination, bile climbed into my throat. He lifted said finger to his mouth, and I spun around with a revolted gasp.

Gag times infinity.

Nonetheless, I forced myself to smile so much that my cheeks ached and even sportingly penciled in a handful of dances on my dance card, which pleased my mother to no end. Zia used to make up names on hers, but Mama would see right through that ploy. She knew *everyone*. While she was preoccupied with greeting a countess, I took the chance to make my escape to a quiet corner of the ballroom.

When the handsome redheaded rogue Lord Blake Castleton strolled into the room and veered toward me with a smile from ear to ear, the first genuine grin of the evening touched my face. "Lord Blake," I greeted him. "I'm delighted to see you here."

He took my gloved hand and bowed over it. "Lady Rosalin, you are a vision in . . . er . . . tangerine."

I rolled my eyes. "It's yellow, and the fruit you're thinking of is a pineapple. Don't worry, I'm distressingly aware of the catastrophic resemblance."

"Well, a girl as beautiful as you would make a burlap sack look like Parisian fashion," he said loyally, and I warmed at the compliment. He was a dear friend, and one I was very thankful for. "Did you save me a dance?" he asked.

"You're welcome to the rest of my dratted dances," I muttered, unable to keep the bitterness from my tongue.

His lip quirked. "That bad?"

"You know I loathe the season with a passion. I'd rather be at home reading about mathematics and calculating planetary trajectories than waiting for an invitation to dance and simpering up at some dimwitted fellow who is only interested in whether my coffers are plentiful and if my hips are suitable for childbirth."

Blake laughed. "What kind of eccentric loves mathematics over a ball? You're a strange girl."

"You act like this is news." I let out an amused huff.

Blake was one of the very few people who knew the real me, and I suspected that I was one of the few who ever got to see the real him. He was silly and jovial with everyone else, but yet, we could have intense conversations about philosophers like Immanuel Kant and the impact of moral law for hours on end. In hindsight, perhaps I had been unfair in opining that only girls had unrealistic expectations to bear. Much like me, Blake was a walking contradiction.

Grinning, he held out a hand as the introductory strains of music for a quadrille started, and he sketched a bow. "Come on, then, my lady. Dance and simper with me, and let's make everyone green with envy, shall we?"

CHAPTER FIVE

A centripetal force is that by which bodies are drawn or impelled, or any way tend, towards a point as to a center.

—Isaac Newton

My stone-faced tutor narrowed his eyes in suspicion, his gaze dropping to the book on the table between us and then rising up to my face. "You read the entire thing? In three days?"

Staring back with a neutral expression, though my head felt as befuddled as it usually did in close proximity to him, I nodded. One would think I'd be used to his beauty by now, but every time I saw him, his extraordinary looks were like a punch to my lungs. I couldn't help thinking that today he resembled a fairy prince from some fictional realm, though he obviously harbored the heart of a villain.

Beauty is but skin-deep, I reminded myself.

Jaw clenching, I tried to knock some sense into my brain. "Yes, but to be perfectly honest with you, I have read it before, so it was familiar."

"And?" he prompted after a beat, and stared at me . . . at my upper lip, to be precise, and narrowed as if something there had confounded him. Skin heating uncomfortably, I pretended to adjust my spectacles as a bead of perspiration rolled down my spine. His gaze was too intense, too perceptive. Had I applied my false facial hair properly this morning? The adhesive paste could also become unreliable with damp, sweaty skin.

Scrunching my nose because of my suddenly tickling mustache, I blinked awkwardly at him. "And what?"

He released an exasperated breath. "What is your opinion on Newton's findings? Surely you have some original thought in that vainglorious head of yours?" He scoffed. "Or are you just like every other spoiled toff here—a waste of resources and opportunity?"

I frowned at the unexpected attack on my character. Well, on *Ansel's* character, though my tutor's hostility was also squarely on me at this point, after our last interaction in the dining room. "You don't like me very much, do you, Mr. St. Clair?" I asked.

Surprise flickered over his face before it was hidden. Perhaps he had expected me to react badly . . . like the overindulged noble he'd accused me of being.

"I think life has been handed to you," he replied carefully. Will and the others were right—he *could* make my life difficult in terms of workload or academic expectations, but as a peer, I would always hold more power than him, simply by being a lord and a duke's nephew in everyone's eyes. The dichotomy in our positions was clear, though arguably, we were both scholars here for the same purpose: to gain an education and challenge our minds.

I had to do something to stop this chasm from becoming unbridgeable.

"You cannot fault me for being born into privilege, just as I should not judge you by your own status or origin," I said evenly. "And if I have wronged you in the past on account of either, then I am sorry." Not knowing all the details of what had transpired between Ansel and him, I struggled to find words that might set us on a sounder path. "People can change, if you give them a chance."

"You've *changed*?" he bit out acidly. "Lord Ansel Chen, whose idea of sport was to direct a scout to spy and steal on his behalf? Whose notion of amusement was to pilfer weeks of important research that didn't belong to him for his own gratification? You almost cost me my position at St. John's when we were both there! Or have you forgotten because it was so inconsequential to you?"

Stunned speechless, I balked at the accusations. My cousin wasn't a thief. I knew that in my very soul. Ansel might be arrogant, but he would *never* take someone's work, or worse, take advantage of a humble, innocent subsizar. Neither of us was raised like that—my parents could not abide by the ill-treatment or exploitation of anyone in service.

Thus far, more out of a healthy fear of discovery, I'd avoided my own scout.

But in truth, he was the only reason I hadn't missed *this* meeting, knocking loudly earlier on my door, which I hadn't opened because Rosalin had been the one to tumble out of bed and not Fake Ansel. The carriage ride back from London had been hard and taken longer than usual because of the poor weather, and desperate to finish my skimming of *Opticks,* I'd fallen asleep the moment my head had hit my lumpy pillow.

At the thought of sleep, I suppressed an untimely yawn that rose from nowhere, but caught my tutor sneering at me, disdain sparking in those frosty lapis lazuli eyes.

"Is all of this so boring, my lord?" St. Clair snapped, venom in the address. "That you cannot even bring yourself to feel remorse for nearly ruining someone's life?"

"Of course not, but I am exhausted from being up all night reading," I replied somewhat calmly, though his scathing tone made me bristle. "I truly have no idea what you're talking about. Ans . . . I would never purposefully harm another student." Thankfully, I caught the near slip of referring to myself in the third person.

"Are you saying you *didn't* sabotage my notes and chances for the Tripos at St. John's?"

My sluggish mind ticked over. I'd have to write Ansel—he was in Italy when he posted his last letter—and hope that my reply found him, or I'd have to talk to Blake and see if he knew anything, though the conversation would be trickier with the latter if my secret was to remain a secret. I trusted Ansel with my life, but Blake adored gossip.

"No, I did not," I said eventually, putting faith in my cousin even though it could be misplaced. But Ansel wasn't *cruel,* and that I knew with every bone in my body.

Somehow, I had to get to the bottom of this if I had any hope of a congenial relationship with my tutor, whose eyes flashed with disbelief before turning speculative.

"I am not sure I believe you weren't involved, when it was

your scout whom I saw loitering outside my rooms," he said. "Though admittedly your shock and sincerity seem convincing."

"I *am* sincere, St. Clair. I swear this much to you." A belated thought occurred to me. "Scouts are sometimes shared, and there's also the possibility that mine might have been in the wrong place at the wrong time. I will investigate this. I can also assure you that the person I am now is not who I was then."

In every possible way.

I was a girl, and Ansel would *not* be having these confusing feelings for his tutor.

My cheeks warmed when my eyes lifted to his, and I cursed my fair complexion, though St. Clair was more focused on the book in front of him than on the unfortunate timing of my blush. "Were you . . . we ever friends?" I blurted.

After a lengthy pause, an incredulous laugh burst from him. "No, Lord Ansel. You and your set would not deign to befriend a mere subsizar."

A knot formed in my throat at that, though James had alluded to the same, as if the menial position were something to be maligned. St. Clair obviously wasn't a subsizar now, but he had worked hard to get where he was . . . earned the title of Wrangler and was on track to become a Fellow of Trinity College. Much like Newton, the accomplishment was impressive. If St. Clair's standing had been threatened by my cousin's perceived actions, no wonder he was so antagonistic toward me.

"What made you switch to Trinity?" I asked, hoping it wasn't an odd question but curious about James's claims.

One shoulder lifted in a shrug. "After completing my degree in natural philosophy, there was more opportunity to become a Fellow in the field of mathematics."

"Just like that?" I asked. Most academics excelled in one subject or another, but Tarik St. Clair seemed to be the exception to the rule. My wayward fascination with him grew yet again. This boy had intelligence in spades.

"Not at all. I had to apply with special approval. Everything requires hard work, Lord Ansel. We are not all related to dukes." Obviously, he was referring to my own sudden transfer, but there was less heat in his words.

"Roz," I said softly. "Call me Roz."

"We are still not friends, Lord Ansel, and I'd prefer to keep our interactions professional," he said after a beat. "You'll forgive me if I am somewhat wary given what"—he paused, staring at me with an unreadable expression—"*allegedly* happened in the past."

That was a start at least . . .

Clearly, I had to *earn* his trust.

Nodding, I offered him a small smile and then focused my attention on *Opticks.* I thumbed to the pages featuring Proposition VIII, which included Newton's experiments to shorten telescopes, and cleared my throat. "I particularly liked his proofs on using mirrored convex lenses to sharpen the colors, with the aperture pointing to a small prism, and his thoughts that the aperture had to be proportionate with the length of the tube to properly magnify the object at rest." My voice became less stiff as I discussed the subject. "To perfect clarity and luminosity."

St. Clair's eyes lit with approval. "Correct. He argued that the different refrangibility of light rays was the true cause of imperfect images."

I nodded. "Yes, that's the degree to which light refracts when passed through an object. And his subsequent proofs showed that varying the lengths of telescopes would help with magnification," I said, pleased that he knew exactly what I was talking about. My heart quickened in my chest. "He asserted that the apertures had to correspond with the square root of the length," I added excitedly.

His lips curled slightly upward into what could almost pass for a smile at my enthusiasm, and I sucked in a breath at how it transformed his entire face from something stern and taciturn into something much softer. He was already unfairly handsome, but gracious, what would he look like with a full grin, completely relaxed and happy?

Stop mooning over him, you ninny! You don't need to make him smile; you need to win his respect.

To distract myself, I turned to page 101 and read, my finger tracing the written words as I did. " 'For Instance, a Telescope of sixty-four Feet in length, with an Aperture of two and two-thirds Inches, magnifies about one hundred and twenty times, with as much distinctness as one of a Foot in length, with one-third of an Inch aperture, magnifies fifteen times.' "

"I gather you enjoy astronomy," St. Clair remarked.

I peered up at him. "I do. The idea that there is this whole universe beyond us—that we are simply one speck in the entirety of the cosmos—is fascinating to me."

"I happen to agree," he said, surprising me. "We are but a

minuscule part. When I look up at the stars at night, there's nothing like it to make a person feel inconsequential."

"Exactly!" I nodded with renewed eagerness, thrilled to find we had that in common. "That's why I hope to build a telescope of my own like Newton did. I want to study what is out there. Perhaps even find something yet undiscovered by others."

"Do you?" he asked, surprise flashing. "That's ambitious."

Self-consciously, I gnawed on the corner of my lower lip and released it the moment his eyes tracked the movement, a glimmer of confusion flickering in their depths.

Botheration!

I had to be more careful. Gentlemen did not nibble upon their lips. No, they scrubbed their chins or their heads or the bridges of their noses, and sometimes excavated their noses like the odious Duke of Renton, though I could not possibly bring myself to do the last.

I lifted a hand to my jawline and patted the facial scruff there while pretending to be deep in thought. "Perhaps so, but I hope to try. Sir William Herschel improved Newton's reflecting telescope by grinding and polishing the mirrors into a parabolic shape instead of a spherical one," I said. "I'm planning to use a similar design to build my own."

St. Clair canted his head. "Herschel discovered Uranus, if I recall from my historical studies, originally named *Georgium Sidus*, George's Star, after the king. It was the first planet to be discovered in a thousand years. Wasn't his sister a renowned astronomer in her own right? Charlotte? Cora?"

"Caroline," I replied, impressed that he would mention her.

Normally, men hardly ever credited any women who made scientific observations. Caroline Herschel was, in fact, one of my personal heroes. "It was actually her discovery of a periodic comet as well as five hundred and sixty missing stars, which she presented to the Royal Society in an index to John Flamsteed's observations, that first seeded my interest in astronomy." I sighed in wonder. "Did you know the king made her the first official professional female astronomer and paid her fifty pounds annually to assist her brother with his experiments? She was thought to be the first woman to receive a wage for her scientific efforts."

"I had heard that," St. Clair said. "Sir William was offered four thousand pounds to build the Great Forty-Foot telescope, and I believe his sister was the one who recorded all his notes and findings. Brilliant family."

"He also came up with the idea that clusters of stars occurred because they were attracted to each other over time," I added. "It's incredibly romantic, as if those celestial bodies were on some similar course, destined to find each other in the infinite space of the universe." I suddenly became aware of his stare and realized what I'd said, along with the warm, wistful tone of my voice. I cleared my throat. "Romantic in a purely analytical sense, of course. Gravity is quite scientific." My cheeks felt like they were on fire, and I ducked my chin to hide them. "Poets love whimsical things."

When I forced my eyes back up, St. Clair's expression was languid, a hint of a smile playing about his mouth. "Did you know Herschel also cataloged eight hundred and forty-eight double stars? They were known as stars that orbited around one another."

"Binary pairs," I said softly.

"Yes."

We stared at each for a long moment in congenial silence, our heads bent over the open copy of *Opticks,* before jerking apart. St. Clair ran a hand through his hair, mussing the carefully combed waves, and leaned back into his chair, his usual unreadable expression taking over.

"Never would have taken you for a stargazer, Lord Ansel."

I shrugged. "I told you. You don't know me, Mr. St. Clair. People change. Perhaps the gentleman you knew before isn't same person you see before you now."

"I suppose I shall have to give you the benefit of the doubt, then," he said, and rose, stretching his arms over his head and rounding his spine. Goodness, I forgot how tall and lanky he was. I stared, hypnotized by his graceful, sinuous movements. Flushing, I tried not to notice how much the muscles of his abdomen bunched beneath his shirt as he reached for the coat hung neatly over the back of his chair as well as his outer gown.

"Have we finished, sir?" I asked.

"Considering it's well past luncheon, yes. Moving forward, we can focus your studies on observational astronomy and celestial mechanics as well as understanding historical context, since those seem to be your primary areas of interest." He leaned over to collect his books strewn across the tabletop and pack them neatly into his satchel. He pushed one over with the tip of his finger toward me. "Let's meet in the Wren Library three days hence."

I pulled the new tome toward me and frowned at the title. "*Principia*?"

"Have you read this, too?" he asked.

"A while ago, but—"

Based on the look of challenge on his face, I didn't need to finish my sentence. "Good, prepare to be thoroughly tested on the laws of motion and gravitational properties next Thursday. Shall we say early afternoon, at two o'clock, directly following luncheon?"

"Wait. Tested?"

St. Clair glanced over his shoulder. "You didn't think transferring here was going to be easy for you, did you, Lord Ansel? We're mathematicians, scientists, and physicists continually pushing the boundaries of what we know and everything else that's waiting to be proven. If you're committed to your education, then I'm here to offer the instruction and support you require. If not, tell me now, and I'll focus my efforts and energy elsewhere. We can have another more appropriate tutor assigned to you. Sir James Lowry, perhaps? I saw you taking meals with him."

The thought of not being able to pick this boy's unique brain left me cold. I'd never met anyone else like him—his wisdom sparkled, and I wanted to learn everything I could about the way he saw the world, about the way he *thought* and how that erudite mind worked. Even with his princely good looks, St. Clair's brain was by far his greatest asset.

I shook my head and stood, gathering the book to my chest and then lifting my chin. "No, sir. I'm up for the challenge."

The corner of his lip curled. "Excellent."

I waited until he left before slumping back down into the chair. I released a belabored groan at my complete inability to think rationally around him because, by everything holy, I should have asked for at least a week, not a scant handful of days. Refamiliarizing myself with *Philosophiae Naturalis Principia Mathematica* was a more daunting task than the last.

Though displaying my acumen and going toe-to-toe with someone like St. Clair was something for me to look forward to. Newton's proofs had been argued and discussed enough over the past century and a half, so our discussion would not be groundbreaking, but at least I would be able to hold my own.

Tapping the book, I let out a laugh as I remembered the many gentlemen over past seasons whom I'd interrogated with my little aptitude tests—one of them, an arrogant marquess, had insisted that gravity was a supernatural force with no basis in science or mathematical law and that I was a heretic for even considering it. That had been eye-opening. He'd delivered me back to my mother with a disdainful sniff, saying that he could never marry an agnostic.

Mama had been horrified at first, but after I'd explained that we'd spoken about gravity, whereupon he'd insisted that such a phenomenon was God's work, she'd been promptly reassured that I'd narrowly escaped from being hitched to an utter dunce. My mother might urgently want my future secured, but she herself was no slouch in the academic department.

Before she married Papa, she'd been a brilliant amateur astronomer. In fact, I inherited my love of the stars from her when she used to tell me fantastical stories as a child of the ancient Greek constellations and the gods behind them, like Orion the mighty hunter and Andromeda, who was chained to a rock to be sacrificed to a monster. Or the myth behind the Great Bear, where the goddess Hera transformed Callisto, who was coveted by Hera's husband, Zeus, into a bear so she would not be so beautiful.

It saddened me that Mama had abandoned her passion after she became the Duchess of Delmont, instead becoming focused on raising a family and shoring up the Delmont name in influential social circles. When I was fourteen, I'd discovered one of her old journals, tracking stars and comets she'd discovered using an old telescope, the same one I'd used to satisfy my own burgeoning curiosity for the starry night sky.

Later on, Mama had never discouraged me from following my interests, but she had always been clear after my initial season that my duty as a duke's daughter would always come first. Like her, my primary goal was to make an advantageous match . . . not to chase uncharted stars.

I increasingly resented the pressure to wed as each season passed . . . especially when *my* perfect match seemed more and more out of reach.

"Roz!"

I jolted at the sound of my nickname.

"We've been looking everywhere for you! Where have you been?"

I stared at Will's flushed face when he poked his head in the doorway. James appeared beside him, shaking with unbridled excitement. "What's going on?" I asked.

"The twins are racing on the River Cam!" Will cried. "Some other students dared them to do it, and those two clodheads agreed."

My eyes rounded. "Swimming?"

"Rowing," Will said.

I blinked—though it was unseasonably warm for late spring, the river would be ice-cold. Not that they would be going into the water, but boats could capsize.

Good heavens, what were Klaus and Kristof thinking?

I felt a grin split my face anyway—I always used to be so envious of the antics Ansel got up to with his set, and though I'd heard rumors of Zia running wild with a few of her schoolmates, leading a group called the Lady Knights, who raced on Rotten Row at midnight and fenced in underground gaming clubs, I didn't have daring friends like that.

I didn't truly have many friends at *all,* only acquaintances.

And *those* were all proper, demure ladies of the *ton,* and the most daring thing they did was try a new brand of tea. Well, I supposed Ela and Zia were different, but they'd come into my life much more recently, when I'd already been hammered and polished into a dutiful young lady. The only thing I'd ever rebelled over was marriage to someone I could not abide.

And now this—impersonating Ansel because I craved *one* grand adventure before resigning myself to my inevitable future.

Grinning at my—*Roz's*—friends, I scrambled up, gathering my things, and raced upstairs to dump them in my quarters before joining the others as we headed toward the Backs. It was a scenic garden area on the western side of the college that bordered the river, though I hadn't had much time to explore it. A crowd was gathered when we arrived, and many wagers were already changing hands.

"Roz!" Klaus said, seeing me. "Fancy rowing with us? We're in need of a fourth."

My jaw slackened as I glanced from him over to the wooden four-rower gig boat to the murky churning waters of the River Cam. Kristof shot me a maniacal grin, and poor Harold, who presumably was their third, had a nauseated look on his face.

Could I? *Should* I?

The water was likely freezing and contaminated with all kinds of vermin and filth, much like the Thames in London, but my blood pounded through my veins in exhilaration at the prospect of doing something so unbelievably bold. So *thrilling*!

When would I have a chance like this again? When would *Lady Rosalin* be able to do something so dreadfully unconventional and audacious? The answer was never. Roz, however, was more than up for the challenge. I'd never rowed in a race before, other than on the Serpentine during leisurely summer garden parties, but how hard could it be?

I shucked off the top later of my academic gown and handed it to a gaping Will before making my way down the bank. "Sure do!"

"You are the man!" Kristof crowed.

A hysterical laugh bubbled up my throat—yes, I was.

CHAPTER SIX

> The philosophers say that Nature does nothing in vain, and more is in vain when less will serve; for Nature is pleased with simplicity.
>
> —Isaac Newton

"I can't believe we did it!" Harold screamed.

Knees buckling, I flung myself to the grassy bank, chest heaving and lungs about to burst beneath my ribs. "By a deuced hair," I panted, smiling so hard that my frozen cheeks ached.

I could barely feel my toes in my boots, but I had never felt so gloriously alive in my whole life! My arms trembled like jelly, as though they were on the brink of falling off. It had taken some coordination to get my oar into a working rhythm with the other three, which had put us behind at the start, but we had caught up to the other boat by a nose at the end. That was mostly thanks to the brute strength of the twins. Harold was even thinner than I was—neither of us was the muscle in that foursome, and he doubled as the coxswain, calling out the action. But as a team, the four of us had done the impossible.

We had *won*!

Klaus hollered, happily collecting the money he had bet on us taking the race before the small throng dissipated and students skipped out on their bets. "Still counts as winning whether it's by a nose or a head or more. We are rich, and we are celebrating tonight!"

"Capital," Kristof agreed, slapping his brother on the back, then loosening his cravat. "We're all going, no excuses," he added with a meaningful look at me.

"I'm in," I said, knowing if I made another refusal, I might not get an additional invitation, and as much as I was afraid to break the rules or get into trouble, I didn't want to miss out on a potentially unforgettable experience. I'd never been to a gaming hell before. The most exciting place I'd ever visited was Vauxhall, which had given me the chance to mingle with people from all walks of life and all stations. And even then, I'd been heavily chaperoned.

I loosened my own cravat and unbuttoned my coat. The cool air was a welcome reprieve on my overheated skin.

"Good idea, Roz," Harold said as he did the same. "I'm bloody boiling."

I felt my cheeks flush as the twins grinned in unison and started stripping off their outer layers. *All* their layers . . . not just unmooring a few buttons from their coats. Mortified, I averted my gaze quickly when they were down to their shirtsleeves, but not before my eyes had gotten a healthy eyeful of their chiseled muscles as they removed their shirtsleeves, too.

Goodness me.

The twins were built, not that I was normally swayed by thick shoulders and cut abdominals. But that didn't mean I couldn't *appreciate* the sight. I was only human. Their display was altogether improper and undignified, but nobody seemed to care that they were shirtless, jumping around and hollering. And there weren't any girls here for them to scandalize any delicate sensibilities . . . well, with one hidden exception, of course.

Half chortling, I caught my breath and composed myself just as the twins converged on Harold, chanting at him to join them. I blanched, wondering if I was next. There was no way *I* was going to take off any of my clothes. No way I *could,* given the scandalous truth that lay beneath all my careful padding.

I stood quickly and made my way over to Will and James before the twins got any cheeky ideas. They were already pestering Harold, who was on the cusp of caving.

"Can we talk about tonight?" I asked Will as we began the walk back to the building. "Will we get into trouble with the proctors?"

Despite my excitement, I couldn't risk getting thrown out of school when this term was all I had. I would never have another chance like this, and I had no intention of wasting it. By the end of the season, I would likely be engaged, and no peer would permit his future wife to dress in men's clothing and pretend to be male for the sake of schooling. No, this was it—my only shot at being an actual Cambridge student.

Will's transparent face looked just as nervous as I felt. "We won't get into trouble if we don't get caught. But the proctors have been growing stricter and stricter of late with maintaining the ten o'clock curfews and reprimanding disorderly conduct."

"Have they?" I blurted nervously.

"Yes," he replied. "Certain proctors have made it a point to get the twins suspended because they're notorious repeat offenders."

"Suspended?" I gasped.

Will nodded. "They won't be—their father donates far too much money to the college, likely as compensation for his unruly spawn—but that doesn't mean the rest of us caught with them might not be punished. Harold was nearly rusticated last term when he and Kristof were caught racing a curricle in the village. It was rather unfair, but well, Harold's parents aren't as influential here in Britain. He only got off because the twins went on a hunger strike in protest. They're deeply loyal." He lowered his voice. "Harold's a subsizar, but don't tell anyone. He's sensitive about it."

"I won't say a word," I vowed, though the revelation didn't surprise me, considering how hurt he'd been by James's disdain. "Isaac Newton was a subsizar here, and he was one of the most brilliant, influential thinkers in history. Harold's in exceptional company."

Will shrugged. "He doesn't want to be treated differently. You saw how James was about St. Clair and the whole status debate. Lots of people think like him. Look at how they treat me, and I *have* a title."

"It's despicable," I muttered.

"Sadly, it's the reality." He wrinkled his nose, sending me a sidelong glance. "If you're worried about going, you probably would not get into any trouble. You're a lord. Your uncle is an influential duke. You could probably get away with just about anything."

If only Will knew the secret I was hiding. Stomach churning, I wondered if I should excuse myself from the festivities. Being suspended or publicly reprimanded could result in my father receiving a summons to speak with the Fellows of the college, and I couldn't have that, especially since the real Ansel was currently somewhere in Spain or Austria. Right now, Papa was blissfully and thankfully unaware of his daughter's wrongdoings as well as his nephew's sly jaunt, and I was determined to keep it that way.

But still . . . a night on the town . . . what an irresistible temptation!

"Are you going with them?" I asked Will.

"I'll go if you do," he said, chewing on the inside of his cheek. "We can keep an eye out for each other, and if you want to depart early, we'll leave before the curfew."

That sounded reasonable. "Then I'm in."

We agreed to reconvene after dinner, which I'd taken in my rooms while poring over the first chapter of *Principia*. Newton truly was one of the most radical and inventive thinkers of his generation, but one of my favorite books on mathematics was written by Émilie du Châtelet. The way she'd translated and expanded on some theories of *Principia,* as well as commented on and clarified several of Newton's principles, was astounding.

For example, a body at rest or in motion would continue its state, unless it was prompted by some other force to change that state. Her book was translated from Latin to French and published posthumously after she died at the age of forty-two. Émilie had perservered, despite all the obstacles against her as a woman. I wanted to be just like her. Innovative. Bold.

And I *would*.

But that didn't mean I couldn't also have some fun while doing so.

A sharp rap on the door had me stuffing the last of my bread into my mouth and hurriedly donning the nearest coat. I checked my face in the mirror, making sure that the new short wig I'd commissioned from London was fitted securely over my own tightly wrapped hair. It was perfect and much sturdier than a hat, which could come loose at any moment with a good yank.

Lastly, I chucked the annoying spectacles onto the bridge of my nose. My facial hair was in place, and for a moment, I looked so much like Ansel that I blinked. With a smirk, and channeling the careless arrogance of my cousin, I snatched up my hat and my coin purse, and sauntered from my room to join Will and the others.

"Where are we going?" I asked the twins as we crammed into a hansom out on the main street—Will, Harold, and me on one side of the carriage, and Klaus, Kristof, and James on the other. It wasn't quite late enough to garner the notice of any vigilant proctors, but we'd still been quiet in the courtyard until we were well away from the Great Gate. My friends looked dapper, their faces excited and bright at the prospect of an evening on the town. Their exhilaration was contagious, and I felt a grin lifting my cheeks high.

"It's a surprise," Klaus said, his face stoic, just as Kristof blurted that it was a new social club and gaming hell. His twin scowled and punched him in the arm, but even Klaus couldn't keep his face from splitting into a smile. "Fine. What he said."

Will frowned. "How are we going to get in?"

"Money talks," Kristof went on, and hefted a fat coin purse from his pocket. "Not social connections or titles. And we have lots of the former, thanks to our winnings today."

The social club in question resembled a tavern from the outside, but the queue of patrons lined up in front had us joining it in a hurry. I spied a few familiar faces from some of the discussions in the combination rooms, but it was more of a challenge to recognize my schoolmates without their academic gowns and tassels identifying them. We were *supposed* to wear our gowns outside the college, but no one wanted to be singled out, for good reason. I wondered briefly if my stern tutor would be here and then laughed.

Tarik St. Clair would *never.*

He'd be pronounced dead before entering a place like this.

Suddenly, a frisson of nerves scattered down my spine, and one glance at Will's very pale countenance had me convinced he was feeling the same onslaught of panic. "Are you well?" I whispered, bumping him with my shoulder.

"I have a bad feeling about this," he whispered back. "With all of us and so many other students here, it seems like a magnet for trouble."

"Stick to the plan," I murmured. I squinted up at the tower clock that was down the street, the hands barely visible though it seemed like it was not far from chiming the nine o'clock hour.

"We'll leave at a quarter to ten. That should give us enough time to get back before curfew."

"Fine," he replied.

"Chin up, Will," I said, and pushed a bright smile to my face. "This could be fun. Let's give it a chance and have a capital time."

"If you say so."

Harold jostled between us with a slightly spooked expression. "Klaus said there are girls here. Women . . . *courtesans.*" The last was whispered in a strangled tone, the rest of his words choked out. "Do you think this place might double as a *brothel*?"

I blinked at the almost-garbled question. I supposed such a thing wouldn't be out of the ordinary—these kinds of gaming hells had a fast reputation. Drinking and gambling went hand in hand with other vices. I'd overheard enough conversations from my cousin and his friends about a few of their escapades in some of the more notorious areas of London.

While most of the aristocracy—and polite society in general—looked down on courtesans and light-skirts, I was of the controversial opinion that a woman could do what she wanted with her own body. If she chose to be a mistress to a man under her own terms, that was her prerogative. While I understood that some women might *not* make this choice themselves and others did only out of necessity, none of them deserved to be vilified.

Besides, many of the gentlemen of the *ton* openly had mistresses. No one chastised *them* for their behavior! I'd heard gossip from the maids, who were dependable fountains of information, about several aristocrats who committed adultery with no care for their wives. Thank God my father didn't. My mother, for all her grace and decorum, would not stand for it.

"Don't worry, Harold," Klaus promised. "We'll take excellent care of you, or at least, we'll find a pretty ladybird to oblige you for the evening."

My snort was loud. "Aren't you studying to be a vicar? Shouldn't you be preaching self-restraint and abstinence instead of moral excess?"

"Consensual pleasure isn't a sin, dear one," Kristof interjected solicitously.

I lifted a brow. "Coitus before marriage *is* according to the Church of England."

The deviant waggled his own dark blond eyebrows. "Yes, but there are many other marvelous appetizers than can be enjoyed before the main course. And besides, those rules are for ladies, perhaps, not for us men," he replied smugly, and suddenly, I wanted to kick him.

I wanted to kick every man standing in this line who might share his odious, archaic opinion that women were nothing but vessels of virtue to be consumed at their leisure, even after the bonds of wedlock. Many of them, most likely.

That would mean a lot of kicking.

"What's wrong?" Will asked, sidling up to me. "You look positively murderous. Was it what the twins said? You know how they are—they say contemptible things to get a reaction."

"My cousin is a lady," I whispered heatedly. "Shouldn't she be deserving of a choice as well?"

He blinked. "To be in a brothel?"

I waved a hand. "To be anywhere, to do anything she pleases. Why are women always viewed as lesser or weaker?"

Will looked genuinely confused. "I don't doubt that there is a double standard, Roz, but that's the way the world works. At least for now until change happens." He shrugged with a wry grin, his round cheeks dimpling. "And sometime in the future when women's voices have as much weight as men's, indubitably, they will outthink, outplay, and outpace us."

I stared at him, stunned. "Do you truly think so?"

"If women are to have the same employments as men, they must have the same education," he said, and I frowned at the familiarity of his words. "Plato wrote that in *The Republic*," he added.

"You're right, he did," I said with a low laugh, clapping him on the back. "Will, if I haven't said it before, you are a true gem. Whatever you do, please never change."

By the time we shuffled to the front of the line, the twins were paying the astronomical entry fee for the six of us. I offered to repay them the cost of mine, but they refused as we entered the building. When we passed through the first velvet-draped arch into the main room of the establishment, excitement filled my blood.

I was instantly assaulted by the smell of cheroot smoke, heavy perfume, and hard liquor. Voices hummed around us, punctuated by high-pitched feminine laughter and deeper chuckles. The lighting was low, and the place was akin to a rabbit's warren, with a dozen hallways branching off to other rooms.

If we weren't careful, we would get lost in the maze.

After being mesmerized by the lush décor of a grand receiving room, I stared at a beautiful woman who seemed to be dressed in only peacock feathers and carried a tray balanced on one hand, admiring her confidence and graceful agility as she weaved through the crowd. Men gaped, but no one did anything untoward. I suspected that had to do with the enormous bodyguard following in her wake, who looked like he could break bones with his littlest finger.

"Will, what do you want to do first?" I said, and turned, only to see that Will and the others had disappeared. A fox-faced man with a thin mustache sneered down at me instead, and I hurriedly mumbled an apology before scurrying away. I didn't like the avaricious look in his eyes. These kinds of clubs attracted swindlers who preyed on unsuspecting youth visiting from the nearby colleges—*pigeons* as I'd read somewhere they were called. Not that I intended to be fleeced, but I was definitely out of my depth.

Gracious, where are my friends?

My gut knotted in alarm at their absence, but they had to be around here somewhere. Following the crowd, I roamed toward the back of the room, where it seemed less congested. To my right, there seemed to be a large dining room with widely spaced tables, and to my left, there was a smoking room filled with plush armchairs and comfortable seating. Neither of them stimulated my interest, so I pressed past them toward a staircase at the end. Perhaps I'd be able to spot Will if I could see from a higher vantage point.

Upstairs, there were more chambers, including a cramped billiards room and several smaller nooks with gentlemen playing backgammon and hazard. Strolling along the plush new carpets, I admired the paintings on the walls—the art was nothing compared with what I was used to in Mayfair—but the portraits were captivating. I turned into the nearest doorway and found myself in a card room. Various games like faro and commerce were being played on baize-and-leather-covered tables while gentlemen lounged indolently, sipping on drinks supplied by smartly dressed waiters.

Now, this was a little more my style. I weaved between the tables. I enjoyed a game of whist from time to time, and while I knew the basics of card games like vingt-et-un, I'd never seen a setting quite like this, with men betting considerable sums. It was rather exhilarating!

I was contemplating sitting and looking for the least crowded table, when a familiar, handsome face caught my eye a handful of tables over.

No . . .

I blinked, convinced I'd imagined him there or perhaps it was only someone who resembled him, but there he was, my nemesis and the coldhearted gent I'd *never* expect to see in a place like this or doing anything remotely fun.

What on God's green earth was *Tarik St. Clair* doing here?

CHAPTER SEVEN

I do not define time, space, place and motion, as being well known to all.

—Isaac Newton

Clearly, I had been wrong about my tutor's extracurricular activities. The soles of my feet were glued to the floor as he brooded over the hand of cards he held, his lower lip pulled between his teeth, and a lock of dark hair falling into his brow. He brushed it back lazily and set his cards down face up. My heart skipped when the dealer folded, and a satisfied smile curled St. Clair's lips. The sight of it made me warm.

Turn around and leave. Pretend you never saw him.

Run if you know what's good for you.

But my feet had other ideas, steadfastly propelling me forward in his direction. There was an empty seat beside him, and before I could stop myself, I cleared my throat.

"Mr. St. Clair, may I join you?" I asked as he turned those sharp blue eyes toward me. They were wide with astonishment, as though he hadn't expected to see me either, but then a careful, studious blankness overtook his features, and he schooled them into that bland, unreadable expression I'd become all too familiar with.

It was a mask he had perfected, I realized—his mien as the scholarly future Fellow of Trinity College. For a moment, I wanted to tear it off, witness more of the genuine person I'd just seen take pleasure in winning a game of cards.

"Lord Ansel," he said after a moment. "What are you doing here? The Master of the College will not look too fondly upon such an outing to a gaming hell."

"Then why are you here?" I returned. "Besides, it's not yet curfew, and as far as I know, it's not a crime to visit a social club."

His eyes flashed at the defiance in my voice, but then he canted his head. "I suppose so, though this is nothing like what you're used to in London. White's and whatnot. At best, this would be a copper hell, quite a step down for you."

I shrugged noncommittally. It wasn't like I could admit that I'd never been to the illustrious and exclusive White's, although my father was a member and seemed to enjoy his time there, along with every other British aristocrat who could afford the membership.

"What's a copper hell?" I asked, and pulled out the empty chair.

He smirked at me before answering, gaze sliding somewhat contemptuously over my expensive coat—*Ansel's* expensive coat—snow-white cravat, and tailored waistcoat. "The not-so-luxurious gambling institutions for us poorer, more common folk."

The dealer coughed and stared at me. "That seat is for

players, sir. The minimum wager is five shillings." I gulped at the amount—it wasn't enormous, but it wasn't small either. I know Ansel's set wagered and lost obscene sums, but the idea of wasting my pin money on a game of chance and not saving every cent I had to buy books or build my telescope was silly to me. The risks were too high, especially when I didn't have an income.

St. Clair sent me a sidelong glance. "Do you play vingt-et-un, Lord Ansel?"

"I've played a hand or two in my time, though I can't say I'm any good."

Despite my distaste for gambling because of the risks of losing perfectly good money, I wanted to tarry a bit longer, to remain in his irresistible orbit. It probably wasn't smart. In such an informal setting, I could very well say or do something that might give me away, but the exhilaration spiraling through me at the thought of being next to him eclipsed all my worries.

"It's simple," he said. "Once you get the hang of it."

I dug into my pockets to place a handful of coins on the green baize and pushed the required sum over to the dealer. "You have to get to twenty-one, correct?" I said to St. Clair, who nodded. "And you win or lose whatever you have wagered, depending on the winning score. If you get twenty-one, it's called a natural, and if you go overdraw, you automatically lose." I released a self-deprecating laugh. "I never know when to ask for another card or not."

"I can help you," St. Clair said and then seemed surprised by his own offer. "If you'd like, I mean."

I wanted to blush and fan my suddenly overheated face, but

I squared up and rapped him on the shoulders instead. *Hard.* So hard that my palm was aching, and I had to hide my own wince at the reverberating pain shooting up my arm. Under all that serviceable tweed, St. Clair was clearly as well muscled as the twins.

"Capital," I agreed much too brightly, and clenched my bruised fist.

The dealer distributed two cards face up to each of the five players on the table. I stared down at mine—three of hearts and an ace of clubs. St. Clair held a king and a queen. Each of his face cards had a value of ten points, I knew, which put him in an enviable position with twenty to win. He smirked, and I tried valiantly not to notice how his eyes sparkled or the surprising peekaboo dimple that appeared out of nowhere. *Gah!* My pulse sped up stupidly as I forced myself to focus on the game instead of a facial indent that should come with its own warning label—beware intense peril to brain.

I breathed out and shook my head.

Pay attention, you silly goose!

Since an ace could count as one point or eleven, I technically had a total of four or fourteen points. The dealer kept one of his cards face down, and the visible one was a jack of spades. I attempted to calculate the odds of winning in my head, though I had no way of knowing what cards had already come and gone. St. Clair might have an idea, since he'd been sitting here awhile, but I would have to wait until the entire deck was shuffled to keep a true tally.

In a normal deck, there were twelve face cards—a jack, a queen, and a king, in each of the four suits—as well as four aces.

All the others counted as the values marked on their faces. Studying my hand, I had to assume that the dealer was hiding at least ten points or had a natural—points equaling twenty-one—which was the whole point of the game.

"Hit," the player on the end said with his total of fifteen, and the dealer gave him another card. He made a disgusted face as a queen put his total to twenty-five. A bust.

"Stand," the gentleman next to him said. His cards totaled eighteen points.

The player to the left of him went over twenty-one by a single point, and he swore loudly. I tried not to gasp as the crass expletive echoed over the table, reminding myself that my usual sensibilities had to be hardened in male company. No flinching over someone swearing or I'd give myself away.

St. Clair chose to stay with his twenty, a wise decision, and then it was my turn. "Hit," I said past the thick knot in my throat. My shoulders hunched as a nine of diamonds appeared. If I counted the ace as eleven points, my tally would be twenty-three, so I would go over, which meant I had to count it as one point. Thirteen it was, then. "Hit," I said again. A two of spades materialized, which brought my total to fifteen.

I wavered. Fifteen was a respectable number, especially if the dealer went over. St. Clair raised a brow but remained silent. Hadn't he promised to help me? But it looked like he was going to watch me make a fool of myself all on my own. Typical.

No matter, I did not need him. All I had to decide was whether I wanted to play it safe or take the risk. I peered at the dealer's face, but he gave away nothing.

"Hit," I pronounced, and waited with bated breath.

The dealer flipped a five of hearts. I exhaled in relief. *Twenty.*

"Sir?" he asked me.

"Stand," I said.

St. Clair indicated he would stay as well and then the dealer flipped his hidden card over. My heart sank as a collective sigh echoed over the table at the sight of the ace of clubs—the lucky bastard had a natural, which meant we all lost.

"Bad luck," St. Clair murmured, though it didn't *all* feel like bad luck when he graced me with a genuine smile of commiseration. Strange that it would take a losing hand of cards to feel like we were on the same side instead of at opposite ends of a competitive pitch. I dug in my pocket for more coins to cover the next round.

I won that game by pure luck with a count of nineteen when the dealer was forced to go over his sixteen to beat my hand. Pleased as punch with my winnings, instead of leaving the table as I probably should have, my body decided to stay put since St. Clair showed no signs of leaving either. Considering the pile of money in front of him, he was doing well.

After another hand, in which my tutor won handsomely, the dealer shuffled a new deck of cards. I sat forward, intent on paying attention to the fifty-two cards that were going to be used so that I could monitor the higher face cards, but after more than a few rounds, I'd already lost track of them.

Drat and botheration!

Though that was likely because I kept getting distracted by the proximity of the boy next to me, and that accursed dimple.

I was keenly focused on not leaning in to inhale his delicious scent. He smelled like a winter evening spent by the fireplace with warm spiced chocolate in hand. On top of that, a loose lock of his dark hair kept falling over his brow, and I itched to push it back. Would his hair feel soft or coarse? Would it be thick or fine like gossamer?

I was much too curious about him for comfort.

Wearing a slight frown, he drummed his long fingers on the edge of the baize-wrapped table. They were strong fingers with carefully clipped nails. Nail health said a lot about a person—bitten nails pointed to an anxious or easily irritable personality, nail texture and color indicated healthy body functions or vitamin deficiencies, and nail length pointed to other traits like practicality, diligence, or indolence. They weren't always an accurate measure, but his nails were short, clean, and square. He had beautiful hands.

"Sir?" the dealer said loudly, just as St. Clair bumped me with his elbow, jolting me out of my woolgathering. Heat singed my neck as I tore my gaze away, and I was deeply and profoundly grateful that my idle thoughts were private.

"Stand," I blurted without even looking at my cards.

"Are you certain about that, Lord Ansel?" St. Clair asked. Frowning, I glanced down and flushed as I realized my count was a measly eleven. I opened my mouth to ask for another card but was silenced by a glare from the dealer.

He cleared his throat with a stern look at me and then moved to the next player. "The gent has already spoken, sir. Play is to you."

While my mind had been wandering, St. Clair's pile of money had steadily increased. Mine had waxed and waned, mostly out of sheer luck and no actual skill on my part. Other gentlemen had been replaced by new players, and I hadn't even noticed. Apart from my last silly blunder, over the subsequent rounds, I'd done surprisingly well, due to the dealer having a run of terrible luck.

I peered at St. Clair, whose concentration remained sharp, his gaze fixed on the cards on the table. For a second, I was sure that I could see his lips moving as though he was tallying something. While I'd had the same thought earlier about keeping track of the high and low cards, I'd never presumed one could do it by a counting system. Was St. Clair using mathematics to gain an advantage in this game? If he was, it was impressive, to say the least.

"Bloody cheater!" the man at the end of the table shouted, standing so quickly that his chair tumbled backward as he slammed his fist down onto the baize. He wasn't as well dressed as some of the other patrons, which meant he was likely gentry or a merchant. It took me a second to realize that he was glaring at St. Clair, who had won the last round and accumulated a large pile of money. "You marked the cards, you thief!"

St. Clair's eyes flashed with rancor, though his face remained neutral. "I beg your pardon, sir. My cards are the same as yours."

"Then you did something," the man snarled. "Memorized and cheated."

"Memorization isn't illegal," St. Clair replied calmly, as if being accused wasn't an uncommon occurrence. "In fact, anyone with half a brain could do it." His lip curled. "Though I suppose you are likely in the minority."

"Think you're so smart, do you? Bloody pencil sniffer." The man clenched his fists, ready to do bodily harm even as the dealer urgently signaled for the factotum, who managed the floor, and was already on his way over with two burly men.

Good, that was good.

But my relief was short-lived, when the player to my right suddenly pushed to his feet as well, pointing at the first accuser's sleeve, where the edge of a card—an ace of hearts—was clearly visible beneath his cuff. "You're the cheat! What's that hanging from your shirt?"

The first man blanched, but then went red. "Mind your own deuced business!"

"Fraud!" the second roared.

A vein popped in the first man's head when he lunged and swung at the second. Cards flew everywhere while more chairs toppled over, the shouting so loud that my ears started ringing. It was suddenly a free-for-all as hands and limbs flew and bodies crashed into each other. Coins clinked as desperate fingers grabbed for piles of money on surrounding tables in the melee. A wave of panic hit me. If this went south and the proctors arrived, I could not be involved or caught in the middle of a brawl.

"Roz!" I heard a panicked voice yelling. My head whipped around. Searching through the mass of colliding bodies, I spied Will's pale face on the other side of the room. The twins were near him, but those two buffoons were grinning and throwing punches left and right. My heart sank. We were all going to go to prison and my woefully brief stint as an independent university student would be over.

My *life* would be over.

"Roz . . . here! We . . . leave . . . ," Will shouted again, but his words were jumbled and broken apart by other shouts in the rapidly worsening scuffle. I blinked, peering through the throng as he struggled to keep someone up at his side. Gracious, was that poor Harold slumped over?

It would be impossible to get to them. My best chance was to stick with St. Clair, who I imagined would not want to be caught either. We both had a lot to lose—a potential fellowship for him and, well, my whole future for me.

"Go!" I yelled back. "I'll find my way out!"

My stomach dropped as I felt a strong hand yank me out of the way of a spray of blood. I almost gagged as the splotch of scarlet bled into the pretty green baize of the card table. Fear tangled with horror as the man who had started it all threw a vicious elbow at the second man, who ended up in a heap on the floor. His bloodshot gaze swung to my left just as St. Clair made a sound like a growl and braced his shoulders, fists flying up at the ready.

"Try it," he said to the man, whose nostrils flared like an angry bull.

My heart hammered behind my ribs. Was he going to *fight*? That pigheaded man was nearly double as wide as we were combined. "St. Clair, no. He's a beast."

Shockingly, my tutor grinned. "Worried for me, Roz?"

I couldn't fully register my glee at the fact that he had finally called me by my nickname, though standing shoulder to shoulder in a scuffle that could cost the two of us everything probably made us the best of mates. "Worried for *us,* yes."

I barely swallowed my high-pitched scream before the man was lurching toward us. Mimicking St. Clair, though I had no idea what I was doing, I threw my fists up to chin level and squared my weight over my feet. But I needn't have worried. With a confident two-punch combination, the boy next to me ducked out of harm's way and then walloped his adversary in the right temple with his left fist and followed with an uppercut to the man's jaw that made his eyes roll back in his head and sent him crashing backward.

My mouth slackened, but I didn't have time to congratulate St. Clair before I noticed a figure looming from the back of us, knuckles raised and heading right for my tutor. *Oh, good gracious, he's going to hit him in the head!*

"Watch out!" I yelled. But when he didn't move, possibly because my warning was lost in the kerfuffle, I had to act. I didn't think—I shoved him sideways, so he wasn't in the direct path of the assailant, rammed my fist up and out, and hoped for the best.

"What the hell?" St. Clair shouted as he stumbled and gripped the edge of a table for balance.

When my balled fingers connected with a fleshly thud into the oncoming attacker, I didn't expect it to hurt so much. A shriek bubbled up as I wrenched my injured hand back to cradle it, belatedly registering the man dropping to his knees, coughing, and clutching his throat where I must have made contact. *I did that!*

I only hoped my poor aching fingers weren't fractured, because they bloody hurt!

"You got him," St. Clair said with surprise. "Nice one. Thanks for looking out. I didn't even see him behind me."

"You're welcome," I replied, feeling as though my heartbeat were pounding in each of my sore knuckles.

"Duck!" he shouted suddenly, and I obeyed on instinct just before the legs of a splintered chair—and was that a dratted *tooth*?—flew over our heads. I yelped as my feet slipped out from under me, and I scrabbled with my fingers to catch my fall on the edge of the table. I managed to save myself from tumbling down, but heat exploded over the back of my hand when a piece of shattered glass caught the skin. Blood welled and dripped as I stared blurrily at my split skin.

"Christ, you're bleeding!" St. Clair said before unknotting his cravat and holding it out to me. "Here, take this and wrap it."

Feeling slightly woozy, I took the offering and glanced down at the stripe of crimson. I looped the fabric around my palm, the pristine white soaking up the blood in an instant, and then fought against the ensuing rush of nausea. I didn't do well with blood . . . mine or anyone else's.

"We should get out of here before it gets worse," St. Clair yelled over the noise. The sound of whistles blew through the air—a warning of some sort—and panic ensued. Were those the proctors?

Whirling, I winced and cursed as he unwittingly grabbed my other arm to yank me through a doorway that led to a darkened staircase. I recognized some of the attendants who had been passing around drinks. This had to be a servant's entrance. "Where does this go?" I asked.

"Kitchens, I think," he shot back. "Try to keep up!"

Ignoring the pain in both hands, I pumped my shaky legs faster, taking the narrow stairs three at a time even though I knew in the back of my head that a fall would be the end of me. The kitchens, thankfully, were empty. The servants had likely either disappeared to safety or run upstairs to keep the place from being absolutely destroyed. St. Clair led me through a maze of smaller storage rooms that had bags of grains and then a cramped cellar that was filled with casks. He seemed to know where he was going, though, so I followed, hoping I would not regret it.

Finally, he crashed into a small wooden door, and the scent of the outdoors—a rank alley, in fact—reached my nostrils. I had never been happier to smell such putrid air, and even the sight of a dozen rats scampering down the grease-blackened cobbles didn't dampen my relief. We were out of danger! Now we only needed to get back to the college. I moved toward the alley mouth when St. Clair's soft whisper made me halt. "Wait."

"For what?" I whispered back. "We need to leave this whole area. The proctors—"

"Are exactly why," he interrupted, pointing and crouching down.

Sure enough, I saw three shadows block the light on the street I'd been seconds from running toward. "Is that them?" I asked, dropping to my haunches beside him.

"Or constables."

I blanched. Those were infinitely worse. The proctors were university officials who could only send us back to the college and threaten us with fines or a period of rustication. Neither of those punishments were as bad as being thrown into the local jail. My stomach roiled with dread.

"How are your legs?" St. Clair asked.

"My legs?" With a frown, I blinked.

A gentleman didn't ask a lady about her *legs,* especially when they were alone and unchaperoned in an alley. Outrage and something else I couldn't name jumped hotly in my veins as I peered at him through the glimmering darkness. I opened my mouth, ready to give him the blistering he deserved before I snapped it shut. Deuce it, I *wasn't* a lady . . . I was a young *man.* In the chaos, I had almost made an unforgivable error and outed myself.

"Well? Can you run, my lord?" St. Clair asked again, sounding irritated. Clearly, he was, since he'd reverted to calling me by my honorific. "It's about two miles back to the college from here. Can you make it?"

"A-all the way back?" I stammered. Two miles was a long way for a girl whose only exercise was the occasional quadrille. "Why can't we take a hackney?"

"They'll be watching all the hacks in this whole area," he said. "Trust me, I know how the proctors work."

He would, since he'd been at Trinity much longer than I had. I bit my lip, deliberating. I wasn't athletic by any means, but I would have to do whatever it took to avoid being caught. "I can do it."

I hoped.

St. Clair rose and inhaled a few deep breaths before spearing me with a look I could only describe as one of challenge. But his next words made me grin.

“Race you! If you win, no reading for a week!”

CHAPTER EIGHT

Every body perseveres in its state of rest, or of uniform motion in a right line, unless it is compelled to change that state by forces impressed thereon.

—Isaac Newton

My heart sped, beating in my chest like a hammer against my ribs. I let out the breath punching at my lips, giving myself over to the heightened intensity of the moment.

"You are different tonight," Blake said, eyes narrowed with interest as he pulled me in for the next turn of the cotillion, our right forearms intertwining as we circled each other.

"Whatever do you mean, my lord?" Gracious, even my voice sounded freer and less encumbered by all the rules and expectations of high society. That said, it was *Blake,* so I wasn't too worried about him finding fault with my comportment, but for once, I wanted to enjoy truly letting go during a dance.

A vision of sparkling blue eyes filled my head—would dancing with my tutor be half as thrilling as racing through a village in the dead of night with the threat of being caught at every turn looming over us? It was strange to think that the incident at the gambling den had been only a few days ago. The healing scab on my hand beneath my arm-length glove pulled slightly. Gloves had been a godsend.

Will and the others had also made it back safely, without being apprehended by any proctors or worse. He had left a note tacked to my door, saying that he was never again trusting the twins. I'd laughed and written him a short message, one that I left for my faithful yet anonymous scout to deliver, replying that it hadn't been their fault and to go easy on them. None of our group had been injured, thank goodness.

Unfortunately, I had been summoned to London by my mother, but the incident at the gaming hell had done something unexpected and unalterable to me. All the rigid control I'd held over myself started to fray . . . like a thread being ripped from its confining stitches. Suddenly, I wanted to exist in the moment and experience each second as deeply as I could, even if it was during a simple cotillion. I wanted to be *present*.

Wasn't *that* what life was about?

Newton talked about motion and his theory of being at rest versus the opposite. Instead of being stagnant, I wanted to fly. I wanted to soar and keep soaring, despite the risk of discovery for not being the decorous young woman everyone knew me to be. My newfound thoughts were dangerous. No one in the *ton* wanted ladies who did not behave exactly as they were bred to—smiling when required, speaking when invited, performing like the perfect automaton.

"Something's different about you," Blake said again as he led me off the ballroom floor toward the refreshments room.

"What's going on in that inventive little mind of yours? What are you up to, Roz?"

I widened my eyes innocently. "Moi?"

"Oui, toi," he shot back. "And now you're being cute with the French. Something is up. Your eyes are glittering like you have a secret." His stare intensified as he pressed a hand to his chest, always the thespian. "Be still my fluttering heart. *Are* you keeping secrets from me, Lady Rosalin?"

"Nothing of note, my lord, I promise you," I said, accepting a glass of lemonade and collecting my breath. I was uncharacteristically parched. Perhaps it was because I was actually dancing instead of mapping out the steps like a master cartographer. In truth, the change had been exhilarating.

"I don't believe you," Blake said.

I almost laughed aloud at his peeved expression. "You're imagining things."

"Have you met someone?" he demanded, making me nearly choke on my next sip. "A clandestine lover? You can tell Papa Blake."

"Goodness, you love gossip." I wrinkled my nose. "And please, never refer to yourself like that again."

I watched as a young woman approached, infatuation in her eyes, her dance card in hand. I could sense Blake's reluctance to leave our conversation unresolved, but he frowned at me with a resolute look that said he fully intended to get out whatever secrets I was harboring, one way or another. Smirking, I arched a brow in challenge and was rewarded by a disbelieving snort, his eyes brightening with intrigue. "I knew it, you crafty minx!"

"You know nothing, Lord Blake."

Something effervescent bubbled in my chest as he let himself be led to the ballroom floor by his eager partner. I wanted more than anything to confide in someone . . . give voice to the beautiful chaos bursting inside of me. I was discovering who the real Lady Rosalin was, and it was glorious! It finally felt like I was peeling back all the layers of myself . . . and uncovering all the special, imperative pieces that made me who I was. I enjoyed being seen and being valued by people like Will and the twins.

And *him*.

My inner voice was quick to chide me. *He's not seeing you. He's seeing Ansel.*

The reminder was harsh. But I refused to let my joy be crushed. Regardless of my false outer disguise, it was still *me* on the inside, and that had to mean something.

You're deceiving them all.

I clenched my teeth at the sound of my self-righteous conscience. "Not where it matters," I growled under my breath in a forceful tone, belatedly realizing that anyone who saw me might remark at my state of mind if I kept muttering to myself. "Get it together, for God's sake!"

"Roz?"

My spine stiffened against the marble column that blocked my view of the entrance to the ballroom. *That* voice was one I knew. Panic exploded within me as my two separate worlds converged.

A smiling face peeked around the column, delighted surprise and then dismay running across his familiar features as he took in my profile, the feathers in my hair, and the length of my gown. My stomach dipped unsteadily at the sight of Will but then righted itself when I realized my identity was safe. I was Lady Rosalin.

Will's ruddy face paled to an ashen color as he bowed several times, resembling a chicken pecking at feed. "Oh, my lady. I do beg your pardon. I mistook you for someone else."

I swallowed my immediate mirth at his adorably flummoxed reaction, guessing that he meant my cousin, and kept my face composed. Will would not take it well if a young lady laughed at his expense, and publicly at that. "And who might that be, good sir?"

While it was proper for young gentlemen to be introduced to ladies and not introduce themselves, there was no one around to judge either of us for one small impropriety. I glanced up quickly, searching for my mother in the crowd, but she was in conversation with the Duchess of Harbridge. If Blake had been here, he could have handled the situation more appropriately, but I could see him twirling his partner, his eyes shooting me daggers of doom every time he spun in my direction.

Will cleared his throat. "Er, my lady, may I beg your gracious pardon," he repeated in a croak, sweat breaking out over his brow and his eyes wide. "My friend Lord Ansel Chen. Your voice . . . er . . . is rather similar." He blinked wildly. "Not that your voice is that of a gentleman . . . I mean . . . your voice . . . is lovely . . . he . . . Roz . . ." He closed his eyes and sighed as if the world were ending with the forlorn breath that left his body. "Please just forget I said anything at all."

"Ansel is my cousin," I said gently, taking care to soften the notes of my voice. "I'm Lady Rosalin."

I turned, facing him fully, watching his expressive eyes round at the feminine version of the face he knew. His gaze parsed over my sleek locks, which were pinned in whimsical loops over my crown and cascaded in soft inky waves over my shoulders, to my eyes and then my cheeks and lips that were stained a soft pink.

"L-lady Rosalin."

I nodded. "We do share a strong family resemblance, I'm afraid. Don't be troubled. The confusion happens more often than you know. I realize we have not been formally introduced, but I won't tell if you won't. Who might you be, sir?"

He straightened and gave a smart bow. "Viscount William Humbolt at your service. Lord Ansel has spoken about you." His stare canvassed the crowded ballroom. "Is he here by chance?"

"Alas, no. My father required his presence, unfortunately." I offered him a demure smile, ducking my chin slightly. "I suppose you'll just have to put up with me in his stead. Tell me, my lord, how do you and my cousin know each other?"

"We met at university," he said. "Capital chap, Roz is."

Though my heart warmed at the praise for my alter ego, it also quailed when Blake glowered meaningfully in my direction once more. The minute that dance was done, he was going to stalk over here like a bull chasing a red rag. "*Lord Ansel* is well liked."

My emphasis on my cousin's title did not go unnoticed, and while it was a not-so-subtle reminder to Will about honorifics and the weight people in the *ton* put upon them, it was also a placid prompt for him not to employ the nickname I had foolishly insisted he use. Especially because Blake was very familiar with that particular address for *me*.

Will's throat worked as he gulped. "Indeed, Lord Ansel is the epitome of civility and kindness."

With a nod of regard, I concealed my satisfaction. "Are you enjoying the ball, my lord?"

"Very much, Lady Rosalin."

His cheeks reddened as though the exchange was almost too much for him to handle. He didn't have the relaxed, snobbish mien of many of the younger set of the *ton* . . . that unmistakable air of privilege that most of the young aristocrats wore like a second set of clothing. In truth, he looked like a fish out of water.

That pale blue gaze of his settled on my face, and he cleared his throat with an uncomfortable cough. "You really do look like him. It's in the eyes."

"I'll take that as a compliment," I said, though the intense scrutiny was making me uneasy.

He shot me a shy smile. "It was meant as one. I do mean it sincerely, my lady. Your cousin was kind to me when he had no reason to be. I was not doing well at Trinity. Not everyone is like him." His voice lowered. "Even here. I can see the way that people look at me as though I'm something scraped from the bottom of their shoes." As if he'd admitted something atrocious, Will's mouth snapped shut and his skin went mottled with mortification. "Bloody hell, I shouldn't have said that to a lady. Or sworn. I beg your pardon. *Again*. God, I'm ruining it."

He sounded so furious with himself that I wanted to hug

him, but that would give me away. "Breathe, Viscount Humbolt. The biggest trick is to pretend that nothing is above you. Nothing and no one. Say something silly? Laugh it off as though you meant it all along."

"It's that easy?" he muttered.

"No. But it's much better than berating yourself for being authentic. People are going to think what they're going to think. Their opinions are none of your business."

He bit out a chuckle. "That sounds like something your cousin would say." I froze, realizing that it was true—I didn't disguise my *inner* self. "Are you sure that you and Lord Ansel are not twins? I have two mates who are twins, and they practically finish each other's sentences. It's a little eerie."

I had to agree. The way that Klaus and Kristof sometimes had silent conversations was a bit unnerving. I shook my head. "No, we're not."

"Compassion and intelligence must run in the family, then."

My lips curled, but I lifted my fan to hide them. I liked Will, with his natural lack of artifice, but to fit in here, he would have to play the part, or he'd be ridiculed or ostracized and discarded like a country bumpkin. I didn't want that for him, but I would have to be careful to watch my step and not give away something that only the male version of Roz would know. Lady Rosalin wasn't properly acquainted with Viscount William Humbolt.

And based on his conclusions thus far that my cousin and I were rather alike in face and manner, I would also have to make sure that our personalities were vastly different. I needed to sell the performance of a flippant, featherbrained Lady Rosalin—the *opposite* of Will's version of her cousin.

"How long have you been at university? I do find it quite a useless endeavor." I forced a high-pitched giggle that made me want to roll my own eyes. "All that time and knowledge for what? A gentleman's job is to oversee his estate, to make the right social connections, and to marry well. University is a complete waste of time, if you ask me."

Will's jaw slackened in a strange sort of astonishment. "I suppose formal education isn't a requirement to be a peer, but knowledge is important."

I sniffed disinterestedly with a bland smile. "A title and a fortune are important, Viscount Humbolt. They are the only things that matter, at least according to most of the aristocracy. My cousin is much too foolish in thinking an interest in astronomy will amount to anything." From his stupefied expression, I knew I was laying it on thickly, but that was the point—to detract from any obvious similarities between Lady Rosalin and Alter Ego Ansel.

The music changed, and I was inordinately grateful to see Blake barreling toward us, given the bleak alternative of further repelling poor Will, who was the kindest soul I'd known. The look of disenchantment blooming in his eyes was almost too much for me to bear.

"Who's this, then?" Blake demanded, slinging an arm around Will's shoulders. It was rather uncouth, but Blake did not care in the least what anyone thought of him, which was quite contrary to the advice I'd given Will. Everyone in our set *knew* Blake, however. Throwing an arm around a boy he didn't know would hardly register on anyone's etiquette meter.

"Lord Blake, may I present Viscount William Humbolt, an acquaintance of my cousin at Trinity. He was new to the university and—" I cut myself off from saying that he was also new to the *ton,* because Viscount Humbolt hadn't actually confided that to me . . . but to Roz acting as Ansel. "And he was just saying how well he had esteemed him."

Blake's eyes narrowed. "Don't you mean St. John's?"

Oh, *botheration.* I kept my face neutral and let out an airy laugh. "St. John's, Trinity, it's all the same, isn't it?"

Goodness, this was starting to unravel rather spectacularly.

"You of all people know that they're not at all the same," Blake said frowning. "Didn't you just tell me how unfair—"

Not even thinking of how it would look, I shoved Blake's arm off Will's shoulders and grabbed Will's free arm even as he squawked in surprise. "Come along. It's time for our dance."

"Our d-dance?"

I pouted prettily as I turned, after manhandling him to the ballroom floor. "I thought we could, but I understand if you don't wish to." I stared at him earnestly, feeling Blake's smirk boring into my back as if he *knew* I'd run away. "It will help you settle in, I promise."

Will nodded, acknowledging the boon I was offering him. "No, of course I want to. Thank you, my lady."

As the strains of music started, I let out a slow exhale. That was close. *Too* close.

Blake was going to be a problem. I could feel it.

"Your cousin is delightful."

Distractedly, I glanced up from the book I was trying to finish reading in the next hour before my meeting with St. Clair while simultaneously stuffing my face with food and squinted at Will. Sadly, I hadn't won the wager for our race, which meant no reprieve from reading. "My who?"

"The beautiful Lady Rosalin," Will announced, plopping down into the chair beside me in the dining hall. "She was at a ball that I was invited to, one you missed, might I add. Was everything well with your uncle? It was a pity you had to miss the fun."

The twins immediately perked up. "You met the cousin?" Klaus demanded in a loud whisper. "Do tell, Will! What's she like, and more importantly, what does she look like?"

"Yes," Kristof urged, his wide smile much too devious for my liking. "Give us specifics," he said, moving his hands in an hourglass shape. "Dimensions. How are her—?"

I cleared my throat and narrowed my eyes. "Oy! She's a lady, and I'll thank you to keep your unflattering misogyny to yourselves."

"We don't hate them," Klaus cried in affront. "We *love* all ladies."

Kristof nodded sagely. "We are devoted philogynists."

"Admiration and lust are two different things," Harold pointed out, cramming his mouth with a piece of roasted chicken. "You don't even know her, so how could you admire her?"

Klaus rolled his eyes. "That's *why* we are asking Will his opinion."

Will flushed when the curious focus of four pairs of eyes, not including mine, was back upon him. "She was fine," he muttered. A chorus of boos from the twins had him shaking his head. "Long black hair, dark eyes. Nicely dressed. Pretty. Looks a bit like him"—he cleared his throat, with a jerk of his chin in my direction—"but without the excellent brain."

I almost chortled at that but kept my head buried in my book. At least my tactics were working to keep my identities separate.

"The best kind!" Klaus remarked and pretended to swoon. "Beautiful but brainless."

I scowled at him. "Did you just call my cousin stupid?"

"*I* didn't. Will did."

Will chose that moment to choke on his mouthful of split pea soup, the contents flying everywhere. Staring at the splotch of green sludge on the corner of my sleeve, I made a gagging noise and reached for my napkin. But when I glanced up, both the twins, who were sitting directly opposite Will, had pea spatter all over their faces, looking equally sickened and speechless.

I couldn't help it—I started laughing. And then everyone else burst into laughter, even poor Will, who seemed mortified and could not stop stammering his apologies between snickers. The amusement died down as a long shadow cut across the table.

"Lord Ansel, you're late."

Still swiping at my stained cuffs, I blinked up at St. Clair owlishly and craned my neck to peer around him at the clock along the far wall at the end of the dining room. He was right.

It was past two o'clock! How had that last hour disappeared so quickly?

His lips tightened at my lack of movement. "Library. Now."

He was already marching out when I opened my mouth to apologize even as I jumped up, sloppily gathering the book and the rest of my things. My stomach growled as if protesting the fact that it hadn't been fed enough, so I stole a fresh roll off James's plate and shoved it into my mouth.

"Hey, that was mine!" he snapped. "Get your own!"

I sketched a theatrical bow. That was one of the things I loved about being a boy—absolutely no one sitting in my vicinity cared about whether one was being a mannerless swine or not. Will could spit half his soup over the table, and we would laugh uproariously about it. But I could not even imagine Lady Rosalin or any ladies of her acquaintance behaving similarly. My mother would have a coronary if she saw her precious, perfect daughter with half a bread roll sticking uncouthly out of her mouth, crumbs falling everywhere. And yet, I had never been happier to defy the rules that governed my alter ego.

"Thanks, mate! I owe you one," I told a seething James—who seemed much too angry over a trifling piece of bread—as I hurried behind St. Clair toward the library. "See you later, lads," I said to the others. "Duty calls."

"More like penance," I heard Harold mutter.

I bit back a chuckle. He wasn't wrong.

Despite our unexpected moment of bonding last week, I had a feeling St. Clair was going to put me through the wringer, and while I had gotten some refreshed reading of *Principia* done during the carriage ride to and from London, I wasn't close to being finished.

St. Clair didn't seem like the type to accept or appreciate any excuses . . . not even wildly inventive ones that involved juggling secret identities and switching lives between Cambridge and London, which required the patience and planning of a master engineer.

I sighed and braced myself. This was what I'd signed up for, and the only thing to do was to keep moving forward even if I wasn't prepared. It was written in the very book I carried—one could only stay in motion if one *kept* in motion.

If I stopped . . . the game would be over.

CHAPTER NINE

We are certainly not to relinquish the evidence of experiments for the sake of dreams and vain fictions of our own devising.

—Isaac Newton

Hustling out to the lush green quadrangle of Nevile's Court while brushing the remaining crumbs from a scone off my cravat and making sure my gown, gold tassels, and cap along with the rest of my disguise were firmly in place, I finally caught up with my tutor inside the Wren Library at the top of the black marble staircase. He strode down the black-and-white diagonal-checkered floors, light streaming in from the huge windows on the east and west sides.

I felt a brief twinge of disappointment that only men were able to enjoy a place that most women, if given the chance, might love as well.

One day, perhaps.

I swallowed my usual rush of wonder at being within these hallowed halls with their polished woodwork topped by plaster busts of philosophers and mathematicians, filled with so much knowledge and history. The walls on each side of the long rectangular room were lined with oak bookshelves all the way up to the sills. At evenly spaced intervals, elegant racks winged out toward the middle of the room, forming three-sided, book-filled celles, or nooks, where a person could sit to read or study. On each side, there were fifteen celles, which included a reading desk, a lamp, and benches.

Right now, some of them were filled but most were empty. St. Clair kept walking toward the gorgeous stained glass window at the south end. There were two rooms on either side that had doors, unlike the rest of the open study nooks, and he walked into the one on the west side before closing the door behind us when I followed.

The room was small, and his presence seemed to dwarf it. It didn't help that all I could smell was him—that divine chocolate-and-snow scent that made me feel warm and breathless. Even though his frosty demeanor was the opposite of warm.

"Sit," he said, indicating the wooden bench closest to the door and walking to the chair on the other side of the reading desk. I jumped at the terseness of the abrupt command. "What are the three laws of motion?" he asked without preamble and without waiting for me to get settled.

Still standing, I gathered my thoughts for a second. "Er, firstly, an object will not change its motion until another force pushes or pulls it. Secondly, the force on an object is equal to its mass times its acceleration. And thirdly, for every action, there is an equal and opposite reaction."

Thick brows rose as he leaned back in his chair and crossed his arms. "Excellent. Of all the theories covered in the book, which is the one that stood out the most to you?"

My brain decided right at that moment to go blank as I sagged down into the seat opposite him. "In *Principia*?"

"Were you reading some other book perhaps, Lord Ansel?" The slightest hint of amusement in his words had me peering up at him, considering it wasn't a tone he typically reserved for me or how he'd started this session.

Usually, he was blunt, mocking, or caustic. Or all three. But there was no mockery on his face, only what appeared to be genuine interest in my answer. I frowned. Was this a trick?

"Er, no, sir?"

"Then which idea in *that* book was most appealing to you?"

I composed myself and exhaled a breath. "Considering the main theory pertains to the law of universal gravitation, then I would have to say that what appealed to me the most was understanding how motion and gravity impact the movement of visible celestial bodies like planets, comets, the Earth, and the moon." His intense gaze bored through me as I went on. "Every object in the universe pulls on every other object with the force we know as gravity. When things are closer together, the pull is stronger, and when they are farther apart, it's weaker. The bigger the objects, like the sun, the stronger the pull. Gravity keeps the planets in orbit around the sun."

"So, everything has gravity," he concluded.

"Yes, even the two of us, to each other and to the Earth. The Earth keeps us grounded, and though we have some pull on it as well, it would be impossible to feel because of the size of it versus the size of us."

The image of standing chest to chest with him floated

through my brain. The truth was I was already caught in his orbit, like an obsessed entity circling the biggest, most beautiful star in the sky. I don't know why the image made my knees weak, but it did.

"You mentioned having a particular interest in astronomy." When I nodded vigorously to hide my inconvenient attraction, he dragged the book toward him and flicked through the pages. "That's why I chose this material for our discussion. So how much of this did you actually manage to reread?"

I blinked in wonder—he'd chosen the subject matter because he knew it would be of interest to *me*? I wanted to be suspicious of his motives, but something fluttered to life in my chest, something that felt too much like tiny butterfly wings beating.

No, no, no.

I squashed the feeling instantly—Isaac Newton was practically a staple in mathematics, physics, and astronomy. Perhaps St. Clair simply wanted to get the measure of me to see how serious I was, not because he *cared* about my interests.

"Most of it," I admitted and flushed. "I'm a fast reader."

A small chuckle left his mouth. "You know, I find myself consistently surprised by you, Lord Ansel. You never struck me as particularly devoted to study when we crossed paths in the past. In fact, you seemed to be quite the scoundrel, more interested in social intrigues with your mates and being properly idle than receiving an actual education. Tell me, what changed?"

My breath left me in a hiss. It wasn't as though Ansel was planning to return to Cambridge, considering he'd already fulfilled the residency requirements, and St. Clair wasn't wrong about my cousin's proclivities, so in the interests of nurturing this fledgling camaraderie, I opted for honesty. "When I was younger, I used to be afraid of the dark, but my mother told me that it's only in the true depths of darkness that one can really see the stars. I remember looking for them then, these tiny celestial bodies that transformed the night sky, and I was fascinated with how they came to be. I wanted to know more about them. Perhaps even discover one of my own someday . . ." I swallowed, trailing off, suddenly worried that in being too honest, I hadn't sounded like Ansel at all. Unsettled, I cleared my throat. "I suppose I realized that I had a unique opportunity to learn from the greats, and I didn't want to squander my remaining time before my uncle called me back to my familial duties."

"I can appreciate that," St. Clair said staring at me thoughtfully. "Is that why you want to build your own telescope?"

I gnawed on my lip. "Someday. I think I want to prove to myself that I can do it."

"Why prove it to yourself?"

Because I'm a girl with a brain, who is just as competent as any boy here, and not some arbitrary abnormality.

"I suppose it's a personal objective," I told him instead. "To see the stars with something I've built."

"I think it's a great plan. Ambitious, as I've said, but great."

I blinked, an idea forming . . . one that scared me, but it was an achievable goal. "Do you think such a thing could be part of my assessment at the end of the term?"

He paused, then said, "I'll consult with one of the Fellows, Mr. George Peacock, and let you know."

We lapsed into silence, and when I looked up again, I found him staring unwaveringly at me with a gaze that seemed to delve right through to all my secrets. Or perhaps I felt that way only because I had the foolish inclination to confess them all to him. I shoved my spectacles up my nose. "Is everything all right, sir?" I asked, worried that my facial hair might be migrating again.

His lean throat bobbed as he swallowed. "Before we continue with the reading assignment, I wanted to thank you again for last week. I could have been badly hurt if you hadn't seen that punch coming, and my whole career, everything I've worked for, would have been in jeopardy."

I was shocked but something deep inside me tightened and warmed. "You're welcome, and don't worry; your secret is safe with me. I expect you would have done the same in my place. In fact, I should be thanking you for getting us out of there. I would have been in a similar boat if I'd been caught." I smiled. "So, I suppose we helped each other, Mr. St. Clair."

"Since we've been bonded in blood and apparently are going to be friends now, you can call me Tarik." He glanced at my hand resting on the table. "How's your injury?"

I blinked at him, stunned by the invitation to use his given name, before following his stare to the wound I'd sustained at the gaming hell. I smoothed my fingers over the back of my hand, feeling the tight, scabbing skin. Thankfully, our family physician had said I hadn't needed stitches. I shook my head sadly at him and let out a dramatic sigh. "It was a rather narrow escape from certain peril, but the doctors said I will live, although they've stipulated that mulish, hard-nosed tutors will need to be exponentially more tolerant of their charges."

"Mulish and hard-nosed, am I?"

"Capitally."

When his face broke into a gloriously unbridled grin and displayed that dratted dimple, those pesky wings in my stomach started to flutter again. I ducked my head lest he see my infatuation written all over me. A brusque and stern Tarik St. Clair was dangerous enough, but this affable and charming version of him would be Lady Rosalin's utter undoing.

Heavens, I'm in so much trouble!

I was almost tempted to ruin the moment with contempt or disdain, to bring my prior tutor back—because at least if he loathed me or mistrusted me, I could keep him at a safe arm's length. And then I could convince myself I didn't need to earn any of those riveting dimpled smiles or desire his sincere claims of gratitude.

He's your tutor, nothing more!

"What about you?" I blurted, hoping to distract myself. "Why did you choose to study mathematics at Trinity College? I know you said that there were more potential opportunities as a Fellow, but surely you had some interest in the field before that." I coughed. "You're ridiculously astute on the subject."

That bright gaze collided with mine, conflicting emotions ebbing and flowing in it, and for a moment, I thought I had snapped the tenuous bonds of our friendship, but then he shrugged one shoulder. "I was originally the recipient of a small scholarship to St. John's. My father worked at a gaming hell in Paris, and the owner of the club there, his brother-in-law and my uncle, was a transplanted Englishman, a former subsizar of St. John's himself."

"Your uncle went here?"

"He earned a fellowship after years of study and taught Latin at St. John's College for a time before joining my parents in Paris to strike out on a new business venture."

"So, you're French?" I asked.

"Half, yes," he replied. "My mother was born in England, though she lived with my father in Montmartre until she died of consumption. My father passed not too long after." He smiled fondly, his eyes glossing at the memory. "My parents might not have had much, and our apartment was little more than an attic, but they were a love match. He always knew he would follow when she departed this earth. They were les âmes soeurs, as he used to say. Soulmates." He let out a low and embarrassed laugh, a faint flush dispersing across his cheekbones. "Now who's a romantic?"

It was a reference to the time we'd spoken of Herschel, when I waxed poetic about the gravitational movement of the stars. My heart clenched, a strange yearning rising in my throat. Did he want to follow in his parents' footsteps, too, and fall in love with someone who was his perfect match? Find *his* âme soeur?

This was one of the times when I wished I could have been here as myself—that he could see the true me. Then I could let my admiration and esteem for him show . . . and perhaps even have those feelings returned. My throat tightened with an impossible ache for a dream that could never be. There was no way I could admit who I really was. So, for now, my affections would be wholly unrequited.

"I'm sorry for your loss," I said quietly.

His mouth creased. "It was a long time ago, but thank you."

"Did you grow up in Paris, then?" I asked, curious to learn more about him and enjoying this glimpse behind his usually impenetrable, aloof façade.

His eyes lost some of their melancholy. "Until I was sixteen. I attended a lycée where I learned Greek, Latin, philosophy, science, and mathematics. At St. John's, I discovered I had a particular aptitude for the latter and found myself at Trinity. Mr. Peacock expressed a decided interest in me after I completed the Mathematical Tripos in second place."

That reminded me of my conversation with James. His remarks about St. Clair not succeeding on his own coattails didn't quite ring true. "Are you friends with Sir James Lowry?"

Distaste ran over his face. "Why do you ask?"

"He said he took the Tripos in the same year as you. It's interesting that you both ended up here from St. John's. Did Mr. Peacock invite him to Trinity as well?"

"Not exactly." St. Clair's mouth went tight but then he shook his head. "Look, Roz, keep your wits sharp around him."

"What do you mean?"

A muscle flexed in his jaw, and St. Clair pushed the book in front of him over to me. "He will do anything to get ahead." He cleared his throat. "But we are not here to gossip, and I don't wish to speak out of turn. Let's get back to your studies. Can you identify another mathematician who challenges or expands on Newton's theories?"

I frowned at the abrupt turnabout. There was obviously some history there, as James hadn't been charitable in his remarks about St. Clair either. Competition between boys could be just as bad as between girls . . . or even worse, it seemed.

I shook my head to clear it and refocused on Newton. "Yes. I once read the work of a Frenchwoman named Émilie du Châtelet, who expanded on some theories of *Principia*. She commented upon and clarified several of Newton's principles in her own words, which made a lot more sense to me."

He nodded. "Ah, Voltaire's mistress."

I huffed. "Why does every woman need to be in the shadow of some male? Shouldn't she be known in her own right as a scholar and mathematician?"

"I hardly think she stood in his shadow," he said, his eyes flashing with something like admiration. "She was a brilliant mathematician, and *Institutions de Physique* was an excellent book. And you're right, her understanding of Newton's mechanics was unparalleled." He grinned at my instant mollification. "I only mentioned Voltaire because he once called her 'a great man whose only fault was being a woman.' "

"That we can agree upon, though shouldn't she be great in her own right despite her sex? The mind has no discernible sexual identity. It simply *is* . . . before it becomes distorted by social rules and expectation. A superior path for men, a lesser one for women. It's conditioned behavior, shaped by morality and ethics, when it should be shaped by caliber," I said the last word with such fervent bitterness that he cocked his head, eyes huge.

"You seem very passionate about the subject."

I wondered how much I could say without giving myself away. There was a line between advocating for my principles and drawing too much interest that might not bode well for me. St. Clair was nothing if not keenly perceptive.

On the one hand, he could also be a man who thought a woman's place was at home, though on the other, I suspected he was someone who might value, or even share, my provocative opinions, since he seemed intrigued, not outraged. Most gentlemen would be scandalized at the mere suggestion that women, God forbid, might be deserving of the same education as them.

"I am," I said slowly. "My cousin Lady Rosalin and I used to have lively discussions about geometry and celestial calculations, until her focus became securing a good marriage by being the type of girl society expects her to be as an heiress. Arguably, if it were truly a question of aptitude, *she* would be here, not me."

"Does she enjoy science or mathematics, then?"

"Categorically adores them," I replied. "She used to solve all the mathematical puzzles in the weekly periodicals and does nautical calculations in her spare time for fun. She would thrive in a place like this. Perhaps one day, women will be allowed to study here, though I suspect it won't be in our lifetimes." I waited with bated breath for his reply, knowing it would shape everything I felt about him. He could be the most handsome, cleverest man in all of creation, but if he turned out to be a bigot, it was something I would never be able to abide.

"Sooner rather than later, I hope," he said, and I nearly let out an audible sigh. "It is an irregular opinion, but I, too, believe that the mind is molded from birth and is nurtured by the environment that surrounds it. Beyond the anatomical size difference, when a world is divided by the sexes, it's a foregone conclusion that the brain will be, too." His expression was energized. "To make up for my insensitive comment about Émilie earlier, did you know that her father recognized her genius at age ten and arranged for private astronomy lessons? He, a French peer, chose to nurture her brilliance."

He waved an arm between us, pointing to himself and then to me. "You and I are given these opportunities by default of being male, ones that some willingly squander, while mothers, daughters, and sisters must unfairly languish in a future that has been charted for them. They don't have open-minded fathers like Émilie's. The brain is elastic and pliable, and hungry to learn, *regardless* of sex. It absorbs what we choose to feed it."

My jaw nearly dropped in stupefaction. By God, he was mesmerizing, his wise words falling from his lips like love sonnets. In all the years I'd been out in society, I had never heard a man speak so sincerely about equality between the sexes, especially as it related to intelligence or skill. It was as though the sentiments had been snatched straight from the depths of my own soul.

"Precisely," I breathed.

"Give a girl a telescope, and she'll discover the world."

In the future, if I ever looked back as a grown woman, this was perhaps the exact moment I think I fell irrevocably in love with Tarik St. Clair.

"Or have her build it herself," I said, and then swallowed past a lump the size of London when his eyes caught and held mine, and the butterflies in my chest exploded.

"Yes," he agreed. "Is that why you've become intrigued by astronomy, and you're interested in building one?" he asked insightfully. "For her. Your cousin?"

For a moment, I'd completely forgotten I wasn't Rosalin. "Partly, yes."

"Another surprising discovery about you, Lord Ansel," he said with a shake of his head. "That's rather selfless and generous. It's why you changed colleges, isn't it? I must admit I wondered what could have been a catalyst for such a move. I unfairly assumed you had been forced into rustication from St. John's and convinced your powerful uncle to enroll you elsewhere to finish the term." After a beat, he stuck his hand out over the surface between us, expression solemn. "You were right all along—and I was in the wrong. I *didn't* know you, and I didn't give myself the chance to get to know you. May I ask your forgiveness?"

I clasped his hand, trying not to shiver at the indelicate rasp of his smooth, bare skin against mine. My pulse streamed.

You're Ansel, you're Ansel, you're Ansel, I chanted to myself.

I gripped extra hard, shook like my life depended on it, and then dropped his warm, calloused palm. He didn't have the soft hands of a nobleman; they were rough to the touch . . . hands that told a story of a hard worker.

"Forgiven and forgotten." I forced a jovial expression to my face. "So, what does the great Mr. St. Clair intend to do with his life? Do you plan to become an academic Fellow like your uncle?

Terrorize, I mean *influence,* the malleable young mathematical minds of the future?"

He laughed. "The easy answer is yes, but I suppose it would be ungracious if I wasn't as honest as you've just been," he said. His cheeks reddened, and my curiosity spiked when he took a few more minutes to form his reply, seeming unusually shy. "The more complicated secret answer is that I wish to open my own exclusive social club."

Lips parting, I blinked at him. That was . . . not what I'd been expecting.

He paused, folding his lips between his teeth, those flags of color on his cheeks darkening as he shifted in his seat. I'd expected him to say something along the lines of specialized mathematical research or that he was developing some fantastic secret invention or writing his own version of *Principia*. Not that a social club wasn't an intriguing or impressive idea, but they were a dime a dozen. Most men's clubs promoted idleness and indolence where aristocratic or wealthy gentlemen lauded themselves on how smart and wonderful they were.

It was frankly . . . disappointing.

"Go on," I told him. "Tell me more."

A tiny frown marred his brow at the baffled expression I couldn't quite hide, but then he sat forward with purpose. "It wouldn't be just social, but academic also, with meeting rooms for philosophical societies or national organizations for scientific disciplines and the like. And it would include both men *and* women. There'll be salons for theoretical and speculative discussions, a full library, exquisite food with a French chef, as well as spaces for leisure and entertainment, including exclusive card rooms with high-stakes gaming."

Well, that changed things. The idea was both brilliant and provocative.

"Women, too?" I asked, surprised.

His smile grew wider. "Why not? Women bring a unique perspective to the world. Perhaps if I am ever successful, you can invite your cousin. She would be able to participate in intellectual discussions in whatever manner she wished."

My brows lifted, though my pulse started to hum an excited rhythm. "But it's not the *done* thing."

"Perhaps it's time for a change, then," he said with a shrug. "What's the point of not being bold, of not breaking with tradition? The worst that can happen from reaching too high is that I fail." He glanced at me with a wry look. "Then again, unless I can attract enough investors, I fear my idea won't get off the ground at all."

"Investors?" I asked.

"Opening a social club, and one with such unique requirements as the one I intend to build, will take lots of money. Alas, I'm not a rich man nor an aristocrat who has the ears of such people."

I stared at him, a marvelous idea forming. "But *I* am," I said slowly.

"You are what?"

My smile was so wide my cheeks ached. "Hear me out."

PART II

Be not afraid of greatness . . .
Some are born great . . .
Some achieve greatness . . .
And some have greatness thrust upon them.

—William Shakespeare, *Twelfth Night*

CHAPTER TEN

When a body is falling, the uniform force of its gravity acting equally, impresses, in equal particles of time, equal forces upon that body, and therefore generates equal velocities.

—Isaac Newton

Our plan was audacious. Bold. Categorically dodgy.

If we were discovered, there would be hell and more to pay. But Isaac Newton allegedly said no great discovery was ever made without being bold. I wrinkled my nose. The quote wasn't exactly that, but I was sure it was what he *meant*. One can't achieve greatness, in discovery or otherwise, without some measure of brashness.

So here we were . . . being brash.

I swallowed hard. Hopefully, not foolish.

St. Clair—*Tarik*—had been resistant at first, and it had taken hours to convince him that my plan could work. We were going to hoodwink the *ton*. My own disguise had worked so well at Cambridge that I figured a similar *smaller* disguise could work to give him access to the bottomless coffers of the aristocracy, to get what he wanted and needed to achieve his dream.

Not that he knew that *I* was in disguise, but semantics.

As a socialite, I had excellent insight into how people worked, having navigated the *ton* for three seasons prior, and presenting a convincing argument to Tarik was as easy as breathing to me. Within moments, he was hooked by the possibilities, though he remained dubious, arguing that he was a commoner with no significant income to his name and people would see right through the charade.

I'd countered that he conducted himself like an educated gentleman, thanks to his formal instruction at Cambridge, spoke multiple languages, could converse on any subject, and it was only a matter of clothing and the right introductions to high society . . . which would be facilitated by *me,* Lord Ansel's lovely and charming cousin.

Tarik had balked at the cost of a fashionable new wardrobe, the façade of his new identity, which I said I would handle. Luckily, I convinced him to consider it as an early investment into his club, which I would hopefully recoup as a minor stakeholder in his business. Tarik had relented only after a very lengthy argument where I held that this was in no means charity and was in both our best interests. I admired how much pride he had—he hadn't seen it as a handout. He'd insisted that if his venture failed, he would repay it as a loan.

I had graciously conceded the point.

In truth, I was helping myself as well—because this term at university would not last past June, but if there was an academic and social club that women could look forward to being welcomed at, that made any future of mine better. The idea of a hospitable place where my ideas could be heard as *myself*—a woman wearing a dress and not having false facial hair or spectacles to disguise my appearance—was every female scholar's dream.

Certainly, women with literary interests had formed their own informal movements, like the Blue Stockings Society, which focused on female education, charity, and cooperation, but they existed at the fringes of men's spaces, in drawing rooms. Their voices weren't as amplified as they deserved to be. And while some educated men of letters supported them and participated in their literary conversations, it wasn't a conventionally accepted thing.

What Tarik was trying to do was nothing short of remarkable, and I wanted to be part of it. The concept of his club was truly innovative.

And it deserved to have a chance of success.

As my carriage came to a halt on Bond Street in a flutter of ruffled skirts, I caught a glimpse through the window of my tutor standing like a statue in the gentlemen's part of the shop and felt a glimmer of relief that he'd come. He looked totally out of place in his well-worn, serviceable brown tweed, but at least he was there. Roz had set up a rendezvous with his cousin, Lady Rosalin, to meet him at their family's dressmakers to have clothing sized and ordered.

"Here we are, my lady," Anna said, handing me my reticule as the coachman opened the door. Though Anna knew of *my* ruse as a student at Cambridge, I did not confide in her about my audacious plan with Tarik. While I could take responsibility for the consequences of my own schemes, I could not in good conscience expose Tarik to someone he didn't know or trust. *I* trusted Anna, but this new subterfuge didn't involve only me—and the more people who knew about it, the riskier things became.

"Thank you, Anna."

Hit suddenly by nerves, I lifted my chin and bolstered my flagging confidence. Still, I felt nervous to meet Tarik as myself, even though I'd gotten to know him so well through my alternate identity. *Rosalin* was a stranger to him. I felt naked without my mustache and spectacles, and I desperately wanted to make a good impression.

I wanted him to be intrigued by me. The *real* me. Because I greatly esteemed him.

Even if he didn't know it. He was everything I'd yearned for and never found.

Hope fluttered in my chest on gossamer wings as I smoothed my fingers over my dress again and fussed with an errant lock of hair that would not stay put. Goodness, would he even think I was pretty? My cheeks warmed. I knew it was a shallow thought, but that didn't negate its lingering presence in my brain. What if he thought I was unattractive? I blinked. Did Tarik even *like* girls? I didn't want to be presumptuous.

Enough, Rosalin. Either he will like you or he won't.

Inhaling a deep breath to quell my lingering fears, I strolled into the shop with Anna at my heels.

"Lady Rosalin, how lovely to see you!" My family's longtime modiste, Madame Marchand, greeted me happily with a kiss to each cheek as was the French custom. She was a well-known dressmaker for many affluent ladies in the *ton,* and her husband, Monsieur Marchand, was a renowned tailor for the gentlemen. They owned the largest dress shop on Bond Street, which was divided into two boutiques with separate entrances. Their fitting and sewing rooms encompassed the middle.

"Come, Monsieur Marchand is waiting with the young gentleman, Monsieur St. Clair. May I get you some tea?"

"Non, merci," I told her as she led us down a well-lit corridor with framed drawings of their combined designs. Some of them had even been featured in *Ackermann's Repository,* a popular, fashionable monthly magazine.

"How is your maman?" she asked. "I haven't seen her since the start of the season, though her order was very large. Such a stylish woman!"

"Mama is well, quite busy as you know," I said, stiffening instantly at the thought of the duchess finding out that I was here commissioning clothing for a strange boy, but it was unlikely she would return to Marchand's anytime soon. The expenses would be put on Ansel's account, which was managed by my father's solicitor. I knew my cousin would not care.

"We were delighted to get the letter from Lord Ansel about his friend, a young nobleman from Paris," Madame Marchand said. "It's truly generous and wonderful that your family is taking him under your wing."

I felt Anna's curious gaze flick to me as she overheard that, but I only nodded. "My cousin has close friends all over the world."

Ansel's letter, ergo *my* letter, had instructed Monsieur Marchand to outfit our dear family friend with no expense spared, which I'm sure had *delighted* the couple very much. To make sure that my parents would not be contacted to confirm the instructions in the letter and ensure it wasn't a fraudulent one, I had made an appointment to be here, to shore up the ruse.

The story I had concocted to support Tarik's position in the *ton* was that he was the son of a rich French businessman and was wrapping up his education at Cambridge. A wealthy backstory shored up by a connection to the Duke of Delmont would give him added legitimacy; not that his own humble origins weren't enough, but aristocrats were a privileged and exclusive bunch. They would not give Tarik the time of day if they didn't believe he came from *somewhere* of note. The nephew of a former university Fellow turned Parisian gaming den owner did not quite have the same ring to it as a French magnate. The only things aristocrats loved more than titles was money.

And I would be sure to confirm that Tarik possessed an obscene amount of it.

We hustled into the storefront where Madame Marchand's husband and my tutor, who struggled to keep his face neutral, were waiting. While the husband-and-wife pair put their heads together with their staff, consulting magazines and pulling out various lengths of fabrics, I walked over to where Tarik stood. Outside of his university gown and plain garments, the quality of his clothing was unremarkable, though in relatively respectable condition. They would not pass muster in our circles, however, which was the reason behind a completely new wardrobe for the rest of the season.

He needed to be *noticed*.

Approaching him where he stood looking out the large bay

window to the crowded street beyond, I coughed delicately into my gloved fist. He glanced over his shoulder, turned, and stood stock-still. My entire body froze, along with everything around me, as my senses narrowed down to one single thing. *Him*.

Those lapis lazuli eyes met mine, and I sucked in an inaudible gasp when they stared at me with an electric intensity I hadn't felt before. And I *wasn't* imagining things—the heat of them seared into my skin as they took in the long dark hair that tumbled in inky skeins over my shoulders and nearly to my waist, the excellent cut of the ruffled pale-green-and-cream dress, from its puffed sleeves all the way down to the tips of my polished walking boots, and then back up again to my pristine white gloves, beaded reticule, bodice, and face.

They settled on my eyes and lips, studying my features with a familiar scrutiny that made flames ignite beneath my skin. Surely, it wasn't polite to stare so long, but I was also willing to wager that what had felt like hours had been merely seconds.

Would he recognize me?

"Lady Rosalin, I presume?" he said softly so that the owners of the shop did not hear. We were skipping past formalities for the sake of time, especially since we required everyone else to think we had already been introduced by Ansel.

Since we were both unwed, Anna remained demurely a few feet away as chaperone, which did not put us in indecent territory. I nearly snorted—I'd been with said gentleman behind closed doors *alone*. Not that he or anyone here knew that. I'm certain that if Ansel had thought twice about what such a deception entailed, he would have said an emphatic no. Thank goodness boys were not used to thinking about all the rules that unmarried girls my age faced.

"Mr. St. Clair," I said equally softly. "It's wonderful to finally meet you. My cousin has spoken quite highly of you."

"Has he?" he asked with a slight raise of his brows. He looked so incredulous that I wanted to laugh.

"Did you expect him to say something untoward?" I asked. "Ansel can be hard to read at times, and often comes across as arrogant, but when he speaks well of a person, it is usually genuine. What did he tell you about me?"

"That you're very intelligent," he replied. "He did not, however, say that you would be . . . so comely as well."

With that one sentence, every bone in my body melted. "You flatter me, sir. My cousin and I look tremendously alike."

"He is annoyingly handsome," Tarik agreed as he bent over my hand and lifted my gloved knuckles to his mouth. My eyes widened. Where had he learned *that*? Not that I would have seen Tarik St. Clair in any social setting where he would be greeting a lady of my station. Everyone at Trinity was male. I caught my breath as the heat of his lips seared through the soft fabric, and I pinned my lips together so no sound could escape. He glanced up, those eyes crashing into mine again, mischief in them. "Though I dare say, you're a much lovelier sight than he is."

My cheeks flamed as he stood at his full height, a few inches above me. I kept my voice low. "Thank you, but you don't have to oversell it. I've already agreed to help the two of you with your nefarious plans."

His expression grew serious. "Are you certain, my lady? I do not wish to cause you any unnecessary strife. Your cousin was simply trying to help me gain a foothold—"

I lifted a palm between us. "I'm aware of why we are here. We can discuss when there aren't so many ears listening, if that suits you. For now, we have a long and tiring afternoon ahead of us." I pursed my lips and nodded toward the tailor and his wife. "For you, rather."

"Thank you for doing this, truly," he said. "May I interest you in a stroll to the park after I am finished? I would welcome the chance to get to know you better. Your cousin has told me of your interest in astronomy."

I glanced up at him with a smile. "If you can manage to walk properly at that point, Mr. St. Clair, I would be delighted to accompany you."

His extraordinary eyes bulged comically, but I only laughed.

Several hours later, most of which I spent reading, the Marchands had declared they were finished with measurements. Biting back my giggles at Tarik's exaggerated movements, I watched as he rolled his shoulders and pretended to check his arms for injury.

"I feel like a human pincushion," he grumbled as we stretched our legs, walking through the neighboring Hyde Park. The ever-vigilant Anna followed us at a discreet distance.

Parasol in hand, I peered up at him, once more struck by the change in him. He wore a brand-new suit that Monsieur Marchand had on hand for a gentleman who had supposedly lost his entire fortune in a hand of cards at a gaming hell on the west side of London and was unable to pay his accounts. The tailor had deftly and expertly altered the suit to fit Tarik to perfection. He looked quite handsome and dapper.

It was truly shocking what a new set of elegant clothing did for a man, but considering I had never seen my tutor out of his academic gown or in any fancy clothes, it was no wonder that I was in a state of enchantment. With his height and lean figure coupled with his dark, wavy hair; rich brown complexion; and flashing eyes, he looked exactly like the wealthy member of the gentry we were portraying him to be.

The ladies would be swooning when he entered ballrooms, of that I had no doubt, and the younger set of gentlemen would be clamoring to know who he was and how to align themselves with him. Half the battle was confidence, and Tarik St. Clair had that in spades. I had no idea how a man born of humble origins could have such innate self-assurance, but he had never struck me as someone who was lacking in conviction.

It was still early, before most of the fashionable people came out to promenade on the paths through the park, so it wasn't too crowded just yet. Not that I minded. Since part of the mission was to have Tarik be seen by influential people, it would be an easy start. At least before the Marquess of Ridley's ball next week, where he would make his grand, official, splashy entrance into high society.

My companion made another noise of discomfort that dragged me out of my thoughts. He tugged at the silky folds of his cravat and ran his gloved fingers over the frock coat he wore. His little groans and his constant adjustments made me want to giggle.

"The fitting could not have been *that* bad, sir," I said, keeping my mirth to myself. "The Marchands are professionals who have done this hundreds of times already this season. Trust me, anywhere else would have taken weeks or months. There's a reason they are called the best. As it is, they will have coats, waistcoats, breeches, trousers, shirts, with all the accoutrements, and arrange for shoes, hats, and accessories delivered to you within the week."

"Truly, I am grateful, but if I ever see another bolt of fabric, I might revolt. Does a man actually need a dozen waistcoats?"

"If he wants to be remembered, yes," I said with a surreptitious sidelong glance at the embroidered cobalt-blue waistcoat he wore, which made his eyes blaze.

He snorted. "Looks are fleeting. I'd much rather be remembered for my character and my mind."

I couldn't help it anymore—I laughed. "Then you would be better off courting someone other than the aristocracy. Most of them are a bunch of strutting peacocks. Sure, there are a select few who understand that the measure of a man or woman goes far beyond their appearance, but for the majority, first impressions can seal a newcomer's reception."

"I suppose. Still, that doesn't account for why a man must be poked and prodded for hours on end, simply to impress a few dandies."

I rolled my eyes. “Ladies’ dress-fitting sessions take days; yours took only a few hours. Imagine how women must feel to achieve the standard of perfection we are held to.”

“I cannot conceive that it takes long for you,” he said. “To achieve perfection, I mean.” It took a moment before I realized that he was complimenting me again. Faltering, I sucked in a breath at the warmth in his eyes. Gracious, was he *flirting* with me? For a second, I’d forgotten that we weren’t in Cambridge, and I wasn’t garbed in my usual disguise.

No, I was in a dress, and I was a lady . . . and someone I truly esteemed was reciprocating my interest. I’d fantasized about such a scenario for so long that I almost did not know how to react or respond. I blushed daintily, and unlike the times at Trinity when I’d ducked to hide my pinkened cheeks, I let him see them. “You’re very kind, Mr. St. Clair.”

“Tarik, please, and I’m only being honest.”

“I could not address you by your given name, sir. It would not be proper.”

I could feel his smile, and it took everything in me not to stop and stare so I could memorize every inch of it. “Not even when we are alone like this?” he asked softly.

“We’re not alone, Mr. St. Clair. We’re surrounded by a few other people strolling in the park on this fine afternoon who are pretending not to notice us while cataloguing every step we take for dissection later. Not to mention, my lady’s maid, Anna, is right behind us.”

He glanced over his shoulder to where Anna was trailing us. “She’s very serious about her job.”

"Most chaperones have to be, lest a young woman's virtue be snatched out from right under her nose and her reputation be forever tarnished."

"In broad daylight?" he asked with some incredulity.

"You would be surprised at what some unscrupulous rogues might attempt to do to compromise a young heiress." I pointed at a small copse of trees. "Last year, Lady Simone, the daughter of an earl, was escorted into that very glade by a fortune hunter who hoped to get her into a compromising position. He failed, thanks to her very vigilant chaperone. A few years ago, another young lady snuck off to Vauxhall with her beau, and they were forced to marry when discovered. The scandal was interminable."

His expression was thoughtful. "I admit, I've never thought about the rules of your station and how they applied to the safety of young women until your cousin Lord Ansel and I discussed it. He was especially cross about the fact that women are not permitted to attend university and intimated that you would thrive there, given the chance. But I supposed I always assumed the rules were too rigid and prevented girls from having the same freedom or opportunities as boys."

"They are, and they do," I said. "But it's the violence and ill will of some men that make them necessary, especially when a girl is out and about on her own. Society needs to change and hold the men accountable. As a matter of fact, one of my dearest friends had a boy lie about her past, and her entire reputation was ruined. Everyone believed that something untoward had happened between them and my friend was sent away to a girls' seminary instead of coming out to high society as the daughter of an earl. Just like that, her life was finished. All because of one boy."

"That is utterly appalling," he said, horrified.

Pursing my lips, I nodded. "It was, but everything turned out all right in the end. It's a long story, but she returned to London to reclaim her reputation and take back her rightful place in the *ton*." I smiled at him. "You'll meet her, I hope. Her name is Lady Ela, and she's married to a very influential young man in the *ton*, the Marquess of Ridley. Win their support, and you'll be guaranteed success."

"It's that easy, is it?" he asked.

"No, Mr. St. Clair. Nothing is ever easy, but as a very smart man said, 'more is in vain when less will serve.'"

He stopped so suddenly that I'd walked a few steps more before realizing he was no longer at my side. I turned and nearly stumbled over my feet seeing the wide smile on his face. "You quoted Newton."

I shot him a teasing grin of my own and canted my chin. "Surprised, Mr. St. Clair?"

"I should not be, considering everything your cousin has shared," he said, shaking his head in wonder. "But is it too soon to admit that I might be smitten?"

My cheeks flamed at the admission, my heart thumping in my chest. "You do not even know me, sir."

"True, but it's strange how much I feel like I do," he said. "Your cousin . . . you're very similar, but so different. I can't explain it without sounding foolish. Even this conversation feels outlandishly familiar and comfortable as if we've already spoken at great length, though I can't imagine how." He raked a hand through his hair, the loose waves falling every which way. "In truth, I feel like I've known you my whole life, and I know that's an extraordinarily peculiar thing to say to someone I've just met. Forgive me, if I am overstepping."

"You're not," I whispered, staring at him. "I know exactly what you mean."

"You do?"

The desire to confess the whole farce sat heavy on my tongue, but it would ruin everything. I wanted St. Clair to have a real chance to fulfill his dream. If there was anything I could do to make a difference with the limited power I had, I needed to do it. I shrugged easily. "Perhaps we knew each other in another lifetime or somewhere else in the cosmos. The universe is infinite, after all."

"No," he murmured. "That's not possible."

"Why not?" I asked, my heart stopping.

His eyes were filled with wonder. "Because there's no other universe or lifetime in which I could ever forget meeting someone like you."

CHAPTER ELEVEN

But if I have done the public any service this way, 'tis due to nothing but industry and a patient thought.

—Isaac Newton

Will stared at me, his round face wreathed in disappointment. "Wait, you're going to be gone for the rest of the term? How is that even possible? What about examinations?"

"My uncle is the Duke of Delmont," I replied as I packed up a few of my belongings. "He gives a significant endowment to Cambridge. I have important duties I must attend to in London. As far as examinations, I don't have to take them. They're only a formality."

I had no legitimate reason to take the tests, other than to prove something to myself, especially since Ansel was on track to graduate with an ordinary degree, the one most aristocrats aimed for with the minimal amount of study and effort. *He* had nothing to prove or to gain. In fact, he probably would have received his degree anyway without me being here this term.

"And your tutor?" Will asked. "Surely he has something to say about your departure?"

"Mr. St. Clair will accompany me to make sure that I stay on track with my studies. It has all already been authorized with the Master of the College. My uncle submitted the formal petition, which was approved." The letter with my father's stamp was yet another crime I added to the litany of the ones I'd committed since setting out on my adventures, but was it really hurting anyone? The college was still getting its money, and Alter Ego Ansel required formal approval to continue his course of study while I was in London. I stopped my packing to glance at Will. "I will still see you in town. It's truly not the calamity you're making it out to be."

"I don't want to lose my friend," he said morosely, and his sad admission made my heart twinge. "I know the twins and Harold and James are my mates, but you're the only one I've felt close to, since well . . . you know, the viscountcy."

I understood what he meant. All the other peers here gave him a wide berth, as if they instinctively knew he wasn't one of them. Luckily, none of them were part of my immediate set or I'd give them a piece of my mind.

"You won't lose me and you're going to be fine. I'll only be a few hours away. And who knows? I may be back before you know it."

"It's already nearly June," he said. "The term is over next month."

I moved to stand in front of him, swiping my forearm across my sweaty face. "Will, pull yourself together, for heaven's sake! This short absence won't be the end of the world. I'm still enrolled and have no intention of withdrawing before the end of term. We have many weeks left."

In truth, staying in London for a fortnight or two felt like a bit of a much needed reprieve. The lengthy trips back and forth had started to take an unexpected toll, and keeping up the pretense of being two people was much more difficult than I'd anticipated. I'd slipped up several times in recent days due to exhaustion.

"This is how it's done all the time with aristocrats who have obligations in London during the social season. With any luck, it will only be for a short while." As I spoke, his stare settled on my mouth . . . my upper lip to be precise, and I frowned at him. "Are you even listening to what I'm saying? What is so interesting on my face?" I groused.

"You have a bald spot in your mustache," he said.

I blinked at him and immediately covered my mouth with my palm. "What?"

Glancing down, I found the rogue tuft hooked to my sleeve. In dismay, I pressed my fingers to my lip, locating the smooth patch, and attempted to brush some of the remaining hairs over it. The sweat must have dislodged them somehow or maybe the adhesive paste was reaching the end of its life.

"I pick at my facial hair when I get anxious. More of a reason for me to leave now," I explained hastily, knowing it was a rather flimsy excuse that a child could see through, but either Will was too overcome with emotion to make sense of it or he chose to ignore it. "It's a nervous condition like biting your fingernails," I added.

"I'll tell the lads you said goodbye," he said in a forlorn voice. "They will be miffed they didn't get to see you off." He perked up, eyes brightening. "Maybe we can all come visit you in London. Can you imagine? They would love that!"

They *would,* but I didn't want to risk them exposing Tarik, not that any of them knew we'd come up with a creative slant for the aristocracy about his personal history. He absolutely could have rich parents in France whom no one knew about. And perhaps they'd been estranged for a time, which was why he'd come to Cambridge on a scholarship and was working his way up to a fellowship. We could easily navigate any overlap, should that happen.

But I had a sneaking suspicion that Will and the others' presence would only needlessly complicate things, not just for him but also for me. Managing my personas of Ansel and Rosalin while in London would take a lot of finesse and perfect timing, and my new friends—the twins especially—had a way of stirring up trouble, and I was tempting fate enough as it was.

I nodded noncommittally. "We shall see!"

Grabbing my traveling bags, which held most of my male clothing, I took my leave of Will with a firm handshake, and for a moment his eyes glossed over, and a sniff escaped him before he squared his shoulders and attempted—futilely—to hold it all in. *Goodness, he's a sensitive chap.* I wasn't one for making friends easily, with Blake being my only constant, followed by Ela and Zia, but Will had grown on me like a giant Cavalier King Charles Spaniel.

If, for some unforeseen reason, I never came back here, I'd miss him terribly.

I patted him on the shoulder, nearly squeaking as he yanked me into a bone-crushing hug. "I know you can't come to the Marquess and Marchioness of Ridley's masquerade, but Lady Zenobia's engagement ball is after that," I wheezed while trying to breathe. "I'll make sure you get an invitation."

"Thanks, Roz," he said. "Can I help you carry those?"

Not wanting to make things worse while he looked like he was on the verge of tears, I shook my head. "No, thanks, mate. I've got it."

Hefting the heaving portmanteau and my satchel full of books without gasping for breath was a feat in itself, but I managed. I could have gotten help from my scout—whom I still hadn't officially met, though I could not determine if that was because of him or me; we seemed to be purposefully adept at missing each other. However, I had two perfectly healthy arms and decided to use them—a decision I was regretting by the time I made it to my plain family coach, which I'd commandeered for my journeys to and from London. Tarik was already waiting, a booted foot propped up against the wheel, and I felt my heart leap at the sight of him.

Anna, hidden under a face-concealing bonnet, since technically she should be with Lady Rosalin, glowered at me from her position on the bench up front, where she was ensconced next to Henry. I flinched at the judgment on her usually pensive face. She had made her stance very clear about me traveling with an unwed gentleman inside an *enclosed* carriage, and I had countered that he thought I was my male cousin, so it really wasn't breaking any rules.

"But you are a *lady*, Lady Rosalin," she'd argued a few hours earlier. "A fact that you seem to have forgotten in the last month or two of your charades."

"It's a few hours, Anna. My virtue will survive."

Her mouth had tightened mulishly. "And both Henry and I shall lose our positions should any harm come to you. Or should your tomfooleries come to light. I know who he is—I saw him at the modiste. I don't know what you're up to, my lady, but you are playing with fire every single day that this scheme of yours continues."

My stomach had dipped, knowing she was sharp enough not to miss who he was. "Nothing will happen, I promise. St. Clair is a gentleman. He'll be prepping and quizzing me for examinations. If I am in trouble, I will bang on the roof. You and Henry are right there, and besides, your future husband is an expert marksman."

Finally, she had relented, though it was with plenty of apprehension.

"Ready to go?" I asked Tarik, after Henry had stored my bags.

He frowned at me, eyes dipping to my upper lip, and I panicked when I realized he was looking at the bald patch Will had mentioned before. "Shaving accident," I said, adjusting my spectacles. "Lucky I didn't slice my lip off with the razor."

"Do I even want to know?" he muttered, shaking his head.

"Forgot to strop the blade," I explained after we climbed into the carriage, thinking frantically back to when my father's valet used to shave his beard and I'd been a very curious little girl. The blade had to be stropped before every shave to make sure that it was sharp. Tapping the smooth spot with the pad of my finger, I made a mental note to compensate for the expected regrowth over the next few days, if and when I dressed like my cousin.

"Don't you fancy nobs have a valet for that?"

I snorted and sat on the velvet-covered bench facing him, noticing for the first time how small the spacious interior seemed with his presence barely a few feet away. I could understand why Anna would be worried, given the situation. No wonder Ela and Keston always looked slightly rumpled whenever they traveled anywhere together, even if it was within Mayfair—they probably could not keep their hands off each other in such an enclosed, *private* space. Heat bloomed in my chest.

You're Ansel. Behave.

"Some of us *nobs* can handle our personal hygiene ourselves," I said. My eyes fell on the enormous stack of books on his side. "Are you planning to start a traveling library or become a book salesman?"

Blue eyes narrowed on me as the coach jolted forward in a smooth rocking motion. "This is a working journey, my lord. A few weeks away won't make me neglect my duties. Even while we are in London, my job is to make sure that you earn your degree."

"You do realize that that's a forgone conclusion?" I replied. "Lords are not required to take the examinations to be honored with a university degree. It's a formality."

His right brow rose. "I didn't take you for a lily-livered weakling. Are you afraid you won't pass a formal assessment?"

Perhaps I was a little scared of failing, especially if Tarik was going to be the one getting me ready for said assessment. I didn't want to fail in front of him or disappoint him by being incompetent. "Well, we're not all brilliant Wranglers who have aced the exceedingly arduous and challenging Senate House and Mathematical Tripos examinations, are we?"

"And how do you think I was able to do that?" He patted the mountain of books beside him. "Patience, attention, and *study.*"

I scowled. "Says the Fellow."

"Not yet," he said. "I still have a few steps, including completing my master's degree. You have no reason to be afraid. As far as mathematics, you know the basics. I've seen your answers scribbled to mathematical problems in the periodicals, like what is the square root of one hundred and forty-four and how is it derived, or define the terms *diameter, radius*, and *circumference of a circle*? You already know Latin, so for the classics, I'm certain you'll be able to handle the translation of a passage of Homer or Virgil. For moral philosophy and theology, I'd ask you to define the role of the church. For science, name five of the planets from the solar system or define gravity." He shot me a reassuring look. "The latter which you have done brilliantly before. And lastly, for logic, perhaps what is rhetoric and provide an example."

Snorting, I shook my head at him. "You mean using the pragmatic influence of words, as you have just done, to convince or persuade someone of an argument?"

"Full marks!" He grinned, eyes shining. "See, you're passing already and you're not even trying."

He reached for a scroll I hadn't noticed that was beside him on the seat, and I stared at him curiously as he unrolled it. There were several sheets of paper with diagrams, drawings, and numerical markings, but I couldn't make heads or tails of them upside down, until he pulled and flipped the bottom sheet around. Was that an illustration of a *telescope*?

He noticed my stare with a smile. "You asked about being assessed on building your own. Mr. Peacock approved it."

I gulped. "He did?"

"Yes. While we are in London, you are going to do just that," Tarik pronounced in a tone that brooked no argument when he saw my face. "I have a list of requirements for a basic Newtonian reflecting telescope, materials needed, and step-by-step instructions." He handed them to me across the narrow space. "Study these for now, and let me know if you have any questions." He pulled out a notebook and a pencil.

"What will you be doing for the journey, then?" I asked.

"Refining my business plan for my club, from possible available properties for let in London, approximate square footage, architectural designs and a few idea sketches, financial estimates, navigating any legal hurdles, things like that," he said, pointing to a thick packet with a sheaf of documents. "Preparation is important in any venture."

"Oh," I said, somewhat mollified that I wouldn't be the only one suffering for hours. "Do you have a name yet? Or will you name it after yourself like all the other gentlemen with clubs?"

He exhaled, turning to a page in his notebook that had a neatly penciled list. "I was thinking of The Collective," he said. "I wanted something that would provide an idea of what I hoped to accomplish. An assembly of like-minded people—erudite, cultured, refined."

"The Collective," I echoed. "It's simple, yet powerful."

He circled the name in his book. "Thank you. Now stop stalling. I plan to quiz you on everything in those documents."

"You wouldn't!" I frowned at him, but he only lifted his eyebrows.

The next hour or two passed in silence as I perused the scrolls, jotting down notes of my own while attempting to memorize all the different parts of the instrument—eyepiece lens, primary and secondary mirrors, a papier-mâché tube, and a wooden mount. It was a daunting prospect, but the more I read, the more excited I became. Before it had only been a general idea, but now with everything explained so clearly in front of me, the vision was becoming a reality.

After a while, I glanced up and nearly swallowed my tongue. I'd been so engrossed in my work that I hadn't noticed Tarik had removed his coat and rolled up his shirtsleeves to his elbows while he worked. My breath caught in my throat as my eyes devoured the expanse of rich brown skin, from the elegant fingers I'd already obsessed over to the fascinating topography of his muscular forearms. I'd seen the twins fully shirtless on the River Cam, and not even that could make my mouth drier than it became at the sight of Tarik St. Clair's bare arms.

Good God, is it boiling in here? Beads of sweat broke out on the back of my neck, and I squirmed uncomfortably, causing the sheaf on my lap to scatter to the floor.

"Are you well?" Tarik asked, leaning down to collect and hand them back to me.

"You took off your coat," I croaked like an imbecile, gaze darting anywhere but his forearms as I took the papers.

"Oh, sorry. I didn't think you would mind. It's hot in here." A line appeared in his forehead at my reaction, which was either frantic or unreasonably hysterical. He pointed to his coat. "I can put it back on, if you like. Is that a thing? An aristocratic thing I should be aware of? No coat removal in hot coaches?"

"No, no," I assured him, trying desperately to not ogle him like a predator eyeing its next meal every time he moved his dratted arms. "Only in mixed company, of course. Wouldn't want to injure a young lady's delicate sensibilities. It's a wonderful idea. I shall do the same."

My words emerged in a nearly unintelligible jumble as I shucked out of my coat as well, trying to ignore the fact that Anna would have conniptions if she had an inkling of what was happening. Under these layers of satin and wool, I was still me, and not only was I in close quarters with an unmarried gentleman, but I was *undressing*.

Not that he knew, of course, but the reality still applied. I was an unwed girl. And clothing was being removed. It was scandalous in the extreme, and yet, I could not bring myself to care. In fact, I would be eternally happy if he removed more layers so I could ogle my wicked fill, but just in case, I reached up to crack open the small window on the upper wall opposite the coach door. That should cool things down a bit . . . including the minor immolation occurring in my own body.

Tarik cleared his throat. "Speaking of young ladies . . . your cousin is lovely."

"My cousin?" I echoed.

"Lady Rosalin." Those high cheekbones reddened. "She came in your stead to the tailors' to help me with the small mountain of clothing required for the season. We went for a walk in Hyde Park afterward."

"And?" I asked, deeply curious but also not wanting to appear too interested. "She didn't say anything horrid about me, did she?"

"Only that you were an insufferable jackanapes." He laughed when I snorted. "I'm jesting. Your family is clearly close, you two especially, it seems."

Closer than you think . . .

If he discovered the truth, I would be lucky if Tarik ever spoke to me again, but that was a problem for later.

"We are inseparable," I said, tongue in cheek. "So, what did you think of Rosalin?"

Those blotches of color deepened in his skin, making me warm inside again, and I had to force my face to remain neutral. "She's brilliant as you said. Charming. Amiable. Pleasant to look at."

"*Pleasant,* that's it?" I prodded before I could stop myself.

His entire face flamed as he tugged on his cravat. "Fine, she's the most beautiful girl I've ever seen!" he admitted. "Which I'm sure is strange since you two could practically be twins. And I truly hope to see her again, if she would welcome it."

I wasn't sure what would emerge from my mouth—a scream of joy or a sigh of delight—so I kept my lips sealed against the excitement bubbling up into my throat. He thought I was *beautiful*! And brilliant. I wanted to bask in the sensations flooding me like a balmy river on a summer's day, but it was all I could do to keep my face inscrutably blank.

"Is that going to be a problem?" he asked quietly, peering at my stone-faced expression with his worried one. "I don't want to risk our friendship, if it will."

I shook my head quickly. "Rosalin has her own life. If it's my approval you need to make your intentions known, you have it."

I was aware that my reply was more than a little self-serving, but I'm sure the real Ansel would have said the same, along with something on the lines of, *Hurt a hair on her head and I'll make you regret it*. As much as he teased me and pretended to loathe dancing with me, my cousin was deeply protective.

But even as I parted my lips to say something similar to Tarik, I knew there was a far greater chance of me hurting *him* irreparably. I also couldn't bring myself to shut down his affections or warn him off and say that my father would most likely be marrying me to a peer at the end of the season. Secretly, I wanted him to court me . . . even if it couldn't go anywhere.

I just wanted to know what true courtship would be like. *Feel* like.

"Although, hurt one hair on her head, and you'll find yourself in a world of trouble," I added sternly, with a narrow-eyed stare for good measure.

"I give you my word," Tarik said solemnly, making my stupid heart flutter. "I promise to be the perfect gentleman."

"I'm sure you will see a lot of each other during the next few weeks," I said. "And besides, we need her help to make sure you meet the right people in our circles, especially when I'm called away by my uncle for my other duties."

While my baby brother, Bowen, was my father's heir apparent, since he was still in leading strings, it was important for Ansel to understand what was required as duke, not that anything was going to happen to my father, but he liked to be prepared. I would also have to be Alter Ego Ansel sparingly in London, as anyone who did know my cousin, like Ela or Zia, or Keston and Rafi, would see right through the subterfuge. Thus, Lady Rosalin would have to do most of the work at balls and events.

For once, however, I was looking forward to the season.

CHAPTER TWELVE

I shall not mingle conjectures with certainties.

—Isaac Newton

The large ballroom of Ela's house in Grosvenor Square was packed to the brim, and still more people were entering at the top of the stairs. She and Keston had gone all out for this masquerade ball, with the lavish décor of golden columns and wreaths of flowers and ribbons stretching across the tops of the walls in between them. No expense had been spared. The floors had been polished, the chandeliers sparkled with hundreds of lights, and an orchestra played at one end while dancers in beautiful gowns spun with their intricate masks and costumes.

After three full seasons, I should have been used to the extravagances of the *ton,* but I was strangely nervous, mostly due to the presence of the gentleman at my side. I hadn't been able to take a full breath since Tarik had arrived. He wasn't staying with us, of course. That would have been impossible to explain to my parents, not to mention the gossip it would have caused . . . and *not* the good kind. People in the *ton* loved to speculate.

So, while Ansel wasn't in town, Tarik would avail himself of my cousin's pied-à-terre at The Albany in Piccadilly, which was exclusively for bachelors. Like other gentlemen his age, Ansel kept the set of apartments for prestige and privacy, as well as proximity to the gentlemen's clubs of St. James's and Pall Mall. He was a young man who needed his own space, after all. Though the place was rented annually and his to command, it was currently vacant, and I was certain my cousin would not mind.

Once more surreptitiously using my father's stationery and his seal, I was able to write a letter to the management at The Albany to let them know about Ansel's guest—Mr. Tarik St. Clair, by way of Paris—who would be staying for a fortnight, possibly more, in his apartments. I was turning into a regular forger, but I promised myself that this would be the last time.

I'd been to The Albany once. Women weren't allowed and could visit only by strict invitation. But as far as I could remember, the accommodations were luxurious and included a bedroom, dressing and drawing rooms, and a study. Tarik would also have shared access to a butler, cook, and valet, and all his new clothes from the Marchands had been delivered there.

"Is it always such a crush like this, Lady Rosalin?" Tarik asked, his voice deep and sonorous in my ear.

I turned to him, breathless at how debonair he looked in a set of raven-black formal wear with a dark silver waistcoat, snowy-white shirt, and cravat. Beneath his tailored evening coat, fitted black breeches hugged his long legs, and his new dress shoes shone. A black domino covered the upper half of his face, leaving that square jaw and those lips on display.

With his eyes currently shaded by the mask, I realized I had never noticed how finely shaped and plush his lips were, and now I wished I could go back in time so I wouldn't fixate on yet another perfect feature of his. Or how they might feel against mine . . .

Stop it.

"Usually for some of the more popular people in the *ton,*" I replied in a hoarse voice. "Everyone always hopes to get an invitation, but this is certainly the most crowded it has ever been. Last year, the prince regent attended, and the newssheets went wild. Though I suppose Prinny's the king now."

He sucked in a gasp upon hearing the prince regent's well-known nickname. "Will he be here tonight?"

"One never knows when it comes to him, though it's a quieter season with the death of his father. I doubt he will leave the palace." I let out a small laugh at Tarik's wondrous expression. "I'm sorry that Ansel couldn't be here to greet you, though he said he might show up at some point during the evening."

Tarik's lips pursed. "And I'm sorry that the introductions have fallen to you yet again, my lady. I do not wish to be a burden or to keep you from enjoying the evening as you undoubtedly would be without me like a millstone at your side."

"I don't mind," I said. "Usually, I'm quite bored at these things."

He shot me a skeptical look. "Truly? I assumed gentlemen would be lined up out the door to write their names on your dance card and you would be whisked away until your toes were aching from so much dancing."

Another genuine laugh left me. "Believe it or not, Mr. St. Clair, but I have scared away nearly all of the eligible gentlemen here. Most of them do not like girls who are outspoken, you see. And well, usually while I am dancing, I do tend to enjoy a spot of conversation instead of remaining meekly silent. I'm not a mute puppet to be moved around and look pretty."

He canted his head, bright eyes sweeping me from behind his mask. "You do look very pretty this evening, Lady Rosalin, though from the little I've come to know of you, I could never call you a puppet."

"Excellent, you've passed the first test," I said, smiling at him.

He reared back. "*First* test?"

"Shall we see how you fare in a waltz next?" I said with a nod, hearing the soft measures of music. "Or will you end up in the wasteland of London gentlemen who cannot seem to perform two tasks at once? Are you up for the challenge, sir? I am a harsh taskmaster, I've been told."

Tarik bowed and extended a gloved hand, his mouth quirking with amusement. "Challenge accepted. I would be delighted to demonstrate my skills."

In all honesty, as he led me to the ballroom floor, I wasn't anywhere near ready to perform a waltz—the most intimate of all dances—with Tarik St. Clair, but the minute he grasped my hand and waist, time seemed to stop. Everyone else in the ballroom disappeared, and it was only us moving to the ethereal strains of music and the three-count measure that I swore my heartbeat was imitating.

"Where did you learn to waltz?" I asked him.

He smirked, making my pulse trip—that look should be illegal. "Is that question your next test?"

"Are you going to answer it?" I countered.

He spun me effortlessly in the first turn, making my breath catch, the press of his fingers on the indent of my hip providing only the gentlest guidance. "Paris. My mother loved to dance, and I was her second-favorite partner, whenever my father was working, which was often. She taught me all the steps, all the court dances, all the country dances, even ones from other countries."

"Oh? Which ones?"

"Dances from India, where my grandparents were from, and from the Americas and the West Indies. She loved music from everywhere—the sounds of the tabla, lute, tambourine, bamboo flutes, and maracas."

His words had a hypnotic quality. "That sounds incredible," I murmured. "Did you learn to play any of the instruments?"

"Some."

He guided me across the floor for a few beats of music. Neither of us spoke, but our silence had a language all its own—the movement between our bodies, our breaths, and the rustle of our clothing. I felt more at home in these moments of quiet in Tarik's embrace than I ever had in anyone else's.

What if we had met *here* during the season, instead of at university? What if he were a gentleman of good station, and not just in nobility of character? One could argue that the latter was more important, but in the *ton,* status and rank mattered. Titles and wealth mattered. It was infuriating, and yet not something I could easily or effectively change . . . not as a duke's daughter who was expected to make an excellent, society-worthy match. A part of me would wholeheartedly choose him, with nothing, over a peer with everything.

Idly, I thought back to the tests I'd formulated to determine my perfect match what felt like an eternity ago, and felt a wry smile touch my lips.

- *Scholarly aptitude and ability to engage in intellectual discourse—multiple questions in mathematics, physics, and philosophy*
- *Progressive stance on women's status and rights in the aristocracy*
- *Emotional breadth and depth—must be compassionate and kind*
- *Political views in favor of changing antiquated laws*
- *Physical compatibility*

Deep down, I already knew that Tarik would meet every marker I'd set. The evidence of some of them had somehow come to me at various points over our interactions while I had been at Trinity. Even without a title, he was smarter and more educated than most of the gentlemen our age. But that was the bitter rub—he *wasn't* a nobleman—so the whole test would be moot.

Still . . . it didn't hurt to imagine.

"Mr. St. Clair," I said, catching his gaze. "Answer this question for me, if you please. If a man is forty years of age and his son is ten, in how many years will he be three times as old as his son?"

He let out a chuckle. "Five years."

"How did you arrive at that number?" I asked, astonished and yet unsurprised at how quickly he'd calculated the correct answer from a recent problem I'd solved in a weekly periodical.

His hand tightened as he drew me a few inches closer, making me inhale sharply as his breath coasted over my ear. "If *x* represents the number of years in the future, then the man is forty plus *x* and the son is ten plus *x*. Ten plus *x* equals three times ten plus *x*. Expand the equation to find the value of *x*, so forty plus *x* equals thirty plus three *x*. Forty minus thirty equals three minus *x*, and we get ten equals two *x*, therefore *x* is five."

Be still my quivering heart . . .

"Capital," I whispered as he widened the gap between us once more. "Next question. Can we trust our senses to provide knowledge of the world?"

He smirked. "Ah, a philosophical question. John Locke, I presume? All knowledge comes from experience, and our senses are how we interact with the world, in which repeated observations can indicate patterns. Descartes, however, argued that reason was more reliable than the senses." I nearly stumbled as his lips grazed the sensitive skin of my lobe. "I trust my senses to inform me that you enjoy being in my arms, my lady."

He wasn't wrong. My brain went inconveniently askew as the singular snow-and-chocolate scent of him chose that very moment to remind me of how close we were. For most of my dances, *especially* the waltz, I remained the requisite twelve inches away, holding myself as stiffly as I could. Nary a gentleman could enter my sacred dance space. Now all I wanted to do was erase the distance between us.

Focus, Roz!

My next question was on women's rights, though I already knew his stance on those. No man would argue so passionately for women to attend university without supporting equality of the sexes. I was also familiar with his capacity for compassion and empathy as well—I'd learned that just in the gentle way he'd spoken about his mother. I cleared my throat. "How do you feel about changing antiquated laws?"

"Anything that's for the better gets an unequivocal yes from me. Better working conditions for the common man, proper education for children, safe harbor for women who lack opportunities." He paused, and I could feel his body stiffen. "Emancipation in the English empire. We have been fighting for it in France for decades."

"Emphatically agree," I said.

"A person should always strive to leave the world a better place than they found it, in my humble opinion," he added.

That warmed my heart—it was a true mark of character when someone thought of others and the wider world more than themselves. The last thing on my list was the matter of physical compatibility. Given the heated state of my blood and the heartbeat that pulsed thickly between my ears, attraction wasn't something I had to worry about. On top of that, Tarik wasn't one step from the grave. He was in possession of all his teeth, he had no cases of gout that I could discern, and he did not treat me like a brainless damsel.

When the waltz came to its conclusion, he escorted me off the ballroom floor toward the refreshments room. Clearly, he was thoughtful, too. I thanked him as he handed me a glass of lemonade, which I drank thirstily.

"So," he asked with a slight smirk. "Did I pass muster?"

"We shall see, sir," I said in a teasing voice that had those pretty eyes flashing in mock affront.

"I wager no one has ever solved that problem as quickly as I did."

"Don't be cocky. You'll ruin it."

I smiled at him, only for the amusement to be wiped off my face when I saw who was headed in our direction: Blake, along with Keston and Ela, as well as Rafi and Zia. There was no way to avoid any of them, and I had been expecting it, but I had hoped for some more time alone with Tarik before we were bombarded . . . and separated. In truth, I did not want to share him with anyone, not even my closest friends. I did not allow myself to ponder on what that meant about me.

"Hullo, sweeting," Blake said, reaching us first while the rest were waylaid by other guests. Tarik instantly stiffened at the informal and much-too-intimate endearment. "Who do we have here?" Blake drawled.

I scowled at him. "It's Rosalin, as you well know, Blake, not sweeting nor darling or treasure or sweet chuck." I turned to Tarik, who was clearly sizing up the new arrival—the way he stood so tall and intimidating had my breath shortening. I blinked—I'd never seen him with such a rigid jaw and oozing tension. Surely, he wasn't *jealous*?

"Mr. St. Clair, may I present Lord Blake Castleton, a longtime *friend*." After the emphasis on the last word, I glared balefully at Blake, who was smirking as if enjoying his little game far too much. "My lord, may I present to you Mr. St. Clair by way of Paris. He's the nephew of a French count and heir to a shipping magnate. We met several months ago at a house party. Mama introduced us."

I could feel Tarik's curious stare, since that hadn't been what we'd discussed. *Ansel* was supposed to have introduced us, but of course, he didn't know that Ansel wasn't even here in London. And the French count idea had been spontaneous. When he had arrived earlier, I had introduced him to Mama as Ansel's mate from Cambridge, but as anticipated, she'd been too preoccupied with the arrival of other guests to interrogate him thoroughly.

Using Ansel now would have been disastrous, especially if some unintentionally helpful soul mentioned that he was on his grand tour. With Tarik's presence in London, everything was infinitely more complicated, and I had to navigate all the intricate lies I had constructed.

"A pleasure, Mr. St. Clair," Blake said.

Tarik canted his head, a slight frown marring his mouth as he studied my friend. Did he recognize him? Blake and Ansel had both attended Cambridge, while Keston and Rafi had enrolled at Oxford, though like most of his ilk, Blake had barely deigned to attend any of his classes. I knew that for a fact because he loved boasting about it.

Agitated, I opened my mouth, preparing to redirect the conversation, but Tarik seemed to relax. "Likewise, my lord," he said.

Blake's eyes shifted to me, narrowing, and then back to my companion. "A house party you say. Which one?"

"One you clearly weren't invited to," I retorted, earning myself another brow-raising glance from Tarik.

Blake was the closest thing I had to a male best friend, but to anyone else, especially during *ton* events, he seemed to behave like a suitor, which I encouraged. That was his role, of course, designed to chase off fortune hunters, old decrepit peers, prepubescent heirs, and the like. Usually, I enjoyed our intrigues, since I had no interest in getting married. But now I wanted to kick him in the shins.

However, I didn't have time to do that, as the others arrived, their faces inquisitive, unused to seeing me with a handsome young man our age. Despite loudly bemoaning my solitary existence and pretending to be enamored at every turn, I rarely showed favor to *anyone* at these social events. I performed the introductions again. Tarik seemed much more at ease with the other two gentlemen than he'd been with Blake.

"So," Ela said softly, sidling up to me and drawing me to Zia, a few feet away from where the boys were already in conversation. "Here you are on the arm of the most gorgeous boy I've ever seen, well besides Keston, of course. Wherever have you been hiding him?"

Zia grinned, her eyes lighting with mischief. "Yes, Rosalin, where have you been keeping that fine specimen?"

I felt my cheeks burn at her singsong, teasing words. "I haven't been *hiding* him. He's been at university in Cambridge, dozens of miles away, and he's here now to make social connections for a business venture. Stop inventing melodrama that doesn't exist, for heaven's sake."

"Oh, wait a moment! Is *he* why you've been running back to Newmarket every chance you get?" Ela asked slyly, and I cringed internally. I hadn't realized anyone had been keeping track of my movements, though I supposed my absence would have been noticeable to my two closest female friends.

"I have an ongoing charity obligation," I said.

"Must be hard work, that *charity*," Zia teased, with a sidelong glance to Tarik. "Looks like it might take quite a lot of time and effort on your part. Not that I blame you. A girl could climb your charity like a tree."

"Zia!" I couldn't help it, I giggled. "And honestly, aren't you engaged to Rafi? You should be only interested in climbing your own tree."

"I have eyes," she said, while Ela cackled.

Grinning, Ela leered at me. "Her *own* tree? Does that mean you admit someone else with eyes like a tropical ocean is *your* tree? And *has* there been climbing?"

Tarik's eyes were prettier than *any* ocean.

Heat ignited under my skin on the heels of my thought at her much-too-obvious innuendo. Climbing sounded a lot like kissing, but I wasn't going to go down that path, not when the idea of it made me much too breathless. Tarik wasn't *my* anything, and yet, I relished how that sounded, like I had some sort of claim to him. "I'm not a gardener, Ela," I said primly. "There's no climbing either."

"Would you *like* there to be climbing?" Zia pressed.

I shook my head, certain that my face was the color of beetroot. "You two are incorrigible. Tarik is a friend, nothing more."

I knew my mistake the moment the two syllables of his given name left my mouth. Both their eyebrows hiked to their hairlines, and I wanted to kick myself. "*Tarik*, is it?" Ela commented, exchanging a wicked look with Zia. "Sounds like someone has been doing a little gardening after all, don't you think, Zia?"

"Who's been gardening?" Blake interjected, gazing down from his height into our tiny huddle. "Rosalin doesn't like to get her hands dirty."

I glared at him while the girls erupted into giggles. "Go away, Blake. The boys are over there."

"But girls are so much more fun," he said in a dramatic whine. "Besides there's always juicy gossip. Don't be mean."

"God, you're such a child," I said, happy to redirect the conversation.

The look in both the girls' eyes told me the conversation was far from over, but everyone in our circle knew that Blake had the loosest lips this side of the channel and usually was the one who knew most gossip. I couldn't risk having him getting ahold of any information about Tarik. Though from his speculative glances over to where Tarik was obviously talking about his social club plans to Keston and Rafi, who both appeared rapt, I might already be too late.

Ela leaned in. "You do look well, Rosalin. It's nice to see you . . . so lighthearted?"

"You do seem happier than usual," Zia remarked. "Is your father still planning to marry you off this season, or did you somehow find a way to get out of it?"

"Does said happiness have to do with a certain guest of yours?" Ela interjected.

I could sense Blake's immediate interest, so I shook my head emphatically. "Of course not. He's an acquaintance, and besides, Papa would hardly approve of someone without a noble title. You know how he is, protective to a fault, and wants to make sure I'm taken care of and not swallowed up by a fortune-hunting opportunist."

"It's not always about bloodlines," Zia said. "I'm engaged to a mere mister."

As dukes' daughters, Zia and I were closest in status in our friend group. I let out a small snort. "For *now.* Rafi is heir to his uncle's viscountcy, and even if he wasn't, he's as rich as Midas."

There was no argument to that. Rafi Nasser had been the catch of the century, but he'd only ever had eyes for Zia, his best friend's little sister. It didn't hurt that he was handsome, obscenely rich, and heir to a title. Alas, Tarik was not in the running for either of the last two, unless he made his fortune himself, which I had no doubt he would one day. He was too brilliant not to. But I doubted the *probability* of success would be good enough for my father.

"Excuse me, Lady Zenobia?" a feminine voice interrupted.

Zia's eyes widened in recognition at the pretty Indian brunette. "Oh, hullo, Lady Petal. How are you?"

Lady Petal Joshi was one of the girls who'd attended Zia's finishing school before her own parents had caused a scene about controversial reading material and removed her from the school.

The book had been *Frankenstein; or, The Modern Prometheus,* which I'd read the second it had been published. In my opinion, it was hardly polemic, but the gothic novel had ruffled a few feathers because it was about murder. Little did anyone know that a woman—*gasp*—had written it. Though that was a secret, according to Zia.

Lady Petal giggled and blushed. "Well, thank you. I overheard you talking about the new gentleman with Lord Ridley and Mr. Nasser earlier, and Lady Rosalin saying that he's an acquaintance and not a suitor, so I was wondering if I could possibly have an introduction?"

As her request sank in, I didn't want to explore the bitterness that shot into my throat like poisonous acid. I was having a hard time keeping my reaction off my face or refraining from giving this troublesome, obnoxious busybody a piece of my mind. How dare she stick her nose in where she didn't belong?

Tarik was *my* tree.

But Blake's shrewd gaze was fixed on me, that vexing smirk hovering over his mouth, as if he was slyly waiting for my reply and daring me to refute my earlier words. I shrugged as if I didn't have a care in the world. "Of course, Lady Petal," I told her in the pleasantest voice I could manage. "I'm sure he'd be delighted."

But never had any words tasted more like ash in my mouth.

CHAPTER THIRTEEN

> The alteration of motion is ever proportional to the motive force impressed; and is made in the direction of the right line in which that force is impressed.
>
> —Isaac Newton

I was up to my elbows in flour and water making this deuced papier-mâché tube. I was certain I had gotten globs of the cold, sticky mixture on my face and possibly inside my shirt, because something clammy and lumpy kept sliding down beneath the band over my chest. But there was no way I was going to clean that up with Tarik on the other side of his drawing room.

We were at Ansel's apartments at The Albany. I had arrived with a cap pulled low, smart men's clothing I had purloined from my cousin's closet from the residence in Mayfair, and a repaired mustache and spectacles in place. I had managed to hoodwink the building staff into thinking I was my cousin, well enough to allow me entry to the building. While I had to use my persona sparingly in London for reasons of discovery, I supposed it was also ideal for Ansel to be seen with the new gentleman temporarily staying in his pied-à-terre.

People with undue suspicions caused problems.

Speaking of my cousin, I had written Ansel a long and very detailed letter, explaining the mess into which I'd gotten myself. The last correspondence he'd sent me had arrived with a Greek address, so I'd used that. I also wanted to know when he planned to return, because if he did while I was pretending to be him, that would be an utter disaster. Hopefully, he'd stay away from London until after Mama's annual ball, as that would be ideal, but I had no way of knowing. The truth was that it was getting harder and harder to play dual roles. I was constantly anxious I was going to give something away.

Wiping my sleeve across my brow and dislodging my spectacles, I squinted at the instructions on the rolled papers Tarik had given me. I'd managed to locate a mirror with a five-inch diameter that had been ground into a spherical shape, as well as a sliding focuser from an instrument maker and a smaller flat mirror to reflect the light to the lens, which I'd sourced from one of Ansel's old pairs of spectacles.

The papier-mâché part of the process was slow. To shape the tube, I started applying old newssheets and paper scraps dipped in a thickened paste I'd made from heated flour and water around a three-foot-long greased metal pipe. I'd already painted the innermost sheets of the base layer black to minimize reflection, but once the outside hardened properly, I'd coat it with varnish and tie it with some cloth strips at intervals. Brass fittings would go at either end, one for the primary mirror and lens and one inside to secure the secondary mirror.

"How's the progress?" Tarik asked, walking to where I was hunkered over the table.

"Messy," I said, wiggling clumpy fingers.

He laughed. "I can see that."

"Glad my pain and suffering are amusing to you."

Tarik smirked as he crouched down beside me. He was so close that I could see the sapphire and navy striations in his bottomless blue irises. God, even his eyelashes were obscene, thick and dark, making him look as though he used a liner of kohl like Ela was fond of wearing. A lock of silky, dark hair flopped into his brow. "If Newton could make his own tools, then so can you. I believe in you, Roz."

The sound of the nickname made me jolt. At least he called me that only when we were alone, and I was dressed as Ansel. It would take a lot of explaining if he did it in front of people who knew Ansel and had never heard that nickname. It was one that Blake used often with me as Lady Rosalin when we were by ourselves, however.

"Speaking of belief in someone, how did it go with Keston and Rafi the other night?" I asked. "Sorry I couldn't be there, but Rosalin mentioned that you seemed to be in a deep discussion."

"Lord Ridley and Mr. Nasser?" he clarified, and I nodded. "They're very smart gentlemen and seemed positive about the venture. They both said that the academic forum for discussion was a unique idea and wanted to see more of it in society. They also liked the idea of it being open to both men and women, but they foresaw problems with gaining approval and a possible foothold."

I wiped the gunk off my hands. "The older aristocrats are set in their ways. Did they seem interested in investing? They're both quite wealthy and Zia has mentioned that they are always on the lookout for new ventures." I blinked in dismay, realizing that *Ansel's* mates would have confided directly in him, not Zia, but Tarik didn't seem to notice anything out of order. I exhaled, relieved.

"Yes, I believe so," he said. "Lord Blake as well."

There was a strange intonation in his voice that I instantly picked up on, but Tarik didn't say anything more as I put away the last of the paste and tried to clean up some of the mess. Since he had access to a shared housekeeper here, I didn't have to, but I also liked picking up after myself. Luckily, I had set down some extra sheets of newspaper, so cleanup was quick. I washed my hands and returned to the drawing room. I needed a proper bath, but there was no way I could take one here.

"Roz," he said softly.

I glanced over, hearing the subtle hitch in his breathing. "Yes?"

"Do you think that your cousin is interested in Lord Blake? She said that they were friends, but they seemed . . . intimate, like they might be more than that."

My heart started a drumming cadence behind my ribs at his cautious words. How much did I want to reveal? Did I say that Blake had been the closest to the perfect suitor until recently? Did I mention the ill-fated kiss we had shared one season at Vauxhall? I sucked in a breath to keep my tone calm. "Blake isn't the type to settle down, and honestly, he'd be interested in you just as much as he'd be interested in her. They're friends. Good friends, and ever since her first season, that's all it has been."

"What happened the first season?" he asked, not missing a thing.

I cleared my throat. "I believe they might have shared a brief embrace."

If I hadn't been looking right at him, I would have missed the darkening of those eyes at my answer. Tarik *was* jealous of Blake. I ignored the small thrill that gave me because even if he was resentful, it hadn't stopped him from dancing with Lady Petal, who'd turned herself into a girl-shaped barnacle the entire evening.

"Why does it matter?" I asked. "You seemed to be enamored with Lady Petal, at least according to the scandal sheets."

He huffed an embarassed laugh. "Gossip flies quickly here. Honestly, I was . . . hoping . . . ," he trailed off, shooting me an odd look. "Never mind."

"No," I said. "You were hoping what?"

He scrubbed a hand through his dark hair with a frustrated noise. "Nothing. Lady Petal was fine. Good-natured and sociable. A capable dancer and she seemed interesting to talk to."

A better dancer than me? I couldn't bring myself to ask the question, knowing it would be decidedly strange coming from Ansel. He wouldn't give a hoot whether one girl was a better dancer than the other, even if one was his cousin. "Do you think she's pretty?" I pressed.

Tarik flushed, making me scowl. "Pretty enough, I suppose. She's charming and wants to see me again. She asked if I would call upon her this week."

"Well, good for you. Enjoy your time with Princess Charming." Inexplicably peeved, I reached for my coat and hat. "I better be going. My uncle has some ledgers on the estate he wants to go over with me, his steward, and his solicitor. I'll be back to finish this when I can."

He frowned. "Roz, wait. What's the matter? Did I say something off-putting?" When I didn't answer, he moved to block my path to the door. "You don't fancy Lady Petal, do you? I don't want to step on your toes or cause any confusion."

It was on the tip of my tongue to lie and get Petal out of the picture, but all it would take for Tarik to verify the truth was to ask anyone, even Petal herself. She'd been smitten with Ansel for years, but she wasn't his preference whatsoever. Perhaps I should introduce her to Will, which might distract her with another option. I warmed to the idea for reasons I did not wish to dwell too deeply upon. I had no right to be jealous when I could not consider Tarik's suit, but my stomach still tightened at the thought of Petal's simpering advances.

"No, of course not," I said. "We're not a good match."

"Why not?"

I stopped at the door, peering over my shoulder. I couldn't resist a parting jab, repeating words Ansel had once said. "Ever heard the saying 'Empty vessels make the most noise'? She'll talk your ear off with nothing valuable to say, but I suppose some gentlemen like that." I shot him a sharp look. "Besides, what if your wandering attentions affect my cousin? You did give me your vow, if I recall, that you would not harm one hair upon her head."

He blinked owlishly at me. "I assure you, I'm *not* interested in Lady Petal. I just hoped that perhaps Lady Rosalin might have shown me more attention . . . if there was competition."

I wanted to laugh, but instead, I thought diligently on what my cousin would say. Or any boy, for that matter, who did indeed often attempt such ploys to sway a lady's interest. Girls did it, too.

"Be yourself, mate," I said eventually. "You don't need to play games."

I swallowed that down like the bitter medicine it was, knowing I was the one playing the most dangerous game of all.

Tarik sat forward, elbows on his knees, and listened, enthralled. I'd heard Zia play the piano before many times, but for anyone who hadn't, her talent was truly extraordinary. She played the usual piano pieces to start the musicale at her home—Mozart, Schubert, Beethoven—her fingers dancing over the keys with practiced elegance. Her mother and her fiancé both looked on with pride as most of the spectators who'd been invited to their soiree enjoyed the blissful music.

"By God, she's amazing," Tarik whispered when she finished playing *Sonata Pathétique*. "I didn't know human fingers could move so quickly."

"She's very talented," I agreed. "But just wait."

He glanced incredulously at me. "There's more?"

"Watch."

We both went quiet along with everyone else when Zia stood and thanked the audience. "Now I shall play an original composition," she said shyly, her gaze flying to Rafi, who gave her an encouraging nod. They were so in love it was nauseating, but I couldn't help feeling happy for my friend that she had found her perfect person.

My gaze darted to Tarik, and I felt my lungs squeeze with a painful yearning. The hope fluttering in my chest was impossible to extinguish, despite the odds stacked against us.

"What is she doing?" Tarik whispered as Zia proceeded to place a bolt, a piece of rubber, and a sheet of parchment on the inside of the piano on the bare strings.

"She's preparing the piano for her piece," I explained softly. "It takes some getting used to, because the altered notes are so discordant, but the overall effect is transformative."

Instead of watching Zia, I watched him, and I could have sworn that his jaw fell open when she began to play again. It was a far cry from the beautifully harmonious melodies of Beethoven and Mozart, but it was mesmerizing in its own way. The sounds were percussive, ethereal, and otherworldly. Zia had been making a name for herself in smaller London theaters with her special style of playing, and I loved that for her. It took great courage to put oneself out there, and she was doing it without apology.

I wished I had half her bravery. Instead, I was hiding my true self at every turn.

This deception felt . . . cowardly.

I shouldn't have to conceal that I was an intelligent scholar and pretend to be my cousin just so I could experience what being valued for my mind felt like. The whole notion upset me so much that when Zia's last original piece was finished, I leaped to my feet and escaped onto the balcony, tears burning my eyes. I hauled deep breaths into my lungs, trying to escape the cloying sensation across my ribs that everything was going to go south . . . and that I would soon be found out and exposed.

"Are you well, Lady Rosalin?" a quiet voice asked.

"I'm fine, Mr. St. Clair. Perhaps simply overcome by all the emotion. Powerful music can do that, you know?"

"I understand. The performance was very moving."

Tarik came up to stand beside me at the balustrade above the gardens, the moonlight shining down from a cloudless sky and outlining his features in silver. He looked like a serene, self-assured prince, surveying his domain, while I felt . . . small and invisible. *Unseen.* I couldn't breathe! Couldn't be myself or who I wanted to be.

"Do you ever feel trapped, Mr. St. Clair?"

"Tarik," he corrected softly.

It still wasn't proper, but we were alone so I let his name tumble over my tongue in the soft tenor of my true voice, the sound like the best kind of sugared treat. I savored it. "Tarik."

"I do," he said. "Trapped by circumstance. By wealth. By station. By birth. It's unfair to want things that aren't accessible to us simply by nature of who we are. A commoner cannot access the same things that a peer might."

"Like what?" I whispered, meeting those blue eyes.

He opened his mouth and closed it, looking impossibly pained for a second, as if he wanted to get something off his chest but couldn't bring himself to do it. He exhaled heavily. "Sometimes I wish I had been born under different stars. That I'd been born to privilege and could reach for anything I wanted."

"It's not always so easy under these stars," I whispered. "We don't get *everything* we want. We still must follow the absurd rules of society that the powers of fate could give two flailing shits about."

Tarik released a bark of laughter at my unexpected swearing. Face alight, he stared at me, so many unsaid things flying between us in that endless moment. Two star-crossed souls destined to pass each other like ships in the night because of class boundaries that held more weight than the possibility of true happiness.

"Do you want to leave?" he asked me impulsively. "Go someplace where there are no rules? Where it's just the two of us in our imperfect skins with no stations, no expectations, and no differences?"

What he was suggesting sounded impossible, but I could not help nodding, desperate to escape the shrinking walls of my prison, which were slowly suffocating me. I'd broken so many rules already. What was one more?

"Yes, I do."

With an irrepressible grin, his eyes sparking with excitement and something else I couldn't quite read, Tarik grabbed my hand. "Tell the duchess that you don't feel well and will be retiring to your residence. And then meet me down in the courtyard as soon as you can."

"What are you going to do?" I asked, stopping at the balcony doors.

He winked. "Get us transportation, of course!"

Tarik's *transportation* turned out to be a hackney at the end of the street that was heading to London's West End. When I had claimed that I had a headache and needed to leave, Mama had frowned, but I assured her that I would be fine at home with Anna. We lived only a few blocks away, after all. Our coachman would drive me to our residence and then return for the duchess.

Luckily, I had avoided both Zia and Ela, who would have undoubtedly seen right through my story. I couldn't fib to save my life with the two of them. I'd also felt slightly guilty about involving poor Anna, who would be none the wiser as to my whereabouts, but a chaperone was the last thing I needed. That was the problem with having a taste of freedom as my Ansel alter ego . . . I wanted that as Rosalin.

"Where are we going?" I asked Tarik as the hackney made turn after turn, my heart pounding a fast cadence the farther we went from Mayfair.

"Somewhere fun in Covent Garden. You're safe with me, Lady Rosalin," Tarik said, his face earnest. "Do you trust me?"

I stared at him—this boy whom I'd gotten to know over the past few months, albeit not fully as myself, but that didn't impact how I felt putting my trust in him as a young lady—and nodded. "Yes."

"Good," he said, and grabbed my hand just as the carriage pulled to a stop outside a building that housed a bustling theater, according to a worn blue awning. People crowded the streets . . . aristocrats, gentry, and commoners alike. Others shouted their wares for sale even at night, while drunk people stumbled between bars on the dirty cobblestones. It stank, and yet, the place was alive with laughter and shouting, the sounds of its residents having a wonderful time. Wild fiddle music poured out of a nearby tavern's entrance, and I held Tarik's palm tightly as he drew me down the steps to the open door.

"What are we doing here?" I asked in a hushed breath.

"We're going to have an awful drink or two," he said, and my eyes rounded. "But at least we can be ourselves. Two people away from the pressures of life, society, and the weight of expectations."

I stared at him, his words settling somewhere right in the middle of my chest and loosening a knot in my gut.

"Have you been here before?" I asked him, excitement bubbling up inside of me.

"A few times."

It was yet another thing I didn't know about him . . . his familiarity with rowdy London taverns in more colorful parts of the city. But I did not feel afraid, not when he was at my side. He handed me a brown ale with an inch of foam at the top and clinked our tankards together. "To life!"

"To life," I echoed. "And impossible dreams," I added before taking a huge gulp and nearly choking on the bitterness of the drink. "What is *in* that? Acid?" I spluttered.

Tarik chuckled, the rich sound of it warming me like sunshine as he reached forward to wipe a stripe of white foam from the top of my upper lip with his thumb. "It gets more palatable the more you have."

"It's disgusting," I pronounced, smacking my lips and grimacing at the sour taste sitting on the back of my tongue. "But I love it!"

"That's my girl," he crowed.

Somewhat stupefied by the unexpected declaration, I gaped. Was I *his* girl? Or was I nothing but a pleasant distraction while he found investors for his social club? Was he truly interested in *me,* or had I become an excuse to pass the time in London and visit old haunts like this one? Did it even matter? Knowing I wouldn't find any agreeable answers right at that moment, I let the musings go.

"There's dancing!" I exclaimed, watching some of the younger people in the adjoining room lifting their skirts over their ankles and cavorting around each other in a boisterous country reel. "Drink up, good sir!"

He downed his ale, and I valiantly attempted to do the same, but it was much too unpleasant for me to swallow all at once. I made an excellent effort, however, with more of it staining the silk of my gown than I could consume. No one here cared one whit that someone had spilled ale on their dress. "I win!" I said, holding up my nearly empty tumbler. "Now let's dance!"

"I don't know these steps," he protested as I dragged him to the worn wooden floor, where people were already lining up for a rousing Scotch reel.

"Neither do I," I replied, and threw my hands up into the air. "But that's half the fun, isn't it? Not knowing what you're doing and letting the music take hold of you!"

"Lady Rosalin . . ."

I pouted prettily. "Don't be a spoilsport, Mr. St. Clair."

He sighed, his eyes falling to my jutting lower lip. "Don't give me that lip, for the love of everything holy. Bloody hell, why can't I say no to you?"

Beaming, I batted my eyelashes. "Because I'm adorable?"

He shook his head in resignation. "Because you're adorable."

We followed the lines of dancers, the women circling the men, skipping in a loop that closed in, then opened up. Tarik joined the men, and we ended up facing each other, his face so bright and unguarded that I found myself hooting as our legs kicked out, and then our arms intertwined like vines as we spun and spun and spun. The music was ceaseless, a visceral drumbeat that echoed in my soul, in my bones, in my very pulse. Until the roof and the lights made me dizzy . . . and all I could hear was my own giddy laughter.

Tarik twirled me in his arms, and I was lost and safe and the only place I desired to be. I never wanted him to let me go. "Your eyes are so beautiful, did you know?" I told him with a soft hiccup when we slowed, the last strains of music fading. "They're endless like the depths of an ocean shot through with rays of sunlight. I could stare at them forever."

We paused for a moment as he drew me back to a small alcove on the far side of the adjacent room where it was less loud. A cup pressed to my lips. "Drink this; it's water."

The cool liquid slid down my parched throat. "Do you not believe me? About your eyes?"

He smiled, that torturous dimple flashing. "I do. I love yours, too."

"Why?" I wrinkled my nose. "They're so boring. Just plain dark brown." I nearly poked myself in the eye, but he redirected my wrist at the last moment, saving me from injury.

Tarik cupped my cheeks. "On the contrary, chérie. They're a deep, intense, mesmerizing brown with flecks of chocolate and honey that I would willingly drown in if I could."

Stifling a snort, I giggled and then blushed hotly as the French endearment lodged itself deep. "Sometimes you say the most romantic things, monsieur!"

"It's the truth."

"Say that in French," I said dreamily.

"C'est la vérité, ma belle."

That velvety accented voice calling me *his beauty* at the end made me feel like swooning. "You think I'm beautiful?"

His eyes softened. "Oui. Plus que les étoiles dans le ciel."

More than the stars in the sky.

Gracious, who knew that my buttoned-up tutor had such a charming, fanciful side? Brimming with elation, I flung my arms around his neck, reaching up on my tiptoes as we swayed together to the strains of the fiddles in the other room, which had shifted to something softer and sweeter. I pressed my cheek to his chest, lulled by the sound of his steady heartbeat.

"What if we could run away? Go live in a tiny village somewhere. You could teach and write a book on mathematical theories, and I would invent magnificent telescopes, discover a thousand stars and comets—" I broke off. "Since it will be just the two of us, I suppose I could keep things tidy and cook."

Lips twitching, Tarik shot his brows high. "You can cook?"

"Well, no. But I can learn," I said brightly. It couldn't be so hard, could it? Half of doing anything was having the confidence to start, though in my befuddled state, I wasn't *quite* sure what that would entail. "Wait, can you?"

"I know a few French dishes."

I scrunched my nose, deep in thought. "Perhaps if we don't want to starve, you might have to be the cook at first and then you can teach me. There! It's settled."

"You've thought this through," he said smiling.

"One can accomplish quite a lot with thorough planning."

He chuckled, his blue eyes warm and open as we swayed back and forth. There were a few couples near us, dancing as scandalously close as we were, though there were no vigilant patronesses to frown or warn us about remaining twelve inches apart. I felt happy and unfettered in a way that I had never been, not even at Trinity.

"I suppose that's fair," he said. "So, do you truly want to be a star-and-comet hunter? Is that your dream—to discover celestial bodies?"

"One of them. Did you know Caroline Herschel discovered *eight* comets?" I sighed and pulled away from him to spin myself slowly while staring up at the peeling patchwork ceiling as if I could see to the infinite night sky beyond it. "A tiny woman with huge dreams who persevered through illness and adversity and didn't let anything stop her. I want to be remembered for something great like that. Can you imagine a comet named after *me*?"

"I believe you will achieve whatever you put your mind to," Tarik said, studying me from where he stood near the alcove, one lean shoulder propped up against the wall. He sounded sincere. *Genuine.* I loved that about him—he didn't diminish my dreams or belittle my ideas like most of the other older gentlemen in the *ton.* My good cheer soured at the thought of my future.

"Alas, if my father marries me off to some old goat of a peer, he will determine the freedoms I have."

"He intends to marry you off?"

I nodded. "At the end of the season to someone of his choosing, unless I can find someone suitable enough for him before then."

"What does suitable entail?" he asked.

Something in his voice made me pause and glance at him, but instead of being open, his face was back to being annoyingly unreadable. I almost told him to get rid of his Trinity face but stopped myself at the last second, reminding myself that I was *Rosalin,* not Ansel. Thanks to that dreadful ale, my thoughts were so muddled that I'd almost given myself away again!

I shrugged. "Suitable to me, or suitable to the duke?"

"Both, I suppose."

"What *I* want is someone who is smart yet handsome, decisive but thoughtful, adventurous but also safe, a brilliant, inventive mind steeped in compassion . . . a boy who would help a girl escape the pressures of her life, if only for an evening." My reply emerged in a garbled rush, and I swallowed past the lump in my throat. "You, if I'm being honest." The words were a wistful whisper I wasn't even sure he could hear, but from the intense way Tarik was staring at me, I was certain he had.

He'd lost his coat at some point, and his sleeves were rolled up again, exposing those strong forearms. His cravat was gone as well, putting his bare neck on display. It gleamed with perspiration from our dance, his muscles flexing. He'd be barred from a London ballroom for such unforgivable impropriety, but I couldn't bring myself to ponder the asinine rules of high society. Here, other gentlemen in this tavern seemed to relish being in a state of undress. The women, too, were displaying a shocking amount of cleavage and skin.

But I only had eyes for him, and he only had eyes for me . . .

"And the duke?" he said softly.

Bridging the gap between us, I moved closer to him. I caught my lip between my teeth, my eyes burning. Because even though everything about him was perfect for *me,* he'd never be enough for the Duke of Delmont. "Titled. Influential. A match to strengthen our position in the *ton.*"

"I see."

He *didn't* see. My eyes watered, but I forced the tears back. Or perhaps he did and knew nothing could ever become of us. Of *this.* And that was why we were here, outside our lives and respective stations, hoping for a sliver of time that was just ours.

The tension between us was palpable as we inhaled the same air, our lips nearly close enough to kiss. One step more and they would be touching. Blood rushed in my ears as I contemplated doing just that, but I nearly jumped out of my skin when a loud crash of breaking glass reached us, and the moment was lost. I shuffled back, hauling air into my aching lungs.

Kissing him would be a mistake, something we couldn't come back from.

Not even while we were pretending to be . . . *not* who we were.

Despite the loud clatter, the music and dancing in the adjoining space didn't stop as I took belated stock of where we were standing, trying to distract myself. I blinked and sipped my water. The more of it I drank, the clearer my mind became, and when Tarik handed me a refilled glass, I took it gratefully. A clear head meant no more foolish blunders.

Like kissing.

I glanced up at him. God, those pillowy lips were perfect for it.

Stop gawking, for heaven's sake!

Hot-cheeked, I guzzled my water and surveyed the tavern instead. This place was like a warren of tiny rooms. Peering over to the right, I took in the sight of green-baize-covered gaming tables in the next hall and felt an indecent thrill spark inside me.

"Look! There are card games here. Shall we try? Do you know how to play vingt-et-un?" I asked my brooding companion, with a wide, innocent stare.

"I don't think that's a very good idea."

Since it worked so well for me last time, I pouted again. "One game, please, Tarik? Girls never get to play like this. Do I need to make my lip quiver to convince you?"

"You fight dirty." A sound like an aggrieved growl rumbled through him, but it turned into a grumble of resignation. "Very well. One game, but my word goes. If we need to leave, we leave. You must promise me you will do as I say."

Hiding my glee, I stuck out my hand for him to shake. "I promise, monsieur."

CHAPTER FOURTEEN

> Therefore to the same natural effects we must, as far as possible, assign the same causes.
>
> —Isaac Newton

My first thought was that this was nothing like the gaming hell in Cambridge. The fact was this crowd was rowdier, rougher, and infinitely more dangerous. But I was with Tarik, and he would never let any harm come to either of us. Greedy eyes tracked over me, taking in the fine cut and fabric of my gown, and other details that marked us as possible pigeons, while we threaded our way through to a table with a pair of empty chairs.

The dealer sported a huge mustache that I couldn't help staring at. Though his face was weathered and hard, he had kind brown eyes, I thought. But in places like this, kindness would be construed as weakness. Perhaps it was just my overactive brain trying to convince me that I was safe and not allowing me to give in to the primal instincts that warned me to flee.

One game . . .

"Betting limits are twenty pounds, minimum is fifty pence," the dealer said, and my eyes widened at the maximum number.

Twenty pounds was no small amount, barely less than the *annual* salary of some working-class people. But the maximum bet was only set by the house so that they could cover any losses, which meant that they probably did quite well as a copper hell. "Payout for a natural is two to one, and one to one for a win."

I took stock of the players. The man at the other end of the table looked like one of reasonable means. The second player, a woman, was dressed well at first glance, but her hem was slightly frayed, and her embroidered collar worn. The third man was a gentleman dressed like us who appeared to have deep pockets, based on the pile of money in front of him.

"Place your stakes."

Before the dealer handed out the cards—two per player and one for himself, the wagers were made. Surreptitiously, I followed Tarik's lead and bet only the minimum to start.

An hour later, our single game had turned into several. I won some and I lost some, while Tarik seemed to be consistently losing, though his wagers were small enough not to hurt. After a while, I grasped that he was doing it on purpose. When all the cards in the deck were dealt, the dealer shuffled a new set of cards, and play resumed.

Tarik sat back in his seat, a tiny smirk playing about his lips, a glass of cherry brandy in hand. He looked so utterly relaxed that one might assume—erroneously—he wasn't a threat, but this was yet another of the masks he wore. I suddenly recalled the allegation that had been made back at the gaming table in Cambridge by the man who had started the fight—that Tarik had somehow memorized and kept track of the cards.

So that was why he hadn't been playing or betting seriously before.

He'd been *biding his time.*

Perking up, I paid careful attention as well. My first card from the new deck was a queen of spades and my second was a four, which put my total at fourteen. The dealer showed a nine of clubs. I played the round cautiously. Tarik got a natural, doubling his initial bet. The three other players went belly up and I managed to stay alive when the dealer went over twenty-one with a bust.

A new round was dealt and bets placed. I bet a quid, and Tarik wagered five pounds. I held twenty, and Tarik had five or fifteen, with an ace of clubs and a four of spades. I chose to stand on mine.

"Another," Tarik said.

He received three of diamonds, which put his total at eight or eighteen with the dual value of the ace. I would have stopped with eighteen, but he asked for a card again, miraculously receiving a two. My breath hitched as the dealer flipped his card and showed a six. He drew a five, putting him at eleven. With bated breath, we waited for the next card . . . a king of diamonds. Everyone groaned. We'd all lost.

"House has the luck of the devil," the woman said with a sigh.

I watched as the dealer raked in all the money. From keeping careful track of the cards that had been played so far, I knew that there were more high-value cards left in the deck, which would give us statistical advantage over the dealer. Two more rounds passed with me winning both times. Alcohol flowed freely, and the man at the end grew drunker and more belligerent.

"This game is bloody rigged!" he grumbled. "Highway robbery."

"Place your wagers, please," the dealer said, face tight at the man's behavior.

Tarik speared me with an arch look and pushed most of his winnings into the middle, totaling eighteen pounds. I did the same, though my amount was less, at fifteen. My heart thumped, but our odds were good with the current tally in my head. Better than good.

The man on the end continued to swear, eyes shooting daggers at us as he sneered at the hefty wagers. He was down to barely anything, glowering all the while. "I need a credit line."

The factotum came over, consulting his ledgers. "Ten pounds to Mr. Smith."

Credit was usually extended to players in good standing, who would return to settle their accounts the next day. Or at least, that was how I heard it worked in more high-end clubs. Here, in the West End, the settlement might be in flesh and blood. I suppressed a shiver.

When the man received the money, he shoved seven of the ten into the middle. The woman went with the minimum bet, while the gentleman in the middle played the maximum. Someone let out a loud gasp, and I looked up to realize that we had drawn an attentive crowd. Even the factotum remained close, keeping a vigilant eye on the table, players, and spectators.

The dealer distributed the cards. As I'd expected from watching the previous rounds, most of the cards were now face cards. The foxed player had a total of fifteen, a weak hand, which made him smash his fist onto the surface of the table. Cheers burst from the crowd as I received the queen of hearts and the ace of diamonds—a natural—and Tarik's two cards showed a total of twenty.

If the dealer didn't have twenty-one, I would win forty-five pounds. His visible card was a ten. The chances that he would have a face card were also excellent. Tensions were high—and a lot of money was at stake. The drunk man scowled and hit, receiving a nine, which put him over twenty-one. His face turned puce with rage, but by some miracle, he held his tongue by dousing it with whiskey.

My neck felt hot when the dealer stared at Tarik. "Sir?"

Long elegant fingers drummed on the tabletop. The odds were good, I thought.

"Stay," I whispered to him. "He'll go over."

Blue eyes met mine. "Sometimes you have to risk it all to win it all," he said in a low voice. I wasn't sure if he was still talking about the game or something else entirely. He studied the dealer, head canting slightly. "Another."

A collective gasp went up as my heart fell. Asking for another card when he stood at twenty was audacious. Foolish, even. But when the dealer flipped the card, it was the last ace in the pack—the ace of hearts. The game was over when the dealer displayed his second card, and it was another ten.

Tarik and I had won a small fortune together.

"I know a sharp when I see one, you cheating bastard!" the

drunk at the end slurred, pointing a finger at Tarik and then at the dealer. "He's in on it, too! The whole house is crooked!"

"Sir, calm down," the dealer warned, nodding to the factotum, who handed him a new deck.

The drunk man bared his teeth, spittle flying everywhere as he lurched unsteadily to his feet. "Don't bloody tell me to calm down! Rigged, I tell you!"

Dear God, not again!

But unlike the last time, the factotum nodded at two enormous men, who strode through the crowd to escort the troublemaker out of the room. He sputtered his outrage, but they didn't care, lifting him up between them and practically dragging his carcass away.

I turned to Tarik with a wry grin. "I'm starting to think that you are the common denominator here, sowing chaos in your wake at gambling dens."

He stared at me in confusion, and I recognized my mistake much too late. The last time we were together, I hadn't been Lady Rosalin. "I beg your pardon?" he said.

"Oh, Ansel told me about your brawl," I rushed out quickly, my stomach dropping.

Tarik cocked his head. "Did he now? That's rather curious."

The way he said it with the slightest hint of disappointment had me wavering. Why would he be disappointed? I blinked. Botheration, it was supposed to be a secret, wasn't it? *Roz* had promised not to tell anyone. I racked my brain to come up with any excuse Tarik might accept for the broken trust.

"Yes, well, his hand was injured," I explained. "I hounded

him until he confessed what had happened but also swore me to secrecy, don't worry."

"You play a lot better than he does," Tarik conceded after a beat, though that look of disquiet remained. "So have you had your fill, or shall we continue?"

"Perhaps one more game," I said, eager to spend more time with him before we were both forced to go back to reality.

However, play seemed to be paused. The factotum was in quiet conversation with the dealer a few feet away from where we sat, their gazes occasionally flicking in our direction . . . specifically to *both* of us. When he signaled for the two security guards to come to his side, I couldn't help frowning. I could feel Tarik's unease when the factotum approached us, his face giving away nothing though his shoulders were stiff and his stance was distinctly menacing.

"Sir," he said. "Can you come with me please? You and your companion." My frown deepened at the request, though it sounded more like a command than anything else, especially with the two men looming behind him like ominous shadows.

"May I ask why?" Tarik asked.

The factotum's mouth flattened. "It's a private matter. You must come with us." The men at his back flexed, and my entire body stiffened at the silent threat.

Tarik's reluctance to go with them was clear, and I realized that what happened behind closed doors might not be so savory in a place like this. Patrons could be beaten to a pulp, or the house could take our money with no one the wiser. We didn't have any protections. Well, technically, *Tarik* didn't. If needed, I had the protection of my station and my name, and though the aristocracy might not be revered in this part of London, that was still something.

I had limited power, but I wasn't afraid to use it, not in this circumstance.

And if news got back to Mayfair, I'd deal with it then.

"Unless you can tell us what we did wrong," I said in a clear voice, rising to my full height as Tarik followed my lead, "you have no reason or cause to detain us. And neither of us *has* to do anything."

Calculating green eyes flicked over me. "This is a private establishment."

"Then we shall leave."

A smarmy grin overtook his face. "Not until we have a little chat, miss. You understand."

Tarik's fists clenched, but neither of us would be any match for the two enormous men. I understood all too clearly what was happening. They did not want us to walk out of here with the small fortune we had won, even if we had done so fairly. Calculating odds was not a crime, but they did not like being undermined of potential profits by clever-minded players. If Tarik had been alone, his winnings might have gone undetected, but with the two of us winning such large amounts, it had drawn notice.

"Either you let us leave, or you will find my father's solicitor on your doorstep, and I assure you, if this is indeed your establishment, it will be shut down first thing tomorrow and everything in here will belong to him." I paused for effect. "The Duke of Delmont."

Recognition flared in his eyes. Oh, he knew who that was. There wasn't a business owner in London who didn't know my father, considering his fleet of ships brought in many of the goods from the Far East. He was responsible for almost all the fair-trade laws in place in Parliament and took harsh measures to battle piracy and profiteering from illegal practices.

"Pay back your ill-gotten gains, and you're free to go," the factotum said through a clenched jaw.

"Fine, we don't want any trouble," Tarik said, reaching into his pockets, but I know he was capitulating only because he was worried for my safety. Although it was the principle of the thing. There was no law preventing a person who was good at addition from gambling.

"No." I stopped Tarik with a hand to his arm. "We played, and we won."

"You were keeping track," the factotum snarled.

I snorted. "Everyone does, sir. Is that not the point of the game? To add numbers until a sum of twenty-one is reached?"

"That is not what I meant. You kept a tally."

I feigned confusion. "Of my cards? Well, of course I did. A good player must have proper count of their cards to win, good sir. Surely, that is the goal of vingt-et-un."

Face reddening, he curled his lip back over his teeth. "You're mocking me."

Perhaps I'd overdone it on the innocent indignation.

"If you feel mocked, sir, then you must look inward, as I have certainly no idea what you mean," I said primly. "However, if you do insist on detaining us, then *I* must insist that the Bow

Street Runners be summoned by our coachman, who is waiting outside. And if you intend on threatening my fiancé or me, prompt measures will be taken, I assure you."

My coachman was nowhere near Covent Garden, but *he* didn't know that. I didn't dare look at Tarik after the last declaration, though I could feel the immediate sweep of his stare. I kept my chin up and my demeanor fierce. Any glimmer of weakness would be exploited.

"Leave," the man bit out. "And don't come back."

I smiled. "With pleasure."

The two burly men stayed close to our heels as we walked to the entrance. I didn't miss the look that the furious factotum exchanged with them, nor was I unaware of the avaricious glances of some of the seedier patrons who had noticed us pocketing our winnings. If we didn't come to harm at the hands of the two men tailing us, there was a good chance we would be followed and robbed by others. A hundred pounds was a fortune to many people in this area, and we were plump targets to thieves.

As we exited to the street, I pointed up one of the roads. "There's the carriage," I lied loudly, and grabbed Tarik's hand. I sucked air into my lungs as we hurried away, hopefully toward a thoroughfare where we could actually get a hackney. Seven Dials was a warren of streets one could get lost in, and obviously, I was not familiar with this part of London.

"That was brilliant!" he said, squeezing my palm. "*You* were brilliant! I thought we were done for! I wasn't quite ready to give up any of my fingers."

"They do that?" I asked in horror.

"So I've heard."

I blanched. In hindsight, perhaps we should have forfeited the winnings and left. "Is anyone following us?" I asked.

Tarik glanced over his shoulder. "No, but I have no doubt *someone* will."

Sure enough, it wasn't long before we heard footsteps on the cobblestones, ones that were much too fast to be anything but cutpurses in pursuit. Tarik tightened his grip on my hand, and we both upped our pace. My delicate dancing slippers with their leather soles would not last on these streets, but I didn't have much choice.

Footsteps grew louder and closer.

"This way," Tarik said urgently, yanking me down the mouth of another alley.

We darted through the narrow streets, though I was already hopelessly lost. My feet were aching, my heart was hammering, and my lungs were shrinking with each panted breath. And yet, we couldn't seem to shake our trackers—their footsteps persevered, getting even closer!

"Here!" Tarik panted, shoving us into a recessed doorway that seemed to lead to an underground cellar. The sound of scampering and squeaking behind the door instantly grabbed my attention. *Good heavens, are those* rats? A shudder rocked through me. Tarik's tall body crowded mine. "Don't move, and don't make a sound."

I could feel the thrum of my heartbeat in my ears as the darkness and silence enveloped us. I didn't dare breathe as the sounds of approaching people grew louder.

"Oy, you see 'em?"

"Check over there!"

"I think they went this way, lads!"

It was difficult to pinpoint how close they were, but after what seemed like an eternity, their voices faded, until it was deathly quiet. I became acutely aware of Tarik plastered up against me, and even though my heart rate should have been calming, because the immediate danger had passed, it wasn't. In fact, it sped up like a runaway horse. My palms were glued to his chest, and I could feel his own unsteady pulse.

I forgot about the possible rodents . . . about everything.

He smelled so good, that delicious chocolate-and-snow scent of him invading my nostrils. His cravat had disappeared, and I wanted to lift my chin and bury my nose in his neck, but of course, that would be unseemly. Though no one was here but us.

"I think they've gone," he whispered, leaning down so his breath feathered against my temple. My entire body trembled at the barest contact of his lips, heat sparking through me in a shower of embers.

"Tarik . . ."

The groan that left him was pained. "I love when you say my name, Rosalin. May I call you Rosalin?"

"Yes." I could barely speak as his nose trailed a heated path down my neck. It was untoward and wicked, and I wanted more.

He inhaled deeply. "How do you smell so good? Like roses and fresh rain."

I gasped when his lips grazed the edge of my jaw. Instinctively, I tilted my head to the side to give him better access. My fingers inched upward, dancing over his muscled biceps and strong rounded shoulders to wind in the soft curls at his nape. It was so wrong . . . and yet felt so incredibly right. If we were seen together, my reputation would be irreparably shattered.

But who would discover us here? Tangled in each other's arms? Shrouded in the darkness as we were? We were nothing but shadows.

Tarik pulled away to study me. He scoured my face so intently butterflies exploded in my stomach. I licked my lips and felt his gaze settle on my mouth. The fact that I could barely make out his features added to the allure, to the thrill of this illicit interlude.

"What are you doing?" I asked him softly when he didn't move.

"I want to kiss you so badly," he whispered, and my breath hitched.

My eyes fluttered closed. "Then kiss me."

CHAPTER FIFTEEN

> Absolute, true, and mathematical time, of itself, and from its own nature flows equably without regard to anything external.
>
> —Isaac Newton

Tarik St. Clair's lips on mine felt like a fever dream. Like two planets colliding in the eternity of space. Like defying gravity.

It started soft, the barest featherlike brush of his mouth against mine as he pressed a kiss to each corner and then to the middle, the plush contours of his lips fitting snugly against mine. I let out a dreamy sigh as he slanted his head, and suddenly, the tip of his soft, damp tongue flicked over my bottom lip. I jolted, but my fingers dug into his collar, holding his mouth to mine as I mimicked the motion, tentatively tasting him, too.

Tarik groaned, his mouth opening wider, welcoming my entry. My tongue swept shyly against his in a sleek, decadent graze. He tasted sweet, with hints of the cherry brandy he'd sipped in the card room. He wrapped his arms around me and deepened the kiss, exploring me with a tenderness that made me breathless. I couldn't even function, my entire being swept up in the staggering sensation of being consumed by him.

This kiss completely eclipsed the unremarkable one I'd had with Blake. Not that I should be thinking about another boy while kissing Tarik, but I couldn't help comparing the two, since I'd only ever done this once before. Blake's kiss had been barely tolerable, while Tarik's was like a comet streaking across the night sky, incinerating everything in its path. Including me.

And all I wanted to do was burn.

His hands gripped my waist, winding into the fabric of my gown as if to anchor us from floating away. Everything inside me felt like it was on fire as I kissed him back, my lips clinging to his while our mouths entangled in a dance that felt as natural as breathing. Kissing Tarik felt like everything I'd always imagined it to be . . . *magical,* and I never wanted it to end. I wanted to bask in him in forever. I didn't know how long we stood there, locked and lost in each other, but when we finally broke apart, we were both dazed.

Tarik leaned his forehead against mine. "God . . . that was . . ."

"Perfect," I whispered, my lips feeling tender from our fervent efforts. I wondered if his felt the same, and I wished we had more light so I could commit the sight of them to memory.

"We should go," he murmured, with a soft kiss to each of my cheeks as if he couldn't stop touching me. "Before those men come back."

That was a splash of cold water to the face. Reluctantly, I disentangled my arms from around his neck, immediately missing the warmth and strength of his solid frame. But when he grabbed my hand and threaded his fingers through mine, the flutters in the pit of my stomach returned. With his guidance, we retraced our steps quickly and exited at a larger street.

Luckily, we were able to secure a hackney without being seen or chased. Tarik gave the driver my address. I would have to sneak in through the kitchens and hope I didn't get caught.

Worth it.

My cheeks were hot as I gazed at the boy opposite me, knowing that my lips had just been on his, my fingers in his hair, his hands on my waist. Especially when said boy was staring at me like I was everything he'd ever dreamed of and more.

My chest ached.

"Stop looking at me like that," I whispered.

"I can't help it," he said. "I like looking at you." A wide smile made his eyes crinkle at the corners. "Because you're an enigma. A puzzle, and I happen to be very fond of puzzles."

"How so?"

"You're delicate," he began, and I scoffed at that, rolling my gaze skyward before he held a finger up, "but somehow hiding a will of pure steel."

"Hardly," I said, blushing.

"How many young ladies would stand up to a group of ruffians in Covent Garden with absolutely no fear? You're dauntless, and you never do what I expect. You're intimidatingly intelligent and can track a deck of cards like the cleverest card sharp." He blinked and reached into his pocket. "Speaking of, here are your spoils of battle."

"You keep it," I said, staring at the stuffed purse he held. He wasn't poor, but his earnings as a tutor wouldn't be excessive.

"But it belongs to both of us," he said. "If you don't want it, then I don't either."

I thought for a moment, a brilliant idea occurring to me. "Then let's do something amazing with it. Let's donate it to an orphanage to be used to buy books for children, including books on mathematics, science, and philosophy for the older ones and adventurous stories for the younger ones. I think Zia has a connection to the Little Hands orphanage, part of Bellevue Chapel."

He handed the purse to me. "Perfect."

"Are you sure you don't need it?" I asked.

Tarik shook his head. "It feels right for it to go toward the shaping of young minds. They're the future."

He was staring at me again, but now conflicted emotions roamed his face. The whimsical wonder I'd seen before was eclipsed by other things. Likely the same desolate thoughts that were creeping up on the heels of all the good feelings in my own head the closer we got to Mayfair.

We'd both known tonight wouldn't last forever . . .

I was certain my sudden despair and melancholy were written all over me, because Tarik frowned. He opened his mouth. "Lady Ros—"

"No," I blurted out in a breathless whisper, not wanting to hear whatever it was he intended to say, especially if it was regret. "Please don't say that what happened between us was a mistake. I couldn't bear it if you did because tonight was the most extraordinary thing that has ever happened to me, and I never want to forget it."

"Extraordinary?" he asked, though his voice sounded much too forlorn for my liking.

I nodded. "Beyond so. The truth is I don't want to let you go, Tarik. It feels like walking away from this would be the biggest blunder of our lives."

His eyes fluttered shut at the sound of his name. He swallowed, so many sentiments crashing and tangling in his expression when those eyes opened. "I'm not who your father would choose for you, Rosalin. I cannot offer you the life you deserve."

"I don't care," I said urgently, leaning forward to grasp his hands. "We will figure it out."

"You're a lady, accustomed to all the finer things in life. Diamonds, jewels, fancy balls, carriages, a glorious home. I can't afford to give you any of those things."

"I don't need any of that as long as I have you," I replied, but I could feel him pulling away with every ragged heartbeat between us.

His voice was soft. "Rosalin, I'm common born. Even if I am wildly successful with my business venture, the fruits of my labor are far away. Years, even."

"Then we'll talk to my father, and I will wait as long as it takes. Because I have no doubt you'll succeed."

Face tight, he exhaled. "Even if your father agrees, which we both know he won't, what of your friends in the *ton*? Lady Ela? Lady Zia? Your cousin Ansel? Even Lord Blake. You'll stop seeing them and going to grand parties and balls because you'll have given up the life of a lady? I could never make you do that."

As his words sank in, underscored by his defeated tone as

though he'd already given up on the idea of us, I bit my lip so hard I winced. "Do you think that's all I want? That I'm so shallow? In truth, I would live in a hovel if I could look up at the stars every day with the person I cherish most in the world." I sucked in a breath as the possibility of us shone like a beacon of hope in my imaginings. "The promise of more is worth any sacrifice, is it not?"

His fingers squeezed mine, that beautiful face sad and solemn. "Have you ever gone hungry? So hungry that you drank water just to fill your belly from one day to the next, not knowing how or when your next meal would come? Have you done the one thing you swore you would never do—steal—just to snatch a burned crust of bread to feed your siblings?"

Shocked, I loosened my grasp and recoiled at the insinuation. That I didn't know what it meant to suffer hardship. I might not have experienced it myself, but I wasn't naïve. I knew that there were people in London who were starving—Mama had made sure to educate us on the importance of helping the less fortunate. Several of her charitable organizations regularly donated food and medicine to the poor, and easing the plight of the less fortunate was one of the reasons I volunteered my help at my local parish.

"What do you mean? Have *you*?"

"I know people who have, and I've seen what it does to them." Tarik reached forward and gripped my hands again, despite my reluctance. "I'm not judging you or saying that you don't empathize. I only mean that it's easy to say you could live without something from the vantage point of never having experienced the loss of it. Poverty is adversity at its most distressing. And I would never want anything bad to ever touch you." He squeezed, his throat working with emotion as he fought to get the words out. "No, if you were mine, I would want to give you everything . . . a life of love and laughter, and especially one without discomfort. You deserve that and more."

"Is that what you want? For me to be yours?" The feelings flying through me were exhilarated one moment and despondent the next. It sounded like he wanted to pursue a future with me while trying to convince himself and me that he was not good enough. I had to make him understand that he was. "Because I want *you* to be *mine*."

One side of his lip curved up into a half smile as he reached out to cup my cheek. "You're not afraid of anything, are you?"

"*Me*? I'm terrified of everything," I sputtered. "I'm terrified of who I am, of my future and being auctioned off to some poxy peer, of not taking chances . . . of what's happening between us right now . . ." I trailed off, the words sticking like honey in my throat. "And most of all, of never feeling like this ever again. I don't want to lose you." I whispered the last bit, my eyes lifting and colliding with his just as the carriage came to a halt.

"I don't want to lose you either."

I turned my face into his palm. "Then don't."

"It's that easy?" he said softly.

"Nothing worth keeping is ever easy. We have to fight for what we want, even when all the odds might be against us."

He exhaled, staring at me with that same look of wonder. "I've never known anyone like you, Rosalin. So full of optimism and hope. Utterly indomitable. I want you to know that no matter what happens, I'll never forget what you've done for me. I owe you and Roz so much."

My heart, flying so impossibly high, sank like a stone as the cold weight of reality hit with those words. He *didn't* owe me anything, much less my lying alter ego. Heavens, I had to be honest. I had to tell him the truth of who I really was.

"Tarik, I need to tell—"

But the moment was lost when the coachman rapped sharply on the door, making us both jump. And then Tarik's lips were erasing the sense from my brain as he cupped my cheeks and kissed me passionately. He pulled away much too quickly for my liking.

"Before you go, I want to request you meet me next Saturday evening," he said huskily.

I blinked. "The night of Mama's ball?"

His eyes gleamed as he reached into his pocket and pushed a folded piece of paper into my palm. "Yes. Instruct your driver to take you here. It won't take long, I promise. We'll both be back in time."

"What's this?" I asked, staring down at the neatly written but unfamiliar address.

"Something I wish to do for you in return."

CHAPTER SIXTEEN

Errors are not in the art, but in the artificers.

—Isaac Newton

A very, very cross Anna had scolded me ferociously, once to make sure I didn't ruin my gown for the evening after her painstaking efforts to get me ready for the ball, and then again, when I told her that she had to remain behind and not accompany me on whatever secret adventure Tarik was planning. She still hadn't forgiven me for the last time I'd slipped away to go to Covent Garden with said young man *without* a proper chaperone, especially when she'd caught me red-handed, sneaking back into my room.

"I don't like this one bit," she'd said under her breath so the other maids couldn't overhear our conversation.

"I'll be careful, I swear, and Henry will be driving me there," I'd replied. "If Mama asks, tell her I'm helping Lady Ela with an emergency."

She'd scowled. "I don't like lying to the duchess, my lady. And you know what will happen if you get caught. A march to the altar will be the least of your worries. Don't you think you've taunted fate enough?"

"We won't get caught, and I'll be back in time."

I *hoped*.

But as Henry ferried me to the address on the piece of paper Tarik had instructed me to give to him, my nerves were hard to contain. Henry had informed me that it would take about forty minutes to reach the destination. While we drove, I switched out my beaded dancing slippers that had been dyed to match my gown with the ankle boots I'd carried in a satchel, since I had no idea where we were going.

At first, I'd thought it was Vauxhall Pleasure Gardens, which had given me a wicked thrill, but we weren't heading south of Mayfair, more to the east. Thankfully, I'd brought my cloak with a deep hood, if I needed to conceal myself for any reason. A girl had to be prepared.

As the journey continued, I stroked the soft silk folds of my dress, willing them to stay wrinkle free. I wouldn't hear the end of it from Anna if she saw a single crease in the pale lilac fabric. The dress was embroidered with cream-and-gold flowers along the bodice and the hem, with a pearl-and-amethyst beaded strip across the waistline, and accompanied by elegant elbow-length cream gloves that covered my arms. My hair had been intricately wound and pinned with silk flowers, and a circle of jeweled amethyst and pearl clusters attached to the ebony strands. Anna had scolded me to keep my coiffure in place, too, or else . . .

I snorted. My lady's maid could be rather bossy sometimes.

Dappled late-afternoon daylight glimmered through the

coach windows, but by the time we arrived, the twilight would already be creeping in. I wasn't afraid—Henry was an excellent shot and could thwart any potential highwaymen—but my pulse still raced with a combination of exhilaration and apprehension. I peered out the window when the wheels finally started to slow, and sucked in a breath at the sight of the sprawling brick buildings with their multi-domed roofline.

My heart stilled and then sped up.

Goodness, he didn't . . .

But clearly, *astonishingly*, Tarik had.

I disembarked outside the Royal Observatory, and there he was, waiting at the entrance in his formal wear for the ball later this evening, looking so achingly handsome that he stole my breath clear from my lungs. For a moment, I forgot about where we were and only stared at him, like he was the center of my universe.

His jaw slackened as he took in my countenance, his gaze dropping from the jewels glinting in my hair to the soft folds of my gown and climbing back up. "You are,"—he choked in a dazed tone—"by the stars above, you're the loveliest girl I've ever seen."

"Thank you," I said, cheeks warming at the smitten expression on his face. "You look nice, too."

Nice was too banal of a word to describe how incredibly dashing he looked in his raven-black evening wear, with his snowy-white shirt and cravat, and a navy, silver-threaded waistcoat that resembled the night sky speckled with stars. His tousled, dark waves, which I now knew were indescribably soft, blew in the slight breeze, and his eyes sparkled like backlit sapphires.

Finally, I found my tongue, which had found itself glued to the roof of my mouth. "What are we doing here?"

"It's a surprise," he said, offering his arm to me as he led us through the doors. "Come on. We are on a strict schedule."

I frowned. "It's a research facility. Visitors aren't allowed inside."

"There are always exceptions," he said quietly, leading us toward a somber-faced man who stood some length away. "I want to introduce you to someone. Mr. Pond, this is Lady Rosalin Chen, the Duke of Delmont's daughter. Lady Rosalin, may I present Mr. Pond, the Astronomer Royal."

I only kept my mouth from falling open in sheer awe with effort. "Mr. Pond, it's an honor."

He smiled. "The honor is mine, my lady. Mr. St. Clair tells me that you have an amateur interest in astronomy," he said, and my gaze shot to Tarik, who nodded encouragingly. A part of me knew that news of my spontaneous visit might get back to my parents, but I didn't care. I'd deal with it if it did.

"I do," I said breathlessly. "One day I hope to catalogue stars and comets like Caroline Herschel."

"Remarkable woman just like her brother," he said with a nod, and ushered us toward a narrow corridor. "I shall leave you in Mr. St. Clair's capable hands."

"Thank you, sir," Tarik said.

With a smart bow, Mr. Pond took his leave, presumably to

continue the work that was going on in the observatory to chart and track celestial data for timekeeping and navigation. Just because we were here didn't mean the scientists stopped what they were doing—their celestial-measurement efforts were too important to the navy and maritime navigation. I was very aware that we were intruding in a space not designed for ordinary citizens.

Dumbfounded, I stared at Tarik when he took my arm once more to lead me in the direction the Astronomer Royal had indicated. "How did you do this?" I whispered. "John Pond is notoriously reserved in his dealings with the public and purported to have a temper."

"My mentor and one of the Fellows at Trinity, Mr. Peacock, arranged it via a letter of introduction at my request," he replied softly.

"Why?" I asked.

"You know why," he said. "For you. This is your dream. You helped me find mine, and I wanted to help you discover yours."

I swear to God I nearly melted. My mouth opened and closed as I stumbled, my knees going inexplicably weak at the sheer sweetness of him. "Tarik, I . . ."

"Thank me tonight," he said with a grin and a swift kiss to my temple. "We're late!"

We hurried through the building, though not so fast that I couldn't take in all the charts and instruments that were used for measuring positional astronomy in the different rooms. The building was dimly lit with a minimum of light, the stone walls covered in maps, logs, clocks, and star charts. We stopped to stare in utter amazement at the Troughton Transit Instrument, which was a large brass-and-steel telescope permanently mounted upon a stone pier that had been built four years ago. It was used to measure and track stars crossing the meridian line, in order to determine Greenwich Mean Time. Since the astronomers were already actively working in silence, Tarik and I only observed, but still, it was astounding to watch history being recorded.

"This way," Tarik said, herding me in another direction to climb the steps to a nearby tower.

The scents of oil and ink filled my nostrils as we entered a room with a seven-foot reflecting telescope, similar to the ones William Herschel had designed, its long brass tube resting on a stone pier. I exhaled, noticing there was only one scientist in here, standing near a large refracting telescope. He spotted our arrival and beckoned us over.

I blinked and stared at Tarik with wide eyes, hope exploding in my chest at the chance of possibly looking through the view-finder. "Could we . . . ?"

He winked, his lips curling into a knowing smirk. "Anything you wish, chérie."

"Mr. St. Clair, my lady," the man said bowing and canting his head. "I am Alec Biggs, at your service. Mr. Pond asked me to assist you this evening. Welcome."

He accompanied us around the room and then indicated the large mural quadrant with a set of wooden steps beside it that took up nearly the entirety of one wall with its large triangular brass frame. "This is used to track and trace the stars, noting infinitesimal movements with precision. It's how we create the navigational maps for nautical use."

"That is amazing," I said breathily.

He pointed out celestial star maps that had been meticulously drawn that hung on the far wall before returning to the instrument he'd been standing beside when we had arrived. "This is a Dollond refracting telescope used for planetary, lunar, and double-star observations. The lenses are five inches in aperture. The mount here is clock-driven so we can track the movement of the stars across the cosmos."

I listened in rapture. "May we look, Mr. Biggs?"

He pointed to the viewfinder. "Please, go ahead. It's currently positioned to Jupiter."

Jupiter! Practically vibrating with excitement, I put my eye to the lens. After waiting for my vision to get used to the aperture, and gently adjusting the focus, I gasped at the horizontal grayish bands on the surface of the spherical planet as well as its four moons, three on one side and one on the other. "Oh my God, it's incredible. Tarik, you must see this."

He took his turn, and then I went back for another longer look. "Jupiter is the largest planet in this solar system, and that's why we can see it relatively clearly," I murmured. "Galileo Galilei discovered the moons in 1610, over two hundred years ago. He thought they were stars at first, and then realized they revolved around the planet."

"Did you know it's the fastest rotating planet?" Mr. Biggs asked.

"Truly?"

He nodded. "It takes about ten hours for a full rotation."

"Marvelous," I whispered. Mr. Biggs clasped his hands behind his back, waiting for me to finish my extended perusal, taking in everything including the strange red spot I noticed between the horizontal bands. "It's so fascinating."

"Let me know if you have any more questions," he said. "I shall leave you to explore at your leisure while I continue my work on the mural quadrant."

Tarik's eyes were warm as he stared at me, walking forward to take my shaking hands in his. "Newton also used Jupiter's moons as evidence of gravitational theory, similar to the Earth and the sun."

I nodded. "Proving that it's universal."

"Correct. I have one more thing to show you," Tarik said, leading me over to the first reflecting telescope we had seen. "Go on, have a look."

His lean frame bracketed mine as I leaned down to the eyepiece and let the image come into focus. What appeared to be a bright star at first, slowly separated into two distinct stars, one a reddish orange and the other a glowing cobalt blue. I carefully adjusted the focus, sharpening the picture so the brighter star took on a more golden hue. "Is that . . . Beta Cygni?" I whispered.

"Yes, Albireo," he said softly. "Twin stars."

My eyes stung, feeling like they were glossing over, and for a moment, the image blurred. I had no idea why I was crying, only that I had never imagined ever seeing such a thing so clearly. "A binary pair," I murmured in wonder, remembering the conversation we had had about double stars, though I'd been Ansel then and couldn't bring it up now. The twinge of guilt deepened, feeling much heavier than usual.

"The Astronomer Royal James Bradley discovered it was a double star in 1753," Tarik said. "And Herschel himself observed it two and a half decades later."

When I was finally able to tear myself away from the telescope, I leaped into Tarik's arms and pressed my lips to his before even realizing what I was doing. I felt his surprise as I peppered his face with kisses between words as he laughed and spun me in a slow circle.

"I. Cannot. Believe. This. You. Are. Unbelievable," I said between kisses.

"I take it you enjoyed your surprise, then?" he asked, chuckling, when I stopped to draw a full breath.

"Enjoyed it? I loved it," I exclaimed. "You've outdone yourself, and I have no idea what I even did to deserve something this special. Being here is a dream come true."

He smiled, eyes twinkling. "Good. I meant it when I said that you deserve to have everything you ever wanted. And now we must get the most beautiful girl to the ball before her coach turns into a pumpkin."

"Dear God, what time is it?" I asked. I was so wrapped up in the whole experience that I hadn't even checked the clock.

"It's only nine. We will be back before ten."

Together, we retraced our steps back to the front entrance, and after making our goodbyes and giving fervent thanks to Mr. Pond, we exited to where Henry was patiently waiting with the carriage. Before long, we were on our way back to Mayfair.

Once more, I switched out my shoes, this time for my dancing slippers while Tarik watched me with interest. I could feel myself blushing even though I was fully covered by the length of my hem and stockings. But something about the nature of it felt much too intimate for the interior of a coach.

"You have tiny feet," he said when he saw me blushing. "I suppose it was smart to keep your gold-and-silver slippers safe, unlike the maiden from the story, who lost hers."

"A gentleman would not stare, you know."

His brows rose. "Good thing I'm not a gentleman, then."

"You're supposed to be pretending to be one, aren't you?" I retorted and then wrinkled my nose at what he'd said about the slipper, and earlier about the pumpkin. "Did you reference *Cinderella* by Charles Perrault?"

He smirked. "Does that surprise you?"

"Well yes, you're a mathematician," I said. "With your studies, how on earth do you have time for fairy tales?"

"Everyone should make time for fairy tales," he responded sagely. "They teach important moral lessons, inspire imagination, bridge cultural gaps, and provide hours of reading entertainment. In *Cinderella,* one learns that grace is of more value than beauty, that compassion and empathy are the true signs of one's character."

I had to work to keep my mouth from falling open.

"I prefer the bloodier ones," I shot back, grinning. "Like the version of *Cinderella* written by the Brothers Grimm that published about eight years ago. The sisters cut off their toes and heels to fit the slipper."

Tarik laughed, the sound low and rich and full of something I could not name but that made me shiver all the same. "You're a violent little creature, aren't you?"

"A rose without its thorns is hardly a rose," I quipped.

"Just so." Tarik canted his head and leaned back against the seat. "I suppose there is also a moral to that story, considering the sisters were so dishonest as to injure themselves to fit into the slipper. Their eyes were pecked out for their deceit."

The guilt I'd felt before about my deception returned in force.

My eyes probably deserved to be pecked out.

Dear God, how am I ever going to tell him? And will he forgive me?

The ball was in full swing by the time we arrived, with dozens of carriages lined up and down the street. I smoothed my dress for the hundredth time and patted my hair to make sure everything was in place. I was slightly rumpled from the journey as well as leaning over the telescopes, but nothing that would be noticed by anyone other than Anna. I draped my cloak on my shoulders and pulled the hood over my head.

"I'll meet you in the ballroom," I told Tarik, deciding to descend first so we didn't arouse any unnecessary gossip.

"Wait." He gripped my fingers and pulled me back toward him into the darkened interior of our coach, pressing a quick but heated kiss to my lips. "Will Lord Ansel be here tonight? I haven't seen him in a while, and we really must discuss his progress. Mr. Peacock required an update."

I bit my lip so hard I tasted blood. How on earth was I going to be my cousin tonight? And there would be no good reason why he wasn't at our family's ball. Illness, perhaps? My mind raced and my belly churned with nerves.

"He should be," I said brightly, knowing I probably should have confessed everything then and there, but it didn't feel like the right moment. I was starting to doubt that there would ever be a *right* moment. The fear of jeopardizing our rapport and his obvious esteem toward me was too much to bear. I didn't want to ruin a perfect evening.

Later. I'll explain it all later.

"Rosalin," he said and when I turned the carriage door handle, his smile was dazzling. "Save me a dance."

"All my dances are yours, sir," I said, and meant it. There was no one else worth dancing with.

My insides buzzing with a nauseating mix of exhilaration and anxiety, I walked briskly up the footpath and entered through the kitchens, hurrying past the bustling space. I discarded my cloak and dashed up the servants' staircase to my bedroom, where Anna was pacing a hole in the plush carpets. Her face was so red she looked like she'd rubbed beetroot juice all over it.

"Good heavens, my lady," she hissed, eyes widening comically when she caught sight of me slipping into my chambers. "Where in creation have you been? I've been having conniptions for hours, and the duchess is convinced I'm lying to her, which

I *am*. Father, forgive me." She made the sign of the cross and stamped her feet in a fit of frustration that made me want to giggle, but it would be in awful form, so I kept my lips zipped shut. "And *then,* Lady Ela and Lord Ridley arrived *without* you."

My mirth instantly vanished. "Oh no."

"Indeed," she pronounced grimly. "But by the grace of heaven, I narrowly avoided chaos by waylaying the marchioness's maid in the foyer and begging for Sally's assistance to explain your continued absence to her mistress."

"And did she?" I asked, wondering in a mild state of panic if my mother was going to storm into my room and demand to know where I'd been if I hadn't been with the Marchioness of Ridley.

"Luckily, *yes.* Lady Ela helpfully informed the duke and the duchess that you were en route with Lady Zenobia because of a gown emergency. Right now, Sally is waiting for the lady to arrive to inform her of the plan."

My breath rushed out. Okay. That was good. I was safe for the moment.

Suddenly, my heart quaked. "Wait, did you say the *duke*? Has Papa returned?"

"Yes, just this evening. His ship put into port earlier than planned. Don't worry. He, too, is unaware of your tomfooleries."

Grinning, I threw my arms around her and squeezed. "That is why you are the best lady's maid in all of Britain!"

"Flattery will not get you anywhere, my lady," she groused. "Let me look at you." She adjusted my bodice and smoothed down the skirts, before fussing over one or two loosened strands of hair. "Excellent. Are you wearing lip stain?" Her eyes narrowed on my mouth.

I blinked at the odd question. "No?"

"Your lips are quite red," she muttered, staring at them again and frowning until I had the urge to cover my mouth with my palm. "I hope you're not coming down with a cold. Chapped lips are quite unbecoming, though yours look rather swollen to tell the truth."

Oh. *Oh*. The realization washed over me, my cheeks aflame.

"Now your face has gone red, too," Anna exclaimed, and shoved the backs of her knuckles to my forehead. "Do you have a fever?"

Blushing harder, I swatted her away. "No, goodness, Anna. I'm just hot from rushing around. Truly, I am fine, I promise you."

My lips are red only from kissing and my cheeks are red from remembering how wickedly delicious it was.

That explanation would *not* go over well.

"Quickly, let's slip downstairs before Zia arrives and my subterfuge is discovered," I said, giving myself another quick glimpse in the mirror before sweeping from the room.

I knew I'd have to explain *something* to the girls, but at least it wouldn't be to my mother. Ela and Zia would understand. They'd told a few tall tales themselves over the years. Mama, categorically, would not. I ran down the servants' staircase again to one of the front salons, which was adjacent to the foyer. From there, I would see the minute Zia and Rafi arrived.

Luckily, I had to wait only about fifteen minutes before I saw Zia's distinct head of bronze-brown spirals. Dressed in a gorgeous gold gown that complemented her complexion, she was accompanied by her doting fiancé. My skin heated as I wondered dreamily if Tarik and I would look the same—so in love and happy—and draw the envy of others. Was he already inside? I couldn't wait for our dance.

As Zia approached, she shot me a narrow-eyed stare. Clearly, she had received what I was sure had become a rather cryptic message from Sally—who had been waiting for her outside—that I was to join them. I greeted Rafi with a grin as he shook his head with a resigned look and raised brows. He was very used to his own fiancée's penchant for mischief, so it was a relief that he remained silent.

"You will explain later," Zia told me under her breath in no uncertain terms.

I nodded. "I will, don't worry."

As we strolled into the ballroom, the majordomo announced our names, and I immediately felt my mother's stare crash into me from across the room where she was in conversation with my aunt. Following Zia and Rafi, I kept my face serene, with my chin high and a placid smile on my lips.

Nonetheless, I was instantly accosted by my mother at the bottom of the stairs and steered off to the side. We still stood in sight of many guests, but she had an uncanny ability to speak without moving her lips, especially if one was getting chastised. Ansel and I had often joked that she would have been a gifted ventriloquist in another lifetime.

"Rosalin!" she hissed. "What is the meaning of—?"

But I was saved from having to answer as my father strolled to his duchess's side, a small smile on his handsome face. "Papa! You're back!"

"Hullo, my girl. You're looking exceptionally radiant this evening." A glance that missed nothing panned over me, and I gulped, folding my still-bruised lips between my teeth. "I've received reports from my steward that you have finally been receptive to a gentleman's suit. An influential young Frenchman from a noble family is my understanding?"

I cringed inwardly at that last bit, considering my liberal embellishment of Tarik's lineage. Had Blake been the one to inform him of the last bit? It also wouldn't surprise me that my father's staff had been keeping an eye on my progress during the season in his absence. Thank goodness I'd been extra vigilant with my second identity. "Yes, Papa. I intend to introduce him to you this evening."

"Now is as good a time as any," he said. "Let's meet whoever put that besotted look on my daughter's face, shall we?"

A blush lit my cheeks. "Of course, Papa."

My mother opened her mouth to argue, but buoyed by my father's approval, I retreated to find Tarik. Both Ela and Zia were waiting for me a handful of steps away, though I couldn't stop to talk to them. Ignoring the justified outrage on both their faces when I skated past, I shot them an apologetic glance and continued my hurried tour of the ballroom, searching for one person. But Tarik wasn't anywhere to be found.

I spotted my lady's maid near the open doors to the terrace.

"Anna, have you seen—?" I didn't have to finish before she pointed outside. Her ashen expression said it all . . . that something was *dire*. My heart palpitated when I finally saw Tarik, and then dropped when I registered the four boys he stood with.

Oh no.

Blake . . . and Will with the bloody twins.

Panicked, I hastened toward them through the terrace doors, hoping to deter the unavoidable collision of my two worlds, but from their perplexed expressions and the stricken look on Tarik's face, I gathered I was much too late. Even the darkened, overcast sky threatening to open up portended something horrible.

"A French count's nephew, you say?" Will blurted. "Since when?"

"But weren't you a subsizar at Trinity?" Klaus demanded, staring at Blake, who must have attempted to perform introductions, not knowing the Trinity boys would have already known each other.

"And Roz's tutor," Kristof added.

Shit, shit, shit.

"Yes, where's Lord Ansel?" Tarik said, his skin flushing. "He can explain."

Blake frowned as his auburn brows shot up. "Ansel's in Greece, mate. He's been gone since April."

"No, he's here. He's at Trinity." Tarik's expression was slightly wild with the panic I was already feeling, though for different reasons. "There's Lady Rosalin, his cousin, ask her. She knows."

Those blue eyes collided with mine, the relief in them swiftly followed by confusion at my complete lack of surprise after

Blake's revelation and the immense culpability I could not hide for the life of me. I gulped hard, blood rushing in my ears as my friends stared.

Blake turned. "Roz?"

The nickname was the match to unlit tinder. I flinched.

Jaw slackening, Tarik went pale, and I could see the exact moment my house of cards started to topple. *"Roz?"* he echoed softly.

"Wait," I begged, hand reaching out even as he reared away, horror bleeding over his features. "I can explain . . ."

PART III

Oh, what a tangled web we weave
When first we practice to deceive!

—Sir Walter Scott, *Marmion*

CHAPTER SEVENTEEN

> If you be affronted, it is better . . . to pass it by in silence and with a jest, though with some dishonor, than to endeavor revenge . . . If you can keep reason above passion, that and watchfulness will be your best defendants.
>
> —Isaac Newton

Every so often, I had the awful dream of being naked in front of the entire *ton* during my come-out. All the guests would be dressed in their finery, and when it was my turn, instead of descending the staircase wearing the most beautiful gown, I wouldn't have a single stitch of clothing covering me. I'd be exposed to all and sundry, and everyone could clearly see each imperfection, each blemish, and each secret flaw I tried so valiantly to hide. They would know that beneath all the silk and jewels, I was nothing but a fraud. The way I'd always felt on the inside—like I never belonged in the first place.

Well, *this* was exponentially worse than that.

My eyes were locked on Tarik, all the words of explanation lodged in my throat like jagged rocks. I could feel Will's baffled stare and the rapt interest of the twins, as well as Blake's riveted curiosity. Of all the people here, he knew me best.

At least, until I'd met Tarik.

But my brain was clogged with so many falsehoods that it was difficult to sort through them all. The lives of my Ansel alter ego and Lady Rosalin were colliding in a manner that made it impossible to separate them . . . and yet, I had to. For everyone's sake.

"Rosalin," my mother's voice called out, and my eyes fluttered shut as I knew my father wouldn't be far behind to witness this absolute catastrophe. Sure enough, hushed murmurs through the ballroom preceded the duke's approach.

"Castleton," my father commanded, making me jump, as he bore down on Blake, whose gaze went wide. "What's this I hear about Greece? My nephew has been at university. My solicitor has been receiving regular reports from the Master of the College."

My jaw clenched. Someone must have overheard Blake's careless words and scurried over to tell the duke.

"Uh . . ." Blake's mouth opened and closed like a dying fish, his face going an awful color of puce at the secret he'd inadvertently revealed. "N-nothing, Your Grace . . ."

"Speak up, boy," my father said in a low voice that did not bode well for anyone. It was when he got quiet that people had to worry. As Ansel's best mate, Blake would know that better than anyone, considering how much trouble he and my cousin had been in over the years.

You could hear a pin drop as Blake licked dry lips. "H-he's . . . No, it was a silly jest . . ."

My father's eyebrows jumped to his hairline.

I am so cooked.

In my peripheral vision, I could see necks craning as people strained to see why the duke and duchess had marched outside to the terrace. Could this get any worse? How many people were going to behold my impending downfall? My palms were clammy, my nerves shot to hell as I ran through each scenario that could save me, discarding them as quickly as they rose.

Somehow, I had to come clean *without* ending up in disgrace.

Without *Tarik* being a casualty of my hubris.

I sucked in a breath. "Papa, this is all my f—"

But the whispered start of my confession was overshadowed by a sudden rumpus in the ballroom, music petering out and the sounds of chatter rising anew as someone unexpected burst in through the upper doors. "By God, is this a party, or is this a *party*?"

We all swiveled in shock at the very familiar voice.

And there stood my cousin at the top of the stairs in all his dandyish glory, and the unexpected answer to my very fervent prayers. Goodness, I had never felt so relieved in all my life.

Had he received my letter? I hadn't wanted him here for the ball, considering the knife-edged balancing act of my two identities, but in truth, his timing could not have been better . . . not that it would save me from what was to come with Tarik, but at least my father was one less calamity to worry about. My cousin descended the staircase three steps at a time like an uncultured lout, and the crowd parted to let him through.

He embraced my mother, kissing her on the cheek. "Auntie Susu, don't you look radiant."

"Ansel, dearest, we do not conduct ourselves thus," she chided him, smiling, and I could hear the sudden intake of breath from behind me like another nail in my proverbial coffin.

"Sorry, Auntie," he said jovially. "Hullo, Uncle. Took me forever to get here. My sincerest apologies for being late."

"Clearly, you're not in Greece," the duke said, eyes narrowed as he glared at poor Blake, who visibly quailed from the withering blast of irritation.

Ansel shrugged with a relaxed grin. "Of course not, Uncle. I wouldn't dare miss Auntie Susu's ball." He embraced his own mother, who appeared beside my parents, delighted to see her son.

He looked good. His sleek black hair was longer and curling over his shoulders, his dark eyes sparkling with happiness and good health. I didn't dare look at Tarik or my Cambridge friends, whose gazes I could feel flocking back and forth as though trying to work out a difficult mathematical puzzle. It wasn't all that difficult.

When faced with the true version of my cousin, the differences were small but noticeable to a discerning eye. People who knew us would *know.*

Because Roz looked like me . . .

Pale, dark haired, dark eyed, and deeply, unforgivably guilty.

My father cleared his throat, with another annoyed look to Blake, and signaled for the orchestra to resume. My aunt and mother followed him, though Mama kept glancing back at Ansel as if she suspected something troublesome might occur but her usual decorum prevented her from causing a scene in front of guests. For once, I found myself grateful for societal expectations. The boot might drop tomorrow, but it wouldn't today.

"Ansel, mate," Blake said, slinging an arm over his shoulder with a wary glance to the duke to make sure he was otherwise occupied before dragging my cousin inside. "Next time send a messenger, will you? Your father nearly skewered me."

At the last moment before closing the terrace doors behind them, Blake turned to spear me with a look that said I wouldn't be getting off scot-free either, but it wasn't him I was worried about. Anna shot me a sympathetic glance, but I couldn't even draw comfort from that. I knew I would have to face my fate eventually, so I sucked in a breath and pivoted.

My Cambridge friends were still gaping at me, though I wasn't sure if they were gawking at Lady Rosalin or the truth about my deception that was now coming to dreadful light.

Feeling like a coward, I felt my knees wobble before meeting Will's stare next. His blue gaze swam with bewilderment, but he wasn't stupid. It might take him more time than Tarik, but he'd figure it out eventually. The Ansel who had appeared on the terrace might have resembled the false version that I'd been pretending to be, but we weren't *identical,* and my cousin certainly was not the *Roz* my new friends had gotten to know.

"Will?" I whispered, resting my palm on his arm.

"Roz," he said softly, face still wreathed in confusion. "I don't understand. Who was that gentleman who claimed to be your cousin? And why are you wearing a gown?"

Not why did you lie to us and pretend to be a boy . . .

My lashes dipped as my eyes stung with helpless tears. I hadn't meant for any of it to end up like this.

"Because she *is* a girl." The sentence, delivered in a vicious monotone, came from the boy standing to my right. Tarik. I lifted my guilt-ridden gaze to his. "Isn't that correct, Lady Rosalin? Or should I call you *Roz*?" The last was hissed with so much venom that I flinched, the ire in his expression like razor-sharp blades.

His lip curled. "Were you so idle and bored in your fancy mansion with your middling daily amusements that you decided to take on a whole new identity for the fun of it? Toy with people's lives because you could?" He blew out a harsh breath. "You claimed you weren't a thing like the Lord Ansel Chen I knew, and you're right. You are much worse."

"It's not like that," I whispered urgently, my heart squeezing. "Please give me a chance to explain."

At that exact moment, like an ill-fated, portentous sign, lightning forked across the sky, and the overcast clouds rumbled ominously. Everyone else but the two of us fled indoors, and we stood there like two immovable objects, frozen like stone statues, when the skies opened up and a deluge broke free. I didn't even care that I was being soaked or that I was in danger of being struck by lightning.

"My lady, you have to come inside," Anna urged through the cracked door.

But I could not move.

The intense blue gaze I so loved felt like shards of ice skewering me in place. "It was *you*, all along. *Lying*."

"No, it wasn't all lies. Tarik, please—"

But his eyes flashed when I whispered his name, his face laced with betrayal as he spun on his heel and marched off into the arbor in the downpour. With a hand in the air to Anna as well as Will and the twins, who were peering from behind the terrace doors, to stop them from following us, I rushed behind him, uncaring that I was without a chaperone or that my reputation was at stake. I'd much rather *that* be flayed than my character, as insignificant as it might be to him. It was important to me. I had to make sure he understood.

That he knew how *sorry* I was.

His steps were quick and frenzied, as though he were being pursued by the devil himself. In truth, with the storm upon us, that was how it felt even as I begged him to slow down or stop. My pleas fell on deaf ears as if all he wanted to do was to get away from me. But I was too stubborn to let him, too proud not to attempt to explain my reasoning, and too scared of losing him forever not to follow. Not to *try*. My dress was soaked through, my hair was plastered to my skull, and I was certain I looked like a drowned rat, but none of that mattered.

"Tarik, wait!"

"Go back inside, Lady Rosalin," he snarled, stopping so abruptly that I nearly crashed into him. Rivulets of water streamed down his face, his clothing drenched and waterlogged.

"No, I have to explain!" I shouted as a crack of thunder obliterated my voice.

"You've done enough," he yelled underneath the sound of the rain and rolling thunder, his eyes burning with fury and so many other emotions I could barely pick them apart. "I told you things I've never told anyone else. I *trusted* you."

"It might have started out as a ruse, but it was still me. I need you to believe that, and I would never betray your trust," I said wildly. "I told you things, too, that no one knows."

"But not that you were pretending to be a man to enroll in university?"

Fisting my hands, I stared at him. "You *know* women aren't allowed to attend. You *know* the challenges my sex faces. Is it such a stretch to imagine that one of us might pretend to be male just to have the slimmest chance to learn? Many have done it, like Sophie Germain and Émilie du Châtelet. I am not the first!"

"And that makes it acceptable?" he shouted over the rain as he marched deeper into the arbor.

Stubbornly, I followed until the thickness of the trees blotted out some of the downpour. "Of course not, but perhaps you can be brought to some level of empathy to understand what kind of risks have to be taken so we can be treated like equal citizens."

He raked a hand through his wet hair. "You lied to me."

"And you didn't?" I accused him, referring to his embellished affluence. "You didn't see a way to crack open some of the doors that had been previously closed to you? To create opportunity out of a system designed to be against those without influence, wealth, or power. How dare you accuse me of something while you wallow in hypocrisy?"

"It's hardly the same thing," he bit out.

"Isn't it?" I demanded just as bitingly. "You invented a new identity to infiltrate the *ton* to get investors for your project. I invented a new identity to pursue educational opportunities. Why is your offense forgivable while mine is not? Because I'm a *woman*?"

"No. It has nothing to do with your sex." Nonplussed, he stared at me in silence, rain still soaking us from the branches above as we stood in the middle of the arbor withering beneath the rage of a summer squall that mirrored the storms inside us. "Was all of this some kind of game to you?" he asked in a broken voice.

"You know it wasn't," I replied, throat thickening with emotion. "None of it was a game. I never expected to meet anyone like you or to feel like I had somehow found my place in the world. For the first time in my life, I felt like I belonged somewhere. With people like me. With you." I felt my tears coming, though they were hidden by the rain. "Do you know how heady that is for a girl who has felt out of place her whole life?"

"I understand that more than you think," he said. "Why didn't you tell me?"

"I *couldn't,*" I replied. "As my tutor at Trinity, you would have been obligated to report me, report that I was impersonating another student, and I didn't want to lose my chance to be at Cambridge. I also didn't want to lose the only boy who has ever remotely cared about me. Whom I care"—I swallowed hard—"cared about, too. You were the closest thing to a match I could ever dream of."

He laughed hollowly, then his mouth flattened into a hard line. "You and I both know I could never be a match for you. Your father would never allow it."

"I don't care what my father wants!" I shouted. I stepped close then, water pouring into my eyes, and yet, all I could see was him. I fisted my hands into his wet clothes and yanked him toward me. "Don't you get it? I only want you. And even if you hate me right now, I know you want me, too."

His eyes flamed with passion and anger, everything raw and real twining between us. His heartbeat hammered above mine as I shoved myself to my tiptoes and slammed my mouth to his. The kiss felt more like an attack than something delicate—a clashing of lips and teeth. A battleground of power underscored by stubborness. We both didn't want to lose.

And then suddenly, Tarik's palms came up between us to cup my cheeks, his fingers achingly tender on my skin, and his mouth softened its assault. He caressed my lips and soothed with his tongue, and it was all I could do not to melt into a puddle at his feet.

We kissed for what seemed like hours, learning and mapping each other with soft swipes and gentle nudges through the last of the rain, until nothing more fell from the rapidly clearing skies. By the time we finally broke apart, I was shivering in my damp dress though I had never felt warmer. Our eyes and bodies remained locked together until the sound of a shout made us both startle.

"Rosalin! Where are you?"

That sounded like Blake. God, I had to be in so much trouble, but I couldn't bring myself to care, not when Tarik was holding me like this.

"I'm so sorry," I whispered to him.

His thumb stroked over my cheeks. "I'm . . . sorry, too."

"What are you sorry for?" I asked, catching the note of regret in his tone.

He stepped back, hands falling and leaving me bereft of his embrace, as ice slivered through me. I couldn't read his eyes, but his palm slid over his mouth. He rubbed at his lips as if trying to erase the feel of me. "We shouldn't have done this."

"Kissed?"

But before he could answer, Blake appeared in the arbor with Anna and Ansel in tow. The expression on Tarik's face was nothing short of murderous. Blake's gaze swung between the two of us, and for once, he read the situation for what it was. None of his usual playfulness was present.

"I care for her like a sister, St. Clair, nothing more," he said quietly, and then looked to me. "Your parents sent me to find you. You need to come back with us now before the gossip gets any worse."

Resigned, I nodded. "Fine. Give us a minute, please."

Not meeting my eyes after they retreated a few feet away, Tarik ran a palm over his wet hair. "I need space and time," he said slowly. "Time to figure this out." He shook his head. "I can't just forget that any of this happened, that you pretended to be a whole other person."

"I was still *me*!" I said, desperation taking hold as the tenuous thread between us started to fray. "That was my brain, my opinions, my sentiments, *my* heart."

"You lied for months, Rosalin," he said tiredly. "And you're right, I did, too, and I have to take accountability for my choices and actions. I'm sure Lord Ridley and Mr. Nasser will change their minds about the proposition and have something to say about my duplicity. You can't build anything good off a lie."

"But what if the lie is a necessity?" I asked.

He exhaled. "No situation should justify telling a falsehood, even if it might be convenient or helpful to do so. I was wrong to do what I did. And so were you."

A tear slid down my cheek, no longer hidden by the rainfall. Sorrow shone in his glassy blue eyes as we stared at each other in silence. "So, what happens now?"

"I go back to Trinity and hope that none of this follows me there," he said.

"You're going to leave just like that?"

He huffed a humorless laugh. "No, not just like that. But in a way in which I can protect myself. I'm not a toy, Rosalin, and neither is my heart, though we both find ourselves painfully at your mercy. I need to reconcile my truths and you need to do the same. Perhaps I was merely a diversion for you, after all, and none of this was real."

"How can you say that? *Everything* was real," I croaked, wondering if heartbreak was unendurable, because everything inside of me felt like it was splintering apart, without any hope of ever being repaired. His heavy words were like sledgehammers against the fragility of blood and bone. "You are wrong, Tarik. You know you're wrong."

"Am I?" His smile was sad. "My wish is for you to be happy someday, Lady Rosalin, and that you find whomever it is you were looking for."

My tears rolled down my cheeks unimpeded at the formal address, as he distanced himself from me . . . from us. As though he were saying goodbye. I knew I had crossed lines, but surely everything he'd come to know about me might be enough to convince him that we were worth fighting for. That *I* was worth fighting for.

But in the end, I wasn't.

Standing there in the cold and the dark, I stared at him as he walked away from me forever, the answer to his wish glued to my tongue.

You . . . I was looking for you.

CHAPTER EIGHTEEN

> Truth is ever to be found in the simplicity, and not in the multiplicity and confusion of things.
>
> —Isaac Newton

"You need to eat, Rosalin," Ela cajoled, to which I ducked and buried my head beneath the counterpane, which smelled distinctly sour.

"And leave this bedchamber before it starts stinking of bed piss like a sick room," Zia added, wrinkling her nose as if the odor was more pervasive than just on my bedding.

"Zia!" Ela chastised, which I also would have done if I had the will to care. Ela lifted a bowl of broth that one of the maids handed her, the smell of it making me feel instantly nauseated. "Please, Rosalin. Just a spoonful or two, and I promise we will leave you alone."

"I'm not hungry," I said.

"She hasn't eaten a proper meal in days," Anna said, her low voice missing its usual caustic edge. One would think she'd be furious now with my apathy, but she only sounded worried. "That's why I sent the message to you."

It had been a week or two—perhaps more—since the ill-fated ball that had ruined my life. I hadn't taken to my bed in a fit of self-pity, but the despair I had felt had been unimaginable to bear. I wanted to sleep it away like Little Snow-White in the fairy tales Tarik so esteemed. But perhaps that was a bit melodramatic.

Admitting to my best friends that I had schemed and lied had felt unconscionable. After I'd done it, I hadn't been able to look any of them in the eye. And so, I'd hidden like a coward and refused to see anyone, until Anna sounded the alarm.

"You need to wash, Rosalin," Zia said. "You smell like ten-day-old stockings sitting upon a round of moldy cheese left in the sun."

God, she was histrionic—and obsessed with old cheese and smelly stockings.

I seemed to recall an old duke suitor of hers whom she'd described similarly. Come to think of it, that also sounded exactly like my moldy old suitor, the Duke of Bentley. Did all old dukes smell like stockings and cheese? I bit back a ragged laugh. Was *that* now in my future? I'd take the prepubescent nose-picker himself, Renton, over him in a heartbeat.

Too bad I didn't want either of them.

When Zia cleared her throat expectantly, the slightest twinge of shame rolled through me. I honestly could not remember the last time I'd left the bed, much less to bathe properly. Ducking my head to my armpit, I sniffed cautiously and grimaced. She wasn't wrong. Not exactly moldy cheese-stockings but not fresh roses either.

"Will you termagants leave if I promise to have a bath?" I muttered, peeking over the bedclothes with a shamefaced scowl.

"And eat a meal," Ela added. "A full one, not just a nibble or two."

I huffed a breath and regretted that, too. I'd have to give my teeth a good scrubbing as well. Nothing like falling apart on the inside to mirror it on the outside. "Fine."

"And we will wait right here to make sure that you hold up your end of the bargain," Zia said firmly. "We know all the tricks in the book." She peered at my head. "And wash your hair! It looks like a deranged rodent made a nest on the top of your head. And no boy, I repeat, *no boy* is worth weeping over to the point that you have snot trails crusting your cheeks."

My hands flew to my face, and finding only smooth, uncrusted skin, I let out a curse. "You're the worst!"

I turned in my bed to meet those glacial amber eyes that glittered in an unsmiling countenance. Zia scrutinized me and placed her hands on her hips. She was a force to be reckoned with on a regular day. Today, she embodied a cyclone bearing down on me without remorse or mercy. I was too tired to argue, but the truth was I'd grown sick of my own company.

Gingerly, I hobbled out of bed while Ela and Zia made themselves comfortable in the small sitting salon adjacent to my private chambers, and I glowered at Anna. "Turncoat."

Anna's smile was spare as she led me into the bathing chamber to the steaming bath. "Turncoat or not, my lady, you needed help. I was worried that your deep, incurable melancholy would send you to the lunatic asylum for hysteria, but then I realized I would never be so lucky to finally be rid of you." She sniffed dramatically.

"You love me," I said.

For once, she had no scathing retort, which made me falter. "And you should be glad I do, my lady. Anyone else would have left you to rot in your own putrescence."

I let out a horrified giggle. That was an impressive word choice, but it did not surprise me. Anna also loved to read, though her tastes ran to novels and verse instead of textbooks. For a second, I wondered if, like me, she'd had any dreams of education beyond becoming a lady's maid. She was obsessed with poems and usually carried around a notebook that she scribbled in. Maybe when Tarik finished his club, a woman like her might be welcomed for poetry discussions.

My heart clenched at the thought of him. He hated me—not just for lying to him but for ruining his chance to secure investors for his own social club. My already-swollen eyes stung, the pressure behind the bridge of my nose building. Deuce it, I was *done* crying!

Don't think about him.

I inhaled a handful of bolstering breaths as I stepped into the soothing, warm rose-and-vanilla scented water. With a sigh, I leaned back as Anna washed my greasy hair, combing through the tangles with a gentle hand. She might be frustrated with me and have an unnaturally sharp tongue, but she was never cruel.

"There, doesn't that feel better?" she asked, after she'd lathered my locks and rinsed them clean. "Now let's get you up and moving. I told Cook to make your favorite steamed buns."

The thought of food, for once, didn't make my stomach roll. Instead, it rumbled.

After I dressed in a soft navy day gown, with my hair left loose over my shoulders to dry, I joined my friends in the antechamber. Zia was in the process of stuffing an entire steamed bun into her mouth, practically moaning at the flavor of the sweet pork filling.

"Those are mine," I said petulantly.

She rolled her eyes. "Thought you were on a hunger strike, which means these are for public consumption."

"Don't make me fight you, Zia," I warned, having had enough of her incessant needling.

She grinned. "*You* want to fight *me*?"

"If you steal my food, I am going to have to teach you a lesson," I threatened. "You're not the only one who has been learning things in secret."

"There she is," Zia crooned. "I was wondering where our friend had gone, cowering and hiding in her room like a little mouse when Ela and I both know you are anything but, even if you play the part of the demure, obedient lady so exceptionally well."

I knew why she was goading me, of course. She wanted to make me vexed enough to feel something more than numbness. Perhaps she understood more than she was letting on. Both she and Ela had had their share of tribulations, especially when it came to the gentlemen they chose. But sadly, it wasn't the same. There was no way Tarik would ever forgive or trust me again.

Heavy of heart, I approached my friends and sat in one of the plush armchairs, reaching for a plump bao and tucking my knees beneath me. "I wasn't cowering. I was . . ."

"Hurting," Ela said softly. "I understand that all too well. Our circumstances are somewhat similar. When I thought I'd lost Keston by pretending to be Lyra, I felt helpless." She exhaled roughly as if the thought of what had nearly come to pass was much too painful to remember. "But you're stronger than you know, Rosalin. We all are."

"I'm not as strong as the two of you," I murmured. "You both won the loves of your lives. Rafi turned out to be the rock you needed, Zia, and Keston loved you enough to forgive you, Ela, because deep down, he always knew who you truly were. You both have your happy endings while I'll probably be betrothed to Bentley or Renton within the month." I couldn't keep the morose expression from my face. "And Tarik hates me."

The sound of his name on my lips felt like knives through my chest.

"Do you want to talk about it?" Zia asked.

There was nothing on earth that would make me *want* to talk about him, and yet, I knew I should. Somehow, I had to purge all the chaotic feelings that were rioting inside me, and who better to tell than my friends? They were here for *me,* not because they had nothing better to do. I opened my mouth, just as my bedchamber door crashed open.

"You better be decently attired," Blake drawled, right before walking in like he owned the place. My cousin followed on his heels with an exasperated look.

"Honestly, we all know he's an uncouth boor," Ansel said by way of apology.

Blake grinned and sprawled on the sofa, kicking one leg out

and immediately stuffing a whole bun into his mouth. "Mmm, so good. Can we get more of these? Where's my darling Anna? Can we have Cook make some more?" he called out. "I know you're lurking in here somewhere, protecting the questionable virtue of this degenerate pretender!"

Anna appeared, thank goodness, though she went pink at Blake's overly flirtatious gaze. Lord, was no one safe? Anna was betrothed to Henry for goodness' sake. She still shot Blake a smile and practically skipped off to do his bidding.

I scowled at my friend. "Not everyone is like you, you libertine! And my virtue is decidedly *un*questionable, thank you very much."

He snorted. "Oh? Then why was a certain gentleman looking at you as if he wanted to devour you whole in the arbor . . . as if said virtue was hanging on by the skin of its teeth?"

I blushed, my cheeks heating. "You are truly a wretch! There was no devouring. Or skin or teeth. Or any of it!"

"Thou dost protest too much," Zia said smirking.

I aimed the full force of my glare upon her. "Not a word."

Ansel walked up behind me and propped his chin on my head. "Seems like you've cocked it good and proper, Cousin. You promised me you wouldn't get caught and that no one would suspect a thing."

I huffed a breath. "I suppose I bit off more than I could chew."

The girls frowned in unison. "Wait, Ansel knew all along?" Ela asked, pouring three steaming cups of tea before handing me one.

"How do you think he was able to live his best life in Europe?" I replied, glancing at him. "Was it everything you hoped for?"

"And more," my cousin said. "Life-changing."

Much like Cambridge had been for me.

With a sigh, I blew on the hot tea as Blake grunted with disbelief. "So let me get this right. You pretended to be your cousin? As in a *gentleman*?"

"Like it's hard?" I scoffed as Zia and Ela dissolved into giggles. "You walk around swaggering and talk about yourselves ad nauseam. Pretending to be a boy is easy."

"Not so easy if you got found out," he shot back.

Oh, I wanted to stomp over there and punch him right in his infuriating nose. "Thanks to *you*."

He pressed an aggrieved palm to his chest. "Me?"

"You were the one who told them that Ansel was in Greece! Why couldn't you have just stayed quiet? You're always blathering, Blake, like your mouth is a bloody broken faucet. You're worse than half the women in the *ton,* I swear—" I broke off, registering the hurt on Blake's face much too late.

"It's not his fault, Roz," Ansel said gently, lowering himself to the carpet beside my chair and propping his elbows on his knees. "He can't be responsible for your actions."

Disgusted with myself, I closed my eyes, pressing the bridge of my nose hard with my thumb and forefinger. "You're right. I'm sorry, Blake. I didn't mean it."

"Forgiven," he chirped, happy again now that one of the kitchen maids had delivered a freshly steamed basket of bao.

"Just like that?" I asked.

He shrugged. "Sometimes the hardest part of apologizing is the apology itself. You don't have to overthink it, Roz. If you're sorry, say you're sorry and mean it. Sincerity always comes through, and if someone cares enough to receive your words, then it'll work out. If they don't, then that's nothing you can control."

"I don't think it's going to be that easy with St. Clair," I said, burying my face in my hands, knowing well that Blake was talking about Tarik and not the apology I'd just given him. "You saw him in the arbor. He was so angry that I'd deceived him. I don't think there's any coming back from this."

"Wait." Zia stood so quickly that her chair nearly toppled back, anchored at the last second by Ansel's foot. "You mean to tell me that YOU, Rosalin Chen, masterminded nearly an entire term at Cambridge University pretending to be Ansel Chen, while actively doing reading, coursework, and having academic discussions about what I presume is a strenuous academic curriculum, to the point where you'd made actual friends who seem to genuinely like you, along with a tutor who was very impressed by your accomplishments this term, WANT TO GIVE UP NOW?" She practically bellowed the last part.

"Um, yes?" I muttered, slightly afraid after her unhinged rant.

"No." She shook her head. "I won't allow it. Honestly, how can someone so brilliant be so nonsensical? Not everyone can thrive at university, much less a woman, who isn't allowed to attend in the first place. You're a trailblazer!" Then she turned to Ansel. "No offense, but everyone knows you're not the sharpest tool in the shed, even with your fake spectacles."

"Oy!" Ansel protested, shoving said spectacles up his nose. "I'm sharp, and they're very real."

"Ela?" I asked, ignoring my cousin's outburst.

She threw both hands into the air with a grimace. "Don't look at me. I'm with her. Zia's not wrong. Do you know how *amazing* what you've done is? You did something none of us has ever attempted, proving we're just as smart as men." She stopped, thinking for a moment. "But let's pause briefly. What were you hoping to accomplish? What did you want?"

I shrugged. "I wanted to learn about mathematics and astronomy from the best. I wanted to do something for me before I lost all freedom," I said dismally. "You all know what Papa said. He was going to pick a husband for me by the end of the season if I couldn't find someone suitable myself."

"And your gentleman tutor wasn't in the running?" Ela asked frowning. "Or have I misread this entire situation somehow?"

"He's a commoner," I said quietly. "The thing is . . . we fabricated his origins so he could make some acquaintances to help him get started on his brilliant idea of a social club where men and women would be equally welcomed. The pedigree falsehoods were my idea, not his. No one would take him seriously if he wasn't already *someone* of influence." I huffed. "We might be powerful, but we are as shallow as a puddle in the height of summer."

Blake sat up, his expression thoughtful. "I liked St. Clair's proposal. I thought it was well thought-out, and if he had the proper financials, it could be a windfall for everyone involved. Nothing like it exists in London. Not White's, Boodle's, Danforth's

Den, or any of the others. Ridley and Nasser liked the concept as well," Blake went on. "It doesn't matter to us what his lineage is. I'm only speaking for myself, of course."

"Blake's right," Ela said. "Keston would likely care about the odds of success, growth, and measurable returns."

Zia nodded, eyes shining with excitement. "Rafi, too. And he has more than enough money to invest in anything that takes his fancy . . . or *mine*. And what a brilliant idea, not just financially. Think of the doubled membership by adding women, but also accessibility for our sex to participate in intellectual discussions. Can you imagine attending a literary discussion with Mary Shelley at the forefront? I would positively *die*." She pretended to swoon, and we all smiled, knowing her singular obsession with said author. "I hardly think his lack of a title would matter in this case."

Nodding fervently, Blake demolished another bun and patted his stomach. "Besides, your boy is supposedly on track to become a bloody *Fellow* at Trinity College. I'm quite sure that means he's already outclassing half the *ton* in intelligence."

I bit my lip. He wasn't *my* boy.

"He is a genius," I said through a tight throat.

Dejection hit me like a tidal wave again. Was he thinking about me? *Missing* me the way I was missing him? Everything felt surreal, like I was dreaming or imagining it all. Maybe I would wake up and get in the carriage to go back to Trinity the next morning, and everything would be back to normal.

But that wasn't true. I *couldn't* go back there. Not as a woman anyway. And it wasn't just Tarik and me; Will and the twins knew now as well.

Secrets had a way of coming out . . .

And the truth was I'd already lost Tarik enough opportunities and prospects. I wouldn't want to jeopardize his future at the college, if word were to get out. I'd had Anna scouring the newssheets and the gossip rags, but by some miracle, no one had written about the daughter of the Duke of Delmont dressing like a boy to attend university. But perhaps it was only a matter of time. There was speculation, of course, that I'd cavorted with a footman or spurned one of my suitors, which was why my father had seemed so furious at our ball.

A rap on the door had us all twisting around to see who it was as Anna answered. Mama entered the room in a swish of emerald skirts, and everyone immediately snapped to attention. The duchess had a way of doing that. She wasn't alone either. Dr. Barker, our family physician, followed in her wake.

"Your Grace," my friends murmured, as my mother canted her head in greeting, her eyes darting to me where I sat nibbling a half-eaten bao.

"Good, you're finally up, hái zi."

I gulped at her soft voice. The fact that she was calling me *child* in Chinese was indicative of her unusually frazzled state of mind. "Yes, Mama."

"Dr. Barker is here to have a look at you. When you weren't eating properly, I was worried. He'll see you in your chamber."

The doctor followed as I rose and padded obediently to the bedroom, accompanied by Anna, who stood by the closed door as chaperone. I perched on an armchair near the window as he opened his bag and pulled out his instruments.

"May I inspect your heart and lungs?" Dr. Barker asked in his high-pitched voice, and I gave my consent. It was something I'd always liked about him. He asked every time, which was uncommon. Most male doctors *didn't* ask for permission before they examined a patient. He lifted a stethoscope—a hollow wooden-and-brass tube resembling a telescope that I instantly wanted to study—in his delicately boned hands and placed the conical end to my back and the smaller end to his ear. He listened for a moment and then moved it lower. "Can you inhale for me, please?" When I complied, he listened again and then nodded. "And exhale. Good. When did you last eat?"

"I had a bit of bao when you arrived," I said. "But not much."

"Do you have pains when eating?"

I shook my head. "No, it's not that. I'm just not hungry."

He continued to check my eyes, my throat, and my ears before sitting back. I observed his face as he checked my pulse and temperature. At such close proximity, Dr. Barker's smooth chin and jaw were exceptionally clean-shaven . . . as in *not* shaven at all. His nose was large and his lips quite thin, but he certainly did not have the typical facial stubble of a man.

"The duchess said there was an incident with a young gent, and you might have caught a chill in the rain, but your lungs are clear." He paused, studying my wan face. "The mind, by way of the heart, can certainly have an impact on the body," he said as he closed his bag. "You need to keep yourself nourished, my lady, which means eating a balanced, healthy diet."

"I understand." I stared at him and felt an odd burst of admiration for everything he'd accomplished, every hurdle he'd soared over, and every obstacle he'd faced. Because he'd triumphed in the face of adversity and was living life according to his own terms. I admired that. If we could all live so authentically, people would be so much happier. Alas, not everyone had the means or the forbearance to do so, especially in an unforgiving world.

"Thank you, Dr. Barker."

"You're very welcome, my lady."

After the physician took his leave, I padded back into the antechamber, where he was speaking to my mother as they both left the room. She seemed lighter, which was a relief. I didn't want to cause her undue worry. I sent a reassuring glance to my friends and resumed my meal, making more of an effort to finish it. Their concerned gazes, however, did not relent.

"I promise I am fine," I said.

"Good," Ela and Zia chorused.

Another knock on the door had Anna rising to check again, and I wondered if it was my mother again, but a deep voice from one of the footmen ensued. "There's a young gent downstairs for you," Anna said. "Says his name is Viscount Humbolt and he must see you posthaste."

I blinked. What was *Will* doing here?

Anna pursed her lips. "He's not alone."

My heart shot like an arrow to my throat. *Surely not Tarik?* I shared a wild look with my friends as we collectively shoved to our feet and descended to the main floor like a herd of elephants. But when my eyes canvassed the group waiting in the front salon, the hope in me crashed.

He wasn't there.

Will was accompanied by the twins and Harold. Once more, my worlds were coming together—my old friends and my new ones—though this collision did not fill me with dread. I was glad to see them.

"Roz!" Will exclaimed and blushed. "Er, Lady Rosalin, I mean. Deuce it."

I forced a smile to my face. "Roz is fine."

"Lady Rosalin," Klaus crooned, giving me a once over. "Who knew all of *that* was under the glasses and facial hair."

Kristof made a smacking noise with his lips. "You're looking fetching today."

I let out a huff of laughter. I'd missed them, and it warmed me that they treated me the same. "Stop it, both of you."

They pouted in unison and then set their sights to Zia, who promptly held up a palm. "No. I cannot be responsible for any bloodshed. My fiancé has excellent aim."

Ela shook her head before the twin profligates could even swing her way. "Married."

"What a husband doesn't know won't hurt him," Klaus said, waggling his blond brows.

"Yes, but he'd hurt *you*," she replied with a wink. "And besides, *I* would know."

Good God, the twins were menaces. Herding the rest of us into the already-crowded salon, out of sight of the very curious staff who would undoubtedly report back to my parents, I signaled to Anna to close the door. "Everyone, find a seat."

When that was done, I made quick introductions. "This is my cousin, Lord Ansel, the real one." He grinned with an insouciant wave. “These three are Lord Blake, Lady Ela, and Lady Zia.” Then I pointed to the university boys in turn. “These are my mates from Trinity, Viscount William Humbolt, Mr. Klaus and Mr. Kristof Blendel, and Mr. Harold Jennings.” I exhaled and smoothed my dress, perching delicately on a chair. “Now, what are you all doing here?”

They exchanged a fraught look as Will blanched. “It’s St. Clair. He’s in trouble.”

CHAPTER NINETEEN

If I have seen further it is by standing on the shoulders of Giants.

—Isaac Newton

Dread instantly spiking in my veins, I stared at the boys from Trinity. Klaus pursed his lips, his handsome face wearing a fretful expression that wasn't typical for him. Neither of the twins cared about anything that didn't directly affect them, and they'd never had much fondness for Tarik. "He's in danger of being rusticated," Will continued. "If he doesn't come back to university to face the official complaint levied against him."

"Rusticated?" Ela asked.

"Suspended from the school," Harold supplied helpfully. "Temporarily at least, until he can speak for himself to defend against the accusations."

I blinked—I'd been holed up in my chambers for more than a fortnight. Tarik was supposed to have gone back to Cambridge to check in with the Master of the College. While my presence wasn't mandatory, his was, especially since he was still on track to becoming a Fellow and had specific milestones he needed to meet. "Wait, he hasn't returned? He's been here in London? And what accusations are you talking about?"

Will shook his head, his normally ruddy face pallid. "You know how the gossip mill is. After the ball, word got back to Trinity somehow, and of course, because the competition for a fellowship is so stiff, sometimes people will do anything to discredit others. You know that St. Clair was Second Wrangler, right?"

I nodded just as Zia interjected with, "I beg your pardon, what on earth is a Wrangler?"

Ansel scoffed aloud, and I wanted to roll my eyes. Considering *he* didn't value his education, to the point that he'd gone off on a grand tour, his reaction shouldn't have surprised me. "They are the top students who best the Mathematical Tripos examination at Trinity," he explained. "Basically, the most boring, self-absorbed, zealous pedants you can imagine."

"I like the real Lord Ansel," Kristof crowed.

"Only people who aren't academically gifted denigrate others for being so," I said with a scowl at my cousin before turning to Zia. "The Wranglers are the crème de la crème of the university, and it's extremely prestigious to be recognized as one. Most of them go on to be notable mathematicians and scientists. It's the reason Tarik received his nomination to be a Fellow. He's brilliant."

Will perked up. "Did you know that St. Clair enrolled at Trinity at fourteen? He was one of the youngest students to matriculate. He's one of the most dazzling minds of our generation."

"And yet he wants to open a social club," Blake mused. "Why not invent travel to the moon?"

Klaus let out a guffaw. "Because that's bloody impossible!"

"Nothing is impossible," I murmured, remembering the scientists and astronomers at the Royal Observatory charting stars, tracking data, and breaking earthly boundaries. "Even that. One day, someone might surprise us all. But enough about that, will someone please tell me what the deuce happened with Tarik?" I faltered as several pairs of eyes converged upon me.

"Tarik, is it?" Kristof pounced.

Botheration! I wanted to kick myself. Using one's given name was a familiarity reserved for family, bosom friends, and intimate relationships . . . which my tutor and I weren't supposed to have. I swallowed and cleared my throat. "Mr. St. Clair."

But my cheeks remained hot as though daring me to refute what everyone was already thinking. Ela and Zia already knew, and Blake and Ansel had seen us in the arbor. As far as the Trinity boys, Will's gaze was wide, the twins were grinning impishly, and Harold was blushing.

"Naughty, naughty, Lady Roz," Klaus teased, picking up where his dreadful brother left off. "Who knew the straitlaced St. Clair had it in him? The tutor and the student. He's gone up a few notches in my estimation."

"Focus!" I said, ignoring his teasing. "What's happening at Trinity? Will?"

Will drew a deep breath. "Basically, you know how the Third Wrangler has always been in competition with St. Clair because he's Second Wrangler? Well, when he got wind of the gossip that St. Clair had pretended to be someone he wasn't in London, he used it as ammunition to take out his biggest rival."

I frowned, something tickling my memory, and then it hit me like a punch to the gut. "Wait. Surely you don't mean James?"

The strange expressions of fury and bitterness on my friends' faces as they nodded in unison threw me. I thought Harold was going to cry. "Yes."

For a second, I couldn't reconcile what I was hearing. "*James*? As in *our* James? Redheaded, somewhat snobby, and uptight James? Our *friend*?"

"The very one," Kristof muttered. "Though he's clearly not a friend at all."

"How did he even find out?" I asked.

Harold gave a dejected sniff. "It was me. I'm sorry, Roz. I let it slip when the twins told me what happened after the ball, and I didn't know he'd be so conniving."

"It's not your fault that there's bad history there," I murmured. "They were the same year, correct?"

"Yes, they were at St. John's and then Trinity. He was Third Wrangler after the Tripos," Will explained. "St. Clair was second, which got him significant attention when he went into the Master of Arts program. He was up for recommendation as a future Fellow. James was fuming for years. He felt that he deserved the recognition that St. Clair received. An envy festered within him clearly."

Klaus nodded. "Rumor is that he even tried to discredit St. Clair by paying a scout to spy on him. James was almost found out, too, but the scout mysteriously disappeared."

I blinked. Why did that sound familiar? I racked my brain and came up with the answer a second later. Tarik was quite adamant that he thought *Ansel* had tried to sabotage him by having his scout steal his research notes for the Tripos. How had Tarik come to make that leap of logic? Had James alluded to it to take the heat off himself? Also, hadn't Tarik claimed that Ansel had pushed him into the river?

I turned to my cousin. "Did you and St. Clair ever have an altercation on the River Cam?"

Ansel shrugged. "Not that I can recall, but quite a bit of that time was a blur. Many boys got shoved into the water. Why do you ask?"

I shook my head. "He seemed to be under the impression that *you* told your scout to take his notes for the Tripos."

"That's preposterous," Ansel said, aghast. "I would *never* sabotage another student's work or position. All I remember of him is that he was quiet and barely spoke. In fact, he was much more confident at the ball, and until you asked me the question now, I wouldn't have guessed they were the same person."

"Would your scout have done something like that without your knowledge?" I pressed, frustrated when he shook his head. There *had* to be a link between the two. "Do you know the name Sir James Lowry of Essex?"

Blake whistled, then laughed. "I remember that bloody tosser. He made our lives a living hell, remember, Ansel?"

I'd forgotten that Blake had been enrolled at St. John's for that first two years, before he decided he could get a better education outside of an institution's walls. Blake had always marched to the beat of his own drum.

Ansel nodded, realization dawning. "That rotter kept reporting us to the proctors. He had a chip on his shoulder a mile wide. Threw the *sir* before his name around like it was gold and people were meant to bow. He loathed that we were both lords."

"He would have been in the last year of his bachelor's, the year he and St. Clair took the Tripos," I murmured. "We are talking about the same man, yes?"

Blake lifted a brow. "You said red hair, right? Plus a weasel face? Crooked teeth?"

"Not a weasel, exactly," I said, but I could see it, now that his true nature was being unveiled.

Out of all the Trinity boys, James had been the one I never had a real connection to. I recalled how he'd treated poor Harold and also how incensed he'd become when I'd filched his bread in the dining hall—one would think I'd robbed his pockets of actual coin. It was a small thing, but when someone was pretending to be a different person, small things were usually what gave them away. I should know.

Blake shook his head, peering at Ansel with a grin. "He definitely despised you for nicknaming him Sir Lowly."

"Not one of my finer moments," Ansel said. "How do you even remember these things? Our first year was a haze of drink and wom—" He sputtered to a stop with a sheepish glance at me and the other two girls.

"I remember everything," Blake said sagely, tapping his temple. "Everyone. Every place. Every time."

"You were rakes, we know," I bit out, my thoughts churning.

"But we have much bigger problems than that. Because if James hated you, wouldn't he have known all along that I wasn't the real Ansel? If I truly loathed someone, I would not forget their face, no matter how many years had passed."

The silence in the room was heavy and telling.

Blake swore softly under his breath.

"You're right. This goes deeper than any of us realized," Will said, his eyes round with apprehension.

Even the twins looked perturbed. Because if James knew of my impersonation and was holding that close to his chest like a villain with a winning hand of cards, how and when did he plan to use it? I was the daughter of an influential duke. I remembered his expression when he'd asked about my father, if he was a powerful man, in the dining room and the way his eyes had glittered with . . . *avarice*. Calculation, too. Tarik had said that James would do anything to get ahead . . . Did that include the possible extortion of a duke?

"Does Tarik know any of this?" I asked, not concerned that I was using his given name. If it was true and James had our secrets—*my secret*—in the palm of his hand, then our actual lives were at risk.

"Not yet," Will said. "We haven't been able to find him, and we have looked all over London."

I inhaled and bit my lip before glancing at Ansel. "Have you been to your apartments at The Albany?"

Surprise flared in his eyes. "Is that where he's been staying? Then, yes, and he's gone. The place was cleared out, spick-and-span. If you hadn't said anything, I wouldn't have fathomed anyone had been there. It's empty of his belongings. There's only an unfinished telescope there, tools, and some books."

"Those are mine," I said, heart sinking. I missed the days when I could focus on my small dream to build a telescope while Tarik looked on.

Bloody hell.

How would we find him? London was a big place.

My despair must have shown on my face, because Blake stood up. "We need to divide and conquer." I shot him a grateful look, and his lips curled into a reassuring smile. "It's evening, and if he's in town, my guess is he will be at a club somewhere. He mentioned that he enjoys a hand of cards when things are strained. I doubt he will be able to get into any of the member's clubs like White's or Boodle's, but we should still check those anyway. Ansel can take St. James's Street and Pall Mall. Will and Harold, you can go with him." He paused. "Ela and Zia can check with Ridley and Nasser to see if they know of any other places. Doppelgängers, you're with me." Klaus and Kristof seemed ecstatic at the prospect. "Roz, you can stay here, just in case a foxed lover boy shows up looking for you."

"Why would he . . . ?" I trailed off as the answer became obvious. When people were in their cups, they did unpredictable things. "Ela or Zia can stay here. I want to help. I can't sit here and do *nothing*."

"I'll stay," Ela volunteered, seeing my wild expression. "Zia will check in with Rafi and Keston."

"Thank you," I said with feeling. "Just give me a few minutes to change, and we can go."

The twins sat opposite Blake and me in the coach. It was Blake's carriage, since Ansel had taken ours. I could feel Blake's stare fluttering over the side of my face with equal amounts of curiosity and reluctant admiration.

"Stop staring at me," I hissed.

He chuckled and slapped his palm against his knee. "I wish I could. But with what you're wearing, it's astonishingly uncanny how much you look like Ansel. You pulled the wool over everyone's eyes."

"We *are* first cousins, Blake," I said dryly. "The children of twins. It's not a stretch of any capable imagination, even yours."

"Why the change?" Kristof asked. "You don't need to pretend you're a boy anymore."

"Highborn young ladies do not usually visit the West End, much less unmarried ones without a chaperone," I said, even though I *had* been there before unchaperoned with Tarik.

Blake snorted. "I honestly cannot fathom that you existed like this for months, pretending to be Ansel. No wonder you two and everyone else were so convinced," he said, jerking his chin to Klaus and Kristof, who couldn't stop staring, though for different reasons.

They were used to this version of me. But I'd bet anything they were trying to reconcile the lady I was beneath the spectacles, top hat, and men's clothing now that they knew the truth. I hadn't had time to fit the wig, so my hair was braided and tucked under a hat. I'd forgone the mustache and had barely been able to glue on the false facial sideburns.

I thought that I would have been discomfited putting on the costume, but it had felt like slipping into a comfortable skin. Not the elements of the disguise, but the person I embodied when camouflaged. It was ludicrous how at ease I was . . . like *this* was the true version of me: the smart, scholarly bookworm who preferred to gorge on celestial mechanics and build an amateur telescope rather than wear fancy gowns and dance at a ball.

I didn't want to be a boy. I enjoyed the freedom that came with pretending to be one, but I adored being authentically myself even more. And *this* girl wore what she wanted, built what she wanted, and loved who she wanted. For the first time in my life, I felt *free* . . . and the one person with whom I wanted to share that pivotal truth loathed me.

"Where to first?" Klaus asked, making me jump. "We don't know this area of London very well."

"Good thing I do, lads. Watch and learn," Blake said, leaning back and stretching his long arms.

I frowned at the way the twins were gawking at Blake as if he were some kind of idol and immediately shook my head. Nothing good could come of the three of them together, but right now, we needed to find Tarik.

"There's a tavern near Seven Dials," I said hesitantly. "Blue awning. We could check there."

Blake shook his head. "I don't even want to *hear* how you know about that place. It's a hellhole. Why would he go there?"

"He told me about it once," I fabricated. The chances that he would be there were low, considering the circumstances of how we'd been chased away last time, but I had to make sure, to cross it off the list.

When the carriage finally slowed in front of the familiar building, I bit my lip. I was Lady Rosalin the last time I'd been here and would likely not be recognized in my guise as a young lord, but it would put a damper on things if I were. Ansel and I did look uncannily alike, which could put *this* version of him in trouble if those men were still seeking their pound of flesh.

"Blake," I said quietly, pulling his arm as he went to descend the carriage steps after the twins. "I can't go in with you."

He frowned. "Why?"

"I can't tell you that," I said.

"Can't or won't?"

I sighed. "Both, but suffice it to say that the female side of me might be persona non grata here."

His eyes widened as my words registered. "Rosalin! Tell me you didn't!"

"Fine, I'll tell you I didn't. Scold me later, please," I said, shoving him out of the coach. "Check the gaming tables."

"You are in a *lot* of trouble, young lady," he said, and then grinned. "Only with me, though, because I would never break our sacred trust, but you must tell me everything or . . . I'll spill all your sordid secrets like a cracked teapot."

I rolled my eyes. "You're so dramatic. Go! And Blake?" He turned as I stuck my head out the coach door. "Do *not* corrupt the twins, or I swear I won't forgive you."

His lip curled into a smirk. "But just look at them, they're adorable! And there's two! Don't be stingy."

"No," I said sternly. "Or the only tea spilling to *everyone* we know will be yours."

"Spoilsport." He pouted.

Blake and the twins disappeared into the tavern. Settling back against the velvet seat, I waited and pondered on any other places that Tarik might visit, especially here in the West End. Wasn't there another gambling place that Blake had mentioned when he was talking about liking Tarik's proposal? Danforth's something or other.

My frown deepened as I realized I recognized the name from Zia, of all people, in passing. The place was owned by the father of one of her classmates from her finishing school, Blythe Danforth. Zia had laughingly told us a story of dressing up as a dandy once to infiltrate the place, where she'd almost been discovered by Rafi, who had been a member there. Chances were that Ansel might be a member there as well, since all his mates were.

I knocked on the roof to the carriage. "Hobarth," I called out in a deep voice. "Do you know where Danforth's Den is?"

"Yes, sir. It's at the end of Piccadilly. Not far, about half a mile."

I thought about walking the ten or fifteen minutes, then reconsidered. I wasn't armed, and dressed like this, I was asking for trouble from cutpurses. "Will you ferry me over there in a dash and return for Lord Blake and the boys?" I asked. "They might be awhile."

"Of course, sir."

Blake would be furious, considering I was alone, but Ansel always said it's better to ask forgiveness than permission. The ride to Danforth's was quicker than I expected. I hopped out of the carriage and walked confidently to the entrance, where a small crowd of people were waiting. Mostly men, I noticed. I kept my head angled down and my lips flattened.

The burly man at the entrance eyed me up and down, clearly marking that I was a gentleman of means. "Member?"

My nerves shook. "Lord Ansel Chen," I growled, hoping for a miracle that I wasn't wrong.

The man consulted a leather-bound notebook, his brows pulling low. He flicked page after page, and for a moment, I was worried. But then the man grunted. "Right on through, my lord."

Good God, that worked! I couldn't believe my luck.

I stalked inside and promptly gaped at the extravagant décor. My darling cousin was clearly a libertine to have a membership here—this place was equal parts bordello and gaming hell, all done up in deep lavish reds and stunning golds. It was similar in feel to the gambling den in Cambridge, though on a much more sumptuous, opulent level. Danforth's clearly catered to a certain faction of the elite . . . the part that had money and wanted to spend it on every vice life could offer.

There were women here, too. Though not in the capacity of members, as Tarik had envisioned. Dressed in expensive wine-red gowns like a matching uniform of some sort, they had to be employed by the club. A haze of green discolored my vision. What would be the odds of finding Tarik here drowning his sorrows and flirting with one of them?

Jealousy was *not* a pretty look on me, even dressed as a man.

I quickly canvased the first foyer and made my way to the inner rooms, surveying all the people and searching for the face etched into my brain. He was not on the first floor, or on the second. Just when I was beginning to despair and balefully contemplating the stairs that led to the upper levels, a head of dark waves capping a lean body caught my eye walking toward a table in the main gaming room.

My relief was palpable. I hurried toward him before anyone could take the empty seats. There was not one directly beside him, so I had to be content to sit one player away. Tarik barely lifted his head, even as I sat and placed my bet. I lost the first round to the dealer, completely distracted as my mind tried to come up with something clever to say.

But as I studied Tarik circumspectly, all I could think about was how sad he looked. Sad and gaunt, as if he hadn't eaten properly in days. He wore his new clothes, though they were rumpled and disheveled, his cravat askew and his coat unbuttoned. Regardless, he was still the handsomest man in the room.

"My lord," the dealer said louder, startling me out of my thoughts. "Play is to you."

Distractedly, I stared at my cards. Eleven. I signaled for another without speaking. A queen of hearts appeared. Twenty-one.

"Congratulations, my lord," the dealer said.

"Thank you," I said.

I felt the jolt of Tarik's stare followed by his surprise . . . and subsequent fury. His roiling emotions were tangible enough to sense. My eyes flicked up and to the side slowly. The collision of our gazes was to be expected, since he was glaring at me, but the electric force of it still punched the breath from my lungs. Those blue eyes were glowing like heated stones, incandescent with rage.

At least I still made him feel *something.*

"What are you doing here?" he growled, making the player between us flinch.

"Last I heard, gentlemen have free will."

His glare intensified even as it dropped to my bare lips for an infinitesimal second. "Yes, *men.*" His voice lowered, and I warmed at the fact that even in his anger, he wouldn't expose me. "You should not be here, Roz."

I let my lip curl arrogantly. "Who's going to stop me? You?" I wanted him to stand up and say yes . . . I wanted him to drag me out of there like I meant something to him. Except the boiling ire drained from his face, leaving nothing but a blank, defeated expression that I hated.

"No," he muttered. "I don't care what you do."

Clearly uncomfortable, the man in the middle swung his stare between us. "Would you like to switch places?"

Tarik growled no just as I said yes. The other man stared down into his cards.

"Coward," I said softly.

"Liar," drifted back, and I winced.

The dealer cleared his throat, and play resumed in weighted silence with a new deck. The next few rounds went quickly, and I must have been lucky, because the dealer went bust each time. My mound of money was sizable. Tarik lost, though I wasn't sure if he was even keeping track, betting only the minimum as he was. I was attuned to every single movement he made, even the breaths that left his lips.

To get his attention, I put the maximum bet down on the next hand. Fifty pounds.

That got *everyone's* attention.

His shoulders stiffened at my boldness, but he grunted and stayed focused on the table. By some miracle, I won that hand with a natural, and with a two-to-one payout, that meant one hundred and fifty pounds, but I didn't care about the money. Emboldened, I wagered the maximum again, this time earning myself another grunt and a sidelong glance of warning. My heart thumped with illicit thrill. As pure luck would have it, I received another natural.

One was lucky enough; two in a row drew attention. Not the good kind.

Three hundred pounds in two hands.

"Cheat!" one of the players jeered. "Either he signaled to the dealer or bribed him, but deceit is afoot."

"I think I saw him palming a card," the man between me and Tarik said. "Check his sleeve."

I scowled, glaring at my challengers in turn. It didn't matter that this was an upscale gaming hell; when people started losing, the accusations were bound to fly. "I did no such thing, you lying cads!"

The man who had made the second accusation reached over and started tugging at my coat, as if he intended to pull it off right then and there. I shoved at him, even as buttons of my coat tore loose, and I let out a yelp. I managed to get in a flailing half jab to his nose before his weight disappeared in a second as Tarik let out a roar and practically tore the man away with superhuman strength.

"Get off!"

Howling in rage, the man struck out a wild punch toward Tarik but instead hit the dealer, who had rounded the table to break up the fight with three enormous muscled men. This wasn't like the time in the West End when I was a lady and could throw my father's name around.

One, I was not dressed as Lady Rosalin, and two, many of the people in this gaming hell were likely aristocrats who knew my family. But unlike at the other gaming hell, the guards had the situation in hand in minutes.

"Thank you for what you did," I said to Tarik.

His lips tightened. "I intervened only because I didn't want to go to jail because of a brawl and get thrown out of the college." It was a relief to get more than grunts out of him, but was this when I should tell him that he was already on the verge of such a calamity? I opened my mouth, but he stopped me. "You shouldn't be here."

"I'll leave if you come with me."

A muscle ticked in his jaw. "Rosalin."

"Tarik."

He scowled. "God, you're stubborn. Fine. Lead the way—let's go, then."

A wave of relief rushed through me as we collected our winnings and made our way through the club. A part of me wanted to ask him what he'd do differently than a place like Danforth's, but I wasn't sure he'd be open to conversation. His strong palm against the small of my back steering me through the crowd had my heart singing, but the minute we collected our cloaks at the entrance, it fell away.

Outside, a small crowd had gathered, and I stared in surprise at the handful of men in uniform, the Bow Street Runners, who were observing the entrance of Danforth's Den. Had they been summoned because of the racket?

"He's the thief!" someone accused.

The Runners marched forward, one of them grabbing me by the arm and knocking my hat off in the process. Real fear sluiced through me at the thought of being arrested. "Unhand me. I stole nothing," I shrieked in high-pitched voice, making the man peer down at me, eyes widening in surprise as my unpinned hair tumbled loose.

"You need to come with us for questioning, miss."

Tarik surged forward, ever protective despite his dismissive words. "Don't touch her! She's nobility. I'm the one you want. If you have questions, I'll go with you."

Shrugging off the Runner's hold amidst the gasps of people nearby, I swung around wildly, realization dawning at the choice he was making and what it would mean for him. "No, Tarik. You can't."

"I'm not doing it for you."

It was a lie. I knew that with every fiber of my being. I closed the narrow gap between us. "Who's the liar now?" I asked.

Then I shoved up to the tips of my toes and kissed him hard. I heard more muffled gasps around us, but what did it matter? My so-called reputation was already hanging by the skin of its teeth. Tarik was worth it. His entire body froze but his lips were soft and receptive. At least he was kissing me back. When we broke apart after a handful of seconds, he was flushed. I was certain I looked the same.

"Your hair is down," he murmured.

I shrugged. "So it is. Don't say anything, and don't go anywhere. They can hold you, but they can't keep you without proof of wrongdoing. I'll fix this. And then we need to talk about an old rival of yours."

CHAPTER TWENTY

Plato is my friend, Aristotle is my friend, but my greatest friend is truth.

—Isaac Newton

"Ansel, I need your help," I said to my cousin after I had told everyone what had transpired and they finally left. Blake, as expected, had been outraged that I'd taken it upon myself to go to Danforth's alone, but I was beyond asking any boys for permission at this point.

"With what?" Ansel asked.

I wrung my hands. "We have to get him out. He can't stay there when he's done nothing wrong. Neither of us cheated, but he was defending me. Protecting *me*."

"Roz, I can't work a miracle to get someone out of the custody of the Runners, if they've taken him in. He'll likely be at the Bow Street Magistrates' Court in Westminster, if not somewhere worse, like Newgate."

"Newgate?" I gasped. It was the worst prison in London! I felt my eyes welling with tears. "All of this is my fault. I know I shouldn't have gone to Danforth's alone. I shouldn't have wagered as recklessly as I did. Or even played cards. I should have waited for Blake and gone in there and let the boys get him out. Instead, I wanted to prove to him that he still felt something for me."

"You couldn't have predicted this, even with your addiction to calculating the odds of things," he said wryly.

"What do we do?"

"I don't know. But please don't cry, Cousin."

He looked as helpless as I felt. We were out of options unless we took an enormous risk that could turn out very badly for everyone concerned, including me. *Especially* me. But it felt like it was my only remaining hope. Swiping my leaking eyes, I sucked in a breath and fought with the swelling knot in my throat. "We need to tell Papa."

Ansel's face blanched. "That you dressed like a boy and pretended to be me? And that I *knew* about it?"

"That you went on a grand tour without his approval as well," I added with a sniff.

Ansel paled even further at that, his light brown skin like pasty chalk. My cousin had some accountability of his own to address, continuing his lie by omission even at the ball. Exposing my falsehoods would consequently expose his, and I wouldn't do that to him without his permission.

"He's going to be irate," he muttered.

I nodded. "Probably. I'll try to draw the heat so that the focus isn't on you."

"No, I'm responsible for my choices." He shook his head, removing his glasses and cleaning them. "Someone's future is more important than me being afraid. I should have done the right thing from the start." He shot me a wan smile. "Perhaps it's *not* always better to ask for forgiveness than permission. Sometimes it's better to take the bull by the horns."

"Papa is worse than a bull," I said. "He's a dragon."

"That have horns, too, don't they?" Ansel asked with a watery smile.

I nodded. "Sharp, big ones."

"We're so dead."

We made our way to my father's study, where he would undoubtedly be working. He was used to burning the candle at both ends. Sure enough, there was a light underneath the door. Before I lost my courage, I knocked. "Papa, do you have a moment?"

"Rosalin? Come in," he said, glancing up and frowning when he saw Ansel on my heels. He sat back in his chair and folded his arms, though a small smile danced over his mouth. "Have a seat." Wordlessly, we sat in the chairs in front of his desk. "The last time the two of you came to me together, you'd made the governess leave because you put live frogs in her bed. So, what is it now?" His dark brows rose in expectation. "Has Ansel been terrorizing your young man?"

I cleared my throat. "Actually, it is about him." I inhaled a deep, cleansing breath. "I haven't been completely honest with you."

"*We* haven't been fully honest, Uncle Lan," Ansel said, his face still unnaturally pale, though his voice was strong. "I want to go first. The truth is . . . I wasn't at Cambridge University for the past few months. And I *was* in Greece right before Auntie

Susu's ball. I decided to go to the Continent on a grand tour, while everyone thought I was still here. It was immature and reckless, and I should have asked your permission before leaving England. I'm truly sorry."

My father didn't say anything. The only sign of any reaction was the slight crinkling of skin around his eyes. He steepled his hands over the desk, that dark, unreadable gaze sliding to me. "And you? What do you have to confess? Care to explain how I still received reports about my nephew's so-called excellent progress if Ansel was gallivanting around Europe?"

"I took his place at Cambridge," I blurted. "I pretended to be him and enrolled in another college, while falsifying your approval of the transfer and charges. I wanted to learn about mathematics and astronomy desperately, and it seemed like such an opportunity since Ansel wasn't going to be attending." I swallowed hard. "So, I took it."

In a rush, I spouted out my whole scheme, barely stopping for breath, until the incident at the ball when Ansel had shown up. I explained my idea to introduce Tarik to the *ton* so that he could position his marvelous proposal about the academic social club to potential investors. I told Papa that Tarik had been helping me build my own telescope and had taken me on a tour of the Royal Observatory, where I'd seen the planets and stars. And last of all, I clarified what had happened after the ball.

I hung my head. "I don't know if he will ever forgive me, Papa. But I like him. *So* much. He's the only gentleman who has ever seen me for everything I am, especially what's in my head and heart versus who my father is or how much money we have.

And now, he's in trouble because of me. Because he was *protecting* me from being arrested."

Falling into silence, I waited for my father to speak and his inevitable judgment. "It seems as though you both know that what you did was wrong." He peered at Ansel. "Yes, you should have discussed your interest in a grand tour with me as well as your mother and aunt. Not to mention conspiring with your cousin to willfully deceive the administrators at your college."

"Yes, Uncle."

His stare landed on me next, though it didn't seem as cold or forbidding as I'd expected. "I can't say I am surprised by your ardor for education, Rosalin. You were always in the library with your nose stuck in a mathematics book or participating in your cousin's lessons. *Impersonating* someone else, however, is going a little too far."

"I am aware, Papa."

"Who else knows?" he asked.

"Not many. I thought some would have overheard that day on the terrace, but there's been nothing in the gossip rags. With the thunder and being out on the terrace, we were lucky not to be overheard." I listed the ones who knew, leaving James out, as I wasn't sure how my father would handle someone holding a potentially explosive secret over our family. Over *him*. Besides, we didn't *know* for sure that James was a threat. It was only a speculation.

My father nodded. "I don't condone your actions. They were dishonest and possibly criminal. I've always taught the two of you to look before you leap. Perhaps you need to revisit that lesson in earnest." He exhaled a thoughtful breath even as I withered beneath the weight of his words. "That said, perhaps our hallowed institutions need to start thinking about including women in higher education."

My jaw slackened in shock. "Truly, Papa?"

"Yes, I have always said that women bring a valuable perspective to intellectual discussion. Even your mother, though she has no interest in politics, has her own viewpoints on current policy. The Duchess of Harbridge is particularly outspoken about women's rights and human rights. I will solicit both their thoughts on the matter." He sat back with a solemn expression. "Now, about your young man . . ."

Heaven help me, my heart was going to beat its way out of my chest!

"Papa, I am sorry I lied about his origins. He *is* French, well half, but he's not wealthy." I chewed on the inside of my lip. "He's also on track to be a Fellow of Trinity College." I huffed a winded breath. "The pedigree thing was my idea, not just so he would be taken seriously by the *ton,* but also because I thought you wouldn't consider him as a suitor if he didn't have the influence or wealth you required. I wanted you to like him. To approve of him."

The duke scrubbed a palm over his jaw. "One thing at a time, Rosalin, but a man's character is just as important to me as whether he can provide for you and give you the life you're accustomed to. Though first, we have to find out where he is."

I stared at him in bewilderment. "You'll help us?"

"I am your father, Rosalin. What else would I do?"

"We both thought you would be furious," Ansel said softly.

"Oh, I am quite irate, but this is a learning experience that I expect you two need to reflect hard on before we consider appropriate consequences for your actions."

I gulped, but any punishment would probably be less than I deserved. "Thank you, Papa."

It was well past dinnertime, and Papa and Ansel still had not returned. I waited with my mother, whom Papa had filled in about our conversation, much to her consternation, and whom I was also suddenly looking at with new eyes. I had not expected my father to share such a telling detail about their relationship—that he valued her views even when she wasn't particularly invested in politics. My mother's quiet disposition wasn't a weakness; it was a strength.

One did not have to be loud to be subversive. She listened and then shared her opinions with my father, who clearly *respected* those opinions.

The "Listen more and speak less" adage had never been there to silence me; it was there to arm me. Because *living* was political. How one interacted with the world was political. How one raised and educated one's children was inherently political.

I had been allowed to study with my male cousin.

I had been given free rein over my many so-called failed seasons.

I had been encouraged to read diversely and widely at every opportunity.

Eyes stinging, I recalled my determination to find a spouse who valued me in sentiment and intelligence, who offered me a *true* connection, and who allowed me to pursue my own passions. Goodness, I'd been a fool to think my parents' marriage was everything I didn't want. My mother's passion had shifted to family, and my father had always valued that. Their love for each other wasn't showy like fireworks, but it ran deep, rooted in mutual esteem.

"Mama?" I pressed a hand to the fluttering pulse at my throat. "Remember when you used to tell me stories of the ancient Greek constellations? You had your own telescope and tracked the stars. Why did you give up your passion for it?"

"I didn't give it up, darling," she said after a beat. "My priorities simply shifted. First with you and then Bowen. You became the primary stars in my sky."

"Don't you miss it?"

She shrugged one elegantly garbed shoulder. "There's a reason your father keeps our libraries stocked with the latest editions of books and catalogues by notable scientists and astronomers. He does that for me. You just benefit from it." She let out a soft laugh. "And I'm not completely cut off from that life. Caroline is still a dear friend who keeps me abreast of new developments, and of course, all her accomplishments in astronomy."

I blinked—there was only one Caroline in astronomy worth mentioning. "Caroline *Herschel*?" My voice was a strained squeak.

Mama nodded. "The telescope I had before you were born was a gift from her, one her brother built."

Oh dear *God,* I was going to faint. The telescope I'd used as a child had been built by William Herschel, one of the most brilliant astronomers of our time . . . the astronomer to the *king.* My bones felt like they were made of jelly.

"I see her for tea sometimes," Mama added fondly. "Along with Mary Somerville and Sophie Germain when we are all in town together. Our discussions on science and mathematical law are quite provocative. We share a mutual love for solving mathematical problems in journals."

Spots converged over my vision. I truly was going to expire from a lack of breath. "Mary *Somerville* and Sophie *Germain* have tea with *you*?" My voice sounded like it shifted an entire octave from the start to the end.

The duchess looked at me as if I were addlebrained. "Are you unwell, Rosalin? Should I summon Dr. Barker?"

No. No, Mama. I am decidedly not *well.*

Because my own quiet, don't-make-a-fuss, fashion-obsessed, marriage-minded mother was close friends with my own personal heroes and not just a few faceless charity friends. And she had them over for *tea.* "May I . . . Would it be possible to join you sometime?"

"Of course, Rosalin. You're welcome whenever you like. I'm sure your contributions on the subjects would be appreciated, especially after your recent stint at Trinity. They would find that extremely diverting, especially Sophie, who I recalled might have used a male pseudonym for her analysis and number-theory work in France."

"You're not cross about what I did?" I asked quietly.

"I am more relieved, my darling. Your reputation and future could have been irreparably harmed." She exhaled. "But the truth is women have been disrupting the patriarchy for centuries, whether by pretending to be men or assuming male pseudonyms or publishing anonymously."

My mind was spinning as I considered what I had learned. Honestly, had I been so consumed with my own life that I had ignored what was right in front of me? Mama and I were quite similar, despite our occasional divergences, like fashion. And she'd never discouraged me from following my interests. In fact, the only time we had ever clashed was over the subject of marriage.

"Mama, may I ask you a personal question? Did you love Papa when your marriage was arranged?"

Her smile was warm. "No, but we were great rivals."

I blinked. That was *not* what I'd been expecting her to say. "Rivals?"

"When we were young, our families were neighbors. We had a fierce competition for any of the prizes awarded in the monthly journals to solve mathematical or philosophical problems. He won some, I won others." She stood and walked to the bay window that looked out to the street. "After a while, our families decided that the only way we would stop reviling each other was if we got married. And so, we did." Her mouth quirked. "I love him now."

"Do you think Papa still plans to marry me off to someone?"

She crossed the room to where I was sitting and perched on the sofa beside me. "We only want you to be secured with a partner who can provide for you. Hardship is not something either of us desire for you, though your dowry will stand you in good stead."

"What if I found someone, but he's not titled or wealthy?" I asked.

Her head canted. "Your young gentleman? The one your father went to help?" She paused. "Do you care for him?" my mother asked quietly, and when I nodded jerkily, she patted my knee. "And does he return your affections?"

The truth was, even after our last kiss, I didn't know. And there was no time to ponder a reply before the butler announced the duke's return. I flew up, nerves trembling as Papa and Ansel entered the foyer, followed by my weary, disheveled, cherished tutor.

"Tarik!" I was so happy to see him unhurt and safe that I threw myself into his arms, likely scandalizing my parents and my cousin. Tarik, however, had enough restraint to keep me from embarrassing us both as he returned a brief squeeze but set me back on my feet a respectable distance away.

My father took my mother's hand, brushing his lips over her knuckles. "Dinner and then we will talk." He glanced pointedly at Tarik. "You too, young man. You can wash up in one of the guest rooms. My nephew will show you the way."

I wanted to go with him desperately, but I had to respect the rules of etiquette, even though I had been flouting them so shamelessly for the past three months, from the start of April through to June. A single Easter term that had felt like a lifetime.

Instead of following behind, I went to my own chambers to

change, fussing when Anna insisted on tending to my hair, but the repeated brushstrokes calmed my frazzled nerves. I met her eyes in the mirror as she stood behind me, pinning my slippery locks into intricate loops. "Thank you, Anna. I'll make sure that my parents know you played no willing part in my deception. Your job is safe."

"I know, my lady," she murmured. "I did want to tell you though that your bravery to follow your dreams inspired me to follow mine. I submitted my first piece of poetry to a contest in a periodical." She grinned. "And I won! Five whole pounds! And it will be printed in the next issue. I will be a published poet."

I spun in my chair. "Oh my goodness, Anna, that is wonderful!"

Her mouth made a wry curl. "So, it wasn't all bad. I wanted you to know that."

When she was finished, I smoothed my favorite cobalt-blue dress, which matched the lapis lazuli hue of Tarik's eyes, adjusted my gloves, and made my way downstairs to the dining room, where Tarik and my cousin were waiting. My mother was off tucking Bowen into bed—she loved reading him stories, too, a task most aristocratic mothers didn't do. One more thing we were both lucky for, I supposed.

"Lady Rosalin, you look lovely," Tarik said, strolling forward to take my white-gloved hand.

I blushed. "Thank you, so do you."

He had changed as well—Ansel must have sent a messenger to wherever Tarik had been staying to retrieve fresh clothing. I recognized the navy ensemble as one he had been fitted for, remembering how well the color suited his rich complexion. The ends of his hair were still curled and wet from a bath.

"Was it awful at the Magistrates' Court? What did they ask you?" I inquired in a hushed voice.

"Nothing, especially once I told them the Duke of Delmont would be arriving soon."

I stared quizzically at him. "You knew I'd send my father?"

"Roz," he said softly, making my silly heart quicken. "You adore your father, even if you loathe his stringency. Because your tenacity comes from him. I knew you would ask him for help when you needed it most."

My brows dipped. "But *how* did you know? What if my pride and stubborn nature didn't allow it?"

"You would never let your pride stop you from helping a friend," he said firmly, and I flushed with pleasure at the praise. "And nothing you say will convince me otherwise. By the way, Lord Ansel also informed me of what was going on at Trinity, and my old friend James's accusations."

"What will you do?" I asked, just as my parents appeared. "And James is a louse."

"Defend myself the best I can against the allegations that I've been purposefully lying about my identity to hoodwink aristocratic society and therefore do not exemplify the character of someone who should be a Fellow at Trinity."

I gasped. "They would oust you for that?"

"They have done it for much less."

We followed my parents, who both appeared somewhat refreshed, and sat at the dining room table before the first course of white soup was served. My stomach clenched with nerves, but I forced myself to consume a few spoonfuls of the creamy beef broth with almonds before worry stopped me completely. The second course, roasted mutton with minted jelly accompanied by mushroom ragu and creamed asparagus, appeared quickly after.

I was sure Tarik had to be ravenous after his ordeal. We ate in relative silence, taking our cues from my father, until he finally put down his fork to summarize the earlier events of the evening.

It hadn't taken him long to find that Tarik was indeed at the Bow Street Magistrates' Court, being ruthlessly interrogated about cheating during cards—an accusation that had been levied against him by a peer, who turned out to be the gentleman who had assaulted me. My father had informed said peer that we would formally submit our own charges if he didn't renounce his silly claims.

He'd dropped them immediately.

Papa had also made a stop at Danforth's Den, where he spoke to the owner himself and made sure Tarik wasn't accused of anything that might hurt his future prospects of starting his own social club or even returning to Danforth's.

I suspected that Mr. Danforth had been quite obliging as it was rather useful to have a duke in one's debt . . . or perhaps better yet, to not have one as an enemy. My father was a powerful man, but hearing him use his considerable influence to protect *me* as well as a man he didn't even know was humbling . . . and made my heart feel quite warm.

My appetite slightly restored, I was able to eat a tiny bit more of my meal, and by the time the dishes were cleared, my relief as well as my gratitude to my father were palpable. Without him, the situation could have been so much worse. The disquiet plaguing me had eased somewhat, but we still had to deal with the matter of what James was doing at Trinity to ruin Tarik's reputation.

When the dessert course was brought to the table, a tiny smile touched my lips at the intricate moon-and-stars stamped motif of the traditional Chinese mooncake. Even though it was my favorite—with its refined pastry crust and sweet lotus-seed-paste filling—I could barely stomach more than a bite or two. My nerves were entirely too frazzled.

"What will you do about James?" I asked Tarik while he consumed his portion, and then the rest of mine, with relish. At least one of us wasn't letting food go to waste.

"James who?" my father boomed as he sat back with a glass of claret.

"A student at Trinity determined to besmirch St. Clair's standing," Ansel put in, and then proceeded to explain everything Will had told us. It sounded worse when put so plainly, especially as my father's eyes darkened at the part where James might have known my true identity all along . . . and what he might do with said knowledge. Papa was fiercely protective of our family.

"Mr. St. Clair, you're in quite the pickle," he said in a calm tone that belied his grim expression.

Tarik exhaled. "That's the sum of it, Your Grace. I'll be heading back tomorrow to meet with the Master of the College. My actions are my own, and I must be accountable for them, but

I also won't allow someone to besmirch my name over a personal vendetta. Sir Lowry is undoubtedly embellishing the events. He has attempted unsuccessfully to discredit me before."

"Your integrity is admirable," Papa said. "But it's not just your future at stake. From what my nephew has said, it seems that this Lowry character might have known Rosalin's true identity all along."

"That is correct, Your Grace."

My father's gaze panned between the three of us. "Then that is why I will be going with you."

CHAPTER TWENTY-ONE

> Gravity must be caused by an agent acting constantly according to certain laws.
>
> —Isaac Newton

The Duke of Delmont had been holed up with the Master of Trinity College, Dr. Christopher Wordsworth, for hours, which was not a good sign.

According to the boys, the rumor was Dr. Wordsworth was an austere, devout man who upheld a rather strict moral code at the university. He categorically loathed the twins, whose moral leanings varied by the day. Since Wordsworth was new—he'd only started serving from February—he'd likely be more inclined to protect his position as well as the reputation of the college than be lenient or forgiving.

Which did not bode well.

The rest of us—Tarik, Ansel, the twins, Will, and Harold—waited on tenterhooks in one of the reception rooms of the Master's Lodge. It was one of the few places on the campus that an aristocratic woman was permitted to be in. Women in general were not allowed on college grounds alone, without being accompanied by a man and having express approval. It was absurd how antiquated the thinking was . . . to the extent that women were seen as a corruptive influence on male students. In Cambridge, I read once, a woman had been arrested without cause "on suspicion of evil" for simply existing.

I was glad for my station and the protection of my father's name.

Still, I could be accused of being a Jezebel, appearing solely to corrupt the men. Such an implication wouldn't affect only me; it would affect *anyone* who had been in contact with me.

Meaning everyone in this room.

Was that what James had planned? A claim that I had sown discord?

The accusation of misconduct he'd lodged against Tarik was a grave one. If Tarik received anything more than a disciplinary fine or temporary rustication, his future as a Fellow of the college would be over. Already as it was, the false identity was a perceived mark against his moral character. Tarik had mentioned that years ago there was a student who pretended to be another student to take an examination, and both men were expelled. The deception went against academic integrity.

"Are you well?" I whispered to Tarik, whose handsome face remained drawn.

"Yes, but I fear even the duke's advocacy will not help. Wordsworth is known for his rigorous, unforgiving temperament."

I exhaled. "Does that upset you?"

He shrugged. "It's everything I've ever worked for, so in a

sense, it feels like I'm losing everything." He paused, that blue gaze boring into mine. "Becoming a Fellow meant that I would have something real to offer you. It would have been a respectable position of employment."

My throat tightened as I bit my lip. "Have you forgiven me, then?"

His hand reached across on the bench we shared, his little finger brushing mine. The soft touch made heat spark at the point of contact. No one was paying us any attention, but I felt exposed, as though everyone could see. "I wish you had told me, but I understand why, logically, you could not. In truth, if we hadn't met as friends first, I likely wouldn't feel as I do today."

"And how *do* you feel?" I whispered.

He smiled, his dimple popping, eyes backlit with blue flame. "Infatuated with every part of you—your brain, your wit, your compassion, your beauty." His stare dropped to my lips and ignited. "I wish I could kiss you right now."

My abdomen clenched as his finger hooked secretly around mine. "So do I, but I wouldn't want to corrupt you with my feminine charms."

"If such charms mean an incisive brain that can rival any gentleman here, then consider me thoroughly and willingly corrupted, mon coeur."

"Such sweet nothings, Monsieur St. Clair," I said. "You certainly have mastered the way to this girl's heart."

"Have I?"

"It's yours," I said simply, watching those vibrant eyes flare with an intensity that I felt to my bones. I flipped his palm over and squeezed his hand. "Every beating inch of it. I'm in love with you, Tarik, if that isn't completely obvious by now."

"I . . . Truly?"

Feeling weightless, I nodded.

He opened his mouth and closed it, like a fish out of water, as if his voice was locked in his throat, throttling any reply to my unplanned though earnest admission. I was drowning in that limpid gaze, which revealed his every emotion. We were locked in a trance, the sounds of everyone else fading away, the inches between us vanishing.

"Oy, St. Clair!" Klaus yelled, making us jump apart like we were guilty, which, for all intents and purposes, we probably were. It wouldn't have taken much for our lips to meet. And *that* would have been a scandal for the ages. "They're summoning you. You and Lord Ansel."

Fear pooled in my belly, but I squeezed his hand for good luck as Tarik stood.

"Whatever happens, I'm with you," I promised. "Beta Cygni forever."

That slow-breaking smile was worth everything. He was my twin star. *Always.*

The waiting was going to kill me.

Every minute that passed by didn't help.

And when my father finally appeared with Tarik, I could

tell from their faces that things had not gone as expected. Papa's expression was grim, and Tarik's was dazed, as if he was still coming to terms with whatever life-altering decision had been made.

"I'm out," he informed us dully. "I'll be allowed to get my secondary degree but won't be welcome to stay at the college, and I've lost any chance to be a Fellow. In marginally better news, James Lowry will face immediate expulsion. Ansel provided a statement and evidence of James's own malicious misconduct, stealing my research papers and conspiring to cheat and discredit me. Turns out the college looks a little more severely on breaches of academic integrity than claiming one's family is more well-off than they actually are." He laughed humorlessly. "The duke insisted that such a claim is not irrefutable proof, since wealth can be defined differently. My uncle *is* an entrepreneur. But Wordsworth wouldn't budge."

The idea to introduce Tarik as the nephew of a French count had been mine, but that falsehood had only been made to Blake and my father, if I recalled correctly. Tarik hadn't impersonated or pretended to be a peer. Most of the others in the *ton* had simply assumed he'd come from wealth—an assumption we had not corrected. Still, James's claims citing Tarik's lack of moral virtue based on such a fabrication must have stuck.

"And Ansel?" I whispered, staring at my cousin's nonchalant expression. My father signaled to him, and they both disappeared from the room. No matter what happened, Ansel would be fine. Though he was my coconspirator, he was also a peer, protected by centuries of privilege.

"He will receive his bachelor's degree." Tarik sent me a

reassuring smile. "His work this term really helped him to solidify his learning."

Astonished, I gaped. "*His* work?"

"He nearly finished building an incredible telescope from scratch, didn't you know? It was a rather excellent effort, in my humble estimation. Mr. Peacock confirmed as much."

I blushed, taking the praise and the win for what they were. I had never come to this institution to receive any accolades or degrees. I'd only wanted to prove that I could do the work and be part of something bigger than myself. "So, everything's all right, then?" I asked.

Tarik nodded. "Trust me, Wordsworth wanted to sweep any hint of a woman impersonating a male student, as inferred by James, under the rug as quickly as possible. The impact on the college and university of allowing that to happen under his watch would have been catastrophic to his fledgling career. He'd be finished. In the end, Ansel contested that he'd been here all along and that James was mistaken."

"What if James starts a rumor?" I asked, feeling equally guilty and grateful that my cousin had stood by me. "They can cause just as much harm."

"He won't. Your father threatened that if so much as a lick of gossip ever came out against his family, Lowry would rue the day he'd been born. The duke can be quite an intimidating man. Poor James looked like he was going to piss himself then and there! Even Wordsworth looked like he wanted to remove himself from your father's warpath as quickly as possible."

I laughed at that. My father was rather scary, but he was on our side and that's what counted. The twins informed us that Ansel and the duke had gone to his quarters—ergo mine—to retrieve the trunks that my friends had so kindly gathered.

While the boys dispersed, Will, Tarik, and I left the Master's Lodge and walked over to Tarik's quarters to pack up his belongings. His room wasn't that much different from mine, though it looked a little more lived-in, considering he'd been there longer than me. Still, we were finished within a couple of hours.

"I'll miss this place," Tarik said.

I nodded. "Me too. Especially the library." I glanced at Will, who was on the verge of bursting into tears. "And you, of course. The new best friend I never knew I needed."

"I am?" His lower lip wobbled.

"Yes, now come here and give me a hug before we all start sobbing." Will wrapped those thick arms around me and squeezed. I could hear him sniffling. "I'll see you in town. Don't be a stranger, promise me."

"I promise, Roz," he said. "Thank you for being my friend. I think I would have quit if it hadn't been for you."

I laughed and patted his arm. "Give yourself a little more credit than that. You're a fighter, Will. A fierce defender. A loyal friend with a big heart. You'll figure out your place. Sooner or later, we all do."

After a much longer hug, Will offered to help with the trunks while Tarik and I ferried a couple of his smaller satchels full of notebooks and essays along with his precious copies of Newton's works. I let out a laugh as I traced the embossed cover of *Principia* . . . the book that had brought us together.

“I’ll never regret any of this,” I said as we walked back to his dorm for the remaining items. I received quite a few stares from students in the courtyard, but surprisingly, no one said anything. Perhaps it was because I was with one of the tutors. And as a former Wrangler, Tarik was a familiar face. At least he would leave with his reputation intact. “I know what I did was wrong because of the harm it caused you. But perhaps one day, women will be allowed to enroll here, and there’ll be no stopping us.”

“I believe that,” Tarik said, gathering the last of his belongings.

We went down the staircase and met a red-eyed Will followed by Harold and the twins. “We’ll take those for you,” the boys said, reaching for the rest of the bags.

“Thank you,” Tarik said. “I just want to make sure I have everything. There’s another room I need to check quickly. Will you give me a moment?”

Assuming he meant for me to leave as well, I nodded and turned to head out with Will and the others, but a strong hand yanked me back into the nearest combination room. It was empty and dark, with only sparse late-afternoon light coming in through the windows. I was pressed up against a very warm, very hard chest.

“What are you doing?” I whispered. “We could get caught.”

“This is where we first met,” he said. I glanced over my shoulder, the dark shapes of the sofas and chairs taking form and inciting a memory of my first day here. “You called me aggressive.”

I looped my hands around his neck, since he showed no

inclination of releasing my waist where his palms gripped. "No, Mr. St. Clair, if you recall, I said your viewpoint was aggressive."

"Is it still your opinion that a geometrical method is more rigorous and that there's something to be said for classical construction?"

I traced his jaw with my fingertip. "Classic mathematical methods endure for a reason. But honestly, all I knew was that you were the most beautiful boy I had ever seen and I was certain my infatuation would give me away. You looked like Adonis in the flesh."

"Adonis? Tell me more," he said, bending down to feather a kiss against my forehead.

"And also, the most arrogant." I pushed to my toes to kiss the edge of his jaw where my fingers had traced. "I thought my decision to enroll was done for when I realized how much you detested Ansel, and then you announced you were to be my tutor."

His mouth grazed a path down my temple to my ear, making my breaths shorten to indecent pants the closer he ventured to my lips. "And after that?"

"Instead of quitting, I was determined to exceed your expectations."

His hands lifted to cup my cheeks, making my voice hitch in my throat. "You did. Every last one of them. I've never been prouder of anyone than I have been about you. I hope you know that."

"Thank you," I whispered.

His mouth met the tip of my nose, my cheeks, before finally settling on my lips. I sighed at the soft, sweet feel of him, a sensation that I was already addicted to, as he deepened the kiss.

My hands tightened around his nape, crushing my body to his while he explored me thoroughly, leaving no corner of my mouth untouched.

His fingers crept up into my hair, the strands sliding from their pins like rivers of ink, and he groaned as he speared through the silken locks. When we broke apart, he kept pressing kisses to my throat, one hand tethered in my hair and the other running down the length of my spine, before returning to my lips for one last taste.

"Bloody hell, I'm completely obsessed with you," he muttered against my mouth.

I smiled. "The feeling is mutual."

My entire body was flying in the clouds when the door to the combination room opened, and I nearly shrieked as one of the tutors let out a scream of his own.

"Sorry, don't mind us!" Tarik cried as he grabbed my hand and pulled me to the door. I snorted at the tutor's alarmed expression as we tore past. His eyes widened as they settled on me—a *girl*—in the middle of their prized male sanctuary. Ring the bells! Fetch the pitchforks!

I snorted at the thought of a Jezebel alert going off, warning all and sundry to beware the female wiles lurking in their midst. It truly wasn't funny, but the fear and subsequent demonization of women was categorically absurd. *Suspicion of evil, my foot.* It was simply a way to keep women in the spaces where men thought we should belong.

The kitchen . . . the bedchamber . . . the nursery.

Where I belonged was going to be *my* choice, because I was

ready to kick that archaic expectation right into the Thames. Intrepid women like Wang Zhenyi, Caroline Herschel, Sophie Germain, and Émilie du Châtelet had already carved inroads into male-dominated spaces like mathematics, science, philosophy, and astronomy, and earned recognition for their work.

Just like them, I was going to add my name to the history books.

We caught up with everyone near the Great Gate, where our family carriage with the fancy Delmont ducal crest waited at the main entrance to the college. My father was standing in deep conversation with Ansel. It looked serious but not contentious. I glanced up at the arch that I'd walked through on my very first day here with a strange sense of nostalgia. That moment had changed the trajectory of my life. Not wanting to say goodbye, I dragged my feet to where my friends stood.

I hugged the twins first. "I would attempt to tell you to be good, but I don't want to waste my breath. Instead, I'll just say make good choices."

"We're not that bad, Roz," Klaus said, eyes twinkling.

Kristof rolled his eyes. "Speak for yourself, I always make excellent choices."

"Try not to get rusticated, will you? And you better write me, or I'll tell Blake never to speak to either of you again." The horrified looks on their faces made me burst out laughing.

I hugged the quiet Harold next and wished him the best with his remaining years. We hadn't gotten especially close, but I liked him. And after Will's revelation about Harold's position here, I also had a sneaking suspicion he was the scout I'd never met, which had worked out well for both of us. "Thank you for everything you did for me, Harold," I said quietly, squeezing his shoulder. "I appreciated all of it."

He smiled with a shy nod. "You're welcome, Roz."

Will received one last bone-crushing hug before I disappeared into the coach and let the first tears come. Goodness, I would miss the boys terribly. I'd miss their antics and racing on the River Cam. I'd miss our deep conversations and teasing banter. I'd miss all the heated debates and the luncheon sessions.

After the farewells were made, the duke, Ansel, and Tarik climbed into the carriage. My father sat beside me, facing the other two. I leaned my head against my father's arm. "Thank you, Papa."

"You're welcome, my girl."

The stress of the morning had taken it out of me, and the gentle rocking of the carriage made my eyes drift shut. Before I fell asleep, I could hear the three of them talking in low voices about Tarik's social club, and what he hoped to accomplish. I wanted to perk up to say what an exceptionally clever idea I thought it was, especially with the dearth of public intellectual salons, beyond private drawing rooms, for women.

But I knew Tarik could hold his own. He was a prodigy, after all.

CHAPTER TWENTY-TWO

Useful Things are justly preferable to useless Speculations.

—Isaac Newton

Tarik was once more staying at Ansel's pied-à-terre at The Albany. It would be for the rest of the season until he got his plans together. As it turned out, on the journey back to London, my father had been very intrigued with his idea for his club and was willing to back him on it, once Tarik nailed down more of the pertinent details. That made me very happy, since he would not be going back to France, at least not immediately, unless he couldn't find a job.

I had no doubt he would prevail either way.

I glanced over at him, where he was writing copious notes in a small book, ink stains all over his fingers while calculating sums of projected figures in his head. His sleeves were folded back over his elbows, and I lost myself in the mesmerizing landscape of his defined forearms, from his long, elegant fingers to his slender wrists and the ropy musculature that climbed to his rolled cuffs. It was unfair how delicious they were.

"You're ogling his arms again," Anna whispered into my ear.

"I was not! I was staring into space. Far away, beyond the walls of this building. Thinking about the practical application of this telescope," I scoffed, dragging my eyes away and focusing on finalizing the telescope with its brass fittings. The mirrors had been secured, including the inner one, which was mounted at a forty-five-degree angle facing the primary mirror. The eyepiece was the next bit to be attached and then aligned with the internal mirror. Once that was done, connecting the focuser with its sliding tube was the last step.

"Sure, you were." She handed me a handkerchief with a mischievous grin. "For the drool."

"You are incorrigible, Anna," I protested, ignoring the handkerchief, but I swiped my arm over the bottom half of my face anyway. When Tarik lifted laughing blue eyes to mine, my blush deepened. I'd been squarely caught, though it wasn't anything new. It was not my fault that the boy had perfectly sculpted arms and seeing them writing out sums was a certain form of blissful torture for me.

"How's the assembly?" he asked.

"Nearly done," I said. I probably would have been done an hour ago if I hadn't been lost in wicked daydreams about his forearms, but nobody needed to know that.

"I am excited to see you test it out, though it looks rather overcast outside at the moment," he mused, peering through the window. "We might have to wait for a clearer evening."

The weather was so unpredictable in England, but I was eager to use my painstakingly crafted instrument. I'd wait for a break in the clouds if I had to, but there was no way I wasn't exploring what this beauty could do. "I spoke with one of The Albany's managers, and apparently, there's a maintenance portion of the rooftop on this building. If the weather improves, we could try to set the telescope up there."

"Certainly," he said. "How far off are you?"

"Not far."

His mouth quirked. "Let me wrap up, then, and I'll help you carry it upstairs."

Tarik had surprised me by constructing a sturdy frame for the telescope, with clamps and brackets to hold the instrument in position.

Next was the collimation, or centering of the optical components. Squinting, I peered down to the tube to make sure the reflection from the primary mirror was visible and centered, before aligning the secondary mirror to make sure that light was meeting the eyepiece. I focused the telescope on a teapot that was on the stove, fiddling with each of the positions until I was satisfied that a clear image was visible.

Somewhat stunned, I slumped back in my seat, staring at the finished product. I had built a telescope! *Me!* The sense of accomplishment was surreal.

"Are you ready?" Tarik asked, coming up behind me and studying the final result. "It looks great."

"Thank you," I said. "I'm nervous. What if it doesn't work?"

"You're a scientist," Tarik replied. "You step back, reevaluate the data, make the necessary adjustments, and then repeat the experiment."

"It's that easy?"

His lips brushed the top of my head. "A very clever, very beautiful young woman once told me that nothing worth keeping is ever easy." I smiled at the memory. "If we don't persevere in our studies, in the pursuit of truth and knowledge, and learn from our failures, then we are no better than the most ignorant of society."

God, Zia was right—when he spouted wisdom like that, I wanted to climb him like a tree!

Instead, I maintained my decorum. By a hair.

"Very well," I said primly. "Follow me. Anna, you can stay here until we return."

She frowned. "My lady?"

"I assure you that if my virtue was going to be ruined by this gentleman, he would have done it long before now. Fortunately, Mr. St. Clair is a man who values explicit consent, and I haven't *quite* lost my head to him yet."

My heart though . . . well, that was another matter.

We climbed the stairs to the rooftop, and by the time we reached the highest level, we were both panting with exertion. Though Tarik was certainly worse off than me, lugging the unwieldy stand. My telescope didn't weigh that much, and it was only three feet long. We opened the door to the wide space. The sky was black with only occasional sparkling stars and the sporadic view of the moon. When it was visible, I could see the spires of St. Paul's cathedral in the distance as well as the glitter of the Thames threading its gleaming path through the city.

I picked a spot on one corner of the rooftop. "Here, I think," I told Tarik.

He hefted the frame into position and then helped me attach the telescope to the brackets he'd glued into place. I tinkered with the positioning a bit and checked the collimation again before directing it right to the moon. It wasn't quite full, but I hoped that we would be able to see some of the craters on its surface.

"I can't do it," I whispered to Tarik. "You look first and tell me if it's fuzzy and terrible."

One glance at my fraught expression had him nodding. He bent over, peering through the eyepiece, and I held my breath. He adjusted the focuser and seemed to spend more time than usual centering on the image. Was it *that* bad? Had I failed in properly installing the mirrors? It seemed like an eternity before he stood, his face displaying nothing.

"Oh, no. You're wearing your card sharp face."

He smiled. "Your turn."

I swallowed and approached the eyepiece. This moment felt momentous. When I lowered to it, my eye getting used to the white image reflected to me, I could barely hold back my gasp. It was the moon in all its beautiful, silvery glory, showing the craters and the mountain ranges, displaying long shadows over the uneven, jagged surface. It was in waxing gibbous phase, which means more than half of its shape was visible and shaped like a bright oval.

"Oh my *God,*" I whispered. "Isn't it beautiful?"

"Yes, she's the most beautiful thing I've ever seen," Tarik said in a voice that didn't sound like he was making a scientific observation. I turned my head to see where he was looking, and it wasn't at the moon. His attention was focused on me.

"I meant the moon," I said as he bracketed me from the back and bent past me to take another look.

"I know. But I meant *you*." Tarik rose and gathered me close, one arm banding about my waist and pressing my back into his chest. He nuzzled my nape, nose tracking along the column of my throat to my ear. "You did it, chérie. I am so proud of you."

"Thank you. I couldn't have done it without you." I grinned and turned in his arms to face him. "So, did I pass your final examination, Mr. Tutor?"

He grinned back and pulled me close. "I believe the subject matter requires some light tweaks. It's a matter of position, you see." One hand slipped under my jaw, fingers cupping the back of my head as he arranged me where he wanted me to be, my chin tilted up. "Like so."

His thumb grazed over my bottom lip.

"There, that's perfect. Only I don't know if the aperture is correct."

I giggled. "The aperture."

"Of course," he said peppering kisses over my face. "The size of the aperture determines the power of the resolution."

"Tarik?" I murmured.

His mouth feathered over mine. "Oui, mon amour?"

My body shivered at the endearment. "Will you just shut up and kiss me?"

Thankfully, he obliged, and then we were both blissfully silent for quite some time, standing there above the streets of London, where only the moon and the stars could see us.

A fortnight later, I was practically a moon expert.

I had my amateur telescope pointed to the night sky any chance I could get. I'd also recorded my findings in a notebook, though they weren't anything remarkable or not catalogued before. Still, they were new to me. I painstakingly tracked the shadows of the mountain ranges through all the many phases of the moon I could see, noting all my observations, no matter how small. Part of being a good amateur astronomer, besides having an excellent grasp of mathematics, physics, and celestial mechanics, was to pay attention to detail and data. I didn't expect to discover anything new, but honing those skills was just as important.

Once more, however, it was overcast, and I wasn't in the mood to do anything. Zia and Ela, on the other hand, were insistent that I could not stay at home and pretend to emulate a sloth. There was apparently some secret soiree that a select few had been invited to and that I simply had to attend. However, I didn't see the need to socialize and impress any gentlemen in the *ton,* now that my father had relented on his threat of marrying me off.

There was only one gentleman I wanted.

And just as I suspected, Tarik had categorically impressed the very hard-to-sway Duke of Delmont with his final proposal. So while the former was off trying to finalize a property lease for his new space with the duke as well as my cousin, Blake, Keston, and Rafi, all of whom he'd become quite close with, I'd hoped to spend a cozy evening reading the latest treatise on celestial mechanics by Pierre-Simon Laplace in bed. *Bliss.*

"This is the event of the season," Zia coaxed, reminding me that she was still there.

"I don't care about the season," I said with a shrug. "What on earth is a secret soiree anyway? People will do anything for attention. Are we honestly yielding to this?"

Ela pouted, making me narrow my eyes, because she wasn't one for theatrics. That was usually Zia's job. "This one is special. We can make it a girls' evening, just the three of us, spending time together like we used to before boys."

They weren't going to let this one go, I realized. "Fine. What is the dress required?"

Zia and Ela exchanged a nonplussed look that made me frown again. They were behaving rather peculiarly. Anna was more helpful when she cleared her throat and politely interjected, "Nice but warm, my lady, so perhaps a pelisse will be warranted. I gather you may be outside for part of the soiree. And the address is a few miles east of London proper."

"Outdoors in the evening?" I asked, surprised. "Have I seen that invitation? I don't recall anything so specific."

"It's with the others, my lady," Anna said.

Zia threw an arm wide. "You know how these eccentric aristocrats are. There might be garden games and whatnot."

"You and Ela are acting very strangely."

Ela smiled, showing all her teeth, an expression that made me release a horrified giggle. "No stranger than normal. Very well, we will be back here in two hours to collect you."

"Why does that sound ominous?" I asked.

Zia rolled her eyes and waggled her fingers as my friends swept from the foyer in a flash of muslin. "Because we are secretly abducting you?"

I shook my head at her, not sure if she was joking. Zia had a quirky sense of humor, and considering she and her little band of lady knights had *robbed* her brother and his friends once upon a time to save an orphanage, I wouldn't put it past her to kidnap anyone.

I was hoping to hear from Tarik by the time I finished getting ready, but there were no messages. I quelled my disappointment. He'd been very busy over the last two weeks, setting up various contracts and agreements with Papa's solicitor to get his business idea off the ground.

Having the enthusiastic backing of the Duke of Delmont opened many doors in London, including those of other aristocrats who wanted to be part of such an intriguing concept. Though there were still many who snubbed their noses at the inclusion of women, not just as members but as bona fide academic colleagues. We didn't need them; we only needed a few.

I loved that Tarik was trying to be the change the world needed.

Anna put the finishing touches on my coiffure, which was a new style. Half of my hair was pinned up and the other half left to fall like a curtain of black silk around my shoulders. It was a pity that Tarik would not be attending tonight's soiree—he was obsessed with my hair. I made a mental note to request this style more often.

The dress Anna had chosen was one I hadn't worn before . . . or seen before, come to think of it. It was an elegant dark silver silk ensemble with a sash of seed-pearl beading settled under the bust and delicate embroidery of tiny stars and phoenixes over the bodice and hemline. The stitching was exquisite.

"Where did this come from?" I asked. "I don't recall ordering it."

Anna lifted one shoulder. "It was delivered with the rest of your things, my lady. Perhaps the duchess commissioned it? The phoenix is a symbol of harmony and prosperity in your family's customs, no?"

It was. The fenghuang bestowed harmonious blessings on the kind and honorable. Perhaps my mother *had* commissioned it, though the symbolism was mostly used for bridal wear in Chinese culture. I supposed I was grateful it wasn't pineapples.

In the foyer, Anna deftly fastened a plain but gorgeously made charcoal pelisse with wide sleeves over my shoulders and then threw her cloak over her own shoulders. Her eyes sparkled with an unusual amount of cheerfulness. "There. You are a vision, my lady."

"Is it too much for the soiree?" I asked. "I feel overdressed for a garden event."

She shook her head and ushered me out the door to where Ela's carriage was waiting. The girls were already inside. Since Ela didn't require a chaperone, as she was married, she could technically *be* a chaperone for Zia. I still required Anna to accompany me.

"Where are we going?"

Zia wrinkled her nose. "Settle in for a bit. It's near Windsor Castle."

"The king's residence?" I asked with a gasp. "My gown is lovely, but it's not a court dress."

"No," Ela said noncommittally. "A bit north of there."

Something felt decidedly odd. The girls lapsed into chatter about the remarkably clear weather, the end of the season, and plans for Zia's upcoming nuptials. Contrary to everyone's expectations, and also typically Zia, she was having an intimate summer wedding at her father's ancestral seat in Berkshire. Her residence was a few miles farther east than Windsor.

When the coach started to slow, it was in front of a large brick house with wide windows.

"Here we are. You and Anna, go on in. Ela and I will be there shortly," Zia said with a distressed sound that sounded quite theatrical. "I need assistance with a tear in my gown."

I blinked. "Anna can help."

Ela shook her head, shooing us off. "I'll take care of it."

Again, decidedly odd.

As we descended the carriage steps, the house windows were lit from within, but there didn't seem to be any other carriages in the drive. Were we at the right address? Approaching the door, I knocked tentatively when Anna pointed explicitly at the entrance. When the door opened, my jaw slackened.

"Tarik! What are you doing here?" I blurted, noticing his elegant ensemble. "Did you come for the soiree as well?"

He took my hand and drew me inside. "You take my breath away, mon coeur, every time I see you," he said, kissing my knuckles. I blushed at the husky endearment. I loved when he called me his *heart*. "I want to introduce you to someone. This is Miss Caroline Herschel."

I blinked. And blinked again. Had I heard him correctly? But then the tiny older lady, who was barely a few inches over four feet, smiled. "Lady Rosalin, it's a pleasure to meet a fellow lover of astronomy and, of course, my dear friend Susu's daughter."

It was the hunter of comets herself.

I sucked in a wild breath that didn't come close to reaching my lungs and swayed on my feet, only to be bolstered by a grinning Tarik.

"Miss Herschel, I am a *devoted* admirer of yours," my voice emerged as a squeak. "The eight comets you have discovered, the catalogue of stars . . . I . . . I . . ."

She patted my arm fondly. "There'll be plenty of time for us to chat later. I believe your young man planned this surprise very carefully."

I was shocked to say the least, but my stare swung to a smug Tarik. "There's no soiree, is there?" My question was rhetorical. "How did you know—?"

"Your mother arranged it, but this isn't all of the surprise. Come on." He took my arm and led my numb body to the back garden of the Herschel home.

Oh, my giddy stars . . .

All the blood felt like it was leaving my body in a rush as I stared up and up and up at the largest telescope in the world, built by Miss Herschel's brother, William, and commissioned by the late king for over four thousand pounds. The tube was forty feet long and surrounded by conical-shaped wooden scaffolding. The mirror alone was forty-eight inches in diameter. I openly gaped, not even caring that my mouth was hanging open.

Tarik tugged gently, and I followed in a daze. "Are we going up there?" I asked in a breathy voice, staring at the viewing platform near the upper end.

"Of course we are."

I was even more breathless by the time we stood on the platform, the sky above us littered with stars, the moon just rising to the east. I was about to look through the personal telescope built by the man who discovered the first new planet since ancient times. The moment was surreal. "What is it pointed at?" I murmured.

"Look," Tarik said.

I put my eye to the finder and gasped at what appeared to be an indistinct smear on the velvet background of stars. "Is that . . . a *comet*?" I tuned the focus and stared in rapt delight at the hazy nucleus with a glowing tail that reached out behind it, almost like a bluish plume. It was the most glorious thing I had ever seen. "Which one is that? What's it called?"

"It doesn't have a name yet. I was cataloguing celestial bodies to have a few for you to look at with your telescope when I detected a faint luminescence that seemed to have a noticeable motion near Cassiopeia, unlike the fixed stars around it. I spoke to Mr. Pond at the Royal Observatory, and it is indeed a comet. I observed and tracked it for a while, but I wanted the discovery to be ours. I was thinking we could use your middle name to identify it."

"My middle name?" I asked, gaping at him while my brain tried to process the unbelievable information that this was an *undiscovered* comet. "Don't you want to use yours? You saw it first."

"I want to share the discovery with you." He shrugged, a flush cresting his cheekbones. I couldn't help the warmth that spread through me. "Mine is Étienne, by the way."

It was such a French name, and I adored the way it rolled off his tongue. "My middle name is Zhenyi, after the Chinese scientist. She was a famous mathematician and astronomer who proved the movement of the equinoxes and wrote about lunar eclipses."

"I shouldn't be surprised," he said. "Very well, we shall name her C/1820 X1 Zhenyi-Étienne and send our observations off to the Royal Society."

I stared at the comet again, noticing that it had moved slightly. *Astonishing!*

"I have one more surprise," Tarik said softly.

I straightened with a laugh. "I don't think I can take much more."

He pointed to the lower platform, where, to my shock, I saw the telescope I had built resting on its very small frame. I pursed my lips as he led me down to it. "I think gazing through that will be a disappointment after the Great Forty-Foot."

"It's yours. You built it. It should never feel less than."

Such a sweet thing to say, but wrong, nonetheless. I moved to the eyepiece and maneuvered the tube in the direction of the comet. I frowned. The focus seemed to be off—the clarity would not be the same as the previous telescope, but since the comet was visible with the naked eye, it should be more than a fuzzy, odd-shaped white blob.

"Something's wrong," I began, lifting my head, only to see Tarik standing at the other end of the tube. "What are you doing? You're blocking my—"

My words cut off abruptly as I noticed what he was holding up in front of the telescope.

A ring . . . a rose-cut diamond cluster ring.

An *engagement* ring.

"Tarik?" I wheezed.

His eyes shone with so much emotion that my knees nearly buckled. "Lady Rosalin, I'm certain you already know that my heart is yours. We are binary stars, forever destined to be gravitationally bound in orbit around each other. You are my other half; the girl who makes me feel seen and cherished and present." He smiled as tears of joy sprang from my eyes. "You must know I love you. Would you grace me with the honor of giving me your hand in marriage?"

I couldn't speak.

"Say yes and put the poor sap out of his misery!" someone shouted from far below us, and I glanced down, sobs clogging my throat at the sight of a small crowd gathered there.

"Blake!" Zia squawked. "Don't ruin their moment, you brainless clod!"

My parents stood with my baby brother, Bowen. Then there was Blake, Ansel, Ela and Keston, Zia and Rafi, and even my friends from Trinity, Will, the twins, and Harold. My faithful lady's maid and groom, Anna and Henry, grinned up at me. And Caroline Herschel herself smiled like a tiny benevolent angel.

My eyes tracked back to the boy patiently waiting for my reply, all the love in the universe shining in his gaze. "You planned this."

"I had help," he said. "From your mama, your friends, and even the duke, who only reluctantly gave his permission after hours of my groveling and signing a contract in blood stating that I will never let you want for anything or so help me God." I let out a choked laugh. "So would you make me the happiest man in the world, Lady Rosalin Zhenyi Chen?"

I stared at the boy I loved most in the entire cosmos.

"Of course I will." I laughed through my tears as he kissed me. Cheers from below filled the air. "But first, I have a few very vital questions for you that may impact my decision."

He smirked. "Another examination?"

I nodded solemnly, mentally flying through the specifications of my marriage plan and checking off each one. Scholarly aptitude and ability to engage in intellectual discourse—*check*. Progressive stance on women's status and rights in the aristocracy—*check*. Emotional breadth and depth—*check*. Political views in favor of changing antiquated laws—*check*. Physical compatibility—*extra check*. I blushed at the last. "Possibly worse than the Tripos," I told him.

Tarik held me close, wearing that smile I so adored, his bright blue eyes sparkling with challenge. "Do your worst, my lady. I look forward to proving my worth."

I wanted to tell him he already had, but where was the fun in that?

"Very well," I said, thinking hard, though it was quite impossible with the smitten way he was staring at me. "How many prime numbers exist between one and one hundred?"

"Too easy." Grinning, he peppered my brow, cheeks, and lips with kisses instead, and it was only when we had climbed down the tower to my friends and family that I realized he had kissed me exactly twenty-five times . . . the correct answer to my question.

"Did you answer me in kisses?" I asked as we reached the bottom.

"Impressed yet?"

I pouted. "I should have said between one and one thousand."

My very creative and clever fiancé winked. "According to the Sieve of Eratosthenes, then I shall owe you one hundred and forty-three more."

Sieve of Eratosthenes . . . Be still my beating heart.

It was a simple ancient algorithm from a Greek mathematician in the third century BC that said any multiple of a prime number could not be a prime number. As two was a prime number, then four, six, and eight or any other multiples of two would not be prime numbers, and so forth.

Who said mathematics couldn't make one swoon?

Because after nearly four interminable seasons, I had truly, *finally,* found my perfect match.

EPILOGUE

All bodies whatsoever are endowed with a principle of mutual gravitation.

—Isaac Newton

London, 1824

YOU ARE CORDIALLY INVITED

to

A NOVEL EXPERIENCE

AND GRAND CELEBRATORY BALL

AT THE COLLECTIVE

Pall Mall, London

I stared down at the white-and-gold invitation, immense pride filling me at what Tarik had achieved at long last, four long and challenging years later. After many setbacks with property acquisition as well as the process of getting funding into place; working with architects and master builders; finding dependable tradesmen for various parts of the contruction, including carpenters, masoners, plumbers, and painters; and sourcing materials like stone and timber, we were finally ready for the big day.

The grand opening of the official clubhouse for The Collective had arrived at last.

Feeling much too emotional, I sat in my dressing room, allowing Anna, who was still my lady's maid but also now a proud multi-published poet, to do the finishing touches on my hair. She and Henry had married soon after Tarik's proposal, and Henry continued to work for my parents, though he did drive us occasionally into town. He and Anna lived in a small cottage on the property Tarik and I owned, which wasn't too far out of London, in the Westminster area.

Ironically enough, our home was in Datchet near Windsor Castle, where Caroline Herschel had once lived with her brother for a few years. Sadly, she'd moved back to Hanover, Germany, after he died two years ago. Continuing to be inspired by her, I was now the proud discoverer of several more comets, star clusters, and nebulae and was in the process of composing my own book, called *A Treatise on Celestial Bodies*, featuring a graphic representation and history of the various constellations visible in the night sky.

It was a work in progress.

"How do I look?" my husband asked from where he stood at the bedchamber door. He was so tall and handsome that I had to force myself to start breathing again.

I grinned as Tarik crossed the distance between us. "Like the gorgeous new owner of the most exclusive club in London."

"*Co*-owner," he said, those blue eyes sparkling like jewels when he bent to kiss my cheek. "My wife, the singular Lady Rosalin Chen St. Clair, also shares that title."

"She sounds quite stubborn," I teased, smiling and thanking Anna, who was accustomed to our spontaneous displays of affection and left the room with a playful eye roll.

"I prefer tempestuous," he countered, offering me his hand. Taking it, I rose as he moved to stand behind me, nuzzling my nape, which was on display with the updo Anna had fashioned. "I love your hair like this, where I can admire this elegant, graceful neck of yours. After your clever brain, it's my favorite part of you."

"We're going to be late if you keep doing that," I said breathlessly. The more he nibbled and planted tiny kisses along the length of my throat, the more said clever brain decided to go on hiatus. His eyes met mine in the mirror, so much love in them, it made my heart swell. "And it's your special day. We cannot be late."

"*Our* day, chérie." His gleaming gaze swept down my figure, from my crown to the tips of my slippers. My gown for the opening was a rich purplish blue that matched his eyes almost perfectly. Clearly, he approved. "Toujours si belle, plus que toutes les étoiles dans le ciel."

No matter how many times I heard my scholar tell me that I was more beautiful than all the stars in the sky in his velvety French accent, it never ceased to make me weak in the knees. Tarik reached in front of me and draped a glittering sapphire necklace over my collarbones before fastening the clasp at the back. The deep blue gems caught the light and shimmered.

"What is this for?" I asked with a gasp.

"Do I need a reason to shower my beautiful wife in jewels?" he said, knuckles turning to graze my cheek as I spun in his arms.

"Tarik, I don't need extravagant—"

He cupped my face between his hands and kissed me, silencing my protest. When I was blissfully compliant, he continued, "I wanted to mark this new chapter in our lives. You've given me everything I could ever want and more. When it felt like I would never get here, you stood by me, encouraged me, believed in me. *Loved* me."

"And I always will."

Gracious, my heart felt like it was ten sizes too big for my chest. I threw my arms around his neck and sealed my mouth to his once more. What felt like an eternity later—we were most certainly going to be late to our own party—my husband led me down the stairs to the waiting carriage.

Tarik and I had gotten married three years ago in a small ceremony, and while our lives had not been easy—high society had had many choice things to say about Lady Rosalin Chen marrying a commoner so far beneath her station—we had survived the gossip. With careful planning, my substantial dowry had served us well. Some of it we'd used to live, and the rest we'd invested into our joint venture.

Just like the first comet we had named together, The Collective was ours.

My very stubborn husband had absolutely refused to claim it as his own.

Though he had started The Collective two years ago, using a rental property in Westminster in order to guage interest and membership for his idea, particularly as it related to a space for intellectual discussions as well as entertainment, the unique concept had taken off, and by the end of the first year had a thousand members, with a six-month wait list.

With my father's powerful connections as well as those of the Duke and Duchess of Harbridge—Zia's parents—we had many founding members in the aristocracy who had been excited at the prospect of a club that celebrated the arts, sciences, and engineering. The idea of a nonpartisan club was revolutionary . . . where membership depended on achievement rather than circumstances or birth or personal connections. Tarik had methodically curated the statistics and sought reliable investors to fund the final construction.

As we pulled up in the carriage on Pall Mall, which was already crowded with members and guests arriving for the inaugural ball, I smiled in awe at the palatial structure. The four-story building was designed in a clean, symmetrical neoclassical style—featuring Roman and Greek aesthetics—with pale stone, large windows, marble columns, and a decorative frieze, featuring the gods and goddess of wisdom and knowledge from all around the world, including Athena, Saraswati, Minerva, Ganesha, Thoth, Ahura Mazda, Omoikane, Mimir, Quetzalcoatl, and Nabu. The latin quote "*hypotheses non fingo—I frame no hypotheses,*" by our favorite mathematician, from *Principia,* stood proudly above the entrance.

The inside was as impressive as the outside. The dining and drawing rooms with plush, elegant furniture had multiple fireplaces and pleasing views over the extensive landscaped back gardens. Lavish kitchens completed the ground floor. In addition to numerous well-appointed discussion salons on the second floor, there were separate music rooms for concerts and a window-filled massive ballroom.

The next floor featured the gaming rooms, with tables for whist, faro, quinze, and hazard; the adjacent billiards and smoking rooms; and a stocked library and an art gallery. But the pièce de résistance was the private observatory dome constructed on the topmost floor of the building—yet another of my darling husband's gifts to me—the St. Clair Observatory with telescopes donated by my friend Caroline.

Suffice it to say that The Collective had been a labor of love.

"Are you ready, chérie?" Tarik asked softly, threading his fingers through mine.

"Yes." I squeezed his hand and stalled him with a palm to his chest. "Before we go in, I want you to know how very proud I am of you. Even with all the dissent on admitting female members, you did not waver. You did exactly what you envisioned and you never compromised the integrity of your dream."

Those crystalline blue eyes glistened with emotion. "Thank you, mon coeur. Je t'aime."

"I love you, too. Always."

Hand in hand, we exited the coach up the marble steps and into the grand foyer for the first official ball of The Collective, to celebrate the opening of the club's permanent location. As we entered the opulent ballroom, the welcome cheers were deafening. I had tears in my eyes as I saw our family and friends, older, wiser, and still living their best lives.

Keston and Ela, the Marquess and Marchioness of Ridley, had twin girls three years ago. They were a rambunctious handful. Pregnant again, Ela was absolutely glowing, and her dashing marquess could not be more besotted with his wife, who also led one of the largest charitable organizations in London, dedicated to protecting girls and women who needed legal assistance.

Rafi and Zia, now Viscount and Viscountess Hollis—Rafi's uncle had passed last year from gout—were a renowned composer and sought-after artist. Parents to a handsome two-year-old boy who seemed intent on following in his daredevil mama's foosteps, they were performing in music and art exhibitions at the club over the next few weeks. Zia also ran a foundation for education and literacy with her finishing school friends, Greer, Lalita, Blythe, and Nori—the latter two were still happily in love—called the Reformed Lady Knights, which provided free educational resources and books to children across England.

With the exception of Harold, who had returned to America to become a physician, my friends from Cambridge were also in attendance. Interestingly enough, Will had just proposed to Lady Petal, who had accepted his suit after leading him on a merry chase. To my immense relief, she had finally found her own very loyal, very loving tree!

The twins, to no one's surprise, had abandoned joining the priesthood and were hired as the brilliant comanagers to The Collective instead—the clergy's loss had been our gain. Klaus had gleefully reported that our old nemesis James had been jailed after being found guilty of embezzlement.

Blake, my long-standing best friend, also worked for The

Collective. He was chairman and head of the founding committee, and as a primary investor, responsible for overseeing our rapidly growing membership and ensuring we always had a diverse range of scholars for debate and intellectual engagement from learned societies in England and beyond. As chairman, he was tasked with executing our mission of using knowledge to improve society and leaving the world better than we'd come into it. He showed absolutely no signs of settling down or abandoning his roguish ways.

My cousin-in-crime, Ansel, had gone back abroad, and he was now currently somewhere in China based on his last correspondence. I missed him terribly, but I loved reading about his travel adventures. He was making a name for himself as a cultural explorer and anthropologist.

As we walked through the ballroom, surrounded by so much love and joy, I couldn't help but be thankful for everything Tarik and I had accomplished together. We'd made mistakes, but more importantly, we'd learned from them . . . and kept going.

Tears fell as I saw my mama's beaming smile and my father's proud expression. He'd believed in Tarik, too, at every step of the way, his confidence never faltering. I loved him so much for that, but as he'd said, no woman with probability skills like mine would ever *not* back a winner. They had left my baby brother, Bowen, who was now eight and proving to be yet another mathematics prodigy, at home. I snorted. The apples stayed close to the tree in this family.

After the official toast was made by Papa, my husband escorted me into the first waltz of the evening. As Tarik took me in his arms, I couldn't help remembering the first time we had done this, four years ago.

I tipped my head back and drowned in those lapis lazuli eyes. "Monsieur?"

"Oui, chérie?"

"Do you like puzzles?"

His lips curved upward as he spun me in an intricate turn, the strength in his arms making me lose my train of thought for a second. "I do."

"Two lovers—let's call them the astronomer and the tutor—leave two destinations sixty miles apart. The astronomer travels east at seven miles per hour and the tutor west at five miles per hour. In how many hours will they get to kiss, and how far will they each have gone?"

"Why is the astronomer faster?" he asked with a chuckle. "The tutor has notably longer legs."

"The astronomer is highly motivated for this kiss."

His lips dropped to my lips, and he grinned. "Say the time of the kiss is *x*, then the astronomer travels seven *x* and the utterly smitten but tragically slow tutor travels five *x*. If seven *x* plus five *x* equals sixty, then twelve *x* equals sixty, so the value of *x* is five." Drawing me into his arms with no thought to anyone around us, he grazed the shell of my ear, then my cheek, and then my forehead with his lips. "He kisses the love of his life after five hours, after she has walked thirty-five miles and he has walked twenty-five, even though he'll walk a thousand for her and then a thousand more, whatever it takes to be in her presence once again."

"Full marks," I whispered with a shiver, that mind of his my utter weakness.

"Did you have any doubt?" he asked, and I shook my head. He was the one constant in my world. We weren't even dancing now, only swaying in the middle of the other couples. But this was *our* universe, and we were its nucleus with our loved ones orbiting all around us.

"Gravity is a strange thing, isn't it?" I mused, thinking about life. "It explains the planets in orbit, but no one truly knows how the planets formed."

Tarik pursed his lips. "Scientific laws can explain only so much. I suppose the existential questions about how we came to be here will always persist."

"Perhaps it's a bit like love when you think about it. Transcendent."

Love wasn't a law like gravity; it was the ultimate paradox. It was contradictory and impossible to predict. There were no universal rules governing its existence. It took work and sacrifice. Trial and error. Unflinching persistence. One could only keep it if it was unencumbered. It was beauty and devastation, and every moment in between—and perhaps like the universe of stars, a series of impacts and collisions built and collapsed over time.

It was magical. It was real.

A love like ours was whatever we wanted it to be.

"Your heart is my gravity," I whispered.

My husband smiled. "As yours is mine . . . binary stars, forever."

AUTHOR'S NOTE

Dear Reader,

I can't believe we are at the end of The Diamonds series, but here we are. It is so bittersweet to say goodbye to this incredible group of feisty young adults, but I truly hope you enjoyed reading about their coming-of-age adventures. Writing this particular story for *Rebel Heiress* (an academic take on *She's the Man*, which is loosely based on Shakespeare's *Twelfth Night*) was definitely a challenge, mostly because of all the substantial academic research required to make sure it was authentic for the period! This is an anti-historical novel, primarily because it features an entirely diverse and inclusive cast of characters, which was not typical for the era. But once more, that's the beauty of creating fiction . . . stories have power and hold unlimited possibility. I always want my stories to be inclusive, and for all my readers to see themselves on page.

I love to include real historical figures to make the story feel more authentic. Several actual people from the era had cameos in this novel, including John Pond, the sixth Astronomer Royal from the Royal Greenwich Observatory; Dr. Christopher Wordsworth, Master of Trinity College at the time; and astronomer Caroline Herschel, to name a few. Sir Isaac Newton was a central figure in the Scientific Revolution, primarily known for his discovery of colors in white light as well as the three laws of motion, which laid the groundwork for modern physics. Quotes from his various works were used at the start of the chapters. Arguably one of the most impactful figures in science, I wanted to use his words to underscore some of the choices made by both my heroine Rosalin and my hero Tarik. Copies of his books are still at Cambridge University, which boasts the largest collection of his works, including an annotated first edition of *Principia*.

Many people chose to subvert gender norms during the eighteenth and nineteenth centuries. Charles Hamilton, known as the "Female Husband," married several women in the eighteenth century, while others like Hannah Snell, who enlisted in the army as James Gray in 1789, wanted to be soldiers. Chevalier d'Eon (1728–1810) was a French spy who was born male but identified as a woman in her adult life, Charlotte-Genevieve-Louise-Auguste-Andrée-Timothée D'Eon de Beaumont, and signed her name as Mademoiselle d'Eon. She dueled in a fencing match as a woman at Carlton House for the Prince of Wales in 1787. The physician in this book, Dr. James Barker, is based on a real person named Dr. James Barry, who was assigned female at birth but identified exclusively as a man for his entire adult life. He was a brilliant surgeon who rose to the highest medical post in the British army and performed the first successful cesarean with both mother and child surviving in 1826 in Cape Town, South Africa.

During this period, most aristocratic young women like Rosalin were educated at home by governesses and private tutors, with instruction that was tailored to their future roles as wives and mothers, and included only approved subjects like music, art, romantic languages, and religion. By 1840, 60 percent of women in Britain were still illiterate. Women were not allowed to attend university like their male counterparts, and some subjects like philosophy and science were considered much too advanced for their gender. Young women who wanted to learn other subjects usually took it upon themselves to self-educate at private and public circulating libraries. They would also solve complex mathematical problems in journals anonymously, often entering their names with initials, false names, or not at all.

This was the main deciding factor behind Rosalin's choice to impersonate her cousin and take his place at Trinity College, part of Cambridge University. Women were certainly not allowed to enroll at Cambridge or any other university, at least until 1869 for Cambridge and 1878 for Oxford, and couldn't earn degrees until 1948 and 1920 respectively.

Since my heroine is Chinese, it was important for me to research Chinese scientists who were female and broke gender boundaries just like their Western counterparts. Wang Zhenyi was born in China in 1768 to a family of scholars and was a well-known scientist during the Qing Dynasty (1644–1912). Like many other female scholars across the world, she defied gender conventions to educate herself on mathematics, medicine, geography, and astronomy. Her grandfather was passionate about books and astronomy, and her father was proficient in medical science and mathematics. Following in their footsteps, she read through her grandfather's entire library collection after his death. She also learned martial arts, archery, and horseback riding from the wife of a Mongolian general. At eighteen, she made connections with other female scholars. After marriage at twenty-five, she continued to excel in astronomy and mathematics and even became a teacher to several young men, which was unusual at the time. Zhenyi wrote about the movement of equinoxes as well as the calculation of their movement in her article on celestial bodies, "Dispute of the Procession of the Equinoxes." She also penned several other articles about stars as well as lunar and solar eclipses and conducted her own original experiments and research according to astronomical theories. She recorded her observations on the relationships between the sun, moon, and Earth in her article "The Explanation of a Solar Eclipse." In mathematics, she was exceptionally proficient in trigonometry and the Pythagorean theorem. She also rewrote more complex mathematical books with simpler language and calculations and published her own versions, like *The Musts of Calculation*. Zhenyi was also a poet and wrote about misogyny, wealth, and gender inequality. According to *Notable Women of China* by Barbara Bennett Peterson, He Hong Fei, and Zhang Guangyu, she advocated that we "are all people, who have the same reason for studying." The author of many articles and twelve published books, she died at twenty-nine in 1797.

Sophie Germain was born in France in 1776 to a wealthy middle-class family. Her father was a merchant. When she was thirteen, during the French Revolution, she spent her days in her family's library. Fascinated by a Roman story she found on geometry, she started educating herself, and her passion for mathematics was born. Despite her parents' discouragement, she persevered with her private studies, often studying at night by candlelight. At eighteen, she found a way to get notes from the newly formed École Polytechnique in Paris, even though women weren't permitted to enroll. Using a pseudonym, she submitted an analysis to one of the lecturers. Impressed by her work, especially after learning she was female, he became her mentor, introducing her to many mathematicians she never would have met on her own. In 1804, she started corresponding with a German mathematician, Carl Friedrich Gauss, on number theory, again hiding her identity. It wasn't until three years later that he realized she was a woman. In 1816, she entered a contest on mathematical law organized by the French Academy of Sciences for the third time (the first was in 1811, which she didn't win) and won with her *Memoir on the Vibrations of Elastic Plates*. The prize allowed her to meet many influential scientists and mathematicians as well as refine her work on number theory, and she was the first woman to be welcomed by the Institut de France. Though Gauss, her former mentor, convinced the University of Gottingen to confer an honorary degree to her, Sophie died in 1831 from breast cancer before she could receive it.

Last, but certainly not least, Caroline Herschel was born in 1750 to working-class parents, who encouraged her learning mathematics, French, and music. She contracted typhus at ten years old, which limited her growth, and she didn't grow past four feet, three inches. She lived with her brother William as his housekeeper. Though he was a successful musician, William was fascinated with making telescopes and received a pension from King George III to make more. He was also paid four thousand pounds by the king to build the largest telescope in the world—forty feet—and between 1789 and 1840, that telescope, known as the Great Forty-Foot telescope, remained at the Herschel home in Slough, which my fictional characters visit for the final proposal scene. Though the last actual observation made with the telescope was in 1815, I took some creative liberty to push it to 1820 for the sake of my story. Caroline became William's apprentice, helping him grind and polish the mirrors for his telescopes. She often took over for him when he traveled and eventually the king also gave her a pension of fifty pounds annually—which made her the first woman ever known to be paid for a scientific job. She catalogued nebulae and tracked comets, and by 1820, was a recognized female astronomer and had discovered eight comets herself. She was made an honorary member of the Royal Astronomical Society (RAS) in 1835 and was one of the first women in history to receive an award for her contribution to science. She died in 1848.

The Collective, Tarik's club, is inspired by a private members' club called The Athenaeum in Pall Mall, formed in 1824. This was a nonpartisan club for those with intellectual interests, and it celebrated anyone who achieved commendations in the arts, sciences, literature, and engineering. By December of 1824, the club had one thousand members. Like The Collective, the

Athenaeum clubhouse, built in 1830, boasted a large library, dining rooms, drawing rooms, a morning salon, and a suite of bedrooms. The total cost to build the clubhouse was nearly 43,000 pounds, the equivalent of 8.3 million dollars today, which is how much money Tarik would have needed from investors. However, women were only invited as full members there in 2002, starting as dinner guests in 1972, so it would have been quite progressive for The Collective to have female members so early in 1824. The Athenaeum still exists with over twenty thousand members.

The underlying message of *Rebel Heiress* is about being creative and resourceful when faced with adversity, especially if some hurdles may seem impossible to overcome. It's about how to be thoughtful, intentional, and enthusiastic, especially when advocating for your own wants and needs, and loving yourself just as you are. It's about never giving up on your dreams, even if they seem as inaccessible as the stars. At the end of the day, you are the author of your own destiny. You are the only one who can identify, pursue, and achieve your goals. No one else can do this for you, and like many of the ingenious, diligent scholars described above, occasionally, you may have to go the extra mile to succeed. You might have to work harder than you ever have before. It's worth it. Trust me, any investment in yourself is *always* worth the work.

Hope you enjoyed reading *Rebel Heiress*!

XO,

Amalie

ACKNOWLEDGMENTS

To my very clever and exceptionally brilliant editor Bria Ragin, to whom I can only offer my eternal gratitude for this entire series, thank you for letting me share these stories with the world. The Diamonds has been such a wonderful journey with you, and I am beyond grateful for signing with you and Joy Revolution.

To Thao Le, queen of diamonds, I remain in constant awe of everything you have done for me in this very capricious publishing career. Thank you to infinity for being such an incredible champion and advocate, and for always being supportive of all my unhinged ideas.

To the wonder duo, Nicola and David Yoon, enormous thanks for including me in such a groundbreaking imprint that fights to represent love in all its diverse forms. It is such an honor, truly, to have the Diamonds be part of publishing history and the path you charted.

Thank you to Wendy Loggia, Beverly Horowitz, and Mallory

Loehr for giving my stories such a fantastic home! To the immensely talented Fatima Baig and my incredible designer, Michelle Cunningham, thank you for bringing this cover to such vibrant, perfect life. You nailed it! To all my copyeditors and proofreaders, thank you! Huge thanks to the production, design, sales, and publicity teams for your hard work behind the scenes—I'm truly grateful for your support.

To Katie McGarry, Brigid Kemmerer, Angie Frazier, Wendy Higgins, and Aliza Mann, your friendship keeps me going—there are tackle hugs in your future, be warned. To all the readers, reviewers, booksellers, librarians, educators, extended family, and friends who support me and spread the word about my books, heartfelt thanks for being in my corner for all these years.

To my own diamond in the rough, Cameron, who has never made me feel anything but proud for being nerdy and neurodivergent, thank you for loving me exactly as I am. And to our three children, Connor, Noah, and Olivia, how I love seeing you follow your dreams. I hope you never, ever stop shining.

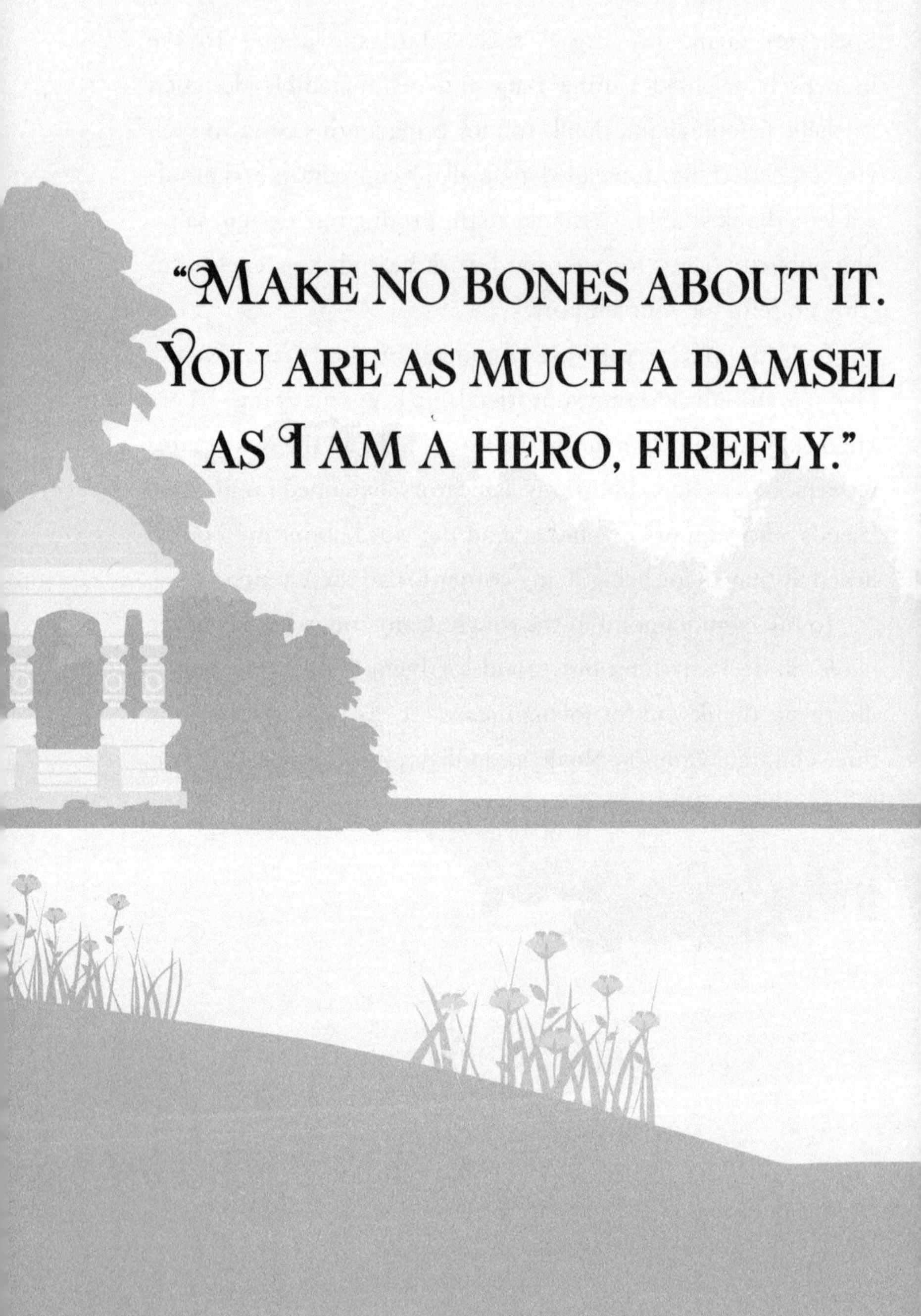
"Make no bones about it.
You are as much a damsel
as I am a hero, Firefly."

Don't miss this swoony companion novel!

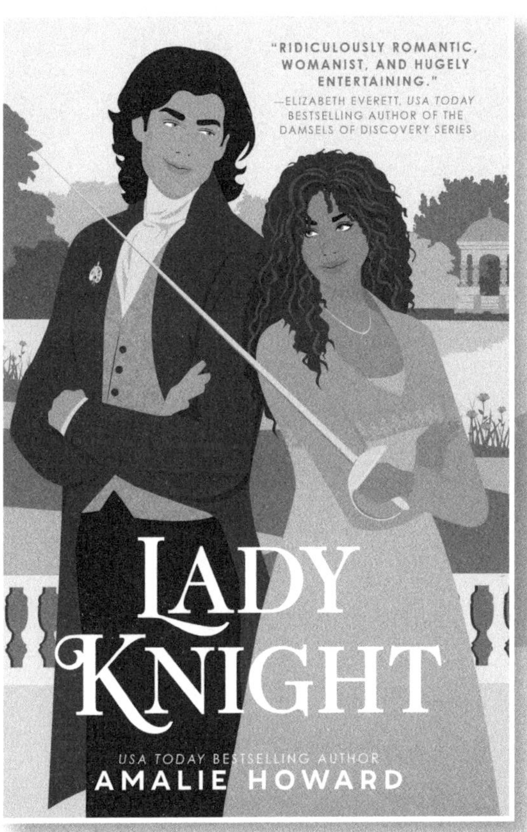

"A lively, spirited read."
—*Kirkus Reviews*

"This book is sure to delight."
—*Booklist*

"A must-have."
—*School Library Journal*

CHAPTER ONE

Strengthen the female mind by enlarging it, and there will be an end to blind obedience.

—Mary Wollstonecraft

London, 1819

The thrill of the hunt was unimaginable. Illicit. *Dangerous.*

Never mind that we'd be the ones chased like plump, juicy rabbits, by the Bow Street Runners no less, if we got caught. Hounslow Heath was known for its crime and the newssheets had written that the authorities were cracking down.

You won't get caught. Focus on the prize.

Yes, the prize was the bounty my brother's friends carried on their way home from what I hoped had been a lucrative evening at their gentlemen's social club. And no, I would not have imagined in a million years that I would be on Great Bath Road with one of my best friends riding toward a carriage ferrying a group of gents at an hour when aristocratic young ladies should be tucked away in their bedchambers, safe and sound, like the precious darlings they were.

Thank the heavens my parents slept soundly and my lady's maid, Gemma, turned a closed eye to my capers. Because instead of sleeping, here I was . . . out of breath, heart pounding, muscles screaming in panic, and yet, so gloriously alive that I'd take this frantic race through Hounslow Heath over another day living the perfectly ordered, lackluster life of Lady Zenobia Osborn—daughter to a duke and undisputed diamond of the season.

Pah! Being a diamond of the first water was categorically overrated.

Especially for the poor twit, being *me,* who had to shoulder that heavy responsibility like a cloak made of nettles. The pressure that it bore was simply too much. Every single gaze was on me this season to find the most impeccable match . . . to be worthy of carrying such an illustrious title and show that I was the true prize.

But I wasn't some silly *prize.*

I was a person.

With a brain, feelings, and a will of her own.

On the surface, I exceeded the *ton*'s requirements. One, I was pleasant enough in looks, except for the dreadful dash of freckles my governess seemed to abhor. She cautioned me daily to stay out of the sun. Not that I ever took that advice; I fed those precious little dots as much sunshine as I could—they were mine and they made me *me.* Two, I was in possession of an enormous dowry. And three, my father was an extremely formidable duke.

Furthermore, my skill at the pianoforte was unmatched, my

manners and breeding impeccable. My education was precisely adequate for a girl of my station—not that I let that stop me from listening in on my brother's lessons any chance I got. Everything else I learned after Keston went off to Eton was thanks to a well-stocked library.

Education was within one's grasp, if one cared to reach for it. Which I had always done without apology. Mathematics, philosophy, science, and other subjects like music, French, and needlepoint that were deemed acceptable for girls and taught by my governess, I devoured them all. I suspected that my parents knew that I was learned, and fortunately, they valued cleverness.

Despite my small personal rebellions, however, I was born and bred to be the perfect debutante . . . and eventually, the perfect bride to some faceless, well-heeled gentleman.

When the plain truth was I wanted more. I wanted *everything.* To write and compose my own songs someday, ones that weren't aristocracy-approved. I wanted to play them on a grand public stage. The idea of a duke's daughter being seen as a plebeian performer was scandalous in itself. While playing in the occasional music salon was appropriate since displaying one's piano skills for the purpose of attracting a husband was highly encouraged, *that* kind of *common* performance would hardly be allowed.

It was a role far beneath my station.

But I loved music, and I wanted to share my compositions with the world.

Why couldn't my parents have been happy with just one of their children being married off? My brother, the Marquess of

Ridley, had become engaged two years ago to a girl he'd been in love with his whole life and nearly lost because of his own shortsightedness. Lady Ela Dalvi was his hard-earned match, and the future Duke and Duchess of Harbridge were utterly besotted with each other.

Then again, Papa hadn't been pleased about the turn of events when his firstborn and heir practically told him to mind his own business during his rocky courtship with Ela. Defying my father's wishes would hardly go over as well for me. Girls were treated as if we were delicate china to be handled with velvet gloves and tender voices. We were only expected to sit quietly and nod and smile. To be the pinnacle of feminine perfection. Whatever that claptrap was.

This was clearly *not* my current circumstance, breaking all those rules!

No. Right now, I was living!

I narrowed my eyes as Lalita cut off the barouche, the three figures inside shouting in confusion as their vehicle pitched to a stop. Even though I was heavily shrouded in my hood, as was Lalita, a frisson of fear went through me. These targets *knew* who I was. Stealing from them wasn't exactly the right thing to do, but they were rich and wouldn't miss the money. I supposed we could have politely asked for a donation, but where was the fun in that?

"Stand and deliver, good sirs!" I shouted in a low voice while I pulled aside the coach, cocking the rifle I'd stolen from my father's collection and loosening the vowels in my speech.

In the late-night gloom, I could see bewilderment dawning on their faces as they whirled to face the business end of my empty rifle. Not that they would know that the weapon was unloaded. Lalita hefted hers as well, though her face had taken on a green hue as if she was fighting not to cast up her accounts on the ground.

Keep it together, Lalita, just a few more minutes. . . .

One of the gentlemen I didn't recognize, though something about him seemed familiar, and the second was Ansel Chen, Lady Rosalin's cousin. The third made my heart flutter and then sink to my toes. Along with Ansel, Rafi Nasser was one of my brother's best mates, and while Rafi was the *ton*'s resident libertine, he was hardly obtuse. In fact, his lackadaisical personality hid an incisive mind, or so I'd observed the past few years. One mistake and I could be discovered.

That would ruin everything.

My brother was not with them, which I counted as a small mercy. I would have been a little more worried about discovery with him there, especially since it wouldn't be the first time we'd ambushed him—but my disguise was solid, thanks in part to his own fiancée, Ela, who was a master of subterfuge. Gulping past the thickening knot in my throat, I squared my shoulders and edged the horse closer.

"What is the meaning of this?" the one closest to me demanded.

"Calm down, Rin," Ansel said through his teeth. I knew the other boy looked familiar he was the elder brother of my other best friend Nori. That made me feel better about robbing someone I didn't know. And if he was with Rafi and Keston's set, he had money to burn, and Nori would definitely approve.

"Bugger off, Ansel," he slurred. "Don't tell me what to do. What is this?"

"It's a robbery, dimwit," Lalita called out, and I nearly laughed out loud at his half-foxed expression. With any luck, they would be too deep in their cups to remember most of this. The coachman blanched and reached for his pockets. "Not you," she told him. "Just the spoiled toffs inside the carriage who can afford to lighten their purses."

Grinning at the coachman's bemused expression, I cleared my throat and threw a sack to the middle of the open conveyance, putting a little mischief in my tone. "Hands where I can see them, kind sirs. Fill the pouch, if you will. You're all much too comely to be shot tonight."

Ansel and Rin complied, though grousing all the while. Most would not put up a fight at gunpoint. My eyes widened at the bank notes, coins, rings, and pocket watches going into the bag. This would be an excellent haul.

When they were done, I let my gaze drift to Rafi, who sat sprawled lazily against the left squabs, his long arms spread wide on either side of him. One would think he was spending an indolent evening in his favorite armchair and not being robbed by armed highwaymen. Er, highway-*women*. I tried not to let myself be too affected by his presence, but Rafi was a person who commanded attention. It didn't help that he'd grown more handsome in the last year, not that I cared, of course. It was a simple observation.

Rafi Nasser always left a trail of broken hearts in his wake . . .

every girl in London wanting to be *the* girl who reformed a notorious scoundrel. Even my own brother had warned me of him, and I supposed it helped that Rafi didn't see me as anything other than his best friend's little sister. Two years ago, during Keston and Ela's courtship, he'd nipped my nascent infatuation in the bud when I'd foolishly let my feelings be known.

I am not interested in courting bratty girls. A cool, disinterested gaze had parsed my excessively frilled figure. *Especially Ridley's little sister. Go back to your schoolroom, Zia.*

I'd tucked my poor, wounded sixteen-year-old heart away and avoided him since.

That open sore of rejection didn't stop him from being unnecessarily attractive, however. Dark stubble crept over a sharp jawline, a bold nose and hooded brows making his features seem more angular in the low moonlight. Thickly lashed eyes—silvery gray in the dappled darkness—shone with something that unsettled me. I resisted the urge to check to see if my cowl was intact, shielding my features from view.

"Come now, don't be shy," I told him audaciously, fighting for poise. "Your pockets seem heavy tonight."

His eyes narrowed as he tilted his head to one side. "Who are you?"

That deep baritone of his descended over me like crushed velvet. "My identity is not important, only your valuables. But if you insist, Lady Knight, it is."

Lalita's gasp alerted me to the fact that naming any names that might lead back to us was not part of the plan. Too late now.

Rafi didn't move from his relaxed pose, a slow smirk kicking up one corner of his mouth. "How quaint . . . lady of the night, I presume?" he drawled, sarcasm dripping from his tone.

I knew I shouldn't engage, but the need to put him in his place was strong. "Knight with a *K,* as in warrior-at-arms, actually. And might I remind you that this is loaded, my lord," I said, knowing full well he wasn't titled as I hefted my rifle. "Make haste. Time and tide will wait for no man."

Something flashed across his face. He sat forward, propping his elbows on his knees, and I resisted the urge to rear back. "What's an educated young woman doing on these roads at night? Don't you know it's dangerous?"

Nerves alight, I tapped the rifle on the edge of the coach. "I *am* the danger, good sir. Now, unless you intend to test my rather excellent feminine aim, I'd advise you to stitch together those pretty lips and divest yourself of your baubles. Patience is not one of my many virtues."

The corner of that devious mouth kicked up, along with my traitorous temperature. "Pretty lips?"

"A euphemism, no more. Now stop stalling."

With that wicked smirk still firmly in place, he reached for the pouch and emptied his pockets. It must have been a lucky night at the card tables. Good for him, and even better for us. When he stretched an arm toward me, my eyes stuck on the large signet ring on his finger. It was his family ring, I knew. But any thieving highwayman worth his salt would never leave such a bounty behind.

"That's a lovely ring."

His eyes darkened. "It's a family heirloom."

"One that will fetch a nice sum."

A chuckle left his lips. "It's much too recognizable to sell, Lady Knight."

"Then perhaps I shall keep it as a memento of our meeting."

Prowling forward, I reached out to grip his fingers with my gloved left hand and grinned as I slipped it off and stowed it into the pocket of my cloak. He lurched forward to latch on to my wrist, making my pulse gallop, but a swift movement of my heel into my mount's flank broke the brief contact. "You won't get away with this," he said in a low snarl that made my already hammering pulse double.

"Already have. Do have a grand evening, your lordship," I purred, and then on impulse blew him a kiss. His nostrils flared, something flashing in those narrowed gray eyes, and for a heart-stopping moment, I wondered if it was recognition. Blowing a kiss was something the Zia he knew would never do, so it couldn't have been that. I frowned when Rafi rose off the seat as if breathing in, and I urged my horse a few more hurried steps back.

Was the rotter *sniffing* me?

I hadn't worn any scent other than daily bathwater, but still . . .

His brows drew down as I moved the stallion farther away and nodded to Lalita, who had remained in position in front of the coach. Together we drifted off the road and into the shadows. Still, I felt the press of that heated silver gaze for a full minute afterward.

"That was intense," Lalita hissed.

Before I could answer, the sound of thundering hooves over the next hill interrupted me.

"Halt! Stop in the name of the law!" someone shouted.

My heart shot into my throat. That voice definitely wasn't from Rafi or the two other boys. That was a cracking order of authority . . . as in the police. Damn and blast, of all our bloody luck! The command had sounded far enough away, but I could not be sure, so I upped my pace and urged Lalita to do the same.

"Bloody hell, who's that?" she yelled.

"Runners or local constables!" I snorted a hysterical burst of laughter through my nose. If I was captured by the Runners, I'd be the pinnacle of ruination. My father would be absolutely livid, and I'd probably be banished to a convent. Half-petrified, I laughed again.

"None of this is funny, Zia. If they catch us, they're going to lock us in jail."

"They won't snatch anyone, Lalita," I yelled back. "Come on, ride faster! We're nearly to the others. And besides, we're the Lady Knights of truth, knowledge, and justice. Nothing bad can happen to us, remember?"

Lalita, one of my close friends from school, had the gall to roll her eyes and let out a snort louder than mine. "You say that every time we're in one of these scrapes. You and these hare-brained ideas are going to get us killed one day!"

"To Valhalla!" I roared.

"You are ridiculous," she said, but a wild answering grin lit her face all the same. "Stop obsessing over those Viking books about shield-maidens."

That would happen only by force. Shield-maidens were magnificent.

Panting wildly, we pushed our mounts to the brink as we darted through the gloomy, deserted fields south of Slough—thank the heavens I'd pored over a hand-drawn map for hours before choosing this particular rural area, west of Hounslow Heath. We'd left our unmarked coach near a respectable-enough coaching inn with two guards. Greer, our resident weapons expert thanks to her avid huntsman father and the last of our foursome, was armed to the teeth.

As soon as I saw the coach around the next bend of the road, I let out a sharp two-note whistle. We had practiced this before, and like a well-oiled machine, the door opened and the attached horses started moving down the street. Nori was on driving duty tonight.

A relieved grin split my face as Lalita and I dismounted, threw the reins of the borrowed horses to a frowning groom in front of the inn's stables, and ran toward our escape route. Jogging alongside each other, Lalita and I climbed in one at a time, attempting to catch our breaths as we slung ourselves back into the squabs.

Lalita wheezed, dark hair clinging to her ruddy brown cheeks. "How did I let you talk me into this?"

"You like helping people," I retorted, lungs burning, my veins mixed with excitement and relief.

"You mean *robbing* people," she muttered.

"I don't enjoy stealing, Lalita. It's a necessity." I shot her a look. "They're rich nobs who have more than enough to spare. And you know why we're doing this. To save Little Hands and Beth. To save *Welton.*"

The spoils of our capers—a large stash of banknotes as well as watches and jewelry to be pawned—would be delivered to Bellevue Chapel, a church that was in danger of closing. Never mind that the money was stolen; it was for a good cause. Our school's future was in peril as well, considering it was housed in the same building as the orphanage. But the children were far more important. Little Hands was their home. Plus, the contribution included most of our own pin money.

Every little bit helped, however.

Even if we had to steal it from our peers. Well, my sibling's peers at least. We'd gotten my brother and Lord Blake Castleton, one of his other mates, the first week that we'd had the brilliant idea to fleece Keston's rich friends who wouldn't miss the coin, then Blake again because he was too easy to rob, and now Rafi, Ansel, and Rin.

Greer stared at us. "What happened?"

"Ran into some Bow Street Runners."

Her lips thinned, eyes going wide. "This far out of London?"

"They must have been scouting or in the area for something else. Word of highwaymen in this particular area is widespread."

It was true; Hounslow Heath was rife with ne'er-do-wells. Which we were not. *Mostly.*

ABOUT THE AUTHOR

AMALIE HOWARD is the bestselling, critically acclaimed author of several novels for teens, adults, and young readers. Her work has won national awards, received starred trade reviews, and been featured in *The Hollywood Reporter*, *Entertainment Weekly*, and *Cosmopolitan*. When she's not writing, she can usually be found reading, being the president of her one-woman Harley-Davidson motorcycle club, or power-napping. She lives in Colorado with her family.

Follow Amalie Howard on Instagram and X at @amaliehoward and on Facebook and TikTok at @amaliehowardauthor.

amaliehoward.com